# THE FATED

---

By

## KATELYNSAM

For more information, please contact katelynsamauthor@gmail.com

First edition: February 2025

*Cover design by Katelynsam*

Library of Congress Control Number: 2024920364
Paperback ISBN 979-8-9915732-2-1
Ebook ISBN 979-8-9915732-1-4

Katelynsam.com

*For Mom and Dad.*
*Thank you for always believing in me and saying just the right things I
need to hear in just the right moments.*

*And for me.*
*For the girl who wrote her first book at twelve and has been giving
everything she's had to be published ever since.*

***And to my reader.***
***There were so many times this book almost but never quite made
it into your hands, so I'm thrilled to be delivering it to you now.
Thank you so much for being a part of making my lifelong
dream come true.***

# CHAPTER 1

## HAUNTED

Even while dreaming, I can never escape *The Fated*.

The ship slices through the fog like a black and white metal beast. Some of its windows glow yellow, ghostly against the dim suffocating backdrop of mist, while others remain dark, and I always shudder from the sense that something is watching me deep from within their churning shadows. Then, like a spirit, I materialize on board, drifting aimlessly, restlessly, towards something I can no longer remember.

With the night wind slashing across my face, I walk the decks of the vessel meant to carry us to paradise. I wander through the ballroom bursting with people in silk, velvet, and chiffon dancing to a familiar melody whose notes echo eerily off the vast ceiling. I pass by dimly lit lounges, their white-clothed tables littered with glasses that never go empty.

Beneath my feet, the ship lurches, and I stumble. Above me, the chandelier tilts, its glittering crystals trembling as if in fright. Around me, people laugh and shout over each other, not caring about the rough waves outside, or the current beneath them rapidly pulling us into the unknown. Into our terrifying, unsuspecting fate.

When I recall my joy at first beholding *The Fated* on the docks, I can't help but scoff at my naivety. At my ridiculous, child-like faith. I should have known, somewhere beneath my intoxicating optimism, that neither I nor anyone else could be saved so easily.

But I didn't know. I could not have begun to imagine what wonder, terror, grief, and yes, even happiness awaited me on that gray endless sea.

For if I had, I might never have dared step foot on that ship.

## CHAPTER 2

---

## GIRL IN THE GILDED BOX

Everything begins when the ticket arrives on a Wednesday.

I'm not at home as the envelope falls through the mail slot of my apartment at nine o'clock in the morning. Instead, I'm miles away, working at the department store near the center of Abeon City and past the river slicing straight through its heart. I might as well be on the other side of The Veil.

Today's shift is every bit as monotonous and agonizing as usual. No —it's worse.

A cheerful ding resounds through the small space as the elevator jerks to a halt.

"Third floor," I say with forced brightness, gripping the handle and sliding the door open with a groan. "Women's wear and accessories."

I have no time to step to the side before the riders stampede by. The toe of a leather shoe nicks my ankle. A woman's satin-covered shoulder slams into mine. My startled gasp is lost amid the clamber of heels on the marble floor and women's cackles.

When I gaze out at the spectacle that is the sales floor, however, for several seconds at least I forget to care.

Palm trees rise over tables hidden beneath rivers of chiffon, velvet, and taffeta. Customers amble beneath arches woven with pink orchids and bluebell flowers. Lixirites as large as compasses glitter a thousand different shades in the light from inside the cases.

Apart from the fabric, none of it's real of course. The palm trees are made of paper and felt. The orchids and bluebells of dyed silk. And given that actual Lixirites haven't been produced on the continent of Zakartha in decades and a single one would be worth more than this entire department store put together—the multicolored gemstones behind the glass are nothing more than masterfully crafted replicas.

As more people shuffle into the elevator, I catch a glimpse of the banner hanging in between the columns past the doors. Colored in bright blues and shimmering golds, it reads:

*New Summer Collection!*
*Buy all the dresses and accessories for your perfect beach paradise!*

Perfect is hardly the word I would use to describe Taldonia, the coastal town thirty miles south of Abeon City where the metropolis's wealthy and famous flocked for summer vacation or weekend getaways to the beach. When I'd travelled there once before with my aunt and cousin, my excitement had quickly dimmed at what greeted me. The brown ocean water was only just a little less murky than the waves lapping the docks of Abeon City. The clouds always shrouding the city from the smokestacks and other pollutants were only slightly less gray and heavy farther south over the gray-beached shores.

Still, I'd trade the department store for Taldonia in a heartbeat if I could.

"Are they making us operate this contraption ourselves now?" a man in the elevator barks, shattering my thoughts. I apologize as I rush to close the door.

The staccato of the second button on the wall being clicked echoes in the impatient silence before the occupants resume conversation.

"Did you hear about *The Fated*?" a woman in a blue hat says to her companion. "It arrived at the docks this morning, and people have already started getting their tickets in the mail."

My heart picks up. The *Fated?* It can't be. She must be mistaken.

Like everyone else, I've occasionally dreamed about embarking on *The Fated's* legendary voyage, about sailing past the Veil's impenetrable storm clouds. I imagined building a new life in whatever world waited beyond—a world of endless opportunities and dreams fulfilled according to all the stories. Then again, I once dreamed about many things.

"I had no idea!" one man gasps, and I can sense the other riders leaning forward in interest. I stop myself from doing the same. "I should hurry home and check as soon as I'm finished here."

"Don't bother," the customer complaining about the door earlier growls. "You'll have a better chance at getting struck by lightning on a sunny day. No one I've known or spoken to has ever seen, let alone gotten their hands on one."

"Well, I wouldn't board that abomination even if a ticket fell into my mailbox," the woman closest to me pipes up. "There's a reason no one who gets on that ship ever returns."

"Why would they?" the first man demands. "The world on our side of the Veil is anything but a paradise. If we aren't worried about soaring prices, we're worried about another outbreak of ebony fever. If we aren't worried about ebony fever, we're worried about the next war. It's obvious from the photos I've seen of that ship that wherever it's taking its passengers must be better than this."

Murmurs of agreement echo throughout the space at his words, and if there was someone who would listen to me, mine would be one of them.

The elevator dings for what must be the two hundredth time today, the clear sound still reverberating through the air as I remember at the last moment to say, "Sixth floor. Housewares and appliances."

"That ship is cursed," the woman beside me mutters to the person next to her as I pull open the door, revealing another level streaked with marble floors and glossy cases. "It's unnatural, appearing like it does out of the mist like a devil from the old world, or worse—"

The rest of her words are lost in the clatter of footsteps and shuffling bags as she, along with the other riders, rushes through the exit before being replaced by more customers. For a moment, I wait in anticipation to see if anyone else will mention *The Fated*. But when conversation erupts on other topics, such as another war brewing between Terratia and Gorinth, the two largest countries in the continents south of us, I can't help but shudder with dread.

I shake my head, vanquishing any more thoughts of war, past or future. I try to cheer myself by instead daydreaming about *The Fated*. Of its sleek decks and glossy windows. Of all the remaining mystery and wonder of the world it carries with it.

And yet...thinking any more about the people lucky enough to be chosen to board makes the already small walls around me feel smaller, my already tight smile even tighter. So, once again I must redirect my mind, shoving notions of a legendary ship and a life of leisure aside until I can finally relax into the symphony of familiar sounds that fill my days.

Even after everything that's happened, everything that's gone wrong, it's still easier to think of my life in terms of music.

The exhausted whir the elevator makes as it descends.

The melodic ring announcing our arrival onto another floor.

The quick allegro of sharp heels and steady thump of oxford shoes as passengers rush out only to be replaced by others.

Then the movement repeats again.

Focusing on the cadence of each noise also allows me to pretend I'm a part of something greater. That I'm a single yet integral note in the chaotic production of the bustling department store. Most of the time it works...that is, until I raise my gaze long enough to see a glimpse of smiling customers, colorful clothes, and faux crystal chandeliers before the door shuts once again, reminding me how isolated I am.

By the time my lunch break arrives, I'm ready to collapse into the nearest chair and rub away the headache I can feel growing behind my eyes. Yet just as I trudge through the doors, I freeze at the sight of the woman in red stalking towards the elevator.

I had hoped today might be survivable.

"Be a dear and take me up to the fifth floor, will you?" Mrs. Savrie, the department store's manager, remarks.

I imagine dashing for the nearest exit. Instead, I mutter, "Of course," before stepping back inside and pressing the golden button with the number 5 inscribed on it.

Seconds pass. Next to me, Mrs. Savrie releases a sigh, and in the reflection of the bronze doors, I watch her eyes bore into the dial indicator above the entrance, willing the arrow to move faster. I will it to do the same.

"The sale looks like a great success," I finally say in an attempt to break the silence. The second the woman's green eyes fix on mine in the reflection, I regret speaking.

"Obviously," she sneers. "But it will be even more of one soon. My daughter, as I'm certain you know, just graduated from the Institute."

An ache twinges in my chest at the mention of Abeon City's renowned conservatory of performing arts. The very school I once believed I would one day call my alma mater. My home.

But Mrs. Savrie pushes on, oblivious to my discomfort.

"People are already praising her as one of the most gifted pianists in our generation," she says. "At my request, she has agreed to hold a short concert in our atrium later today—a spectacle practically guaranteed to bring the entire city rushing through our doors." At her pause, I risk a glance to find the woman tilting her head as if remembering something.

"Actually, when your aunt—being the charitable woman that she is —asked me to give you this job, I believe she mentioned *you* once fancied becoming a concert pianist. Is that true, Miss Obrel? Where on earth could you have concocted such a notion?"

"It's true," I manage despite the weight building in my throat. "It was just...a childhood dream of mine."

My *only* dream.

"Yes, well, dreams are well and good but no substitute for talent,"

Mrs. Savrie says, and I can't help but think that if this had been three years ago, I would have told her exactly how uncreative and juvenile her insults really were. Or better yet, punched the button to the nearest floor and stalked out of the department store forever without so much as a glance back.

But this isn't three years ago, and by the time I open my mouth, the anger has dissipated, leaving me feeling tired and worn like the mat in front of the revolving doors, constantly treaded on by customers and employees alike.

"Of course," I reply, pasting on a serene expression that always fools everyone but myself.

Beside me, the woman huffs almost as if in disappointment before her eyes shoot up to the dial indicator.

"The door," Mrs. Savrie snaps, and too late I realize the elevator has been halted for a while now.

The second I slide open the entrance, she waltzes out, leaving me staring after her.

Trapped alone in the gilded box, as always.

# Chapter 3

## The Ticket

By the time my shift ends, night has fallen. Drizzling rain streaks the trolley windows with raindrops darkened with pollution, dimming the passing city lights into a collage of gold and gray swirls.

The streetcar's steady motion nearly lulls me to sleep when a jingling bell and resulting screech of the wheels against the rails has me surging to my feet once again. As soon as I step outside, I shiver against the chill air. I cough at the fumes from the box-shaped cars racing by.

Across the boulevard, people in faux furs and fine costume jewelry line outside the theater's doors for the Institute's spring performance, and for the thousandth time I wish for a different future, a different life where I was one of the talented students being seen and adored by the whole city.

I quicken my pace. Along the deteriorated glamour that is Pearl Street, billboards and marquees flash at me from every direction, the buildings they are attached to streaked with grime and erosion. People dine inside the windows of a bistro, their silhouettes laughing and raising wine glasses to their lips while outside children beg on the street and a brawl breaks out among those waiting to enter a jazz club.

The capital of Abeon wasn't always like this. Back before the first war between Gorinth and Terratia over sixty years ago, the city had prospered from the Lixirites mined from the mountains at its fringes. But then the Lixirites ran out, and the city's wealth dissolved soon after—which had been followed even more swiftly by the war.

A war that broke out when Terratia invaded Gorinth without warning or reason, it seemed. After all, for centuries Terratia had provided the other country with coal even when the mining destroyed Terratia's land or when Gorinth began treating Terratia less like an ally and more like a tool to be exploited. Only after Terratia laid waste to Gorinth's cities and slaughtered fleeing citizens was the bloody extent of its people's resentment revealed for the rest of the world to see.

And fear.

The war's bombs and slaughtering had all too quickly stretched beyond both Gorinth's and Terratia's borders, but thankfully never reached Abeon's shores. Instead, it condemned the city to an even slower demise from shortages of food, supplies, and medicine it usually received from the southern continents trapped into fighting.

A honk to my right followed by angry shouts breaks my reverie, and I remember at the last minute to turn left on the next street. Block by block, the crowd surrounding me thins until I'm walking through a neighborhood illuminated only by flickering street lamps and dirty windows. From the gray and indistinctive sameness of the buildings lining either side of me, you wouldn't think that they house immigrants from all over the world on this side of The Veil. But that was the nature of Abeon and especially its capital, where over half the population was from somewhere else, and yet consistently dressed in the same style of clothes, ate the same bland food, and amused themselves with the same manner of pleasures.

This had always been the city's twisted charm, I suppose: to transform the extraordinary into the mundane, to saw away at any and every unique and unconventional edge until what was left was indistinguishable and, worse, ignorable.

Few things or people ever escaped this fate. My mother hadn't been one of them.

Neither had I.

Seconds before I pass through the door of a gray building, the rain outside stops altogether, and I can't help but snort in exasperation. *A sign your fortune is about to change for the better*, my mother would say. Along with over a dozen other odd and irrational beliefs passed to her from my great-grandmother, who lived the first twenty years of her life in Lamira, a distant land steeped in superstition.

But I ceased being superstitious years ago.

The creak of the stairs as I climb to my apartment echoes in the quiet—along with the warble of the landlord's old gramophone from his chambers on the top floor.

Usually, the notes would soothe me, but tonight the pitch makes me wince and wish for silence. A wish that goes unanswered given I've barely walked into the apartment when the telephone in my kitchen rings, sending me rushing to pick up the receiver.

"Hello—" I start into the mouthpiece.

"It's a miracle!" my cousin Jaslene's voice shrieks from the other end of the line so loudly that I jerk the receiver from my ear. "We've been *chosen*! I still can't believe it! I would've rushed to the department store to tell you this morning, but Mother insisted I help with the packing while she was busy putting the house up for sale and everything else."

"For sale?" I say, my fatigue dissolving into alarm. "What's going on? What are you talking about?"

"Tickets for *The Fated* came in the mail today!" Jaslene cries. "There's one for Mother and for me—oh, Amarra, please tell me you got one too!"

"I..." my voice catches on the lump growing in my throat as I scan the floor in front of the door for fallen mail. I find none. Around me, the worn walls and uneven floor spin as I grip the counter.

Of course I didn't get a ticket. Of course, out of my remaining family, *I* would be the one doomed to be left behind while my aunt and cousin get to waltz onto *The Fated* and never look back. Never mind the fact that I had been the one to work until my bones ached and the circles beneath my eyes deepened while my aunt and cousin attended tea parties and went to the opera. Never mind that even before my mother died, my life had never been as close to easy as either of theirs.

I'm seconds away from collapsing onto the kitchen tiles and likely never rising again when I spot it. The tattered envelope that's fallen through the mail slot and slid to the far corner of the hallway I failed to notice until now.

"Hello, Amarra? Are you still there?" Jaslene demands, but I barely register her voice crackling on the line. Barely register the receiver slipping from my fingers as I take a handful of steps until I'm picking up the envelope. With trembling hands, I turn it over to find my name along with my street and house number in the center.

No return address spans the upper left corner. It might as well have materialized on my doorstep with the morning mist. Water and dirt stains dot the paper while the edges are folded and worn, as if the envelope endured every element imaginable to arrive here.

Still, when I open the envelope and peer inside, my breath hitches—before stopping altogether as I gently pull out the contents, one of which is a key made of gold. But my eyes instantly move to the piece of paper beneath it.

It's gilded at the edges and corners with old-fashioned script splaying across the page as boldly as the dazzling letters donning the marquees lining Pearl Street. In fact, it looks even grander than an invitation to one of the operas at the Palace Theatre.

As my gaze pours over the ticket, I can barely comprehend both the typed and handwritten words—can barely allow myself to believe them:

*Ocean Ticket No.* 3945

***Congratulations! You are hereby cordially invited to join us on a once in a lifetime voyage!***

*Passenger Ticket for **Amarra Obrel***
*For passage on **The Fated***
*Sailing from **Abeon City**.*
*Pier: **No. 27***
*Date of Departure: **Saturday, March 13th***

*Cabin No. **623***

I stare at the text, afraid to blink, afraid the second I do, the words will melt away like wax held to fire. But when my eyes shut and snap open again, the words are still there, the ink dried. Permanent. That is when it hits me.

I am really boarding *The Fated*. Within days, I'll be standing on its fabled decks and sailing past The Veil to start a new life beyond the world of loneliness and disappointments I know. There had once been a time when I could imagine what it would be like to experience such things as vividly as if I'd already lived them. When, if someone had asked me what paradise was, I would have known the answer in a heartbeat.

Now, however, even with the weight of the ticket in my hand and my name written across the paper, I struggle to dream up the possibilities, struggle to dream up days no longer spent staring at the interior of an elevator, always forced to remain on the outskirts. Forced to remain an observer rather than the star of my own life.

So much time had passed since I allowed myself to dream of my future that for the briefest moment, staring at the thin material in my palm makes me afraid. What if *The Fated's* destination wasn't as grand as all the stories claimed? What if everything *The Fated* promised—happiness, prosperity, fulfillment—would never be mine? What if the woman at the department store earlier was right? What if the ship really was cursed?

A chill shivers over me at the thought. It makes sweat break out along the surface of my forehead and sends my heart throbbing to a painful rhythm.

Yet my fingers on the ticket don't go slack. In fact, my grip tightens because beneath my overwhelming fear is something else. Something stronger. Something I haven't allowed myself to experience in so long that the sensation is unfamiliar. Treacherous, even.

Something like hope.

# Chapter 4

## Leaving

*As surely as The Fated sails.*

It's a phrase every child throughout the world learns early in life. As surely as *The Fated* sails, tomorrow will come and things will get better. As surely as *The Fated* sails, my love for you will never fade. Nothing but birth and death itself was as constant as *The Fated*, which had glided out from The Veil to dock at a different city every sixteen years ever since The Veil split the world in half a millennium ago.

I had only been five when the ship last appeared, docking along the shores of Danmar in the eastern region of Zakartha. I had been too young to understand the news blaring from the radio announcing our neighboring country's attempt to solve the mystery of *The Fated* by sending a fleet of submarines, planes, and airships after it into The Veil. Too young to register the newspaper headlines on how not one vessel or aircraft had ever returned.

The Veil was at the edge of the known world because nothing and no one who ever went inside came back. Not the countless scientists or daredevils that had tried over the years.

Nothing except *The Fated*.

Most believed the ship was from Melanthros, the oldest continent in the world—or it was before The Veil separated us from it. The handful of historical accounts that remained made it sound more like a myth than any location on a map.

Medicines so potent they could cure any sickness. Beaches so spectacular that gemstones more precious than Lixirites and diamonds combined washed ashore with the waves instead of seashells. And technology that was even more unexplainable—compasses that could predict the future, mirrors that allowed people to vanish from one place only to reappear somewhere else, and temples that could trap the most ancient of gods, assuming any existed. Such were the stories that had persisted for generations.

It wasn't surprising then that so many people assumed *The Fated* carried its passengers to a paradise, a place beyond the ordinary, the rational. A perfect utopia only those blessed enough to be chosen would ever be able to experience. Never mind the fact there was no proof the ship had been built in Melanthros at all or that the continent had even survived the formation of The Veil. The slightest chance at a life away from poverty, disappointments, and unhappiness had always been enough to send those with tickets scrambling on board without hesitation.

In less than an hour, I'll be one of them.

The wind howls through the cracks along the edges of a window that's always refused to fully close, making me shiver where I stand packing up the last of my things. Still...when my gaze falls on the sheet music at the bottom of the suitcase, I feel a pang in my heart, and for a moment I yearn not for a ship but for a better, more blissful time.

A memory.

A living room cluttered with cheap souvenirs and reused holiday garlands while snow dances outside the fogging window. In the center of it all, my mother teaching me how to play piano, laughing when my small fingers stumble over the wrong notes and clapping when I succeed in reaching just enough of the right ones to produce a noise almost resembling music.

When I was seven, my mother told me nothing could harm me while I played; not my schoolmates' cutting remarks; not the hunger lingering in my stomach after half a bowl of spinach soup. I had escaped them all through the harmonies my fingers created as they flew across the worn black and white keys.

Carefully, I pick up the papers and brush my fingers over the penciled sketches in place of comments decorating the margins. A pirouetting ballerina to signal a section should be played lively. A trio of feathers to remind me to play the last few measures softly, like a lullaby. If I close my eyes, I can see my mother reaching over the keys to let her pencil dance across the note-filled pages, a contented smile for once on her face.

A sliver of metal gleams in the light, and I glance back inside the suitcase at the small, wooden music box that once played "First and Last Wish," the translated title of the very song composed on the papers in my hand. It's an old Lamiran folk tune. One whose melody was once equally joyful and tragic in parts, given it tells the story of a person's life from birth to death.

That changed decades ago, though, when the famous pianist August Urst heard it on his travels in Lamira before returning to Abeon and rearranging it into a song that was nearly unrecognizable. His arrangement comprised of only the happiest notes that became enshrined forever in records, radio shows, and cheap music boxes like this one my mother bought me when I was ten.

Though I know it is futile, I turn the lever out of habit, and even with no sound, I can still hear the melody in my head. I can still recall the first time I played it perfectly—my own arrangement styled after the original folk tune rather than the false version this music box plays. When all the notes came together, I truly believed I was good enough to build a better life by playing the music I loved so much.

"I'm headed to that new life, Ma," I whisper to the tiny box, as if instead of notes, it now carries messages to a realm I can neither see nor feel but believe in, nevertheless. "I finally made it."

I shut the suitcase with a click, lingering beside my bed to take in the gray dingy chamber one final time. In the corner, my department store uniform hangs from a crooked closet door. Beneath my bed, boxes containing old toys and some of my mother's trinkets I brought when I moved in two years ago remain half-opened and covered in dust. The walls are water-stained and bare, devoid of the colorful pictures from magazines or drawings that had decorated my room in the apartment I shared with my mother.

So many times, this space had felt like both a sanctuary and prison—a place where I could escape my aunt's disapproving eyes, a place where my loneliness grew thick enough to consume my body and soul.

Now the apartment appears as if no one has ever lived here.

I suppose it's fitting, considering this had never been my real home anyway.

Through the window, rare rays of sun pierce the clouds, illuminating the wakening city below for the first time in months. One by one, lights flicker on in the houses across the street as a siren wails blocks away and a church bell tolls.

Time to go.

Grabbing my suitcase, I walk through the doorway without hesitation. I don't look back.

## CHAPTER 5

## NOW BOARDING

The first time I saw *The Fated* was in a history book.

It had been a photo of one of the most famous paintings ever to depict the ship, created centuries ago when *The Fated* still looked like a vessel from old, with gold-embossed sides and sails rippling in the wind like massive wings. I remember feeling awe, a breath-stealing kind of amazement. The emotion quickly plummeted into disappointment when I later saw *The Fated's* modern appearance splayed across the pages of a newspaper, its hull no longer ornate but sleek and sharp like the ocean liners I had glimpsed in the bay.

I'm not disappointed now.

Extending over what must be a thousand feet and rising to at least thirteen stories high, the ship dwarfs the dock like a floating fortress. The sun's rays against the immaculate white paint covering the sides nearly blind me. Still, I squint past the pain, drinking in the rows upon rows of windows winking in the light, the smooth black streaks spanning the top and bottom as starkly as notes on a sheet of paper, and the open decks promising days of endless blue skies and horizons. *The Fated* is written in curving script along the vessel's bow several yards beneath the golden figurehead of a half-fish, half-woman with her mouth open as if in song.

"Amarra!"

A young woman in a rose-pink coat rushes toward me with joy brimming in her eyes and a smile as bright as the chandeliers illuminating the department store.

"Jaslene," I grin.

"It feels like an absolute dream, doesn't it?" my cousin gushes, pulling me into a hug and sending the smell of her lotus perfume flooding my nose. "I considered pinching myself several times on the train ride here, but then I decided if this is all a dream, I never want to wake up!"

"Oh, do stop spouting nonsense, Jaslene," my aunt says, materializing from the crowd to stand over us like we're children again. "You're nineteen years old, and yet you hardly act like a young lady sometimes. Compose yourself for the cameras."

"What cameras?" I scoff when, as if on cue, flashes erupt from the reporters pushing to the front of the metal barricades separating passengers from onlookers several yards away.

For a moment, I can't help but be self-conscious. Standing next to my aunt and cousin, anyone would think we belong to another species entirely. With olive skin the same shade as mine but flawless, ebony hair that cascades in soft waves to their shoulders rather than the wild mess mine tends to become, and elegant custom-made clothes, they've always looked more like someone else's family than mine.

"It's good to see you, Aunt Salenna," I force myself to say when we turn away and start moving towards the dock's edge.

"Is it?"

The coldness in her tone sends my steps faltering. Seeing my aunt never fails to bring a flood of less than pleasant memories washing over me: her disapproval over everything I did in the six months I lived with her and Jaslene after my mother died; her impatience to be rid of me after I failed my audition at the Institute; her condescension disguised as charitableness when she asked Mrs. Savrie to give me a job at the department store to keep me from starving on the streets and embarrassing her further.

But today is a miracle. Today is the start of a new life, and nothing, especially not my aunt's pettiness, will weigh down my spirits.

"Of course," I reply with saccharine sweetness. "Your smile is always radiant enough to brighten my day."

The glare Salenna sends my way could wither stone. She's robbed of a chance to respond though when a commotion erupts at the front of the line full of passengers waiting to board the gangplanks ahead. People's heads turn as a police officer drags a girl with strawberry blond hair back towards the barricades.

"Please!" she begs, her pretty face contorted in panic. "I didn't mean to deceive anyone! My friend gave me her ticket. I swear!"

"No gifts, sales, or trading allowed!" the officer hollers loud enough for everyone to hear. "The only ticket you can use is your own. Otherwise, don't bother wasting your time."

The girl stumbles as the officer pushes her behind the barricades, leaving her looking lost and small amid the countless others who can do nothing but watch as those lucky enough to be chosen board. I can't help but be weighed down by guilt as I take in their slumped shoulders and the desperate envy in their eyes.

There's anger in the crowd too. Shouts and whistles erupt as a group of people charge towards the ship, only to be stopped by more police wearing helmets and strained faces. Forty-eight years ago, when *The Fated* docked in Terratia's capital and war-torn city, onlookers without tickets had made a similar stampede to force their way on board. The occurrence ended in tragedy when the gangplanks collapsed under the weight and sent them falling. Most either drowned or were dashed against the docks and ship's hull like broken shells until the water became tinted with red.

It's not surprising that Abeon City doesn't want to risk repeating such an event, even if this isn't a war-torn capital. At least not yet.

I'm so busy watching the restless crowd behind us that I don't sense the oncoming collision until my knee hits the corner of a satchel hard enough to send papers flying and something solid thudding to the ground.

"I'm so sorry," I blurt out, scrambling to pick up the pages before they grow damp and caked with dirt. I fail miserably.

A piece of metal flashes in the light near my foot, and I bend down to grab a small medallion with a compass design embossed across the front.

"Sorry again," I say, holding out the papers and medallion to their owner, a young man with ink black hair and features so striking that for the second time this morning, I feel my breath being stolen away. "I feel terrib—"

"Don't bother," he snaps, ripping the pages and medallion from my fingers before striding off, making me regret apologizing at all.

I push on, searching for my cousin and aunt, who I've lost in the crowd. I move past more vendors selling food and a preacher praying for our souls until *The Fated* looms before me, tall enough to engulf the sky.

"Amarra, over here!" Jaslene beckons me farther ahead to where she stands beside my aunt who hands over her identification card and ticket to a police officer stationed in front of a gangplank.

I glance at my ticket for the dozenth time to make sure the words haven't vanished, that the name written on the paper is still mine. When I find it is, the tension in my chest doesn't get a chance to ease before I'm passing the paper into the gloved hands of the officer who looks between the photograph and ticket, then fixes his eyes on me.

Hours and lifetimes pass, and still the man does not move, does not smile or nod in encouragement. Instead, his eyes narrow.

That's when I know. This has all been a terrible mistake, and my name was never meant to be on the ticket.

When the officer's arm moves, I flinch—

But he's only shoving the ticket and identification card back in front of my face.

"Next!" he says, waving the person behind me forward.

Stunned, I grasp the papers with trembling fingers as I walk up the gangplank, feeling the chill wind whip across my face while I stare over the rail at the dark waters below.

The toll of a clock tower reverberates through the air, and I glance back to the city once more—to the honking cars, the tired people in coats hurrying to work, and the steel skyscrapers beyond.

I wonder if the next time I step foot on land there will be streets and buildings and cars. I wonder if there will be people waiting at the port as well, except this time to welcome the passengers streaming off the ship and into a better world.

I wonder all of this as I take my last steps on the creaking gangplank, and then when my foot lands on the deck of *The Fated*, I wonder no more.

# CHAPTER 6

## SETTING SAIL

As soon as I step onto the smooth deck, I brace my body for the inevitable roll and sway that signals I am no longer on land but rather at the sea's mercy. To my surprise, the floor beneath me is still, and with every step my legs grow steady once it becomes clear the deck will remain that way.

Past the rows of people filing into the doorway ahead, I barely have time to catch a glimpse of dazzling lights, ornate columns, and raining confetti before warmth rolls over me and I'm inside, gaping at the atrium in disbelief.

Rising six stories tall, the space is a palace of white marble, velvet carpet, and gilded trimmings. A chandelier ten times larger than any in the department store descends from the glass ceiling, its thousands of crystals glittering varying shades of white, blue, and magenta that shift with every angle. A grand double staircase splits against the farthest wall, its balustrade draped with bronze-leafed garland and lacquered ornaments while more people than I could have ever imagined crowd either side, their clothes ranging from shabby coats to beaded silk dresses, as if some passengers have already been here for hours.

Saxophones, double basses, and trumpets ricochet off the walls, and the onlookers crowding the rails on the higher levels dance in time with the lively music. In the center of the first floor, a man with flushed cheeks sways on a ladder while emptying his bottle of champagne into an already overflowing tower stacked with glasses. Far above, a girl in a shimmering dress shrieks in delight as she glides through the air on a makeshift swing decked with ribbons and orchids before other passengers join in.

Around me, the most recently boarded passengers gawk with the same bewilderment I feel. Soon, however, the realization that everything they are witnessing is not some fleeting dream dawns across their faces. I start in surprise when the men behind me whoop in excitement before throwing off their hats and dashing into the fray. Several feet away, the young couple who boarded in front of us grasp each other's hands as they rush into the center of the floor where the man spins the beaming woman into a graceful twirl.

Their joy is contagious. Soon, I too am stepping into the atrium and raising my hand to feel the sparkling confetti brush my fingertips. At the tickle of paper against my skin, I unleash an elated laugh I hardly recognize as my own. The sound is quickly lost among the echoing music and chatter, but rather than being disappointed, I revel in feeling so connected to the strangers surrounding me.

"It's amazing, isn't it?" Jaslene says, appearing beside me to spin under the confetti and lights. "It's just as grand inside as all the legends say."

"No," I breathe, gazing at the water cascading down the edges of the staircase to form a stream that trickles by trees carved from gold and silver. In place of flowers, *real* amethysts and alexandrites dapple their leaves. "It's better."

"It looks more like a circus than a celebration," Salenna says as she stalks along the wall, eyeing the revelers with disdain.

"I think it's wonderful!" Jaslene gushes, grinning so wide that even my aunt loses the will the argue with her.

Within minutes, we've left the atrium and are cramming into an elevator along with seven other passengers weighed down by luggage. I barely manage to squeeze inside before bronze doors emerge from the sides and glide shut on their own.

"Well, what are you waiting for?" Salenna says when the elevator fails to move. "Ask everyone what floor they are going to."

I consider reminding her that as of yesterday, I'm no longer an elevator operator. But when I swivel around to find everyone staring expectantly, I sigh, not wanting to ruin what's still supposed to be a happy moment by making a scene. I've learned from experience that fighting with my aunt on something as insignificant as this would be more tiring than rewarding.

So, I'll play along. For now.

"Where to?" I say, pasting a pleasant smile on my face. After all, I've had more than enough practice.

"Five, please."

"Eight."

"Ten for me."

"Six."

I shouldn't have bothered asking. When I turn towards the wall, the four buttons are already glowing, pressed by the same invisible hand that opened the doors. I glance back to see the others' reactions, but nobody else seems to have noticed as the elevator car launches into motion, raising us upward with a speed and smoothness utterly different from the gentle whir and rock I'm accustomed to. For once, rather than being suffocated inside the close walls, I feel like I'm flying.

The doors barely begin opening before Salenna is stalking past and onto the sixth floor of what looks like a boulevard, with me and Jaslene trailing several steps behind, as always. I can tell from my aunt's proud posture and swift pace that she does not bother to notice the others' curious glances. Does not bother to marvel at the shimmering fountains, the colorful array of bakeries and bistros, or the miraculous nature of being on a ship that by logical explanation shouldn't exist at all.

I do though—and so does my cousin.

"Did you see the saunas back there?" Jaslene exclaims as we leave the boulevard minutes later and enter a hall lined on either side by red doors. "And a pool! Ooh, and a cinema! I plan to visit them all the first chance I get!"

"Calm yourself, my dear," Salenna says. "Just because we've been given a new start does not mean we're free to act uncivilized. Have some propriety—better yet, patience. We will explore the ship in good time."

"I'm pretty sure propriety's the *last* thing everyone on board cares about," Jaslene mutters under her breath, and I don't bother to keep from chuckling.

When I halt before a cabin door with *623* displayed in brass numbers across the center, however, I forget her words entirely. I'm too nervous and excited to see what awaits on the other side, and most importantly, that it's all *mine*. At least for the duration of our journey.

"We're neighbors!" Jaslene says from where she stands in front of the next cabin on the right along with my aunt before disappearing through the entrance with a wave.

Reaching into my pocket, I retrieve the gold key that was mailed with my ticket. I take a deep breath and slide it into the keyhole before twisting the door open.

The interior of the stateroom is sleek and spacious like something out of a magazine—with smooth mahogany walls, dark cashmere furniture, and even a tray in the corner filled with sodas, truffles, chocolate-covered strawberries, and other snacks that make my stomach twist in hunger. A miniature chandelier paints the room in a warm glow. A fresh bouquet of petunias and lilies sweetens the air, which is for once devoid of pollution or staleness. A balcony overlooks the gray buildings and smokestacks beyond that already feel like a world away.

When I come across a door etched with gold and silver starbursts, I fling it open, half-expecting to find my own personal ballroom or library.

Instead, my aunt glares back at me from where she stands in the connecting stateroom.

"And here I was looking forward to some privacy," Salenna says before spinning on her heel and stalking away.

"So was I," I mutter under my breath, my disappointment growing when I search the door for a lock at least—and find none.

Fantastic.

"Look at this, Amarra!" Jaslene gasps, appearing in the entrance less than a second later and grabbing my arm. She pulls me into the next cabin and toward a rounded panel door with her name on it before bursting inside.

When I pass through the entryway after her, I'm certain I must be dreaming.

Unlike mine, my cousin's room back at the townhouse had been fashionably furnished and decorated. But this—this is otherworldly.

Lamps shaped like roses and hummingbirds descend from a high dome ceiling painted with clouds along with the pinks, violets, and oranges of a sunset sky—and coincidentally Jaslene's favorite colors. Sconces glittering with opals drape the walls, reflecting light off the mirrors and the gilt bronze coating the dressers, chairs, and other furniture. A chiffon canopy woven with cherry blossoms—also Jaslene's favorite type of flower—streams over the bed, long enough to brush the porcelain tile floor and silk rug swirling with hibiscuses, carnations, and lilies.

"It's perfect for me, isn't it?" Jaslene squeals, collapsing back onto the satin pillows and reaching for the bowl of candied apricots sitting on the nightstand.

"It is," I agree, eyeing the bowl of candied apricots Jaslene eats from, the crunch of her teeth sinking into the hard surface cracking violently through the space. As a general rule, my cousin doesn't like candied food. In fact, she can't stand candied strawberries, cherries, or any other type of fruit for that matter. Except for apricots.

"Jaslene."

"Hmm?"

"Don't you think this room's actually a little too perfect?" I say. "I mean, what are the odds that whoever designed this room would know the kinds of things you like?"

My cousin shrugs, giving me a look that clearly says I'm overthinking everything. "Who cares?" With a flourish, she launches off the bed and brushes several seashells hanging along the wall before spinning to me, her dark eyes brightening in realization. "Maybe this ship really is *magic*."

"Maybe," I murmur, retracing my steps through the exit as Jaslene continues admiring new details.

I pass a second door with my aunt's name on it that stands propped slightly open, revealing a glimpse of red velvet curtains and classic-styled murals spanning the walls.

Back in my own cabin, it doesn't take me long to locate my room in the far corner. It is so close to the balcony and partially concealed by a lacquered cabinet that for several heart-stopping seconds I fail to see the door entirely. When I do, however, I hesitate, simultaneously excited and anxious for what I'll find inside.

It's even more stunning than I could have imagined. Like Jaslene's room, it feels...personal. Silver stars dapple the arched ceiling painted the same sapphire shade as my eyes, while a crescent moon chandelier covered with diamonds illuminates the space. Similarly to Jaslene's room, a canopy cascades over the bed, except mine is the color of moonbeams and wreathed with tiny lights arranged like constellations. Back in Abeon City, I had often wished I could see the stars, but I almost never could because of the constant clouds.

Then there are the books: shelves upon shelves of them with spines embossed with gold leaves, bronze flowers, and silver scales spanning the entire right wall.

Once again, unease trickles through me at the familiarity of the décor, as if the designer plucked the inspiration from my very thoughts and memories. But I shove the feeling down past my excitement and relief at finally being on board. Today of all days shouldn't be wasted on needless worrying.

After setting my suitcase on the bed, I open it with a click and stare at the meager handful of belongings making up my life. Several of my own favorite books are splayed along the top, their worn jackets nothing compared to those on the shelves surrounding me. Still, my fingers trace fondly over the pages folded at the corners, remembering how the words had provided an escape for me after my mother died and music had failed me.

A total of six outfits are folded neatly inside the suitcase, too—their plainness even now making me cringe in embarrassment. I had worn my department store uniform so often and for so long I hadn't ever noticed my lack of wardrobe until I started packing.

*It doesn't matter,* I try to convince myself, tracing my fingers over the clothes and two pairs of shoes inside. In the atrium, I had seen people in tattered coats, so surely appearances no longer mattered on board, right?

"Amarra, look!" Jaslene cries, emerging in the doorway with two dresses in hand: one cream-colored and covered in silver-white beads, the other peach-hued and overflowing with sequins and fringes. "My closet's full of them! Aren't they gorgeous?"

Without waiting for a response, she whirls, her footsteps pounding across the carpet as she makes for Salenna's room. "Mother, you'll never guess what I found—"

As soon as Jaslene disappears from view, I swivel to face the light blue doors leading to the closet. I hadn't bothered opening them before because I assumed the interior was empty. Holding my breath, I wrap my fingers around the embossed knobs and pull, half expecting to find nothing but naked hangers.

Instead, more dresses than I can count crowd the inside. Hardly believing my eyes, I lift up an amber gown sparkling with crystals and feathers. Next to it hangs a chiffon dress embroidered with vines and forget-me-nots. Silk, rayon, velvet, and satin—there is a garment made from every fabric I can name and others I've never seen before.

In panic, I glance back at the door, fearing someone will appear any moment to announce there has been a mistake and take all these dresses and extravagant things away. But with every moment that ticks by, with every brush of my fingers against taffeta frills and cashmere sleeves, I begin to accept all of this is really mine. On this voyage at least, I will never again have to worry about looking plain or poor. I can dress any way I like. Act in any way I please.

I feel myself sway from the possibilities of such newfound freedom.

I reach for a midnight blue dress with shimmering sequins that catches my eye towards the back, when a high-pitched screech slices through the room, ricocheting off the walls like an inhuman wail before deteriorating into static.

"Where is that coming from?" Jaslene says, rushing into the main area of the connecting cabin followed by Salenna as I do the same.

"Hello, this is the Captain speaking." The disembodied voice emerges from the declining background noise without warning, and the three of us frantically scan the room for anything resembling a speaker. We find none. "Let me be the first to welcome you on board the legendary ship known as *The Fated* and congratulate you on being selected for a once in a lifetime voyage! For the duration of our trip, rest assured, you won't have to worry about the smallest thing. So please relax and enjoy everything our fine ship has to offer!"

The Captain repeats the announcement in a handful of other languages. But I soon block out his voice altogether when the carpeted floor beneath us lurches, sending Salenna and Jaslene stumbling and me falling against a chair. As soon as I regain my balance, I rush through the glass doors and onto the balcony as gray buildings begin drifting by. Far below, onlookers now cover the entire pier. As the ship pulls away from the docks, people cry and cheer.

"I always wanted to know what this would feel like," Jaslene whispers, materializing by my side and peering down at the crowd with a sad smile.

Around her neck, the rose-colored pearl she always wears gleams in the light. She once told me it had been a twelfth birthday gift from her father and a promise to bring her along on the next voyage he took across the sea—a promise he hadn't lived to fulfill.

Sympathy tugs at my heart as I reach out to comfort her, but Jaslene is already pulling away, her expression bright once again as she waves at the people along the docks with her most beaming smile. As if on cue, a pair of biplanes zip by, cameras flashing from the passenger seats.

"I feel like a star in the cinema," Jaslene exclaims.

"Perhaps when we arrive at our new home, you'll become one," Salenna says, the rare affection in her tone making me churn with envy, if only for a moment.

Whistles and shouts erupt from the dock's edge where a man has just dived into the water and swims toward the ship. Behind him, the crowd screams with excitement while more whoops and hollers of encouragement resound from the decks above and nearby balconies as guests too urge him on.

"Someone should lower a rope," I say, scanning the higher levels to see if anyone is doing exactly that. "Someone should help him."

"Don't be absurd," Salenna scoffs. "He'll never make it."

It's true. With every stroke of his arms, the man falls farther and farther behind. Even from a distance, I can feel his desperation and hope with every movement as he is pummeled by wave after wave.

Still, *The Fated* does not slow.

Instead, the ship picks up speed, and all too soon the passengers' cheers turn to disappointed yells and taunts until the man has slowed to an exhausted halt, barely managing to keep afloat as he can do nothing but stare after the ship along with the others.

"What did I tell you?" Salenna says. I don't bother hiding my disgust at her triumphant tone. "He never had a chance. He wasn't chosen like us."

# CHAPTER 7

## DINNER PARTY

The Fated doesn't set sail alone.

Airships, boats, and aeroplanes trail by our side or behind us as we wade farther and farther from shore, the hum of their engines mingling with the sound of waves lapping against the hull and jazz music already echoing from the upper decks. Some are filled with reporters who will snap photos and write newspaper articles dedicated to describing the grandeur of *The Fated's* halls, staterooms, and whatever else they can catch a glimpse of through the ship's windows. Others are crowded with mere spectators who will commit to memory *The Fated's* lights glittering against the waves and the smiles of the passengers dancing along its decks to one day describe to their children and then grandchildren.

Most of these vessels will follow us until we reach The Veil, where they will halt, watching us disappear through the dark wall of clouds and into legend once again for the next sixteen years.

I barely notice them. I barely notice my chattering teeth from the freezing wind, too, or the numbness in my hands as I stare at the man's receding figure in the water until I can see him no more. Still, the memory of him lingers in my mind even as I don a dark maroon dress for dinner and slip my feet into a pair of satin flats nicer than any in the department store. The despair in his expression haunts me even as we pass by things I would have marveled at only an hour ago: a cinema, an arcade, a candy store, an amusement park, just to name a few.

If I were superstitious like my mother and great-grandmother before her, I would have labeled the entire affair as one of many bad omens that would soon follow. As it is, I do my best to bury the memory beneath the countless other infinitely more pleasant thoughts that should be swirling around my head—like how I plan to enjoy my newfound freedom.

Laughter pulls my attention back to where my aunt and cousin stroll in elegant evening dresses ahead of me, their heads bent together conspiratorially as they gossip and stare at a passing woman's old-fashioned bodice and bustled skirt. Like mine, their clothes fit perfectly—as if someone had invaded our closets and measured every sleeve, every bust, every waistline.

As soon as we round the next corner, the most delicious smells assault my senses, and the bodies towards the front of the crowd part just enough for me to catch a glimpse of the dining room—specifically, the first of dozens of tables sprawling with every possible kind of food I can think of and many more of which I've never seen.

Fresh crab legs pile on top of plates next to bowls filled with steaming rice. Pepper and herb-crusted filet mignons sit beside baskets of assorted breads. Platters overflow with pastas and broiled chicken drizzled with creamy sauce. To top it all off, there, scattered in between the countless other dishes are the elegant desserts: angel food cake crowned with ruby-colored strawberries and snowy frosting, soft cookies dappled with chocolate chips and doused in vanilla gelato, crème brûlées, soufflés, and various flavored ice creams.

"Leaving so much food strewn out here like this instead of serving in courses is nearly barbaric," Salenna says before regarding the bottles of red, white, dessert, and sparkling wine scattered across the table along with the other beverages. Her lips flatten further. "There's not even any rosé."

I don't bother to keep from rolling my eyes at this. Only my aunt could find something to complain about now.

"Look, one of the waiters just brought some out," Jaslene says, pointing to a bottle now standing at the far end of the table, the pink liquid inside glimmering in the light.

Instead of looking pleased, my aunt says nothing as she brushes by me with Jaslene close behind. Dozens of other guests follow, hunger brimming in their eyes as they circle around the food like vultures. My cousin and aunt are arguing in hushed whispers by the time I amble to where they are seating themselves at the far end of the table.

"What do you mean you don't have your shawl?" Salenna hisses. "I saw it draped over your arm when we left the room minutes ago!"

"I didn't lose it on purpose," Jaslene pouts, frantically brushing her hands against her arms from the chill lingering in the room.

"Ridiculous girl," Salenna says, earning a reproachful look from her daughter. "How are you supposed to charm our fellow passengers if you are too busy shivering all night?" Her raised voice draws several curious looks from across the table, and she flashes a charming smile before releasing a long-suffering sigh. "Never mind. Amarra will go find it."

"But—" I protest, tearing my gaze from the food merely inches away to glare at my aunt.

She, however, doesn't seem the least bit concerned as she lowers herself onto the seat next to Jaslene. A creak to my left is the only warning I get before I jerk my feet out of the way as an elderly woman pulls out the chair I planned on using.

"Better hurry up before all the spots are taken," Salenna quips as she places a napkin in her lap and reaches for the nearest glass.

Anger, hot and blinding, scalds through me, but any words shrivel on my tongue when my gaze falls on my cousin.

"Please, Amarra," Jaslene says, her beautiful face scrunching into a pout that never fails to evoke my sympathy. My resolve cracks.

"Save me a seat," I snap, drawing an enthusiastic nod from my cousin. I hurry past the entrance and the people milling outside, past the arrays of diners, cafes, and shops spanning the atrium and up the stairs into the corridor leading to our connecting cabins.

The ship lurches without warning, and I stumble over something lying on the carpet. I look down to find a gossamer cloth splayed beneath my feet, its sequins shimmering in the light. Jaslene's shawl. Bending down, I pick it up, resenting how soft the fabric feels against my fingers, how delicate. Only my cousin would carelessly misplace such an item.

I've already taken several steps down the hall when I hear the groan.

The sound is low, lower than the usual creaks and moans haunting the ship. Low enough to send my eardrums pulsing and the hair on the back of my neck rising. The wall sconce closest to me gives a high-pitched buzz without warning before flickering off and on again.

That is when the numbers on the cabin door to my right begin... melting.

The corners and surrounding frame do not budge at all. The white painted wood too remains unmoving. Only the brass figures forming 620 along the surface stretch inch by inch, growing distorted then elongating like unnatural fingers. I gasp, stumbling back.

Voices erupt along the corridor. I glance behind as two couples enter the hall before veering in the opposite direction.

When I spin back to the door though, the brass numbers have returned to normal, their shapes solid and unmelting. Instead of feeling relieved, the sight leaves me unsettled. The deep groaning noise has fallen silent as well, leaving only the normal creaking of the ship and distant notes of saxophones to keep me company.

Had I imagined the whole thing? Surely not, but I don't dare linger long enough to discover the cause. My feet move of their own accord, propelling me backwards, down the corridor, and through the nearest exit.

All too quickly, however, I fail to recognize the dimly lit taverns and pubs that greet me once I descend the stairs to the level I could have sworn the dining room was on. Cackles erupt nearby, making me wince at their pitch. The sound of glass shattering followed by shouts quickens my pace. But as I hurry along the path winding in between various establishments, my surroundings grow increasingly foreign rather than familiar.

Hope courses through me as a passenger services desk materializes into view—only for the emotion to evaporate when I draw close enough to see the "Closed" sign resting on top. Left with no other option, I push on.

One seemingly innocent turn leads me down a dark hall—one I quickly retreat from when I see a pulsing club entrance waiting on the opposite end. Another lands me in a casino filled with glowing slot machines, gem-covered walls, and gaudily dressed people crowding around tables stacked with chips and spinning roulette wheels. I feel light-headed from so many bright lights combined with the disorienting sensation of the floor swaying. When I stumble back outside, I lean against the nearest wall I can find before collapsing altogether.

"Excuse me," I say to the first person who walks by before I can think better of it. "Do you happen to know how to get to the dining room from here?"

Steps in front of me, the stranger turns, his features a collage of dark gold hair, hazel eyes, and chiseled angles.

"If I'm not mistaken, you follow this pathway until you reach the café on the corner, then turn right," he says, pointing in the opposite direction I had been heading. How could I have gotten turned around so easily? I can already envision my aunt's glower when I return. I can already imagine the laughter that will echo across the dinner table as Salenna delivers some deprecating comment about her niece's lack of punctuality or manners. The thought makes me feel the beginnings of a migraine coming on.

"Go past the bowling alley. Then after taking the stairs up two flights and continuing to the end of the Boulevard, you should find yourself in front of the dining room," the stranger finishes, and at my surprised expression, he grins and explains, "Since boarding, I've been exploring as much of the ship as I can."

As soon as dinner is over tonight, I plan to do the same. That is, if I can survive coexisting with my aunt for the entire duration.

And avoiding any more melting doors.

"Thank you," I say gratefully, and the man nods before strolling away. I've already taken several steps when his voice again drifts through the air behind me.

"If, however, you're in the mood for a little more fun, I would recommend trying The Nautilus," he suggests. "I was there myself not an hour ago. The food is delicious, and the company isn't nearly as stuffy."

I whirl, a question on my lips, but the stranger is already turning his back to me, his hands in his coat pockets as he whistles in tune with "Dance 'Til Morning"—a song I hadn't even noticed was playing over the speakers until now.

I shake my head and launch into a brisk walk. Fifteen minutes later, I reach the stairs when something glimmers at the edge of my vision. I halt, peeking past the rail to see the first of several silver-blue letters hanging above the entrance to another hall that is nearly concealed. It's a miracle I spot it in the first place.

My feet move seemingly of their own accord, and as I draw closer, more letters ripple into view above the entrance, spelling out The Nautilus in curving script resembling ocean waves. I yearn to rush inside, to lose myself in the wonders I'm certain wait beyond the doors and forget all about my aunt and the other passengers' judgment. At the memory of Jaslene shivering in her sleeveless dress, though, I climb the stairs. I hurry past people who smile and laugh like they're enjoying themselves far more than I am, and places that look far more exciting than where I'm going to until I'm at last back where I started.

"Amarra!" Jaslene waves, passing through the dining room doors and wearing a wide grin for someone who's freezing.

"Here," I say, holding out the shawl and noticing the navy suit jacket draped over her shoulders too late.

"What? Oh, I'm so sorry you went all that way for nothing," she says, looking anything but as she glances back through the entrance.

"Where did you get..." I start, following her gaze when she gasps, "Don't look now!"

"The young duke two seats down from me lent me this jacket when he saw how much I was suffering," Jaslene explains. "He's from Danmar, you know. Isn't he an absolute gentleman?"

"Sounds like it," I say, ignoring my cousin's command as I peer over her shoulder into the dining room.

A chestnut-haired young man who I assume is the duke watches us with interest from where he sits at the head of the table, the marigold flower pinned to his tuxedo lapel blinding in its brightness even from this distance. Considering Danmar's monarchy ceased having power centuries ago, he's not actually the duke of anything, not anymore—other than likely some estate along Danmar's coast or a fenced-in manor that was passed down to him from his father, great-grandfather, and so on just like his honorary and useless title. But then again, maybe not, considering he decided to board *The Fated* in the first place.

My gaze quickly drifts from him to my aunt, who nods at something the man across from her says, her smile polite but her eyes disdainful. Despite the hunger clenching my stomach, the idea of enduring an entire dinner beneath my aunt's scrutiny fills me with dread. Unbidden, the stranger's words replay in my mind like a recording that grows in volume, refusing to be ignored.

*If, however, you're in the mood for a little more fun...*

"Let's go somewhere else," I say, trying to tug Jaslene with me only for her to jerk out of my grip.

"Don't be ridiculous. We can't leave now," she says. "Things are just starting to get interesting. Besides, Mother would be furious, you know that."

Yes, I do, and the realization satisfies me to no end.

"Tell her not to bother waiting on me then," I say to a shocked Jaslene before spinning on my heel and racing back towards The Nautilus.

# Chapter 8

# The Nautilus

Any moment now, I will touch the ocean floor.

At least that's what it feels like. At first glance, the hallway leading to The Nautilus seems flat. As I continue, though, it gradually slopes down, down, down until I'm certain it will spit me out into the bottom of the sea. But rather than a fathomless black hole, a set of bronze and blue double-doors greet me at the corridor's end. Crashing waves embossed the front, and towards the top I can make out a ship resembling *The Fated* sailing towards a horizon cloaked with storm clouds.

The ominous depiction does the exact opposite of steadying my nerves, but I refuse to turn back now. Thankfully, my hands don't shake when I wrap them around the cold metal handles and pull. With a deep groan, the ornate doors open with surprising ease, and the instant I step through them, I gasp in amazement.

Glamorous people in dresses and suits crowd the space, lounging in booths, flitting between tables, or spinning on the dance floor to a jazz melody pulsing with trumpets and drums. Lanterns shaped like mollusk shells hang along the sides of the room, illuminating the sleek stylized walls bursting with bronzes, blues, and silvers. High above, a massive octopus with rubies for eyes covers the dome ceiling, its intricately carved tentacles curling menacingly towards the celebrating patrons below.

But the thing that immediately grabs my focus is the right wall, which is made completely of glass, revealing the open ocean on the other side. Bright lights shine from the exterior window, bathing the churning water in an eerie turquoise glow and sending its reflections rippling across the floor. I cross the handful of steps it takes until I can brush my fingers against the glass and marvel at the infiniteness stretching out before me. Below, deep-sea coral reefs spread in every direction in a labyrinth of oranges, turquoises, and purples while schools of equally colorful fish along with lobsters and crabs weave in between. Above, the sea's surface bubbles and speeds by, making me nearly reel from the sight's sheer bizarreness.

I turn back to the bustling club, suddenly feeling self-conscious among the people dancing with abandon and chatting with other passengers as if they're old friends until I remind myself that I have no reason to be. I belong here just as much as anyone else. Still, I relax when hardly anyone spares me a glance as I maneuver past the tables until I find a vacant booth in the corner. My jaw drops when I draw close enough to see the plates of fish, steamed vegetables, and sweet and spicy shrimp among the dishes covering the table. Just like the meal in the dining room, the dishes here are still steaming, and the last of my self-control shatters as I waste no time grabbing utensils and begin eating.

Seconds after I do, a glass of wine is set down beside me. "Thank you," I say, but by the time I glance up, the waiter's vanished into the crowd.

Sweet and rich, my first taste of the drink is divine. The second transports me to a state of absolute euphoria—that is, until a musical voice erupts from too close by, instantly shattering my peace.

"Would you mind terribly if we join you?"

I freeze before carefully swallowing the rest of the wine and raising my gaze to meet the dark eyes of the most stunning woman I have ever seen. Dressed in a sleeveless sapphire gown embroidered with gold and white cranes, she looks like nothing short of royalty with her pearl earrings and short hair curled fashionably around her heart-shaped face. Staring at her now makes me feel awkward and inadequate in my velvet dress and jeweled headband.

I blink, realizing I've been silent too long. "Of course," I say, scooting farther into the booth to make room. "I wouldn't mind in the leas—"

"This place is too crowded. Let's go somewhere else," a young man with the same midnight black hair as the girl's interrupts, his eyes skimming over the opulent surroundings with boredom before landing on me—and narrowing.

My smile dies. As does my appetite.

I instantly recognize his chiseled features and even sharper gaze. He's the same man I stumbled into at the docks and whose papers I knocked to the ground. Even worse is the fact that he's just as handsome as I remember: deep brown eyes, flawless ivory skin, and the kind of defined cheekbones that belong to a sculpture or painting heightened with angles. Not to mention a face that would make anyone swoon.

Then he opens his mouth.

"Ah, it's you again," he says, his tone echoing exactly how I feel. "Here to ruin something else of mine? Maybe this time you'd like to spill lemon sauce on my shirt. Or perhaps I could pull out my journal so you could soak it in soup."

I set my fork and knife down with a loud clatter.

"How tempting," I retort, satisfaction burning through me at the surprise that flashes across his face. Still, what remains of my manners pushes me into admitting, "I said I was sorry earlier, and I am. It was an honest accident."

"Fantastic! Now that we've cleared up the misunderstanding, we can carry on with the celebrating."

The tilt of the booth serves as the only warning before another body slides next to mine, and I turn to find myself face to face with a man with pale blond hair and eyes bluer than the sky. He winks and offers a blinding smile before frowning at the otherwise empty table around us.

"You're not one of those few poor souls who came alone, are you?" he asks.

"Don't be rude," the woman chides, sliding into the seat opposite me.

"What?" he says. "It's a reasonable question, considering it's a known fact that families and friends often get tickets to *The Fated* together."

"I'm here with my aunt and cousin," I offer.

"Then I feel even worse for you," the man says, grimacing. "If any of my cousins had tagged along, I would've jumped overboard before we even reached The Veil." He smirks. "Or maybe I would've tossed them over the side instead."

I can't tell if he's joking.

"You're absolutely intolerable," the woman chides but doesn't bother containing her smile as she leans close as if we are old friends. "I apologize for my brother's behavior earlier," she sighs, waving her hand towards the black-haired young man who pulls out a chair and raises the nearest glass to me in mock toast. "He's dreadful at first impressions. And as for him," she nods to her blond-haired companion to my left, "I know it's a challenge, but don't pay too much attention. It only encourages him."

"I assure you, he's never needed encouragement in his life," a fourth stranger with gray eyes and a tweed suit says, smirking, before swiveling to me and placing a rich brown hand on his chest. "Forgive their lack of manners. Let me be the first to introduce myself. My name is Emory Rivers. The beauty to your left and her far less pleasant brother are Miyuni and Kye-Shin Hura, while the charmer next to you is the infamous Leander Scott."

*Leander Scott.* Why did that name sound so uncomfortably familiar? I'm certain I heard it before in the halls and elevator back at the department stor—I gasp, looking at him in shock. "You mean your family is *the* Scotts? The ones who own half the department stores in the city?" I remember the rumors now, the ones claiming the Scotts had more money than the entire continent. "But why would *you* get on *The Fated*? What more could you possibly want?"

"Everything," Leander says as if the answer is obvious. "Freedom from my conniving family. Seeing new sights with only the most beautiful company at my side," he directs the last statement at Miyuni who blushes. "And fame, of course. I plan to start my own business empire when I get to Melanthros or wherever it is this ship is taking us. Mark this day, Miss...?" he pauses, looking at me expectantly.

"Amarra Obrel," I say after a moment.

"Yes, well, mark this day in your memory, Amarra Obrel, because years from now you will be able to tell your grandchildren you had the honor of meeting Leander Scott before he became the most famous man on the other side of The Veil."

Out of the corner of her vision, I swear I see Kye-Shin roll his eyes, but when I glance towards him, his gaze is fixed on something past the window. I wonder if he's even friends with Emory or Leander, or if they've just been thrown together since stepping on board. I have the distinct feeling it's the latter.

"*Amarra*," Emory repeats as if my name on his lips is a puzzle. "If I recall correctly, that means "melody" in one of the southeastern languages—Lamiran, isn't it?"

"Yes," I say, blinking. Startled. "Yes, that's right."

It has been so long since I heard someone speak the translation that I almost failed to remember it entirely. Exactly how much of myself had I lost in the years since my mother died and my dreams been destroyed if I could forget the meaning of my own name?

"I think it's gorgeous," Miyuni gushes with so much enthusiasm that I can't help but study her face for some sign of ulterior motive.

"Thanks," I reply softly when I find none.

"So," the other woman continues, sipping a flute of champagne before giving an appreciative hum. "What kind of place do you all think this Melanthros continent is anyhow? Assuming, of course, that's where the ship's taking us."

"Assuming?" Leander says, nearly spitting out his drink. "It was the only continent on that side of the world when the Veil appeared. What other destination could there be? It's not like this ship just rose out of the ocean on its own one day."

"Why not?" Miyuni says. "Everyone's heard the strange stories about Melanthros and the waters surrounding it. All those tales about fortune-telling compasses and traps for old gods and such. If the people on the lost continent didn't create *The Fated*, then maybe this same magic did."

Magic. Could that explain what I'd seen earlier tonight? Why the door had melted only to return to normal within seconds?

"Magic doesn't exist," Emory says, studying the sharp and angled designs etched along his tumblr glass. "It's just science we cannot understand enough to explain...yet."

"Well, *wherever* this ship is taking us must be a place rich in treasures and resources if the people there can build a ship as grand and invincible as this," Leander says, leaning closer to the table, his blue eyes taking on a hungry glint. "I bet the cities there have streets made of gold and mansions dripping with rubies and emeralds. Real ones, of course, not the garbage sold in those stores back in Abeon."

"What about you, Amarra?" I turn to find Miyuni looking at me expectantly. "Where do you think the ship is taking us?"

Except for Kye-Shin, everyone's attention focuses on me, and the realization that they are actually interested in my response fills me with elation—and dread.

"I don't know," I say reluctantly. "I suppose I haven't really thought about it."

That was a lie. For the last two days and night, I thought of nothing else. At one time if you'd asked me the same question, I would have envisioned a city full of pianos on every corner and in every house. Where the strumming of guitars, ukuleles, and harps drifted along every painted street and vine-covered courtyard. Where families and friends danced in time with waltzes on park lawns and strolled across bridges beneath the stars to nocturnes. So many stories claimed *The Fated* would take us to a paradise, and to me there could be no paradise without music.

But that had been before.

Now I just want a life of ease. Without suffering or struggle. I want to never again be forced to work at a job I hate or be belittled by people like Mrs. Savrie. I want a happy future where I can forget the pain of my past forever. Where I can no longer remember how heartbreaking it is to fail or how paralyzing it feels to be lonely. Where memories of all those nights I wasted practicing the piano are replaced by days spent sipping coffee at a bookstore café, basking beneath a palm tree's shade and my feet in the sand, and doing whatever I pleased whenever I pleased to do it.

The last thing I intend on doing, however, is confessing any of this to people I just met.

"As long as it's a paradise, I can't complain," I finally say instead before adding, "And so long as there's plenty more wine from where this came from."

"Now *that* I'll toast to!" Leander says, raising his own glass and clashing it against mine. As he does, my eyes fall on the square ring on his index finger. Unsurprisingly, it is made of gold just like his watch and is engraved with sleek geometric designs forming the initials LS.

Both Miyuni and Emory raise their glasses in a toast as well, their laughter, along with my own, drowning in the voices, scraping silverware, and other noises crowding the room.

When the jazz music wafting through the air quickens in tempo, Leander bolts to his feet and stalks around the table before extending his hand to Miyuni, his gold watch flashing garishly in the light. "Give me the honor of a dance?"

Her responding smile is dazzling.

"Mr. Scott, I believe that's the best idea you have had all night," she croons, gracefully placing her hand in his as she allows herself to be pulled onto the dance floor where the pair become a blur of spinning legs, silk, and cashmere beneath the lights.

"I guess that's my cue to retrieve more drinks then," Emory says, rising from his seat as well and offering me an apologetic smile. I watch him wade through the crowd filled with people shrieking in laughter or drunkenly singing to music—people I'm rapidly feeling out of place to be among once again.

"I should go," I say, though the instant the words leave my mouth I have no idea who I'm talking to, considering Kye-Shin appears to be occupied with enjoying his dinner far too much to notice or care.

I'm already walking away from the booth when he speaks.

"I wouldn't count on it being a paradise if I were you."

"Excuse me?" I say, spinning around.

"Melanthros," Kye-Shin says, setting down his utensils. "Almost everyone on this ship seems convinced that it's this perfect utopia."

"And you don't," I say, crossing my arms and not bothering to act surprised.

"Not necessarily," Kye-Shin replies, shaking his head. "I think—I hope wherever we're going is better. But then I wonder why *The Fated* only takes a limited number of passengers every sixteen years. Why certain people are chosen while others aren't with no explanation, like some kind of twisted lottery, and what that says about the kind of civilization we're sailing to."

I've wondered the same kinds of things. Everyone at some time or another has, and yet practically no one ever dares utter such doubts aloud. No one, that is, except the man across from me on my first night on board *The Fated*.

And in this moment—on a day that's *supposed* to be full of celebration and happiness beyond belief—I can't help but hate him for it, even though a part of me knows the feeling is irrational.

"Maybe you should wonder less," I say, plucking a chocolate-colored cherry from the plate closest to Kye-Shin's and popping it into my mouth, savoring the darkly sweet taste. "After all, since you decided to come on board, you might as well enjoy the voyage. Or at the very least, have the courtesy to let the people around you try."

I whirl before he can say anything more, stalking through the club even as I feel his glare until the bronze doors slam shut between us.

~

I try to follow my own advice, I really do. I go ice skating, sighing in elation when I glide along the rink as freely as the birds I used to see flying over the river on my morning ride to the department store. I watch a drama at the cinema, amazed when I swear I can smell the fragrance from the plumerias onscreen and feel the unspoken love between the characters as if I am really living their lives. But the exhaustion from the day catches up with me all too soon, muddling my enthusiasm and weighing down my limbs.

Later when I finally return to my stateroom, the connecting door to my aunt and cousin's cabin is still open, but they aren't there, and I can't help but sigh in relief. The wind howling against the window serves as the only other noise in the silence as I wander farther inside to discover both spaces have been cleaned since we left. The clothes Jaslene carelessly threw onto her bed before dinner now hang neatly from the closet while the glasses Salenna sipped wine from just before dinner stand once again by the minibar, their immaculate surfaces gleaming in the light. My bed too has been freshly made, for the covers are unnaturally smooth, leaving not the slightest wrinkle from where I sat or laid my suitcase earlier.

Out of habit, I grab the music box on the nightstand and turn the lever like always when I yearn for the memory of music to overpower my thoughts.

Except this time the song isn't merely a memory.

Soft, clear notes ring from the tiny box for the first time in years, making me nearly drop the object as if it burns. The last time I heard it had been the night I threw it in rage after the audition, breaking it beyond repair—until now. Any joy I feel at hearing the song again, however, quickly dies.

The sound is not the same as I remember. Certain notes drift in and out of tune, falling flat or leaping to a sharp in a way that gives the melody a haunting tone that sounds less like the false happy version made famous by August Urst and more like the original Lamiran folk tune. In fact, it sounds like my own arrangement I had played on the piano hundreds of times.

I recall the cherry blossoms and apricots in Jaslene's room as well as the hundreds of books and constellation lights in mine—along with my unease at how accurately the features fit both our personalities and pasts.

I hurriedly retrace my footsteps, throwing open the door and scanning the hall for any crew or staff member, anyone to ask, anyone to thank.

I see no one.

For once, the corridor is void of laughing people headed to another party or the pool. Their absence overwhelms me with the sensation that I'm the only person here, that the rooms hidden behind the countless red doors spanning either direction are empty. In the distance, I catch a familiar song echoing from the atrium, but the singer's raspy voice is all too quickly swallowed by the sudden creak and moan the ship releases as it hits another wave, as if it's made of decaying bones and flesh rather than steel.

Feeling exposed, I stumble back into the cabin and slam the door behind me. It's only after my trembling fingers manage to lock the deadbolt that I can at last breathe again.

# Chapter 9

## Exploring

"This one's perfect for you," Jaslene says, placing a tiara adorned with aquamarines and pearls on top of my head before grabbing my shoulders and swiveling us towards the mirror.

I blink, hardly recognizing the young woman staring back at me. A woman who wears a cream chiffon blouse and silk trousers rather than an austere uniform or old clothes. Who may still have dark circles under her eyes, yes, but ones that are slowly fading, as well as a smile that is no longer forced.

I never want to let this version of myself go.

"It's not bad," I reply, pursing my lips and mimicking a line I've heard my aunt say dozens of times, "Although it can't possibly compare to the ones offered at The Luxe."

The words barely leave my mouth before Jaslene and I burst out laughing, drawing stares from the surrounding passengers perusing through the jewelry shop. After one last glance, I lift the accessory from my hair and carefully place it back on the glass shelf along with dozens of others twinkling in the light.

"You should have seen her face when I told her you weren't coming back for dinner last night," Jaslene says, adjusting her own tiara studded with diamonds and tourmalines before donning matching earrings and appraising her reflection. "For a moment, I was terrified she would launch out of her chair and chase after you like we were children again."

I laugh at the thought. I'm amused not because it's in itself particularly funny, but rather because Jaslene mistakenly thinks my aunt ever chased after me, that she ever cared enough. I don't have the heart to correct my cousin though.

"How did your little excursion go, anyway?" she asks, dragging my attention back to her fingers as they brush over necklaces strung with ivory, black, and pink pearls.

"Well for the most part," I offer, thinking of The Nautilus's breathtaking view and lively music. Of Miyuni, Emory, and even Leander. "I met some nice people."

"Oh?" Jaslene pauses to admire a gold ring crowned with tanzanites before sliding it onto her finger, followed by a silver one bedecked with beryls and garnets. "Anyone especially charming?"

Kye-Shin's face materializes in my mind, and I will the image to shatter.

"Definitely not."

"Oh, I absolutely can't live without these," Jaslene gushes, placing a third cameo ring on her index finger before holding up her hand to admire.

"You don't have to," a woman several feet to our left says. She motions to the surrounding walls, the action sending the jade beads from her hairpin dangling. "None of this costs a cent. All the jewelry is free, just like the clothes in your closet. You can take whatever you want."

"How can you be sur—" I start, but she is already stalking away, grabbing several moonstone brooches on her way out. Dresses and clothes are one thing, but gemstones?

When she steps through the door, I expect angry staff or security guards in dark clothes to appear and drag her away, kicking and shrieking. I'd witnessed a similar scene at the department store once. But just like the woman said, no one stops her. No wailing sirens accompany her escape. Seconds later, another passenger exits wearing an amethyst pendant around her neck as big as my thumb.

"Look at these, Amarra!" Jaslene squeals, pulling me to another corner of the shop covered with jewelry adorned in gemstones that glitter a multitude of colors in the light.

Lixirites.

"Are these real?" I gasp.

"Of course, they're real!" Jaslene insists. "Just look at them."

She's right. The colors of these gems are far more vibrant than any I've ever seen in Abeon, appearing as a collage of turquoises, oranges, and magentas at certain angles while transforming to twelve different shades of gold at another.

Beside me, Jaslene giggles as she scoops up a ring with a Lixirite as large as my thumbnail to slide on her right hand while grabbing another with a trio of smaller Lixirites to decorate her left.

"Here, take these," she urges, dumping five more rings and necklaces into my palms.

"I don't know," I say, staring down at the Lixirites glittering up at me. I had spent my whole life gazing at luxurious accessories from a distance. Yet now that I can have ones of even greater value and as many as I wished, I can't help but feel...anxious. I can't help but feel as if at any moment, accepting one good thing too many might make every-thing—the jewelry, the dresses, *The Fated*—dissolve like an illusion. Or a dream I wish I'd never woken up from.

"Oh, stop fretting for once," Jaslene insists, clearly not sharing my fears as she switches out her tiara for a diamond forehead band with flamingo-styled feathers. "If you don't, I just might find someone else more fun to spend my day with."

Releasing another laugh, my cousin bolts out the door, barely giving me enough time to slip on a Lixirite bracelet that snatches my eye before I rush to catch up with her.

Over the course of yesterday and today, I've come to realize *The Fated's* layout is a fusion of sorts. The outer edges and top follow the design of a traditional ocean liner with decks, pools, lounges, and cabins connected to balconies overlooking the waves below. The heart of the ship, however, resembles a city. It's made up of a single but multi-floored boulevard that stretches out from the atrium we first saw when we boarded what already seems like ages ago. The boulevard is lined with all manner of shops, restaurants, alleys, street lamps, and other features resembling those one might find back on Pearl Street.

Bakeries melt into truffle shops that stand alongside beauty salons and charming antique stores. The sweetness of perfume fades into the smell of sizzling enchiladas, which then is overpowered by coffee beans, vanilla, baking bread, and too many other aromas to name.

Then there's the music. Couples dance to a tango beneath the courtyard lights of a bistro. A sweeping score blares from the cinema's entrance. Waltzes stream from the carousel with every spin while the strum of a guzheng—a twenty-one stringed instrument I learned is played in the eastern country of Nanshyn from a book I once read—drifts from a teahouse illuminated with swaying lanterns. Underneath every noise, jazz melodies constantly play from invisible speakers, echoing through the atrium like an alternating heartbeat. So many different noises should be discordant to my ears. Yet somehow they aren't. Instead, they meld together perfectly, the sounds of even the most unexpected instruments complementing each other to create one strange but exhilarating symphony.

I love every second of it.

Jaslene pulls us toward the arcade where we marvel at the entrance shaped like the face and mouth of some ancient sea god before we rush inside to play games that burst with colors, whistles, and prizes. Afterward, we explore the Excursion Rooms—living dioramas of landscapes from all over the known world. In the Island Room, we swing from hammocks strung from life-like palm trees that sway in an artificial breeze, giggling all the while. In the Winter Room, we spin beneath the falling snow and make a snowman with a lopsided smile and crooked nose.

Then we move on, rushing along the other floors of the Boulevard with child-like wonder. With every new discovery, I'm certain I have reached my limit of amazement, that nothing else on *The Fated* can possibly surpass all that I have already seen. Yet with every new experience, I never cease being amazed, never cease wondering at the giant squids and tiger sharks that glide through the aquarium, or the floors upon floors filled with shelves of gilded leather-bound books in the library.

"Look, Amarra, a piano," Jaslene gasps as we pass a store filled with harps, violins, tubas, and every other instrument you could name. A grand piano sits inside the window, its immaculate surface glistening beneath the spotlights. "You should play and dazzle everyone with your talent!"

I can't deny that my fingers itch to touch the keys just as my ears yearn to hear the songs I still know by heart. But I hesitate, remembering the hours upon hours I dedicated to mastering every note and measure.

How in the end, they had all been for nothing.

"Maybe another time," I lie, moving away from the music store without sparing it another glance as I pass by a candy shop, then a pizzeria.

"Want to go inside?" I ask when we near a store filled with maps.

Through the windows, I can see they all only depict the known world on this side of The Veil of course. Still, Jaslene once mentioned how she loved poring over maps with her father when he was alive. Seeing the lines and shadows across the paper depicting real places throughout the world had fueled her thirst to travel. They made her yearn to find out for herself how deep the snow in the Roakin Mountains could be to walk in or how refreshing the waters of the Kalaydren Islands could feel against her bare feet.

Now, however, the barest shadow flickers over my cousin's gaze before she shakes her head and resumes her smile.

"Maybe another time," she says, echoing my earlier words before declaring, "Today I'm in the mood for sunshine!"

Without waiting, she rushes to the nearest elevator with me

hurrying behind. We soon forget any mention of pianos and maps when, minutes later, smooth wooden doors open to reveal blinding sunlight. A shocked smile spreads across my face even as I close my eyes against the brilliance. How long has it been since I have seen the sun? Not the occasional sliver of pale rays that manage to escape past the smog and pollution-stained clouds permanently hovering over the city, but rather the real shining light I remember catching glimpses of in my childhood.

The heat dances across my skin, seeping into me, rejuvenating me. A strong breeze sends loose wisps of hair flying around my face, carrying with it refreshing coolness as well as the scent of saltwater. Daring to open my eyes for the second time, I squint against the brightness, forgetting the pain when I drink in the scene surrounding me.

Passengers bustle along the sun deck populated with umbrellas, palm leaf fans, and fruit trays. A group of girls dressed in fitted one-piece swimsuits giggle and splash each other at one end of a pool while on the opposite side, two men in tank-tops and swim trunks bounce a beach ball back and forth over a net. Ukulele chords accompanied by the tropical beat of a steelpan ricochets off the wooden decks and into the sea air, making my soul hum with every note and my feet feel lighter with every step.

"Amarra, over here!" Jaslene dashes to a nearby table strewn with sunglasses and plucks up a pair with large white frames to slide onto her nose. "What do you think?" She poses. "Am I stunning?"

"Always," I say, grinning and surveying the remaining sunglasses until I settle on a pair with dark tortoise shell frames and circular lenses. Simple but fashionable. At least, I hope.

I still can't quite get used to living in such luxury: to having dozens of sunglasses to choose from whenever the day is a little too bright; to passing trays lined with every kind of food and drink imaginable before I even realize I'm hungry or parched. I have to remind myself that this isn't all a dream. I won't wake up to find myself back in my dreary apartment or the elevator of the department store.

Still...I don't dare pinch myself just in case.

"Whatever should we do first?" Jaslene says, grabbing a sun hat from a nearby rack full of over a dozen others and throwing it on as if it were made for her.

My eye falls on the tables lining the deck's edge on the right, crowded with couples wielding paddles. "How about a game of ping-pong?" I suggest, watching their movements with fascination. I had never had a chance to play before. Then again, I had never had a chance to do most of these things. "We could go put our feet in the water too. Or go sunbathin—"

"Arthur!" Jaslene shrieks, making me wince as she waves to someone I fail to spot in the crowd. The movement sends the pearl dangling from her necklace swinging from side to side, glowing in the light.

"Who?" I ask, massaging my still-ringing ear.

"*Arthur*," Jaslene hisses as if it's obvious. "The charming young duke who lent me his jacket at dinner last night, remember?" She whirls to me, her dark eyes brightening. "You don't mind if I spend the rest of the afternoon with Arthur, do you? We have plenty of time to do all the things you want later, okay?"

"I—" I start, but she is already hurrying away, her tulip and sunflower speckled dress gliding behind her gracefully despite her frenzied state.

"Please don't mention a word of this to Mother!" she shouts without slowing. "I promise I'll make it up to you!"

People sitting in the lounge chairs and mingling along the bar raise their gazes to watch as she soars across the deck and into the arms of the handsome chestnut-haired young man like the heroine of a romantic drama. Seconds after they embrace, the pair race hand-in-hand through the double doors and out of my sight once and for all, no doubt on a quest to discover countless other marvels.

Sighing, I grab a strawberry mimosa topped with a mini umbrella from a nearby tray and begin sipping it as I continue my stroll. My eyes drift over the spiraling pool slides zipping with shrieking passengers, buffet stations steaming with fresh beef-stuffed tortillas and pizzas, and ice sculptures of castles and ships resembling *The Fated*. After finishing my drink, I climb the stairs to the upper deck, taking in an azure sky dotted with clouds and sapphire waters stretching in every direction. The ocean's vastness almost stuns my lungs into dissolving, steals my breath away and makes me feel as weightless as the pair of seagulls circling the deck or the handful of airships I spot floating in the distance. Is this how my great-grandmother felt when she crossed the sea to leave Lamira with her family a lifetime ago?

The country they were leaving had been a place of sunshine and palm trees, a place where everyone's skin was tan from basking beneath the sky all day while their feet were strong from running bare against the soft soil and green grass. It was a land where the fruit tasted sweeter than any chocolate and flowers smelled more fragrant than an entire store full of perfume—that is until disease and famine struck.

Left with no other choice, they boarded a ship they believed would carry them to a better life. For my great-grandmother, however, that better life had all too quickly deteriorated into the heartbreak caused by a philandering husband, an ebony fever outbreak, and quarreling children. Three generations later, my mother hadn't fared much better. The possibility of my own journey ending in the same disappointment crosses my mind. The second it does, Kye-Shin's words echo in my mind like a taunt.

*Melanthros...almost everyone on this ship seems convinced that it's this perfect utopia.*

What if we really were wrong? What if I've made a terrible mistake just like my great-grandmother when she embarked on that voyage all those years ago?

No—I refuse to think that way. This isn't simply another ship destined for a known land, a flawed land. This is *The Fated,* and it is bound for a place beyond the mundane world, beyond disappointments and disillusionment and everything its passengers are escaping from. If so many people believed such a thing, then surely it had to be true.

Humming drifts from nearby, and I turn to see a small figure wandering along the deck ahead of me. The younger girl wears a vintage green dress with old-fashioned frills and puffed sleeves as well as a matching bow in her black hair, which whips just past her chin in the wind. She looks to be only ten or eleven, and yet when I glance around, I can find no sign of a parent or guardian. Surely, she hadn't been the only member of her family to receive a ticket. Not when she was so young...

"Hello," I say, pasting on a tentative smile as I approach. Instead of smiling back, the girl halts and runs her gaze over me before crossing her arms and emitting an indignant huff.

"Let me guess, you're going to ask if I'm lost, aren't you?" she snaps, and I have to bite back a grin at the way she straightens her spine to look taller while tapping her foot in impatience.

Up close, her pale skin appears almost sickly against the glow of the tan deck. But there is no mistaking the sharpness in her obsidian eyes.

"I suppose the question was written all over my face," I admit. "But then are you up here...all alone?"

"Not alone," the girl says with a shake of her head before jabbing her finger toward the pool below where several teenagers bellow with laughter as one leaps into the water with enough force to send droplets spraying over nearby sunbathers. "My family's down there, but I don't feel like swimming today, and I wanted some time alone. To think."

I'm tempted to ask what she possibly needs to think about at such a young age. But when the girl raises an eyebrow, as if daring me to say it out loud, I wisely reconsider my reply.

So instead, I say, "Ah, I see." Even though I don't. Then I add, "Well, you chose the perfect spot."

"Is that why you came up here too?" the girl inquires, her expression turning curious. "What were you thinking about?"

"Nothing much," I shrug, gazing out over the rail to several aeroplanes to the east and the flying fish gliding among the whitecaps. "I was just thinking how happy I am."

"You don't look happy." The girl regards me with skepticism, her eyes unblinking in the sunlight. "Do you not like the ship?"

"What? No, I love it, I—" when after several seconds, any half-decent lie fails to form in my mind, I give up trying altogether. "Walking along the deck just reminded me of something—several things, actually.

Memories from my past I usually try to avoid thinking about. Most days, I wish I could forget them entirely."

When I realize who I'm talking to, however, I soften my face into a smile. The last thing I want to do is ruin her mood by talking about my past. "I'm sorry. I feel like I'm taking up your alone time."

"I was just about to leave," the girl says, unperturbed. "I need to be getting back, anyway. It was a pleasure chatting." She delivers the last line with a dramatic flourish of her wrist in a gesture I suspect she's seen only in movies.

"I enjoyed talking with you too," I say, amused. I offer my hand. "My name is Amarra, by the way. What is yours?"

"Lethia," the girl answers, placing her small palm in mine. Her skin is cool despite the sun's heat. Lethia tilts her head as if in question. "Does this mean we're friends now?"

I grin and nod, envious of her childhood innocence. "Yes, I think so."

"Well then," Lethia begins, sliding her hand from mine to raise it in a wave. "See you later, friend."

I return the gesture, feeling lighter as I do. The memories burdening my mind earlier are now nothing more than a distant buzz, like the ocean's surf after the tide has rolled back out, leaving the beach clear and cleansed.

For the first time, I'm not concerned with where *The Fated* is taking us. I can't find it in myself to stress over what sort of life awaits me in an unknown land.

Instead, I relish the sunlight kissing my skin. The gentle rocking of the ship from side to side. The limitless sea glittering against an even more infinite sky. But most of all, the blessed emptiness of my mind.

Right now, I feel as if I'd be happy to remain on this ship forever.

# Chapter 10

## Sea Day

It could be minutes or hours when I finally move away from the rail to wander along the deck again. Voices I recognize too late drift towards me on the wind, and as I round the next corner leading to the ship's bow, an enthusiastic shout shatters my reverie.

"Ah, a familiar face!" Leander booms from the tallest portion of faux turf comprising a miniaturized golf course stretching along the back deck. At my stare, he raises his club and winks. "Remember me?"

I can't help but smirk. "Is that a trick question?" I say, grabbing a tiny piece of toasted bread crowned with balsamic-glazed tomatoes and burrata cheese from a nearby tray. "The more interesting one though is whether or not you remember me?"

"Of course!" Leander replies, offended. "Your name is...Mary? Meira? Emer—"

"Amarra," Emory says from where he stands on the course next to a miniature skyscraper. "Won't you join us?"

For a second, I hesitate. I don't need to glance at where Kye-Shin sits by the deck's edge to feel the intensity of his gaze.

"I was hoping to see you again soon!" Miyuni says, waving from a section of the course I hadn't noticed until now. A short orange sundress drapes over her body, and a matching bandana is tied around her ebony hair. She looks like a model splayed across the front cover of a fashion magazine.

She tosses her club carelessly onto the turf before dancing past a miniature bridge, rotating windmill, and coral tunnel until hurrying to my side. "You snuck out last night before we had a chance to get to know each other. I can't tell you how heartbroken I was!"

"Really?" I ask, skeptical.

"Absolutely," Miyuni insists, wrapping my arm in hers as if we're already kindred spirits. "And I apologize on my brother's behalf for whatever he said to upset you enough to leave without so much as a goodbye!"

She directs the last words to Kye-Shin, who reclines next to the rail reading a book and appearing untroubled by the accusation.

"On the contrary, dear sister," he says, turning the next page without bothering to look up. "We parted on good terms, with Amarra even being generous enough to offer me advice."

"And did you take it?" I say before I can think better of it. "My advice?"

At that, Kye-Shin finally looks up, the heat of his gaze as scorching as the sun's rays on the deck. "It's still under consideration," he says. I swear I spot the corner of his lips twitching in amusement before he returns his attention back to his book.

"Ignore him, please, I beg you," Miyuni sighs, directing us towards the opposite rail. "Sometimes it's the only way to keep your sanity."

"That's funny," Kye-Shin comments. "I once heard one of your suitors say the same thing about you."

Beside me, Miyuni twists around and sticks her tongue out at her brother before saying something in Nanshyn that sends Kye-Shin chuckling, the sound rich and deep. She swivels back to me with a giggle. "Please forgive our juvenility. Whenever one of us starts acting mature, it doesn't take long for the other to bring him or her back down to their level," she confesses with a smile. I can't help but smile back.

"I adore your trousers, by the way!" She eyes the loose pants I absentmindedly threw on this morning. My aunt had found them horrid. Never mind the fact that women, especially those in the working class, had started wearing them within the last several years—or that they were practical, comfortable even.

*Women were meant to wear skirts or dresses, not trousers*, she hissed. Even Jaslene had gawked at them in morbid fascination. From that moment on, I decided they were my favorite piece of clothing.

"From your fashion sense, I can tell we're going to be great friends already!" Miyuni gushes.

"I hope so," I say honestly.

It's been years since I had a friend other than Jaslene. I'd been close with a few classmates at secondary school as well as my music teacher there, but I'd lost touch with them all quickly after my mother died. Afterwards, there had been the shop girls and other staff at the department store who, even when they tried being polite, had always looked at me with some measure of pity or disdain in their eyes.

But not Miyuni.

I tense in apprehension when she climbs onto the rail and leans over the side, her short hair whipping past her bandana as she gazes out towards the sea.

"From this height, I feel as if I could float among the clouds any second!" she says, closing her eyes and holding an arm out for good measure. "It's so exhilarating!"

"Care to challenge Leander's winning streak, Amarra?" Emory asks, reclining at a nearby table as he sips from a martini. With his drink in hand, he motions to where the former heir of the Scott fortune sways in place with his golf club resting against his neck, looking unimpressed. "Unfortunately, Miss Hura and I combined are no match for his skills."

"Considering I'm the three-time champion of Abeon's Northwestern province, I would be embarrassed if you were," comes Leander's modest response.

"You should be ashamed of yourself," Miyuni says teasingly. "Beating a woman who has never even lifted a club before. If you were a gentleman, you would have let me at least win a round."

"And when did you ever expect me to act like a gentleman?" Leander asks with a languid smile that sends Miyuni's pale cheeks blushing.

"I'll give it a go," I say, spinning around to face Leander and Emory's surprised expressions. "Though I've never actually played before."

"There's nothing to it," Emory says, plucking up a toothpick skewered with slices of kiwi, pineapple, and clementine in the shape of a palm tree before popping it into his mouth.

"Nothing except talent and skill, you mean," Leander says, bending down to pick up Miyuni's club and handing it over to me with a wicked grin. "Don't expect me to go easy on you just because you're a beginner."

I can't help but snort. "Thanks for the warning."

In my hands, the club feels strange and awkward, and it shows. On my first attempt, I not only miss the hole but get the ball lodged into the mouth of a miniature tiger along the course. On my second, when the ship tilts without warning, I accidentally send the ball flying, missing several passengers wading in the hot tub by less than a foot.

"Sorry, sorry," I apologize, rushing to retrieve it.

"We're taking our lives in our own hands by staying out here," Kye-Shin remarks as I hurry past. I listen to Miyuni's advice and ignore him. It's anything but easy.

"We should find something more entertaining," Leander says. "Winning all the time bores me."

"There's always the amusement park or the theater," Emory suggests before his voice takes on a humorous tinge. "Or perhaps you would prefer to go back to the Breakfast Room for coffee."

Leander makes a disgusted noise. "Don't be ridiculous!" he growls. "My morning was ruined from listening to that woman hysterically rant about having not seen her husband since they boarded. I'm sure the poor fool is waltzing around the ship with several stunning beauties on each arm as we spea—"

Kye-Shin launches to his feet, his expression alarmed. "He can't be serious," he breathes, and it is only then I become aware of an engine's growing growl and gasps from the surrounding passengers as they raise their eyes to the sky.

I whirl just as an aeroplane blots out the sun, a long rope swinging from its door with a man clinging to its end, his expression determined. Desperate. Almost identical to the one worn by the man who jumped from the docks.

"He isn't planning to board, is he?" someone says.

"What else does it look like he's doing?" another shouts as the plane lowers, bringing the man within thirty feet of the deck. Then twenty-five. Then fifteen.

He's almost within jumping distance when a grating noise erupts from the aircraft, followed by a boom that rattles the air as fire and smoke burst from beneath its left wing.

"Watch out!" someone screams as the aeroplane tilts towards the deck, sending people scrambling away from the bar and out of the hot tubs. The aircraft veers to the side as *The Fated* speeds past.

Kye-Shin breaks into a sprint after it, and I'm running too, pounding along the boards to a rhythm that matches my heart as I race around the corner after him and back towards the main deck. Beyond the rail, the aeroplane careens by, dark plumes of smoke still rippling from it while the rope jerks violently enough to cause the man to tumble into the water, his head sinking beneath the foamy waves.

I wait, not daring to blink. Not daring to breathe. The seconds stretch by, their slowness making me aware of both things that matter and things that don't: the aeroplane swerving past the ship's stern and out of sight; the tropical music still echoing from the deck below; the smell of salt water and burnt metal coalescing in my nose; the coldness beginning to spread throughout my body despite the sun's heat.

Yet my gaze does not waver from the water churning below, its sapphire depths vast. Unknowable. Had *The Fated* somehow caused the aeroplane to malfunction? Had something on this ship purposely prevented the man from landing on board?

"Come on," I hear Kye-Shin beside me urge under his breath, his expression uncharacteristically concerned. "Come on!"

I will the man to splash through the surface any second, for him to kick and struggle to keep up with *The Fated* before inevitably falling behind like the man on the docks if only to show that he was still frantic and fearless and *alive*.

But the water continues churning, its foamy waves vacant of any writhing limbs or mouths gasping for air.

We never see the man again.

# CHAPTER 11

# WATCH PARTY

In many ways, the Breakfast Room is the most impressive place on *The Fated*.

Designed like an enormous kitchen from a fairytale palace, the vast space is all glossy white tiled walls, polished wood, and glittering chandeliers shaped like a bevy of swans in flight. Blue muslin curtains frame windows on each side, while stained glass waves, fish, and seashells span every inch of the ceiling, making the already bright interior dazzle with even more brilliance and color. Despite its name, the Breakfast Room consists of every kind of food imaginable.

In one chamber, a tower of pastries coated with powdered sugar rises to the ceiling, while by each wall, there is a table crowded with platefuls of thin pancakes drizzled with chocolate and strawberries as well as waffles swimming in rich brown syrup. In a second room, the smell of bacon wafts through the air above bright yellow omelets, sizzling steaks, and pan-fried tofu. Still another area contains coffee and tea from around the world along with juice freshly pressed from various fruits, including Lamiran mangos and guavas.

Only four days ago, I had marveled at the twelve-tiered chocolate fountain and over thirty flavors of macaroons. I was convinced I'd stumbled into heaven at the first bite of a warm cinnamon roll drizzled with icing, at the first taste of egg-fried rice seasoned with garlic flooding my senses.

Today, however, I hardly take notice of the biscuits, hash browns, and glazed donuts half-mindedly piled onto my plate. In my mouth, the sugar feels like sand between my teeth, while the sweet taste of a cruller barely registers on my tongue. I'm too distracted by what's waiting for us outside the windows, by the curtain of gray stretching endlessly across the horizon, still distant but slowly growing.

The Veil.

It rose into view earlier this morning, and as soon as it did, the passengers began whispering and jittering with nervousness. Not that everyone will admit it. The half a dozen people at the table sitting next to us shout in laughter, their cackles sounding forced and exaggerated in the muted noise of scraping silverware and moving chairs. Across from me, Jaslene stirs her tea for what must be the tenth time, glancing every second or so outside before she resumes stirring again.

Next to her, my aunt sips something stronger than caffeine from a coffee cup. When her gaze wanders too close to the window, she absent-mindedly pushes the rosemary bouquet decorating the table nearer to the glass. It is as if, like my mother and great-grandmother before her, she too believes the herb will ward away whatever evil might be lurking in The Veil. The observation is unnerving, considering in all the years I've known my aunt, I've never once seen her place any ounce of credibility on the superstitions that clung to our family like ghosts.

I can't decide which is worse: staring at my family or the wall of oncoming storm clouds that would mean certain death for anyone not on board *The Fated*. That might still mean certain death for us all if the legends turned out to be fal—

"Gooood morning!" a voice screeches without warning past the static that ricochets off the tiles and glass. "This is Gerald, your Entertainment Director, speaking! I hope you all had a good sleep last night because on this fifth, and *very special*, day of our voyage, we will be passing through The Veil—the infamous natural phenomenon responsible for sinking many a ship lesser than ours!"

"As if we need to be reminded," I can't help grumbling. For once, my aunt neither disagrees or scolds me.

"—but not to worry, folks, inside these walls you'll be safe and sound! In fact, two hours from now at one o'clock, we'll be hosting a watch party in the Sea Dragon, Neptune, and Siren lounges. So, grab your drinks and strap in while we kick this voyage up several notches of fun!"

Like the Captain, Gerald repeats his message in several other languages before the static and speakers fall silent. The instant they do, the room erupts with voices and activity, as if the Director's announcement has given everyone permission to return to normal, or at least the pretense of it.

"A party sounds exciting," Jaslene says, color returning to her face as she risks a glance out the window. Her gaze quickly skitters back to me. "What shall we do until then? Visit the amusement park? Go to the spa? Watch a movie?"

"Whatever you decide, don't be late for the watch party," Salenna says, grabbing her silverware and cutting a slice of grapefruit, acting as if she was never concerned to begin with.

"Go back to the stateroom and change into something more flattering as well, Jaslene. Since the whole ship will likely be attending, you never know who you might meet or need to impress."

"Impress?" I scoff. "I think everyone will be too busy staring at The Veil to notice or care."

The look my aunt gives me is venomous.

"I'll make sure to change, Mother," Jaslene says before grabbing my arm and pulling me away from the table and the Breakfast Room altogether.

Everything that follows is a blur of activity and restlessness. We skate several laps around the ice rink, spinning and stumbling like the people we watched from the ice cream shop days ago. We watch a comedy called *The Perfect Life* in the theater, eating popcorn and laughing at all the right places beneath the dimmed lights and spinning projector. We even go on a rollercoaster ride at the amusement park. We try to distract ourselves from The Veil's creeping closeness in the drop of our stomachs as we fall and move so swiftly that we no longer know which direction is up or down, forward or backward.

The distractions, though, only last for so long.

By the time we finally pass through the entrance to the Sea Dragon lounge, both Jaslene and I buzz with anxiousness, with more fear than excitement one second then the reverse in the next. Around us, people chat and cackle, but their voices are too high, their conversation so unnaturally normal it borders on absurd.

"You'll never guess where I discovered the most charming little bistro last night," I hear one woman say to another as I pass their table.

"Such fantastic weather for playing tennis today," a man says to a couple in the corner as he downs a glass of champagne. "Fantastic."

Other sections of the lounge are deathly quiet, full of people sitting in booths littered with refreshments and confetti as they stare out the windows. I can't blame them.

The scene before me is one of almost comedic contrasts. The lounge itself is adorned with more decorations than a Welcoming the New Year party. Garlands of golden feathers, silver tinsel, and sparkling stars snake along the walls. Every other minute, confetti rains down from openings in the ceiling, fluttering down onto the women's dresses and tiaras along with the men's tuxes and suits. Lanterns and tissue paper flowers sway along with the ship's rocking while balloons cluster around the buffet tables, seats, and sofas, forming a jungle of latex and ribbon.

But even with all these lavish decorations, my eyes are instantly drawn to the windows lining nearly every wall, to what waits less than a mile beyond the sheets of glass no thicker than my fingernail.

Despite all the research nearly every country had at one time or another poured into uncovering what created The Veil, no one had ever been close to finding an answer. It had come into existence over a thousand years ago, and it stretched around the world with no end. These were the only two things that were certain about it—or as certain as anything could be when it came to all things related to The Veil and whatever existed beyond it. This, I suppose, is why within the last few decades, the majority of the scientific community settled instead on vaguely labeling The Veil as a natural phenomenon.

But there's nothing natural about it.

Up close, The Veil is so much more magnificent and terrifying than any photo or painting I've seen. It appears as a bank of dark gray storm clouds that swallow the sun and sky before cascading like a curtain down into the water. The Veil stretches out endlessly in both directions past the cluster of boats and airships spread out on either side of us, churning and writhing like a living thing. Within the clouds, lightning flashes in bursts of blue and white. Even from this distance static prickles along my skin, curling the already wavy tips of my long hair and sending a shock stinging through me when my hand accidentally grazes a chair.

"Amarra!" I turn, my gaze scanning the crowded room until I spot Miyuni and the others standing beside a window. Like my cousin, she's dressed to impress—or perhaps the satin and sequined dress that glitters like rubies is simply the first thing she felt like throwing on this morning along with the feathered headband dotted with gold pearls and roses.

"Hello," I say, smiling at Miyuni and nodding to Emory and Leander who nod in greeting back.

Kye-Shin doesn't so much as glance my way from where he stares out towards The Veil. Annoyance flares through me, but I shove it from my mind as I focus my attention on those polite enough to acknowledge my existence.

"And who, may I ask, is this?" Leander says, sweeping forward and running his eyes over Jaslene in a way I don't like. "I'm certain I would have remembered if we'd met."

"This is my cousin, Jas—" I start, stepping in between her and Leander, when another voice calls out.

"Jaslene!"

The chestnut-haired young man from the pool the other day—Arthur—waves at us beside a table occupied by my aunt along with several other passengers whose sour expressions I vaguely recall from the dining room.

Jaslene grins, waving back. "I'm afraid I can't keep them waiting," she says, pulling us away before I can protest. "I'll come by later to visit. I promise. Wonderful meeting you all!" In a twirl of beads and silk, she's gone, dashing across the lounge to Arthur, who stares at her adoringly, and my aunt who wears a rare expression of pride I could never evoke.

"Try not to look so disappointed," Emory teases, resting his hand on Leander's shoulder as the former heir frowns, watching her leave.

"So," Miyuni says, sidling up to me and vibrating with the same nervousness that's clung to me throughout the day. It clings to me now too, sinking its claws deeper into my muscles and bones. "How are we feeling?"

"I could be better," I confess. My eyes drift to The Veil before focusing back on Miyuni, the decorations or the floor, or on anything else except the wall of darkening storm clouds getting closer with every second. "If I'm being honest, I just want the whole thing to be over already."

"I've felt the exact same way all morning," Miyuni agrees, her crimson lips forming a troubled line. "It's this dreadful waiting that's absolutely unbearable."

"I agree," Leander bellows, loud enough to make more than a few passengers around us turn. He downs the remainder of his glass and reaches for the whiskey bottle on the table—before swearing when he finds it's empty.

"Out of all the days to run out of alcohol..." he grumbles when Emory hands him another bottle from the table I failed to notice before.

"Relax," Emory says, twisting off the cork lid and refilling the other man's glass before topping off his own. "A waiter just brought this out in time."

"As if it matters," Leander snaps before growling. "Enough of dragging out this wait to pass through The Veil and killing us slowly with suspense," Leander snaps. "I say we head towards the blasted abomination at full speed and be on the other side of it in no time at all!"

"How strategic," Kye-Shin says. "I'm sure that never even crossed the Captain's mind."

"Look!" Emory snaps, pointing towards the window as a lightning bolt whips out from The Veil, striking an airship that's wandered too close. Smoke gushes from the balloon as red and yellow lights begin flashing from the gondola. With horror, I make out passengers scrambling along the decks as the ship plummets toward roughening waters.

A scream tears through the lounge, and everyone whirls just as another bolt of lightning smashes against the window. I tense, expecting the sound of shattering glass, blaring alarms, and agony as the room around us implodes.

But the ship only trembles as the electricity spiders along the glass, illuminating people's faces and the shimmering decorations in a ghostly glow. In the shocked silence that follows, static erupts from somewhere in the walls or ceiling before a voice warbles onto the line.

"Whoooo's ready to get this fun started?" the Entertainment Director screeches, causing me along with several others to throw our hands over our ears. "Great news, folks! The Captain just informed me that today's weather conditions are relatively mild, so your ride will be smoother than usual. Like sailing on glass, if you ask me!

"Now, in case you haven't guessed, all decks and balconies are temporarily closed. But if you're in search of a front-row seat to all the excitement, you can hurry to one of the lounges at the bow of the ship. There's still plenty of champagne and food to go around! Now sit back. Relax. And enjoy!"

As if on cue, a jazz tune starts up. Past the trumpet trills and drumbeats ricocheting off the walls, Gerald repeats the announcement in other languages—as if anyone's calm enough to keep listening.

"I'm going to be sick," a man in the booth next to us blurts before launching from his seat and disappearing through the double doors.

"Coward," Leander hisses, and for a moment I'm tempted to snap at him for such a comment. I would tell him that anyone in their right mind would be terrified, that he is a fool if he isn't.

But when I gaze back outside, the words—any words at all—wither on my tongue. The damaged airship has managed to retreat far enough away from The Veil to land on the waves safely among the line of boats, airships, and aeroplanes that departed with us from the docks. Cameras flash along their decks and windows, creating photos that will be pasted across newspapers, scrapbooks, and cinema screens within the week. The few people whose faces I can make out wave, but the motions are more solemn than cheerful, their expressions more fearful than envious.

For the briefest instant, I wonder if everyone on board has made a terrible mistake. If all the legends and stories have lied and instead of heading for paradise we are speeding towards certain death or something worse—

Then I blink and the ships and aeroplanes along with the ocean and sky are no more, vanished behind the shroud of gray rippling clouds that swallow us whole. One second passes, then two. Apart from the music, a hush falls over the room as no one moves, no one breathes. The walls and floor quake slightly, sending the glasses on the tables clinking and the windows trembling to the touch.

And yet...that's it.

We're passing through the deadliest phenomenon in the known world, and we barely feel a thing.

Next to me, Emory laughs, the sound bright and amazed. The noise shakes the other passengers from their stupor, causing relieved sighs to echo around the room while people smile and cheer, clashing their drinks together in toast or rushing towards the dance floor.

The change hits without warning.

Laughter turns to screams as the ship lurches violently, sending glasses and silverware flying before smashing onto the hardwood floor. I stumble too, reaching for something, *anything* to save me from falling onto the shattered porcelain. But the nearest chair is too far, the edge of the tablecloth I manage to grasp flimsy in my fingers as I tumble down, down, down...

A hand latches onto my arm, stopping me inches away from the shards of a bottle that gleam in the light before pulling me back up and onto my feet once again. I look up to find Kye-Shin's eyes boring into mine, his expression fierce and frantic. *Alive.*

*For how long?* I can't help but wonder.

He releases his hold on my arm just as suddenly as he grabbed it, leaving me feeling unbalanced and shaken.

Around us, the lamps and chandeliers flicker off, drawing more cries and gasps from the passengers as the room is cloaked in blackness except for the lightning that flashes across the windows and the graying clouds —clouds that darken by the second as *The Fated* pushes forward, never slowing. A boom more deafening than thunder sends the windows rattling and the floor quaking as if it will split open any second.

*It's just a storm,* I repeat to myself even though I know it isn't true. I know it can't be true given how beneath my feet, the ship no longer rocks from side to side but instead feels as if it's dropping, falling from an endless height into a bottomless abyss.

I barely register everything—the trembling furniture, shaking lanterns, toppling glasses—all going still before the windows turn black, throwing the world into darkness. The sensation of plummeting continues, like when I rode the rollercoaster earlier but magnified and warped. Pressure builds against my skull, constricting my brain until I no longer can tell which direction is up or down or whether we are falling or flying. Ringing splits through my ears, bringing tears to my eyes and my lips opening in a scream.

Then everything...stops.

No more ringing. No more pressure. No more pain.

*I must be dead.* The words drift half-formed and half-numbly through my mind like an afterthought rather than a realization.

When I open my eyes, the lounge is once again before me, the walls, decorations, and furniture intact, though I have no idea how. The chandeliers and sconces have since flickered back on too, illuminating the passengers hunched over in their booths, at their tables, or on the ground like me. My gaze barely registers these surroundings before fixing on the windows, which are no longer dark but stream with light so radiant it makes me wince and shield my eyes.

Slowly, I rise, the sound of my shoes brushing against shattered porcelain echoing in the space. The noise of my own breathing fills my ears until I step up to the glass...and forget to breathe altogether.

# CHAPTER 12

## PARADISE

Blue skies stretch out for an eternity over a calm ocean as smooth as silk. Perfectly spaced clouds, white and fluffy, glide above, their unblurred reflections in the water making it appear as if there is nothing beneath *The Fated* but air. Behind us, The Veil looms unchanged, a gray blanket of storm clouds that spans the horizon, sealing us off from the known world forever.

It is the most beautiful sight I've ever seen.

"We made it," I breathe, and next to me, Miyuni beams, drinking in the landscape hungrily as if she's afraid it will dissolve any second. I am too.

"Incredible," Emory says while behind him Leander and Kye-Shin step towards the window, both of them for once speechless. Around the room, other passengers are still rising, still blinking at the scenery as if they can hardly believe or comprehend it.

"Cooongraaatuuulations!" the Entertainment Director's voice bellows from invisible speakers, startling half the room and me along with them. "You, my lucky passengers, have successfully crossed The Veil! To celebrate, we are hosting a *boat*load of activities for you the rest of the afternoon and into this evening including parties in the lounges, a scavenger hunt in the gardens, a lottery for a special prize, and..."

I don't bother listening to the rest of his words as saxophones, trumpets, and basses start up again, practically drowning out the speakers. The women sitting on the sofas to my right giggle and reach out to catch the confetti raining down from the ceiling. Whoops and hollers erupt from where another passenger climbs onto a table and pops a bottle of champagne, sending streams of foam and liquid spraying everywhere.

Squealing with glee, Miyuni rushes to the dance floor, and I follow, for once not caring how awkward my movements are or that I can feel my aunt watching, disapproving. Beneath the heat of the lights, I grow drunk from the sheer joy of it all—from singing off-tune with Emory to a song I no longer remember the name of, from fumbling along to a quickstep alongside Miyuni, from laughing with Jaslene until my ribs ache as Leander and Arthur compete to show off who possesses the best dance skills.

Even Kye-Shin, who remains on the fringes sipping a drink, raises his glass when he catches me staring, the gesture and slight smile lifting his lips no longer mocking.

Among the crowd, I make out other familiar and friendly faces too: the woman with the jade hairpin from the jewelry shop lounges on a sofa, rocking her shoulders in time with the rhythm; Lethia pops a truffle into her mouth as she studies a dolphin sculpture made of forget-me-nots along the buffet table; the golden-haired stranger who first told me about The Nautilus leans against the wall in the far corner and nods to me when he feels my gaze.

Around me, the ship floods with music and celebration and *life*— and for once, I'm at the beating center of it all.

"Let's go!" Miyuni cries after what could be one hour or five.

"Where?" I ask, absentmindedly scanning the room for Jaslene and failing to spot her, or Arthur for that matter. Not that I'm surprised. They were likely on the opposite end of the ship by now.

"Anywhere we want!" Miyuni says, lifting the nearest glass of champagne and emptying it in one gulp before wrapping her hand in Leander's and motioning for me, Emory, and Kye-Shin to follow.

High on our own newfound invincibility, we dash through the atrium, dipping in and out of whatever flashy destination catches our interest. We wander through the gardens. Play hide and seek like children among the rhododendrons, ferns, and willows. We explore every corner of the amusement park we come across, winning prizes at the carnival games and riding the huge vertical spinning wheel glowing with lights until our toes tingle from the height.

It's a dizzying whirl of excitement and wonder, and I wish this day would never end. I wish I could always be this content, this carefree.

Perhaps from now on I will be.

"Who knew having so much fun could be utterly exhausting?" Miyuni sighs, reclining on an inflatable lounger and twirling her fingers in the water as she drifts along the pool.

The sun set over an hour ago, replaced in the sky by the moon and stars. Yet for so early in the evening, the deck is surprisingly uncrowded. Two couples recline at a table off to the side, sipping drinks and barking in laughter every other minute or so. A woman drizzles chocolate syrup on her sundae at the ice cream station in the corner, the smell of baking waffle cones drifting past the counter and making my mouth water. Several yards away, another passenger swings in a hammock, strumming his guitar and singing a melody whose notes sound wistful despite the happy occasion.

"You make it sound like an occupation," Emory says, leaning against the side and snatching a shrimp from a covered tray that floats by, its base impossible to overturn.

"And why shouldn't it be? After all, isn't that what paradise is all about? Having so much fun that you're never bored?" Miyuni poses. "Still, I can't help but find the endless possibilities a little...daunting."

"Maybe you just need some more practice," Leander growls, eliciting shrieks and giggles from her as he grabs the edge of the lounger and acts as if he'll topple her into the water.

Smiling and shaking my head, I kick along the surface on my back. I relish the weightlessness of my every movement. Relish the sheer number of stars scattered across the sky in every direction that makes me breathless with wonder. It's been years since the clouds over Abeon parted enough for me to view them, and even then, I can't recall seeing as many as I do now, or them shining so brightly. I've already made out two dots of a bass clef and three tied notes in the constellations when Kye-Shin's face materializes above me, making me gasp and jerk my head above the surface.

"Refreshing, is it?"

I whirl around, wiping droplets from my eyes as I take in his relaxed posture as he sits at the edge, his feet resting on the first step as water undulates around his ankles. The emotions swirling behind his eyes, as always, remain a mystery.

"What?" I blurt before remembering his question. "Oh, yes, it is." I catch my breath long enough to take in his regular attire and dry appearance. "Any reason why you're not joining in?"

Kye-Shin's expression turns amused. "Do I need one?"

I shrug, the action making the waves grow choppy around me. "Maybe you can't swim."

His response is immediate. "I assure you, I can."

"Then maybe you're afraid of—" *Of appearing anything other than aloof or sarcastic. Of actually having a good time.*

But I stop before I can speak any of these things, remembering the feeling of his hand on my arm as he saved me from falling while we passed through The Veil earlier.

"What?" Kye-Shin says, tilting his head curiously. "What am I afraid of exactly?"

Ripples of turquoise light from the pool dance across his face, reflecting in his dark eyes, brushing over his full lips.

"Nothing," I say, shivering from a non-existent breeze and sinking farther beneath the surface. "I doubt you're afraid of anything."

Kye-Shin smirks but doesn't say anything as he turns over something in his hands I hadn't noticed before. Between his fingers, I spot a glimmer of metal.

"What is that?" I ask, curiosity getting the better of me.

"Just something I carry with me," he says, studying his palm. "A good luck charm I found dropped in the street one day, if you can believe it. Take a look if you want."

Kye-Shin tosses the object to me without warning, and I barely manage to catch it before it tumbles into the water. When I open my hand, a platinum medallion stares up at me—the one I realize I knocked to the ground after I ran into him at the docks. Against my palm, it feels cool and soothing.

Engraved lines span the surface, imitating a compass with four cardinal points. Instead of letters, illustrations symbolizing each direction mark the tips: a pair of mountains represent the snow-covered ranges in the northern country of Roakin; rippling waves signify the infamously tumultuous seas stretching along the western coast of Ketris; a rising sun stands for the east; and a plumeria tree, known for growing by the hundreds along the Kalaydren Islands in the south, sits at the bottom.

Slowly, I turn it over, expecting the same image to be mirrored on the back, but instead over half a dozen stars scatter along the surface. All of them are the same platinum color as the medallion except for one inlaid with gold.

"That's the Alexandris," Kye-Shin says. "It's a sort of miracle star famous for leading wayward travelers to some of the greatest discoveries in history, like new continents or caves strewn with diamonds. They say if you ever find yourself lost with no compass or anything else to guide you, just follow the Alexandris, and you won't regret arriving wherever it takes you."

"I've never heard of such a thing," I say, still marveling at the medallion, at the intricacy in every design.

"Well, I'm not making it up," Kye-Shin replies. "You can see it right there. Look."

I follow his gaze to where he points toward the sky.

"Where?" I ask, failing to spot anything distinguishable amidst the constellations. "I don't see anything."

"Come closer, then," Kye-Shin says, motioning me towards him. When I make no move to, however, he sighs. "Don't worry. I won't bite."

"You can't blame one for wondering," I say, and he gives me a glare but wisely says nothing as I wade to the pool's edge next to him.

"It's in a different part of the sky than it was on the other side of The Veil," Kye-Shin says, pointing upwards. "There! Do you see that cluster of bluish stars several inches right of the moon?" I drift slightly nearer to him until I can follow his gaze. After a second, I nod.

"The Alexandris is just below those to the left a little," he says, tilting his head toward me even as his eyes never waver from his target. "Do you see it?"

Finally, I do. True to the depiction on the medallion, the Alexandris glows faintly gold, its light neither brighter nor dimmer than the other stars—but distinctive, nonetheless.

"Wow," I breathe, too late realizing I probably shouldn't act so impressed. From the little I already knew of Kye-Shin, I wouldn't put it past him to lord it over me forever.

"Spectacular, isn't it?" he says, the awe in his tone making me glance at him to see if he's being sarcastic. But for once I can find no trace of cynicism in his dark brown eyes, no slight curve of a sneer at the corners of his lips.

I clear my throat, all at once uncomfortably aware of our closeness.

"Here," I say, causing Kye-Shin to turn, looking confused until I plop the medallion unceremoniously back in his hand and swim away— or try to despite the sudden clumsiness of my limbs and water splashing into my eyes.

I've almost made a successful escape when his voice carries over the water.

"I'm sorry." I swivel to find him leaning his elbows on his knees and peering at the miniature waves. The lightness in his expression has dimmed. "For my attitude toward you soon after we first met—and my pessimism about the future. You were right. While I'm here, I might as well enjoy myself."

Surprise floods through me at his words, followed by guilt.

"I owe you an apology too," I say. "For snapping at you when you were just trying to share your thoughts with me...even if they weren't the kinds of things I wanted to hear."

Kye-Shin nods in understanding. "Believe it or not, I wasn't always this jaded," he says. "I used to write stories about *The Fated* and Melanthros to read to Miyuni before bed, given our parents were always too busy fighting to find the time."

"I'm sorry," I say before I can help it, though my sympathy isn't from personal experience. My own father had left soon after I was born. Even though I should have been too young to remember him entirely, for years as a child, I recalled a shadowed figure stalking out the door and never looking back the handful of times my mother mentioned him.

Across from me, Kye-Shin shrugs. "My parents' incompatibility wasn't surprising, I suppose," he says. "After all, my mother came from Haduko and my father from Senhwon. They are two provinces in Nanshyn that might as well be separate countries altogether, considering they differ in everything from dialects and food, not to mention culture and religion. When both Miyuni and I were born, they couldn't even agree on a common Nanshyn City name for either of us, which is why both our names sound so different."

Kye-Shin shakes his head, clearly trying to rid himself of the memories. "Anyway, since the tales I used to write and tell my sister frequently included castles in the sky and wish-granting mermaids, I suppose I'm to blame for her optimistic expectations."

I can't help but grin at the words, at how they conjure up in my mind the countless nights when my mother had read me stories before bed, too. Like music, they had let me escape to vivid places and more exciting lives.

"Miyuni has wanted to be a dancer for as long as I can remember, you know," Kye-Shin says, drawing my attention back to him and then his sister who has since abandoned the lounger for the diving board. She poses and bows to Leander's and Emory's applause before somersaulting into the pool.

It makes sense now, I realize, given how she was always constantly in motion, constantly expressing herself through the smallest flutter of her fingers or leap of excitement.

"I'm surprised she isn't one already," I say, bringing a laugh from Kye-Shin, but the noise sounds more harsh than joyful.

"Yes, well, she gave it up when our father lost our fortune in a single night of gambling before falling sick. After his death, I tried to support us, but my teaching job barely brought in enough to help cover the rent, let alone dance lessons. Miyuni even took a job as a waitress, but she had never worked before and the manager had no patienc—" Kye-Shin's voice breaks off before he shakes his head and sighs. "She belongs onstage. She always has."

"And you're hoping wherever *The Fated* is taking us can give her that," I finally guess.

For a moment, Kye-Shin doesn't reply. Water on either side of me sloshes to the rocking of the ship, the rhythmic noise filling the silence between us.

"I've seen too much to hope for paradise, but I still *hope*," he says, raising his gaze to me once again. "I don't expect this new world to be perfect. I don't need it to be. I only hope that it's better enough for Miyuni to be able to live her dream."

"What about your dream?" I ask, eyeing the ink stains on his hands. The memory of his angry face when I caused his papers to spill out all over the dock resurfaces in my mind. "It's to write, isn't it?"

"It was once," he says, eyeing the ripples in the water before looking back at me and shrugging. "But it's been years since I was able to write more than a handful of sentences that I didn't hate. It's funny, isn't it? How our dreams can turn on us so easily?"

The words puncture through me like a needle.

"This looks like a riveting conversation," Miyuni says, splashing up to my side and glancing between the two of us mischievously. "What, may I ask, is the intriguing topic?"

"Nothing," I answer a little too quickly. I try my best to look unflustered. From the way Miyuni's grin widens, I know I've failed. "Your brother was just refusing to give me a reason why he isn't swimming."

"Well in that case, all he needs is a little push!" Leander bellows, appearing over his shoulder and nodding to Emory as the two shove him hard enough to send him flying into the pool with a giant splash.

Water rains down onto my hair, splatters into my face and mouth. Yet through it all, I watch Kye-Shin rise to the surface with a shocked expression.

I can't help it. I laugh, the sound loud and soaring until it seems to fill the whole deck and bounce off the stars until my soul reverberates with it, basking in my newfound happiness.

*Because this is happiness*, I realize with amazement as I race Emory to the opposite end of the pool, as I giggle along with Miyuni when Kye-Shin splashes Leander hard enough to send him gasping for air, as I later run with them across the deck with the wind against my skin and the ocean at my side. *This is everything I hoped for.*

By the time I return to the stateroom, it's past one o'clock or maybe even two. Late enough for my aunt to be in bed, no doubt, and most likely Jaslene as well. But when I open the door, the main sitting room isn't dark or silent. In fact, the chandeliers are so bright that for the briefest second, I fail to register my aunt pacing along the carpet and the hysteria in her gaze.

The instant I do, however, the ship lurches, sending me stumbling into the wall and the door slamming shut, trapping me inside. I don't see Salenna move. One second, my aunt is across the room, her emerald gown flowing behind her like a storm cloud, and in the next, she is inches from my face, her onyx eyes searing into mine.

"Where is she?" the woman hisses.

"Who?" I say, confused.

"You little fool!" Salenna shrieks, grabbing my shoulders until her fingernails dig into my sleeves. "Where is Jaslene? I've been waiting for over two hours. I made her swear she would be back before midnight like a respectable young lady. It was a mistake letting her go gallivanting all over the ship with that duke on her own. You should have stayed with her the entire afternoon! This is *your* fault!"

"What are you saying?" I demand, still struggling to make sense of my aunt's panic and fury. The last memory of my cousin and Arthur spinning across the dance floor in the lounge replays in my mind like a scene from a film in the cinema. "You think Jaslene has fallen into some kind of troub—"

"I'm saying," my aunt accuses, "that while you were busy out wasting time with your friends and being too selfish to remember your own family, your cousin has gone missing."

# CHAPTER 13

## LIKE SMOKE

I don't believe my aunt. Not at first.

My cousin wasn't missing. She couldn't be after only a handful of hours. She must have simply lost track of time in the excitement from passing through The Veil, and from the attention of her new suitor. They were both likely still celebrating along with over half the ship's passengers still parading through the halls. I'm certain of it. Or almost certain.

The tiniest inch of doubt and curiosity—but never alarm—keeps me waiting up for Jaslene most of the night. Long after my aunt collapses into bed, I remain on the sofa, fighting heavy eyelids and exhaustion until I at last fall prey to dreamless slumber. When I wake at dawn, my eyes immediately find the door, still expecting the handle to spin and Jaslene to burst through any moment, all smiles and dramatic tales about what kept her away all evening.

She never does.

The day goes by. Another morning of eating in the Breakfast Room. Another afternoon of sunshine along the pool deck and tranquil waters. Another evening spent beneath chandeliers with the most amazing flavors of food flooding my mouth.

Still, there is no sign of my cousin.

Inch by agonizing inch, reality closes in, curing me of any delusions or misplaced hopes until I can no longer deny the truth by the next morning.

Other girls may have disobeyed their mothers, but my cousin would never be one of them. She had tried resisting in the past, of course. Sometimes she aimed a subtly barbed remark at her mother and framed it like a joke, or occasionally, she missed curfew and attributed it to her notorious absentmindedness. In the end, however, she always did what my aunt told her one way or another.

Which meant that my cousin really must be missing if she hadn't returned by now.

How much precious time had I wasted already? I had to find her, and quickly. Because she could be terrified and praying for someone to save her. Because she could be bleeding out with her life slipping away by the second. The possibilities stream on and on, flooding my mind and fueling my fear until I lock them away so I can focus on rescuing Jaslene.

That is, if I'm not too late already.

Another morning, however, seems to have the opposite effect on my aunt whose panic from two nights ago has since subsided into fury and bitterness.

"She's doing this to me on purpose," she says, stalking across the sitting room and pouring herself some coffee as if everything is perfectly normal.

"Don't be ridiculous," I reply in disbelief. "What reason could she have?"

"For attention, of course," Salenna says in disgust, "As if I don't spoil such an ungrateful daughter enough." Her scathing gaze slashes to me. "Or perhaps she's rebelling against everything I've taught her for her own good. Perhaps *you* put her up to it just to spite me."

"You overestimate us both," I grumble, brushing past her. "I'm dialing the emergency number." I pick up the phone from a nearby desk when Salenna crosses the distance between us within a matter of seconds. She rips the phone from my hand before slamming it back down.

"No!" she snaps, glaring at me in betrayal. "This entire situation is embarrassing enough without having the crew get involved. Would you humiliate me in front of everyone on board by making it public knowledge that my own daughter ran away under my very nose? And on a ship of all places!"

"What if Jaslene's in danger?" I say, my anger rising. "What if she was kidnapped or attacked or worse? Perhaps she needs us right now—"

"She doesn't!" Salenna shrieks, her beautiful face contorting into rage before she smooths her expression back into one of disdain. "At least not you. Your influence over her, however minor, has always been especially *un*needed."

I cross my arms and act as if the words don't sting, don't dig through my skin and pierce into some softer tissue inside. I hate this: living in too close quarters with my aunt again as if I never moved out. It's as if I'm back to being newly orphaned, desperate to receive the barest scraps of love from a woman who will never give them to me. It isn't that I blamed my aunt for favoring Jaslene. After all, it was natural she would love her own daughter more.

I just never understood why that meant she had to hate me.

When I don't move, my aunt gives an exasperated sigh. "Listen to me for once, you stubborn girl," she says, reclining on the sofa and for the first time, I notice how unflustered she looks despite her daughter's disappearance—how her makeup is heavy and un-smudged, how her silk gown is every bit as elegant and ornate as her usual attire. I've never been so disgusted at the sight of her. "Within several days she'll return once she grows tired of this little stunt. Just wait and you'll see."

But I refuse to wait any longer.

Instead, I search for Jaslene in the Excursion Rooms where we laughed beneath the palm trees, in the jewelry store and map shop, in every place I think might pique her interest. I look for her dark wavy hair in the auditoriums of the cinema, in the spinning rides at the amusement park. I scour the gardens and decks for her dazzling smile and vibrant figure. When looking fails, I begin approaching passengers with a photo of us taken several years ago on a rare snowy day at the park. In it, we are both grinning from ear to ear like we are back to being children, our cheeks flushed from a snowball fight. The entire adventure had been Jaslene's idea.

"Have you seen this girl?" I ask anyone who glances in my direction. Anyone who will listen as I pass through the atrium.

"Have you run into my cousin by chance?"

"Please, can you tell me if she was here earlier?"

But the people in beautiful dresses and suits just smile and shake their heads, flitting to the next party or sensation without care or worry. When I spot a familiar chestnut-haired young man among the throng of passengers lining up outside an entrance with the words The Morpheus Club in flashing lights above, hope sparks in me once again—then dies out just as quickly.

"I haven't seen Jaslene since we both left the Star-Crossed Café two nights ago," Arthur says when I ask. "I think it was around nine or ten o'clock maybe. I can't be sure. She was actually supposed to meet me at the theater this morning..."

As soon as it becomes clear he can offer me no answers, I turn away, the rest of his words dissipating in my ears as I resume my search. It shouldn't be possible for someone to disappear on board so easily. In the heart of Abeon City perhaps, with its thousands of dark alleyways and hundreds of people living on every block. But not a ship. Especially not *this* ship.

Still, I realize too late how many places on *The Fated* can swallow a person without leaving a trace.

The ship's countless and narrow corridors, which only yesterday I'd found mysterious and exciting in their labyrinthian nature, now seem to stretch out endlessly wherever I turn. The walls appear straight, but something within their makeup must be warped, for noises from opposite ends of the ship bounce off their surfaces to drift through the halls like restless ghosts, making it impossible to locate the source.

Along the ship's edges, hallways wind into hallways with stateroom doors bordering either side, their smooth wood faces revealing no hint of what hides behind them as I rush by. In the center of the ship, even the brightest lights from the shops and bistros along the Boulevard and connecting atrium are plagued by shadows. I never noticed them before, and yet now I can't help but spot them filling the alleys frequently snaking in between the businesses. These alleys, I soon discover, will sometimes veer and spit me back out into another and unexpected section of the Boulevard. In other instances, the passageway I find myself in will end abruptly into a wall, or worse, continue on until the shadows grow into a blackness so thick that fear and self-preservation ultimately send me turning back around altogether.

Then there is, of course, the ocean. The bottomless blue that spreads out on every side for miles upon miles as it churns, dragging anything and anyone unfortunate enough to fall within its grasp down to a realm obscured by sand and decaying matter.

Like an aquatic graveyard.

I smother the thought before it can take shape. I don't want to think about how Jaslene could have all too easily disappeared into any one of these places without so much as a scream or struggle. I don't want to consider that Jaslene's laughter as we watched Leander and Arthur compete on the dance floor will be the last sound I will ever hear from my cousin. That Jaslene spinning in a lilac dress wearing a smile brighter than the stars will be my last memory of her.

So, I keep searching even when my feet ache. I keep moving when my legs grow tired and the dozens of corridors I've passed through jumble together in my mind. I abandon looking only in places I think Jaslene might prefer, and instead scan every scene I stumble across: around the blackjack tables at the casino, in the dimly lit bars of the lower-level taverns, among the shadowed alcoves crowded with couples scattered here and there along the fringes of the Boulevard.

I fail to spot any sign of her.

Had my aunt been right? Was I partly to blame for Jaslene's disappearance? Being two years older, I'd always prided myself on looking out for my cousin as if she were my little sister, and now I've failed her. If only I had refused to be separated from her yesterday, refused to let her slip from my sight. If only I had convinced her and Arthur to join us for a swim in the pool.

If only...

I've never known two more wretched words.

In the end, it's the guilt from my aunt's accusation that pushes me to do the very thing she forbade me from doing. I grab the nearest phone hanging from the wall and spin the rotary dial with shaky fingers until the emergency number is plugged in and the ringing echoes from the receiver.

"Hello, are you in distress?" A female voice crackles onto the line.

"Yes, I need to report a missing passenger," I say, trying and failing to keep my tone steady. "My cousin Jaslene Destan has been gone since two nights ago. She didn't return to our stateroom, and—"

"What is your stateroom number?" the woman asks.

"Um, 623," I say before continuing. "I've been searching for her all morning and haven't found her anywhere. No one I've talked to has said they've seen her eith—"

"Please describe the appearance of the missing person," the woman interjects, and for a second, her impatience and clinical tone grates at me before I force my annoyance back down.

"She's nineteen years old and has black wavy hair, olive skin, and brown eyes. She also wears a necklace with a pink pear—"

"That's more than enough information, thank you," the woman cuts me off once again before her voice turns cheerful. "Rest assured, Miss Amarra Obrel, we will get started locating your cousin immediately. Should we make any progress, we will contact you as soon as possible. In the meantime, please try not to worry and enjoy the numerous facilities the ship has to offer. Have a wonderful day!"

Before I can say another word, her voice clicks off the line, leaving me with nothing but static in my ears and the eventual realization that I never told her my name.

"Excuse me, do you mind if I use the phone if you've finished?"

"Not at all," I say, absentmindedly hanging up the handset and stepping away as the passenger behind me walks up and begins dialing.

"Ah, it's you." I swivel, taking in the passenger's familiar golden hair, strong jaw, and hooded eyes swirling with amber and green that belong to the same man who gave me directions to the dining room the first night. He had mentioned The Nautilus, as if he had known how much I dreaded returning to suffer my aunt's disdain.

"Oh, hi," I say a little awkwardly, forcing a polite smile.

The stranger tilts his head, his eyes regarding me curiously. Their perceptiveness is unnerving. "Everything alright? You aren't lost again, are you?"

"No, I...lost someone actually," I reply, remembering Jaslene's photo in my pocket and holding it out for him to study. "My cousin, Jaslene. She's been missing since two nights ago. Have you seen her recently?"

The stranger leans closer to the picture, his brow furrowing. "Oh yes, I think I remember her now. She was at the watch party the other day, wasn't she?"

"Yes," I say, the last shreds of my hope fluttering back to life. "Did you spot her again any time after that?"

He shakes his head, looking regretful. "I'm afraid not," he says, and with those three words a heavy weight settles over me—a feeling of dread that I might never see my cousin again.

"Amarra!" I spin to see Miyuni along with Kye-Shin stalking towards us while Leander and Emory trail a handful of yards behind.

"When you didn't show up at the bowling alley this afternoon, we were worried," Miyuni exclaims, her lips forming into a pout while her usually warm gaze regards me with something vaguely resembling accusation. "And after you promised too."

"Oh, I—" I begin, suddenly remembering I was supposed see a cinema film with them. "I'm so sorry."

"You look unwell," Kye-Shin, his dark gaze flashing between me and the blond stranger with something like concern. When he speaks again, the wariness in his tone is clear. "Is anything wrong?"

"Apparently so," the stranger says, setting the phone back on the wall. "Considering someone has gone missing."

"Missing?" Miyuni gasps. "Who?"

"My cousin Jaslene," I say. "She never came back to the cabin two nights ago. At first, I tried not to worry. But when she still wasn't back this morning, I started searching for her and have been all day. I've shown her photo to people, but no one's said they've seen her."

"What about the young man she was with?" Miyuni suggests. "The one with the chestnut-hair whose name started with an E or an A. Was it Edmond? Arnold? Alexander..."

"Arthur," I say, running my hands through my hair and stepping closer to a window gazing out over the pool deck. Passengers clutching their hats and towels race to take shelter from the wind and slanting rain. Staring at them, I'm jealous—jealous that the only things they have to fear are getting too wet, too cold.

I spin away from the window, focusing my mind on Jaslene.

"When I talked to him earlier, he said the last time he saw her was at the Star-Crossed Café two nights ago, but he hadn't seen her since. In fact, he was upset that she didn't show up to the theater like they planned earlier today."

Leander snorts. "Maybe your cousin found better company."

"No, you don't understand," I say, growing frustrated. "My aunt made her swear she would be back by midnight, and Jaslene isn't the type to defy my aunt. Besides, she would have told me if she had planned something."

"Have you reached out to passenger services?" Emory asks.

"I just dialed the emergency line to report it," I say, waving towards the phone. "My aunt would be furious if she knew. She didn't want any crew involved. She's convinced Jaslene is doing this just to spite her. I don't think she ever once considered her daughter might actually have been kidnapped or..."

"Murdered," Leander finishes. In response to everyone's glares, including mine, he merely shrugs, and in that instant—in the face of his never-ending smugness and nonchalance with something as serious as this—I hate him. "What? I'm sure you've all thought about the possibility once or twice, and ignoring it won't help."

"And advertising it will?" Kye-Shin says.

"Hush, both of you," Miyuni insists before grabbing my hand. "I'm sure Jaslene's fine."

I offer her a tight smile in return even though I know it's most likely a lie.

"And you are certain your cousin never returned to the cabin either evening?" the stranger speaks up suddenly.

I glance up, puzzled. "No, I was in the main area of our connecting staterooms the whole first night. Then last night, I slept lightly and kept waking up, hoping she was finally back. She couldn't have snuck past without me hearing..." I trail off, a new possibility forming in my mind.

I assumed Jaslene disappeared soon after being separated from Arthur two nights ago. But what if she had returned to the stateroom first? Arthur had said she left the Star-Crossed café around nine or ten o'clock, so she would have had plenty of time to come back to the cabin before my aunt arrived around midnight and I stumbled in hours later.

"What is it?" Kye-Shin asks, making me realize I've been silent too long.

"I don't know," I say in answer to the stranger's question. "Jaslene could have come back to the cabin earlier the first evening and then left again before my aunt or I returned. And then, of course, she could have come back anytime while we were out yesterday. But why would she leave again? And to where?"

Across from me, the stranger shrugs. "It might be worth looking over her belongings," he suggests. "Maybe something in her room could give you a hint about where she was headed."

"When I glanced in her bedroom, nothing seemed out of place," I say, realizing only now how little my observations meant.

I hadn't thought to look closely at my cousin's things because I simply assumed Jaslene never returned to the cabin in the first place. Now that I know she could have, the potential scenarios won't stop streaming through my mind. What if I missed some small but vital clue that would explain everything the instant I laid my eyes on it? What if Jaslene had left me a note, hidden in the folds of her scarves, revealing that this was all some master plan of hers?

"You're right," I say, looking at the stranger in a mixture of awe and relief. "Thank you. Again."

"Helping you seems to be becoming a habit," he grins before he frowns as if remembering something. "I'm afraid, however, our conversation has made me late to a prior engagement." He glances towards his watch in the same moment a gong reverberates from a grandfather clock gilded in gold and sapphire paint in the corner. "Be careful on the stairs."

With that, the stranger turns away. I barely notice something fall from his pocket until the object rolls across the carpet, hitting my shoe.

"Excuse me, you dropped your—" I begin, bending down to grasp the small coin. When I look up again, he has vanished from sight.

"Did you see where he went?" I ask the others in bewilderment.

"Slinking off somewhere that way," Leander says, waving dismissively towards the end of the hall.

"Have you let your drink already go to your head?" Emory scoffs, pointing at the opposite end. "He went in *that* direction. I saw it with my own eyes."

"You're both delirious," Kye-Shin snaps, glaring at the other two. "He took the stairs."

The rest of their ensuing argument fades to the background as I study the bright gold coin in my palm. No, not a coin. An arcade token. I recognize the festive and overly flamboyant style. The image of the stranger standing over a pinball machine or playing a round of bagatelle though nearly makes me laugh out loud.

"What did you say his name was again?" Miyuni asks, rising on the tips of her toes to scan our surroundings for one last glimpse of him.

I open my mouth to answer—then realize I can't.

"I don't know," I admit, scolding myself for forgetting to ask his name both times I had the chance.

"How dashing and mysterious," Miyuni sighs with a dreamlike smile, and next to her, Kye-Shin rolls his eyes in exasperation.

"So, I'm guessing you're headed back to your stateroom now?" Emory says, turning to me expectantly, and I nod.

"With any luck, he's right and I'll find something that will tell me what my cousin could have been thinking."

Even as I speak the words, I cringe at their optimism. I've been searching all day for Jaslene with no success. I was foolish for thinking this attempt would be any different.

"We'll come with you," Kye-Shin offers.

"No," I nearly shout, hating the thought of being a burden, of being someone who is once again pitied. "You don't have to. Really."

"Stop being overly considerate. Of course we do!" Miyuni insists, practically jumping with excitement. "We're your friends, aren't we?"

*Friends.*

The word reminds me I'm no longer the girl trapped in the elevator, ignored and easily forgotten. I am no longer alone.

"Yes," I say past my tightening throat, "Of course you're my friends."

"It's about time that's settled," Miyuni smiles, reaching out again and giving my hand a reassuring pat before pirouetting down the hall towards the elevators with the grace of a ballerina. "Besides, one of us might catch a detail you happen to miss. After all, the more brains there are on a case, the likelier it will be solved quickly. At least, that's what I've gathered from mystery novels."

Next to me, Kye-Shin snorts in disbelief. "Since when do *you* read mystery novels?"

"Whenever I feel like it," Miyuni says. "Though, I must say the storylines are overcomplicated, filled with too much intrigue, and not nearly enough romance."

"You can't be serious," her brother replies before saying something in Nanshyn that sends Miyuni laughing, the sound bright and clear. The familiar rhythm of their banter brings a smile to my face despite the lingering heaviness in my heart.

Once I reach the elevators, I press the bottom button. Seconds after the pale circle lights, however, it flickers off as the ship crashes into a large wave that sends the carpet rolling beneath us and every surface trembling like drums. Blackness engulfs the space as the bulbs behind the tinkling chandelier crystals go dark before flickering to life once more.

"What kind of ship is this?" Leander sneers, stumbling to regain his balance. "It passes through The Veil but can't even handle one small storm—"

A clap of thunder reverberates through the air as *The Fated* smashes into another wave hard enough to send a nearby vase of roses shattering across the floor. Leander's words linger in my mind, and I can't help but wonder if storms on the other side of The Veil might be worse. If maybe they have the power to sink *The Fated* altogether...

The lights shudder off and on again. Past the rumbling, a familiar screech followed by static erupts before a far too cheery voice ricochets off the walls.

"Good afternoon, everyone, this is Gerald, your Entertainment Director, speaking once again. We apologize for today's slightly bumpy ride—"

"Did he just say *slightly*?" Emory cries, clenching the nearest rail to keep from falling as the ship heaves.

"—but please know there is nothing to fear as long as you remain in an enclosed space and away from any of those slippery decks and balconies until this patch of unpleasant weather has passed. Additionally, since we are experiencing a few minor electrical glitches, the Captain recommends using the stairs to avoid any uncomfortably long elevator rides, if you catch my drift. Or should I say *lift*—"

"I'm going to kill him," Leander growls past the Director's cackling. His eyes promise murder. "I don't care if I stumble all over this ship, I'm going to find that sniveling bastard and throw him off the nearest balc—"

"That's a sight I'd love to see," Kye-Shin scoffs, somehow maintaining his balance better than any of us from where he stands with his arm wrapped around a column. "At the current rate your face is turning green, I would say you'll end up rolling right off the ship if you tried. Although now that I think about it, perhaps I could offer you a kick in the right direction."

"Why, you little—" Leander starts, but Kye-Shin barrels on unperturbed even as the chandeliers sway and the ship groans like a dying beast.

"Besides, instead of wasting your energy chasing the unfortunate Entertainment Director, you should be helping us find her cousin," he says, nodding to me. "What floor is your stateroom on?"

"Sixth," I gasp out past my flipping stomach.

"Well then, we better get started," Kye-Shin says, pushing away from the column towards the stairs. "After all, we have five flights to go down, and Leander looks like one is more than he can handle."

Several feet away, Leander grumbles something insulting, but Kye-Shin only grins as he begins descending, followed by Miyuni and the others. I'm the last to leave, and yet when the stranger's words repeat through my mind, I hesitate before the steps, my skin prickling with unease.

*Be careful on the stairs.*

He'd spoken the warning minutes before the lights flickered and the Director cautioned against using the elevators.

So how had he known before everyone else?

# Chapter 14

## In Shadow

To my surprise, rather than dampening the passengers' spirits, the storm catapults them to new heights.

People of nearly every age, appearance, and fashion crowd the lounges and bars lining the various levels of the atrium, toasting each other while liquid sloshes over the sides of their glasses or dancing as chairs slide past, the sound of their legs screeching across the floor drowned out by music and thunder. Somewhere nearby, hysterical laughter and high-pitched voices swallow the crash of plates shattering. Below, ice-skaters slide from one end of the rink to the other every time the ship pitches, while above, passengers take turns flying across the atrium on cloth and rope swings, their faces in varying expressions of exhilaration and glee but never fear.

*The Fated* had survived The Veil after all. A regular storm, even one as nasty and furious as this, couldn't compare.

It is only when we enter a winding corridor lined on either side by cabins that the noise again quiets to nothing but the distant storm's rumble and the ever-constant creak of the ship. I don't realize I'm holding my breath until I open the stateroom's connecting door and relax at discovering my aunt is nowhere in sight. Knowing Salenna, she is most likely lounging in the tea gardens or saunas, convincing herself Jaslene is out gallivanting with a handsome young man rather than floating at the bottom of the sea.

Low buzzing hums through my ears as the bulbs flicker on, casting the cabin in alternating shadows and a soft warm glow. The others fan out around me, ambling past the sofa and chairs while I study the sitting area with new eyes. I search for some detail I might have missed, some sign Jaslene left in a hurry or perhaps was followed when she returned to the stateroom from the café. I can find nothing unusual, though, about the magazines scattered across the coffee table or the drinks and snacks spread along the small kitchen in the corner of the sitting room.

The door's groan accompanies me as I step into Jaslene's room and switch on the lights. The space is every bit as gorgeous as when I first laid my eyes on it. Yet now the porcelain floor and vast ceiling feels cold, more like a museum than a place to live in. Ironically despite her absence, Jaslene is written all over the space: in the satin slippers waiting in front of her chair in the corner; in the silk and sparkling scarves hanging from the closet door; in the romance novel sitting on the night-stand and beside it a bowl of candied apricots that was nearly empty two nights ago but has since been refilled.

No matter how carefully I examine my surroundings, I fail to find anything amiss. As always, whenever we return to the cabin, every possession appears pristine and undamaged, as if my cousin merely waltzed out the door and could easily glide back in any second. I wish more than anything she would.

I'm stepping past the desk towards the closet when my sleeve snags on the flowers in a vase. I spin, throwing my arms around the top of the glass to stop it from tumbling when a thorn-scratches my hand deep enough to draw blood.

I hiss at the sting, my eyes latching onto the culprit. It's a strange-looking plant with thorns snaking along the stem and wine-colored petals so large that they practically smother the neighboring tulips, daisies, and azaleas. Odd that I never noticed it in here before.

"Find something?" Kye-Shin asks, materializing in the doorway.

I shake my head in disappointment, forgetting the flower altogether. "Nothing," I sigh, stalking along the room's edge and brushing my fingers along the shelves and drawers as I gaze around one final time. "Nothing missing, nothing that doesn't belong, nothing left behin—"

My voice trails off as I spot something that looks like Jaslene's clutch on the carpet beneath the dressing table.

"What is it?" Kye-Shin says, alarmed, but I don't dare respond. Instead, I shuffle across the room and pull out the chair before bending down to reach the clutch.

Thunder booms, shaking the walls and floor as, without warning, the ship pitches to the side, sending me smashing into the table just as the cabin goes black. From seemingly miles away, someone calls my name, but the sound drowns in the throbbing pain flooding my head, and for an agonizing moment I can't tell if I am trapped inside reality or nightmare. Strong hands grab my shoulders, pulling me back and upward. Instinctively, I tense, but then a steady voice drifts just above my ear, close enough to make me swallow from nervousness rather than fear.

"You okay?" Kye-Shin asks, and I quickly shake my head, only to wince when the action heightens the pain still ringing through my skull.

"Fine," I manage, but my voice comes out as a whisper. Instead of answering, he remains silent, and I fear he can hear my pounding heart in the darkness.

I clear my throat, hurrying out of his grip and into the cabin's main room with the others. Curtains have since been thrown open to reveal the storm raging outside, and I gape at the mountains of foaming waves so dark they almost look black speeding past us. Wind howls through the slivers between the glass and frames while rain showers the balcony and streaks down the windows like tears.

"What do you have there?" Miyuni says, motioning to my arm, and I realize I'm still clutching the purse in my hand.

"Does anyone have any more light?" I think out loud, and in the dim glow I see Emory reach into his jacket.

"I have always made a point to never to be caught in the dark unprepared," he says by way of explanation as he procures a lighter from his pocket.

"Why is that?" Leander smirks at his friend. "Scared one of the ghosts from the tales our roommates at boarding school used to spout before bed will snatch you away? I never took you for someone foolish enough to believe in such superstitious idiocy."

"Being wary of what is hidden from view is never foolish," Emory replies smoothly. "For even the most familiar things can become alien and dangerous in the shadows."

With a flourish of his fingers, an orange flame bursts to life inches from me, and I slowly raise the object in my hand until I spot the familiar silver and rose beads lining the surface. The instant I recognize it, my heart withers in my chest.

"This is the clutch Jaslene was carrying when I last saw her," I whisper as lightning flashes, illuminating everyone's face in an eerie pallor and revealing expressions that mirror the dread I already feel pooling in my stomach. "She really did come back here before she disappeared."

Thunder rattles the glass doors, drawing my attention to the balcony and waters beyond. Waters that could drag down and crush fleets of ships as easily as if they were toy boats. At the thought of what they could do to one girl's body, I shudder.

Against my control, my mind conjures an image of Jaslene in the lilac dress she last wore standing outside the window, her dark hair flowing behind her as she leans over the rail to study something below. Perhaps she spots the silver scales of a fish gleaming in the sunlight. Perhaps she sees something else far beneath the foam and waves that she can just barely make out if she stands on the tips of her toes. When the ship pitches to the side, it sends her off balance and falling down, down, down...

Or was that still not what happened?

In my mind, the imagined scene changes, and Jaslene is standing at the rail in the same gorgeous party dress with the same gorgeous hair flowing around her, except this time she is no longer smiling or alone. Arthur stands next to her. Too close. Perhaps he lied. Perhaps he never left her alone after all. Perhaps though it isn't him who follows her back, but someone else. A stranger. When Jaslene falls this time, it isn't an accident. The end result, however, is the same. Jaslene crashes into the sapphire waters below as *The Fated* continues beating on, oblivious to the fact it carries one less passenger than before.

*No,* I silently plead even as I feel my body trembling with dawning horror. *Please, no.*

I'm so imprisoned in my rising terror that I barely register the groan of the ship until it grows loud enough to drown out the thunder.

"What is that?" Leander shouts beside me just as my hand turns numb, and when I look down, I see why.

In my palm, Jaslene's purse is melting.

Like the door days ago, its edges soften and stretch. The silver and rose beads detach before sliding down along the sides of my fingers and wrist like tears, leaving streaks as they go. A rancid smell fills my noise, making my eyes water from the stench.

Then without warning, my hand is no longer numb but so cold it burns.

With a cry, I drop the clutch. It lands on the carpet with a splatter just as the ship pitches again, sending the flame shuddering out and all of us stumbling in the shadows.

"To hell with this," Leander growls next to me, his shoulder slamming into mine as he hurries for the exit.

As he pushes past, another streak of lightning highlights the fear contorting his face, the rising hysteria in his eyes as he glances toward the fallen purse before skittering his gaze away. Then he's gone, vanished out the door like a specter as Emory shouts after him. Plates and mugs crash against each other in the kitchen as the ship tilts again. Thunder rattles the windows violently enough to make me fear they might shatter any second.

Without warning, an ache erupts in the back of my skull, heightening every noise to painful proportions. When the dizziness returns, I no longer have the strength to fight against it.

One second I am standing and in the next I'm falling—spiraling further and deeper and out of control until at last unconsciousness swallows me whole.

## CHAPTER 15

---

# MEMORY AND NIGHTMARE

Logically, I should dream about Jaslene. Perhaps it should be of the last time I saw her, repeated like a section of film reel rewound and then played again, every detail crystallizing, every movement painfully slow. Maybe instead I should dream of a happy memory, like the time Jaslene convinced me to call in sick at the department store so we could spend the day watching melodramas, romances, and comedies at the cinema.

But dreams are never logical—which is why instead, in my sleep, I return to the audition.

I remember how the sky that day was bluer than the ocean. The perpetual gray above the city had miraculously lifted, whisking away the cold drizzling rain and replacing it with such bright beaming sunshine that I had been certain it must have been a good omen like the ones my mother often talked about, a sign the fates were smiling down on me that life-changing afternoon.

Instead, they laughed.

Since that day, I'd stopped believing in omens at all.

In this dream, however, there is no sky, clouds, or sun. Only a warmly lit stage containing a grand piano. Like in the actual memory, an eternity seems to pass before I reach it. Rows upon rows of shadowed theater seats pass me, and yet I draw no closer…

That is until I blink, and then suddenly, I'm sitting onstage with the piano spread before me, a collage of keys so white they are nearly blinding and black keys darker than ink. They are warm to the touch.

The beginning note rings through the auditorium like the first bird's song in the earliest hours of the morning. It echoes throughout the vast space, trembling every air particle, like a drop disrupting the smooth surface of a pond. It trembles through me, through the strands of my hair, the cells of my skin, the strong bones of my speeding fingers, and the tendons of my ankles as they propel the pedals extending from the piano's base up and down.

As always, when I play, I feel myself dissolve into the music, feel my soul crescendo with each measure until I'm no longer a single lonely girl but a vital piece of something greater. Something almost divine.

In the audition, I played my own arrangement of "First and Last Wish" modeled after the original Lamiran folk tune. This was the version my mother had gently hummed by my bedside as a child, just as her mother had hummed beside hers. It was also the same one printed across the music sheets my mother sketched breathtaking illustrations on and even danced to in our cramped living room while I played.

In the dream, however, I add variations on a whim. Block chords transform into arpeggios that rise and fall like the steepest mountains or leaves on the wind. Notes and tones never before heard burst into existence, transforming the already stunning masterpiece into a melody with the power to cure any broken heart, relive any moment, or freeze time itself.

As the last note dies across the stage, I become aware of every detail —my heavy breathing, the spotlight piercing my eyes, the almost imperceptible ripple of the curtains as a draft rolls across the stage, cooling the beads of sweat gathered on the nape of my neck.

*This is the moment before my life will change forever*, I think. *This is the moment I have wished for every minute of every hour of every day.*

Beaming, I swivel to the four solitary figures sitting in the sea of seats, more certain than I have ever been they will applaud me. Welcome and accept me.

Yet, just like in reality, I am still not enough.

In the dream, the judges' faces are mostly erased, leaving nothing but empty ovals with frowning lips and voices that flicker in and out of existence. However, just like in the real audition, they tell me there must be some mistake, that I played August Urst's most famous and notoriously happy piece all wrong. Too many of my notes were wistful, even sad.

But when I try to explain that it was my own arrangement styled after the original Lamiran folk tune, they shake their heads, their words hardly sympathetic.

*...are sorry to say you did not make the cut...*

*...simply not a good fit for the Institute...*

*...might as well accept you have no realistic future as a pianist...*

The pain in the dream is always as excruciating as it was in real life. First, there is shock, numb disbelief. Then there is denial, a desperate refusal to understand a truth I know will break me.

Then there is the agony—the burning in my chest and pain of my heart crumbling in on itself. The hope I carried seconds before shatters like the most beautiful, most fragile glass.

Against my will, the body still struggles to fight on. Out of instinct, my eyelashes bat away the tears blurring my vision. Air whistles through my nose as my lungs constrict. The muscles in my calves strive to keep me standing as my knees buckle from the weight of something immeasurable.

All those nights running my fingers over the keys until my dried skin bled. All those days staring at tiny notes zigzagging across sheets of paper until I grew dizzy. All those years dreaming of a future where mine and my mother's stomachs would no longer ache from hunger, where our bones would not shudder from the cold seeping through the cracked floor of our apartment.

All for nothing.

The last things I hear before the high gilded walls collapse inward and water rushes into the auditorium are screeching tires and my mother's cry.

# CHAPTER 16

## DRIFTING

I flinch awake to a symphony of clicks.

Beneath me, the mattress feels unnaturally soft, and after several seconds the darkness recedes enough for me to recognize the silver stars twinkling along the ceiling and crescent chandelier blazing with light so blinding it hurts my eyes.

*I'm in my room.* The realization surfaces from the haze still cloaking my mind.

From the sound of the typewriter outside the doorway, I'm also not alone.

I lurch upward, regretting the action at the ache that pulses through my head, causing the comforter beneath me to blur and ripple like the water in my dream. After I close my eyes and wait for the dizziness to subside I realize my hand is no longer burning. It isn't numb either, and when I raise it to my face, no trace of the melted beads or clutch remains on my skin. I gingerly roll out of bed and shuffle into the main room to see Kye-Shin sitting cross-legged on one of the chairs with a typewriter before him and papers littering the coffee table.

"How are you feeling?" he asks without glancing up from where his fingers dance over the black keyboard with the grace of a pianist. Wide round glasses sit on the bridge of his nose, accentuating his already sculpted cheekbones and bestowing him with an almost romantic air of a writer fully immersed in his craft. It takes me a moment to remember the question he asked me.

"Fine," I say after a too long pause. "I had a restful sleep."

At that, Kye-Shin's brown eyes flash up to mine. I can feel him seeing right through me, puncturing my lie as easily as a pin through a butterfly's wing. Still, the piano and everything tied to it—the audition, the aftermath, my mother—is something I hardly ever speak about, even to Jaslene. Even to myself.

"That's a nice typewriter," I say, anxious to change the subject. "Wasn't it heavy to carry all the way here?"

Kye-Shin shakes his head. "It was made in Nanshyn and designed to be lighter in weight, hardly heavier to carry than a textbook," he replies.

I nod, impressed. "Any better luck with your writing?"

"None at all," he sighs before ripping the paper out and tossing it where it lands among the other crumpled pieces. True to his words by the pool, I can only make out several sentences typed in Nanshyn characters along the pages closest to me.

"You should go to the infirmary," he suggests, glancing at me as if I might topple over again at the slightest tilt of the ship. "Check to make sure you don't have a concussion just to be safe."

"No, I'm fine, really," I insist, throwing my hands out defensively at the thought of someone in a clinical white coat poking and prodding my head for injury. "Going to the infirmary won't be necessary."

Kye-Shin looks far from convinced, but he inserts another paper and resumes typing. I exhale in relief, allowing the rhythmic noise to fill the silence as I try to shake away the remnants of my dream by refamiliarizing myself with the cabin's mahogany walls, dark furniture, and soft lights.

The instant I see my reflection in the mirror, however, I swear at my mussed hair and wrinkled clothes. I'm in the middle of trying and failing to tame my curls and waves back into submission when a new thought forms in my mind.

"Were you the one...?" I ask, motioning vaguely to my room when Kye-Shin glances my way. I take a deep breath and force myself to say the words out loud. "Were you the one who carried me?"

Kye-Shin's typing ceases as he raises his head. His expression turns amused.

"Why?" he asks. "Would it make you feel better if I was?"

"Absolutely not," I snap before I can help it, and across from me the barest smile spreads across Kye-Shin's lips as he goes back to his writing.

I clear my throat and glance around the cabin.

"Where is everyone by the way?" I ask, half-expecting the others to burst into sight any minute. But all the doors remain shut, and the connecting rooms are quiet. For the first time, we are truly alone. The realization sends a shiver along my arms.

"Miyuni and Emory went to get dinner," Kye-Shin says after a moment. "Leander, on the other hand, ran out around the time you collapsed."

I glance back at him. "Why?"

"No idea." Kye-Shin shrugs in disbelief. "Let me get this straight—he calls some poor fellow a coward for feeling sick just before we pass through The Veil. Yet a little thunderstorm sends him fleeing like someone who's seen a ghost."

I recall Leander's shoulder slamming against mine in his haste to get away. I remember the terror written all over his face as he glanced toward the clutch before abandoning us without a second thought.

"So he didn't tell you what he saw then?" I wonder aloud.

"He didn't slow down enough for anyone to ask," Kye-Shin replies, clearly amused—that is until he sees the look on my face. "What's wrong?"

I don't answer. My gaze is already moving to Jaslene's un-melted purse on the sofa. In the light, it looks perfectly normal. Not so much as a bead is out of place.

Was I losing my mind?

But no, Leander had seen it too. Surely that was the reason he'd fled?

"Amarra?"

"I know this will sound crazy," I start, bracing myself for Kye-Shin's disdain. "But this purse melted in my hand just before the light went out."

"Melted?" Kye-Shin repeats, and I don't have to meet his eyes to sense his skepticism.

So instead, I nod, the mere recollection of it even now sending my skin shivering from revulsion and the hairs on the back of my neck rising with unease. "My hand felt numb, then cold. The beads even came off and slid down my fingers, leaving marks as they went." I turn around slowly, at last forcing myself to meet Kye-Shin's gaze. "Like I said, I know how it sounds, but..."

"If it's what you saw, it doesn't matter how it sounds," he sighs. "Besides, we're on *The Fated*, remember? A ship that's very existence defies any sense of logic." He takes off his glasses and rises to his feet before stepping beside me to study the purse.

He picks up the clutch before I can warn him not to, and I tense, expecting the material to melt again and Kye-Shin to shout in pain from its cold burning touch. But the fabric remains intact, its beads in place.

"Whatever caused it to melt must be gone now," he says, handing the purse over to me.

As soon as it's in my palm, I pull apart the clasp to find the contents inside are un-melted as well. I'm not sure if the discovery puts me at ease or disappoints me. An object gleams in the light towards the bottom, and I reach past the lipstick and rouge compact to find it's a token from our visit to the arcade.

Could what caused the purse to melt earlier tonight do the same thing to flesh?

I scramble to push the thought away, but it's too late. The image of Jaslene's melting face bombards my mind: her skin stretching like plasma; her eyes melting into puddles of liquid; her mouth elongating to the floor in an oblong scream.

Nausea overwhelms me as I spin and make for the balcony, belatedly realizing the floor no longer pitches or rolls beneath me. The lights aren't flickering anymore either, and the rumble of thunder is absent.

When I pass through the glass door a handful of steps later, I understand why.

In place of blackened clouds, oranges, reds, and pinks streak the heavens above a calm silver sea, and for a moment I think we might be sailing on an ocean of metallic satin rather than the tempestuous waters that battered us so mercilessly earlier. A chilling breeze slashes across my face as I step onto the balcony, dissolving my nausea as my body instead protests from the cold. But my shivering arms and legs are temporarily forgotten in the face of the sun setting on the horizon.

Sunlight ignites the surrounding waters on fire, creating a blazing golden trail whose end appears close enough for me to reach out and singe my fingertips against. Such beauty captures my breath and steals it away, making me almost forget how so much on this voyage has already gone wrong. Almost.

"Do you think it's hopeless?" I can't help but whisper as Kye-Shin steps up to the rail beside me. "Do you think if we haven't found Jaslene by now it means she's—"

"Only that she is still missing, that's all," he says firmly. "Don't torment yourself by thinking anything else. Not now. Not yet."

*Yet.*

The word lingers in the air, taunting me. Making me again wrack my brain for anywhere Jaslene might still be that I could have possibly missed or failed to think of, but again I can think of nothing. I have never felt so useless in my life.

"Why are you helping me, anyway?" I hear myself ask before I can think better of it. "You barely know me, and you don't even know my cousin."

"I know what it's like to feel responsible for someone though," Kye-Shin replies, leaning his arms onto the rail and gazing out over the darkening waters before looking back at me. "If Miyuni ever went missing, I'd be standing exactly where you are now, searching with the exact same desperation."

I feel grateful at the words—and for his steady presence beside me, which is something I wouldn't have dreamed possible the moment we first met.

"She's as close to a little sister as I've got," I say. "She's my only remaining family member who actually cares about me. After my mother died, Jaslene was the one who tried cheering me up. When my aunt didn't bother to try to stop me from moving out, Jaslene did, crying and begging me to stay loud enough for the whole street to hear."

Watching Jaslene's tears stream down her face as I stormed out of my aunt's townhouse, I'd feared I might never see my cousin again. I was terrified she would hate me for leaving, hate me because she couldn't understand why I couldn't take living under her mother's scrutiny a minute longer.

That fear had thankfully evaporated when Jaslene appeared on my doorstep five days later, demanding we go to our favorite ice cream parlor and then shopping along Pearl Street.

"We'll find your cousin, Amarra," Kye-Shin says, closing the distance between us with a single step that sends the deck creaking beneath his foot and my stomach dropping. Even though only half his face is painted in the light filtering from the cabin, I can see the determination in his dark gaze as it bores into mine. "I swear it."

I don't realize I'm leaning towards him until several loud knocks startle me into straightening. Behind us, Miyuni and Emory wave at us through the glass. When I turn back around, Kye-Shin has drawn away, leaving several steps between us once again. I can't contain my shiver. It's from the growing cold, no doubt.

"We should head in before we both catch our deaths," he says, his expression now unreadable. "Besides, Miyuni will have eaten the entire dessert plate if we leave her alone for long."

I can't help but grin at that. "I'll come back inside soon," I say, placing my hands on the rail after Kye-Shin drifts away.

"Amarra," he says at the last minute, and I glance back to find him standing in the doorframe, haloed in golden light with his profile and face again in shadow. "Your cousin is lucky to have someone like you looking for her."

Before I can reply, he closes the door with a soft click, leaving me alone with the echo of his words. Kind but untrue. If Jaslene were truly lucky, she would have had a cousin who could have found her by now. If she were lucky, she would never have gone missing in the first place.

But I'm only wasting my energy thinking such things now.

To my disappointment, the sun has long since vanished beneath the horizon, the only proof of its existence the streaks of otherworldly orange, green, and violet reaching towards heavens adorned with stars and unnamed planets.

Far below, lights from the promenade deck make the surrounding sea glow green, and I stare, mesmerized at the way the foam rises to the surface and spreads like ever-shifting cobwebs.

The crimson appears without warning.

At first, I'm convinced I imagine the dark liquid trickling from the shadowed edges of my vision and into the light. Yet even after I blink and look away before glancing down once more, the red continues to grow, contaminating the clear churning waters until they are murky and thick like blood. What *is* that?

An earsplitting wail reverberates from the ship, signaling an incoming announcement and startling me so much I grip the rail tight enough for my knuckles to go white.

"Hello, everyone, this is the Captain speaking," the bodiless voice echoes over the balconies and decks, sounding too loud, too abrasive within the vastness of the ocean and sky. "We are currently entering a slightly high-risk area. For your comfort and safety, all passengers should immediately exit the decks as well as your balconies and stay inside until further notice. Within ten minutes, all the doors and windows on the vessel will be sealed, and in order to avoid any unnecessary distress, we would suggest keeping your curtains closed during this period. Please be reassured this is a temporary occurrence and there is no need to be alarmed..."

Not an instant later, the lights from the deck below shut off, cloaking the red waters and me in permanent shadow.

## CHAPTER 17

---

# CABIN FEVER

"**G**ood morning, my fellow stupendous passengers, this is your Entertainment Director Gerald speaking! I hope you are ready for another exciting day aboard *The Fated*! You might have noticed the screens covering all the windows and doors leading outside, but rest assured this is entirely for your comfort and safety as we pass through that slightly high-risk area the Captain mentioned last night.

But don't let the fact that you're stuck inside get you down. We have all sorts of fantastic activities planned for you today, including a Tango party in the Siren Lounge and a showing of the award-winning thriller *No Escape* on the big screen at the Rhapsody Theate—"

The rest of the Director's announcement goes unheard as I rush across the cabin towards the balcony doors and throw the curtains aside. Dread coils in my stomach at discovering that he's right, that the doors are gone. They have vanished entirely behind a gray metal panel that spans the entire length of the glass, concealing any view of the ocean or morning sky.

Fragments of what the Captain said last night echo through my mind, and it is only now as I stare at the solid, unforgiving barrier before me that the meaning behind his words becomes horribly clear.

*...currently entering a slightly high-risk area.*

*... stay inside until further notice.*

*...no need to become alarmed.*

Alarmed by what? The crimson waters I spotted just before the ship lights went dark, or something worse—something so dangerous we aren't allowed to even catch a glimpse of it?

If that is the case, I should feel grateful for remaining blissfully ignorant of whatever else lies outside the ship. I should feel protected by the ornate walls and merciful lack of sunlight.

I feel neither. Instead, as my eyes slide over the dark, unyielding barrier before me, I feel suffocated. Trapped.

A crash erupts from Salenna's room, and I move, racing through the entrance expecting to find something else gone horribly wrong, some other disturbing and unexplainable sight. But it is only my aunt sitting at her dresser, makeup containers and pieces of jewelry strewn along the marble floor where they've fallen around her.

"Well, are you going to help me or not?" Salenna says, glancing at me through the mirror.

For once her tone lacks its usual venom, and perhaps that is why I begin picking up powder compacts and perfume bottles from the floor without complaint. I notice her hand trembles ever so slightly as she reaches for a mascara case, and her gaze flits toward the door every other minute as if Jaslene might skip through it.

*Why don't you look for her then?* I want to grab her by the shoulders and demand. *Why don't you do something?*

I already know the answer is because she is too proud. Too fearful to consider—or at least admit out loud—that her daughter might not be doing this to her on purpose because that would mean she was truly missing, injured, or worse.

So instead, I find myself comforting her by saying, "I'm sure Jaslene's fine." Even though a voice in the back of my mind hisses that I'm a liar. "She'll be back soon. I know it."

"Of course she will," Salenna replies, though it's more to herself than me as she resumes brushing her tangle-free hair and applying lipstick to her already red lips—as if her hands might be scalded should she force them to remain still.

I should leave. I should take this chance to escape before my aunt inevitably directs her anger at me and continue my search for Jaslene. But I have no idea where else I can look for my cousin, and for once as I take in the slight hunch of Salenna's shoulders and the way the action makes her look smaller, I hesitate. I'm unsure of how to comfort the woman who I once thought was indestructible, and yet I cannot bring myself to abandon her all the same.

Such a sentiment is ridiculous though considering I'm certain my aunt would have no qualms about abandoning me.

Around us, the room is every bit as luxurious as she would demand. Velvet curtains cascade from a vaulted ceiling while murals depicting tiered palaces and hanging gardens span the walls. I stroll from corner to corner, drinking in the porcelain jewelry boxes, crystal lanterns, and granite-topped furniture.

"Grab the shawl in that top drawer, will you?" Salenna says from where she still sits at the vanity table, putting on her earrings and glancing at me through the mirror.

Just like she said, when I pull out the dresser drawer, a silk shawl embroidered with black and mauve irises greets me. But it's the small photograph partially tucked underneath it that catches my eye. It's of a man, handsome in features with light hair and eyes that smile at the camera. He's young too, likely only a handful of years older than my own age of twenty-one.

"His name was Florian," my aunt says, suddenly at my side. To my shock, her expression is...wistful. "I met him long before Jaslene's father of course. When we were children, we swore we'd run away together to travel the known world. Venture as far as the Roakin Mountains in the north and the Kaladyren Islands in the south."

"He was your lover," I breathe in realization.

"He was my greatest joy," my aunt replies. "And my greatest regret. But I don't expect you would understand, would you? Not yet."

She's right. The only handful of romantic relationships in my life had been nothing more than passing moods. Frantic kisses beneath a flickering street lamp in the cold. Having someone to talk and laugh with on the trolley—at least for part of the ride. Coffee and movie dates that eventually dwindled down to infrequent calls on the telephone before ultimately fading to silence.

I had never experienced the kind of love I read about in books. Never felt the passion that could make even the most logical people fools or suffered a broken heart like the ones so many singers often lamented about in late night jazz clubs after most of the patrons stumbled home. Part of me wonders if I ever will.

"What happened to him?" I ask, snapping myself back to the present.

"He lost his fortune," my aunt replies after a moment, her expression sorrowful. "Not that he really ever had one to begin with."

"You make it sound as if he committed a crime," I say before I can help it.

"No," Salenna shakes her head. "But marrying him would have been. After watching our father slave away at that wretched shoemaking shop for years only to barely afford to put food on our table and a roof that didn't leak over our heads, I swore I would never be poor again. My children would never know the shame of being pitied at a mere glance because of their worn clothes or the embarrassment for not having enough change in their pockets to buy their favorite candy at the store."

"Your mother never made the same vow," my aunt continues, bitterness seeping into her voice as well as grief. "She was too much like our father. Too much of a dreamer. And you—" she looks at me, and I'm shocked to find something almost like affection in her eyes. "You are just like her sometimes."

Before I can think of how to respond, the telephone in the next room rings, shattering the peace between us.

"You better see who's calling," my aunt sighs, sounding tired for the first time in all the years I've known her. "I ordered room service a while ago. Make sure they haven't lost the food."

Within a handful of strides, I pass into the main sitting room and pick up the phone.

"Hello?" I ask into the transmitter.

"Good morning, this is room service," a smooth male voice announces. "Your breakfast is on its way up to your cabin now. Just listen for a knock on the door, and the table and trays will be waiting for you in the hall. Please call back if you have any questions—"

"Actually, I do," I start, immediately thinking of Jaslene. "Yesterday, I reported a missing perso—"

"—or concerns. Enjoy!"

With a click, the line goes dead, leaving me glaring at the handset.

"Who was it?" my aunt calls from the next room.

"Room service like you said," I answer absentmindedly as I begin dialing the emergency number. "The food will be up in a minute."

It rings three times before a voice answers.

"Hello, are you in distress?"

"Yes, this is Amarra Obrel calling about a person I reported missing yesterday," I say, careful to keep my voice low when I hear my aunt opening drawers in her bedroom.

"Amarra Obrel..." the female voice on the other line repeats as if she's never heard the name before. "Oh yes, you called reporting your cousin was missing. Jaslene Destan, correct?"

"Yes, that's her," I reply, momentarily relieved. "I was wondering if you'd made any progress with your search. I know you said you would call me if you found anything, but I just wanted to make sur— "

"I'm sorry, we haven't located your cousin yet," the woman responds. "But please rest assured, we will notify you as soon as we find anything. In the meantime, have a wonderful day!"

The phone feels heavy as I set it back down. I try and fail to swallow my disappointment.

What had I expected? That Jaslene would have miraculously been found dancing among the other passengers in The Nautilus? That she'd secretly been hiding in the hydrangea bushes spanning the gardens all along?

I'd laugh at my own stupidity if I didn't feel so furious with myself, so helpless.

I don't realize there's anything in my robe pocket until my finger grazes something cool to the touch. How strange, considering I can't remember placing anything inside. Slowly, I lift the object into the light —only to blink in confusion when I realize it's an arcade token. The one the golden-haired stranger dropped in the corridor yesterday. Something about its appearance now strikes me as odd.

An unnamable instinct pulses through me, and I rush to my bedroom and scramble towards the shelf where I placed Jaslene's clutch last night. With quivering hands, I reach inside to grasp my cousin's arcade token and hold it next to the stranger's. I spot the differences instantly.

Jaslene's token is an exact replica of the countless others we plugged into the games at the arcade. On the surface, an embossed version of *The Fated* glides across the sea while sunlight beams through the clouds, showering the ship in its rays.

On the stranger's token, however, an unnamed boat instead sails on the vast ocean, its size so small that the waves look as if they will topple it over any second. Words, too, curve along the bottom of the second illustration, and I have to bring the object merely inches from my eyes in order to make out the sloping script.

*Fortune rests not only on chance but choice.*

Fortune? Among the various games and gadgets Jaslene and I had played or strolled by, I don't remember seeing a fortune-telling machine.

I stare down at the object in my hand, the smallest tendril of hope stirring past my frustration and discouragement.

It's just a token, a strange but meaningless object that surely is unrelated to Jaslene's disappearance. It couldn't be some kind of clue to where she might be.

And yet...

Within minutes, I have thrown on the first blouse I stumble across in my closet, along with a velvet jacket and trousers, before hurrying out of the room and towards the exit.

"You're leaving already?"

My aunt stands in the doorframe of her bedroom, her expression almost wounded. Just like minutes before, the cold marble shell that has always seemed to encase her fractures, revealing a woman underneath who is softer, even capable of kindness perhaps. Someone I might actually want to know.

"I was thinking after breakfast we could go for a walk in the gardens," she continues, wringing her hands and stepping forward. "Or maybe watch the matinee for the new drama showing at the theater. How does that sound?"

The question makes me want to laugh—and cry.

I had wished for my aunt to say these kinds of words countless times. I had dreamed for her to ask me to come with her and Jaslene to whatever fashionable dinner party they were headed for next or go dress shopping with them even if I didn't buy anything. The rare instances when Jaslene actually managed to convince Salenna into letting me join them on an outing, my aunt had acted as if I were a burden, an embarrassment.

Until now. Now that Jaslene is gone. Now that I'm the only person my aunt has left.

Still, as foolish as it sounds, part of me yearns to go with her. Still yearns to be showered with motherly affection and treated, if not like a second daughter, then at least as a niece worth loving.

But I won't—*I can't*—do that to Jaslene. Not now, when she has only me to find her.

"I have to go, I'm sorry," I hear myself say. "But maybe we could go to the gardens and theater some other tim—"

"Never mind," Salenna snaps, any trace of vulnerability in her expression dissolving as her gaze freezes over once more. I know I've lost a chance I will never be able to win back. "Leave then. I doubt I'll notice you're gone anyway."

Without sparing me another glance, she turns and slams her bedroom door closed, abandoning me with nothing but the token in my pocket and my regret.

# CHAPTER 18

## OF GAMES & FORTUNE

Walking through the halls of *The Fated*, you would think nothing was amiss.

The atrium is a symphony of raucous laughter, clinking glasses, and the jazz notes of saxophones and trumpets. The massive winding space is more crowded and darker than usual due to the closed curtains hiding every window. Even the rounded glass ceiling, which always provides a clear view of the sky, has been covered by an exterior roof, throwing the ship into perpetual night.

Lamps glow brightly on each level, causing the marble floors to glisten along with jewels, charms, and other accessories draping the passengers as they amble by. A loud pop reverberates throughout the space followed by amazed gasps and cries as miniature fireworks explode in the atrium's center, showering the air with glittering sparks that streak and loop, forming images of silver dolphins, magenta flowers, and even *The Fated* gliding across turquoise waves.

Only a week ago, I would've found the sight nothing short of awe-inspiring, but now I only feel unease when I watch how people from every level rush toward the edges, leaning over the rails with their mouths open and their eyes reflecting the bursting lights like glossy mirrors. Some are even in costume. A woman in a Nanshyn headdress adorned with gold phoenixes and designed in a style not worn in decades blushes when a man in an old-fashioned top hat offers her a rose. Two men in vintage tuxedos brush past a woman wearing puffed sleeves and hair curled into ringlets. But instead of finding such authentic and carefully designed costumes marvelous, I only feel disgust.

*Does none of it bother you?* I yearn to ask the old woman weighed down with pearls who shuffles past me to gain a better view of the display or the young man frantically flashing pictures several feet away. *Don't you want to know why we aren't allowed outside? Don't you want to know why we can't look out any windows even if we wanted to?*

The urge to demand answers from someone—anyone—nearly has me reaching for them, but I refrain when I imagine the puzzled expression on the old woman's face or the anger in the young man's. They would think I was crazy, paranoid. Neither of them would understand my frustration. Neither of them would understand my fear.

Why would they?

After all, from their placid smiles, I can already tell no one *they* know has gone missing. *They* did not witness the sea turn crimson or melting substances as I had. *They* obviously weren't unnerved at being trapped inside without warning or explanation.

I'm so focused on making my way towards the arcade that I fail to notice Miyuni waltzing out of a shop carrying a fruit bouquet until the other girl waves, calling out to me.

"My goodness, where are you hurrying off to so early in the morning?" she asks, biting into a strawberry carved into the shape of a rose before she tilts her head at me in curiosity. She must see something in my expression, for her brown eyes widen in concern. "Is it about your cousin? Did you find something related to her disappearance?"

I almost nod, but hesitate, the token all at once feeling small and insignificant in my pocket. The sudden realization that it might be a clue to Jaslene's disappearance only this morning had seemed like a gift

—like flailing in the darkness then gazing up and finding a shooting star streaking across the heavens, like wandering lost through the forest and stumbling upon a paved path. How could such a revelation *not* have anything to do with Jaslene's disappearance? At least, that was what I had hoped.

But now, as I stare at the burgeoning excitement on Miyuni's face, I feel less certain. Uncertain, in fact. After all, could I honestly expect a mere odd token to solve my problems?

"It's probably nothing," I say, looking down, embarrassed.

"What is?" Kye-Shin ambles towards us, a coffee cup raised to his lips.

Even so early in the day, he appears as sharp and refined as always with a cream-colored coat draped over his lanky frame and the fringes of his ink black hair partially swept away from his face, making his gaze harder to ignore—as if that was ever possible.

I don't realize I'm staring until he speaks.

"The clue," he says, and for a split second my eyes fall on the slightest curl of his lips before I meet his gaze, heat rushing to my cheeks. Across from me, Kye-Shin raises an eyebrow, amused. "You were talking about a clue, weren't you?"

"Yes. Well, no, I'm not sure," I admit, reaching into my sweater and retrieving the token as if studying it one more time will reveal another hint. Unsurprisingly, it doesn't. In my fingers, the slim piece keeps its secrets well. Right now it's just as much of a mystery as ever, but hopefully it won't remain that way for long.

"Once I reach the arcade, I'll know," I say as if I'm certain, as if I have some semblance of a plan.

"Well then, we'll come along and uncover the truth with you," Miyuni says, wrapping her arm around mine and offering me a piece of pineapple shaped like a hibiscus as we veer around the next bend. Minutes later, we've reached the arcade.

The entrance looks like something from a whimsical dream or a mad hallucination.

Designed like a gaping mouth, the opening is bordered above with golden teeth while the surrounding face is shaded in varying hues of sapphire, azure, and cerulean. Two golden orbs for eyes stare out from under bushy eyebrows, and a pointed nose curves towards the atrium. Locks of hair from his beard and scalp ripple outward like waves. On the head rests a crown decorated with shells, pearls, and fish.

When I first came here with Jaslene, I thought the entrance was breathtakingly wonderful. Now I can't help but stare at details I failed to notice before: the unnatural jaggedness of its teeth; the tips of the crown resembling sharpened prongs of a trident; the vacantness of its pupil-less eyes.

"I swear I'll be seeing that face in my nightmares," Miyuni mutters, and Kye-Shin snorts. I silently agree but step forward, passing through the façade's mouth until I'm among the arcade's bright flashing lights and ringing bells.

A trio of boys rush past, their arms weighed down with glittering prizes. A couple takes turns rolling balls up a ramp and into various rings, shouting in delight when they reach a high-score and confetti erupts from the machine to shower over them. One girl stares at a mechanically operated poster depicting *The Fated* sailing across the open sea. Within it, layers of glowing blue waves ripple as the ship itself rocks from side to side. Even the cotton clouds above appear to roll on and off the screen, and still the girl hardly seems impressed as she regards it with a red lollipop in hand. It takes me seconds to recognize her bobbed hair and old-fashioned dress—one that resembles the green one I saw her wearing last time, except this dress is red.

"Lethia," I say, raising my hand in a wave as the girl slowly turns.

"Hello, friend," Lethia says, shuffling over until she stands before me with wide inquisitive eyes.

"Do you come here often?" I ask, praying she'll say yes.

The younger girl, however, simply shrugs. "Sometimes. I'm here with my brother now," she motions to where several teenagers take turns playing pinball. Lethia twirls the lollipop in her hand as she studies my companions with skepticism. "What are you doing here?"

"Looking for what this goes to." I show her the token. "Is there by chance a fortune-telling machine in here somewhere?"

Lethia scrunches her nose, but shakes her head. "I haven't seen one," she says, sticking the candy in her mouth before releasing it with a pop. "What's so important about this machine anyway? You do know it can't actually tell you your fortune, right?"

From behind me, Kye-Shin's cough sounds suspiciously like laughter—which falls silent when Lethia shoots a glare his way.

"So I've heard," I admit, managing a smile despite my disappointment. "Thanks for taking a look anyway."

Lethia shrugs. "I'm in the mood for ice cream," she says abruptly, stepping around us to stalk towards the entrance. Just before she passes under it, however, she stops and swivels around once more. "If I were you, I would try *The Wishing Well* instead. I saw someone once win over sixty prizes in one round!"

"What an odd little character," Miyuni says as soon as Lethia disappears from sight. "How wonderful it would be to be so young again, with nothing to worry about except finding ice cream."

"As I recall, when you were that age, you constantly worried about becoming the best ballerina in the world," Kye-Shin retorts in amusement.

"Yes, I did worry about that, didn't I?" Miyuni says softly, her usually cheerful tone for once betraying her sadness. "How silly of me."

Wading into the arcade is like wandering through a phantasmagoria of colors, shapes, and sounds. Bulbs of nearly every hue adorn signs, boards, and screens, painting the walls and floor in purples and reds and blues. Whistles, bells, and horns reverberate through the air, accompanied by laughter and shrieks of excitement. People of all ages are occupied with playing bagatelles, crane games, photobooths, mini-slot machines, and countless others—their faces stretched in varying expressions of wonder and elation. Around every corner, there are games I could never have dreamed existed in my wildest imaginations, and yet around every corner, I fail to spot anything remotely resembling what I could be searching for.

"Amarra, over here!" Kye-Shin says, and I hurry past a row of people throwing bean bags at a board decorated with cartoon sea creatures, past a boy and girl mimicking the movements of a dancing marionette dressed in the sequins and feathers of a flapper—until I stumble to a halt along with the others before a rectangular glass case adorned with gold trimmed edges and a lavishly decorated automaton inside.

The unnervingly humanoid figure sits cross-legged, wearing a red and black jumpsuit with a deck of tarot cards fanned out in one bleached hand while the other holds a crystal ball revolving slowly on its fingertips. Its face is concealed entirely behind a gold and red mask in the visage of a medieval court jester, complete with a wickedly pointed hat and a vicious smile twisting its porcelain façade. Where eyes should peer out through the openings in the material, there is nothing but hollow space, as if the true face behind the mask has long since evaporated—or never existed in the first place.

"Fortune rests not only on chance but choice," the automaton speaks without warning, sending me nearly tripping backwards. Beside me, Kye-Shin hisses something in Nanshyn while Miyuni raises a shaking hand to her heart as the jester leans forward until its pointed nose hovers inches from the glass. The head tilts while the chin swivels until the dark vacancy where its eyes should be seems to bore into me. Its carved smile remains unmoved as it asks: "Will you dare glimpse into the future to behold the choices soon awaiting you?"

"Forget nightmares," Miyuni hisses, her face contorting in fear and revulsion. "After this, I won't sleep for weeks."

When the automaton fails to speak or move once more, I step forward, half-expecting the humanoid device to jump through the glass any moment. Instead, the jester remains frozen. Waiting.

Slowly, I slide the token into the slot, watching it disappear, followed by the clink of it rolling into an unseen chamber before silence descends. With growing unease, I realize I can no longer hear the sounds of the arcade: not the laughter, ringing bells, or overly cheerful music—none of it.

The instant the jester automaton speaks, however, all the noises return, and I swear I see its carved smile widen when it draws away from the glass and returns to its original pose.

"You have made a wise decision."

The words barely emanate through the air before the automaton gives a harsh cackle. The jester's mask splits in two along with the rest of its body as the glass case disassembles. The top and bottom vanishes into the ceiling and floor while the remaining parts glide to opposite sides of the wall, revealing an arched doorway I swear wasn't there seconds ago. Royal purple curtains streamed with silver beads cascade over the opening, their edges rippling slightly in an invisible breeze.

"How...inviting," Kye-Shin says, taking in the spliced halves of the jester on either side and shadows seeming to writhe beneath the entrance before regarding his sister and me with a smirk. Neither of us inches forward. "What? No brave volunteers to go first?"

"I will," I say finally, forcing my feet to move one after the other until I stand beneath the doorway. Before my eyes, the opening appears to grow, looming taller and taller, spreading wider and wider until I feel as if the instant I step through, the sheer vastness waiting beyond will devour me body and soul.

*Will you dare glimpse into the future to see the choices soon awaiting you?*

I don't want to dare or choose, not anymore. I *dared* to board *The Fated.* I *chose* to escape to a better life than the one I was slowly drowning in. Isn't that enough? Why should I now be burdened with the knowledge of the future? Why did Jaslene have to disappear at all? For the first time, I can't help but be furious at my cousin—for leaving with Arthur after the watch party, for vanishing and then not being found.

"Amarra?" I swivel to find Kye-Shin regarding me with something like concern. "You don't have to do this. All you have to do is say so, and we can find another way. Find another clue."

There are no more clues, though. No other courses of action unless I follow my aunt's example and simply sit around, waiting for Jaslene to burst into our lives once again. But I have no intention of waiting.

"Thank you, but you're wrong," I say to Kye-Shin. "This is the only way."

For Jaslene. For my cousin. For the only family I still have left.

Which is why I don't hesitate when I step through the doorway and past the rippling curtain.

# Chapter 19

## Choices

A crystal ball levitating in the center of a chamber cloaked in shadows. A deck of tarot cards fanning across a crimson-clothed table like a crescent moon. Wisps of incense curling along walls draped with bronze and beaded talismans. These are the images I expect will greet me as soon as I pass through the entrance.

Instead, I'm thrown into a dark corridor, the temperature plummeting until I have to draw my jacket closer around me to keep from shivering. I whirl, throwing my arms out to brush back the curtains I just passed through, only for my hands to meet air and blackness. The doorway is gone, vanished as if it never existed.

Fear, cold and paralyzing, slithers up my throat.

"Hello?" I say, my voice echoing too loud in the emptiness. I swallow and try again. "Miyuni? Kye-Shin?" But while the shadows around me shift with the ship's movements and groans, none of them step forward to reveal a friendly face.

That's when I notice it. The smell, musty and faintly perfum-ish, like an antique store or old age itself.

The scent is fitting, I soon realize, when I spot the objects of all sizes swinging from thin cords along the walls. With every step closer to a buzzing lamp, I can make out more: a moonstone ring, a silver compass, a violin, a pair of pointe shoes, a leather diary, and on and on the collection goes. Despite the dim light, I can see they are all in decay: the gem is cracked, the compass is rusted, the violin's strings are either warped or broken altogether. For some reason, their deterioration floods me with a seizing horror that propels my feet forward. That sends me rushing farther down the hall to try and escape from the clinking noise the objects make as they swing along with the ship.

Rays of ghostly light writhe at the corridor's end, and despite everything inside me screaming to turn and flee in the opposite direction, my feet continue forward of their own will, dragging me closer to the glow even while my fear rises to a crescendo as I round the corner...

I find myself transported onto a boat, one that feels familiar though I can't place why. But the thought barely crosses my mind before my stomach drops with the violent rock and pitch of the tiny vessel as foam splashes over the sides and onto my jacket and pants. Releasing a shaky breath, I look up—and gape. Before me, a raging ocean disappears into a shroud of fog closing in from every direction, isolating in its thickness. *The Fated* is now nowhere in sight.

A bitter wind beats against my face and yanks my hair while mist showers my skin like tiny needles. Still, through it all, I stare ahead, compelled by a feeling I can't name to peer through the rippling fog, searching for something unknowable.

I never see the wave.

One second I'm on board, reaching my hand out just as the whiteness parts long enough for me to make out something on the horizon. In the next I'm falling through the surface, the water's freezing temperature slowing my movements as I sink below the waves. My lungs scream for air even as I watch the last remains of it escaping from lips to bubble up towards the receding light.

I kick and shout. I beat my arms back and forth as my muscles burn with exhaustion. Still, I continue dropping down, down, down...

I blink and my surroundings have altered again. In place of churning water, smooth mahogany walls rise on either side of me, covered with portraits and mirrors reflecting my dry and unchanged appearance. Slowly, I turn, half-expecting to see the curtains I passed through from the arcade behind me, but there is only a wall covered with dark green and gold swirling paper. No door. No opening. No logical explanation as to how I'm suddenly here.

Am I trapped in another vision? The thought makes me tense, holding my breath as I wait for the scene around me to transform or become distorted in a way that lets me know I've yet to return to reality. But the carpet beneath my feet remains still, the low creaking of the ship and voices from the opposite end of the hall the only noise. Wait... voices?

Half in fear, half in anticipation, I make my way down the corridor until I reach an entranceway and risk a glance around the corner.

I nearly collapse from relief at the sight of Miyuni and Kye-Shin sitting in a connecting room.

"Amarra!" the other girl says. "Thank goodness. We were beginning to worry you wouldn't show up at all!"

"What do you mean?" I ask. "How long have you been waiting? How did we even get here?"

"We don't know," Miyuni says, her features rearranging into a dreamy expression. "It was strange. After I followed you and Kye-Shin through the curtain, I found myself in a ballroom dancing with dazzling lights and smiling people." She shakes her head, her gaze clearing. "Then I blinked and found myself in the corridor you just came from. When I walked out, Kye-Shin was already here. He said he arrived several minutes before I did."

I turn to Kye-Shin, but he isn't looking at me at all. Instead, he stares at the embroidered tablecloth as if willing it to burst into flames or melt out of his view. His features are tense, spooked. Before I can ask him what exactly he saw that could rattle him so much, he launches to his feet, making me wince at the screech his chair makes as the legs scrape across the wood floor.

"Now that you're here we should go," he says, his dark eyes finally flashing to me before he steps around the table. But Miyuni stops him.

"We can't," she protests. "Enzo's already gone to get us refreshments. Leaving now would be rude."

"Who?" I ask.

"Enzo," Miyuni repeats. "It's his stateroom we're inside now."

"Are you seriously concerning yourself with etiquette right now?" Kye-Shin says, suddenly furious. "Does nothing about what just happened bother you at all?"

"Of course it bothers me," Miyuni hisses, glancing around as if this mysterious host will appear any second. "But maybe Enzo can explain everything. Why else would we end up here of all places? We'll just stay long enough to ask him some questions and..."

The rest of Miyuni's and Kye-Shin's hushed whispers recede to the back of my mind as I bypass the table, bookshelves, and display cabinets to wander through another doorway.

The second I do, my jaw drops at one of the strangest rooms I've ever beheld.

Dozens of framed paintings and sketches in varying states of incompleteness cover the walls. The landscapes depict the beginnings of lilac flower fields, evergreen mountains, glowing cities, and bronze canyons that dissolve into white canvas without reason. Drawings of afternoon boulevards and balconies overlooking the sea contain meticulous details in certain segments only to diminish to the most basic of lines in others.

Still, despite their incompleteness, the beauty of the images simultaneously steals my breath away in wonder while calling to mind a memory of a day a lifetime ago. The day my mother had rescued me from the bullies at school and whisked me away to the city's finest art museum, known as The Marvel, where we spent hours roaming from room to room, admiring sculptures hundreds of years old and paintings swirling with color.

"Why are your pictures not here, Mama?" my seven-year-old self finally asked after listening to my mother ramble about countless famous painters before realizing her name was not among them.

When I glanced up, my mother had been wearing one of those smiles that meant she wasn't really happy.

"Because mine aren't pretty enough," she'd said, and before I could declare her paintings were every bit as pretty as the others, she had suggested we go get shaved ice at the park—a suggestion which instantly erased all thoughts of artists and museums for good. That is, until now.

"I have the fresh tea right here!" I whirl, startled to see a man in spectacles hurrying towards us with a silver tray. Something about him is familiar, though I can't pinpoint why. Gray tendrils pepper his brown hair, and when his green eyes fall on me, his smile widens in delight. "And it looks like just in time considering we have another guest." He gestures to where he has sat the teapot along with a plate piled with tiny icing-covered cakes on the table. "Please, help yourself."

At the sight, my stomach growls, all at once remembering I forgot to eat breakfast. Yet I hesitate, the idea of eating this stranger's food without question seeming less than wise given the circumstances.

"My name is Enzo by the way," the man says. "Enzo Harper."

At the introduction, he gives a formal, if somewhat outdated, bow. When my eyes land on the old-fashioned top hat hanging from the corner of the bookshelf to the right, I finally recognize him as the man I saw in the atrium earlier who gave a rose to the woman wearing the Nanshyn headdress. He's still in vintage costume, I see, with a gray waistcoat and a navy cravat that's more befitting of a character in one of the old gothic novels I used to read.

"Amarra Obrel," I offer, forcing my lips into a smile despite my unease. "I'm sorry to ask, but would you actually be able to tell us how we got here? You see, we just passed through a doorway in the arcade and then the next thing we know we're somehow inside your cabin. It sounds crazy, I know, but—"

"Not in the slightest," Enzo insists, waving away the statement as if it's anything but alarming. "You are not the first visitors who have appeared inside these quarters unannounced and with a similar explanation."

"And you find this normal?" I demand.

"Normal? No," Enzo says, glancing up from where he pours the tea.

"But my dear, we are on *The Fated*. Nothing about this ship is normal—or are you telling me that fact is just now grabbing your attention?"

"Well—" I start, only to realize he has a point. "No."

Enzo grins and sighs. "Every once in a while, this ship has a way of turning you around and spitting you back out in the oddest places. In my experience, there is no rhyme or reason to it. It is simply a perk of being on *The Fated*."

"And the hallucinations," Kye-Shin says, unimpressed. "Are we supposed to think of those as perks too?"

"What hallucinations?" Enzo asks, confusion furrowing his brow as the three of us share a look.

"Anyway," Enzo continues, his face turning once again serene. "My door is always open for others to enjoy my rather unique collection." He motions toward the walls. "Since this ship contains an ice-skating rink, gardens, and even an aquarium, why should it not also have an art gallery too? Besides, I am always glad of the extra company."

"How magnanimous," Miyuni says, and I nod in polite agreement before biting into one of the cakes.

"Did you paint these?" Kye-Shin asks, stepping up to a bronze frame depicting a green countryside. "If so, why not finish them?"

Like the others, it's incomplete, with only the right half of the canvas dotted with great oaks and a silver stream trickling through it.

Still, like the others, the parts that are painted are magnificent. I have never been to the countryside but staring at the way the sunlight peeks through the trees' branches to form shadows on the grass makes me yearn for a place I do not know. Curious to learn who the artist was, I search the bottom right corner but fail to find a signature.

"Oh, goodness, no," Enzo replies hastily. "I couldn't draw anything if I tried. No, all these pieces were already in this room when I boarded, but I have enjoyed admiring them even if they are a bit unconventional."

As he speaks, I rise from my seat to peruse the other half-finished paintings and sketches spanning every inch of the wall—every inch that is, except for a large empty space in the center of the room between the other frames. It looks as if a painting once hung here along with the others and was later removed.

But missing paintings are the least of my concerns right now.

"About the other visitors you mentioned earlier," I say, reaching into my pocket and retrieving the photo of Jaslene and me for him to see. "Was one of them this girl right here? Her name is Jaslene. She's my cousin. We've been searching for her for the last two days."

I study his face as I speak, not daring to breathe as I wait for his features to brighten in recognition, for him to tell me that yes, he saw Jaslene here only yesterday or better yet earlier today. The older man's expression is apologetic as he looks up at me and shakes his head.

"I have not seen her," he says, and with those handful of words, I feel the last threads of my hope fray into nothing. It would be easier if he were lying, easier if I could pinpoint the barest hint of deceit in his green eyes. But I find only regret and sympathy—all the proof I need to confirm that the significance I foolishly attributed to the token had been misplaced from the start.

"Well, we've had a charming time," Miyuni announces when the silence grows too thick. She practically leaps from her seat, looking as if she would rather be anywhere else.

"Is the tea not to your liking?" Enzo asks, concerned.

"Oh no, it's delicious. Really!" She says over-enthusiastically. As if to prove her point, she grabs her cup and takes a gulp, wincing at the heat, before adding, "Such a unique taste."

"It is a specialty from my hometown," Enzo replies fondly. "In Tanzet, we grow the finest oranges in the world, so we make a habit of adding a bit of the fruit's flavoring in almost all of our food, including the tea."

"You're from Tanzet?" Kye-Shin says slowly, and it takes several seconds for his words to sink into my mind. When they do, I spin in alarm, my eyes meeting his.

Enzo smiles and nods. "Yes, I've lived there all my life. Well, up until stepping onto this ship, of course. I was certain I must have been imagining things when I saw *The Fated* appear at the edge of the city just before sunset."

"You mean you boarded directly from Tanzet?" I say.

"Indeed," is Enzo's reply. He gives me a puzzled look. "Didn't you?"

"Of course we didn't," Miyuni insists, shaking her head in bewilderment. "That would be impossible because—" She sucks in a breath, her eyes widening in realization.

*Because Tanzet no longer exists.*

The city had been destroyed in the war over sixty years ago. Terratia's bombs and lethal gas had laid waste to entire cities—the first of which had been Tanzet, Gorinth's most beloved city that dated back centuries when emperors and empresses once walked through its vine-covered streets. According to the history books, it had taken less than three days for the entire metropolis to be levelled to the ground.

"How I wish I could have just one more of those fresh oranges now," Enzo sighs wistfully, seemingly oblivious to the fact that the place he speaks so fondly of now exists solely in his memory. "It seems as if it's been ages since I last tasted their sweetness."

"Mr. Harper," I begin, careful to keep the tremble from my voice. "Exactly how long has it been since you boarded *The Fated*?"

"I cannot be sure," Enzo responds, raising his fingers to his chin while his expression turns pensive. "I am afraid time has slipped away from me. I would say a few months. Perhaps longer."

Perhaps at least sixty years.

Yet Enzo looks as if he's at most in his fifties. He couldn't have ever stepped foot in Tanzet, let alone lived there for a long time. More importantly, what was he still doing here if by some possibility he had boarded decades ago? Shouldn't he have made it to paradise by now?

The sound of clinking glass draws my attention to the ceiling where the light fixture sways along with the ship's movements, and belatedly I realize something: the room has no electricity.

In place of bulbs, flames flicker inside the frosted shades like something I have only seen in museums. Slowly, I lower my gaze, drinking in the remaining details of the chamber, realizing their outdatedness: the faded patterned wallpaper; the old-fashioned gilded furniture; the decades-old grandfather clock in the corner, its pendulum deathly still.

Then there is Enzo himself.

Enzo, whose gray waistcoat, cravat, and old-fashioned top hat appear less and less like a costume with every second that ticks by. Enzo, whose memories seem to belong to another era entirely.

"We should be going," Kye-Shin says, launching to his feet. His smile is tight as he nods to the older man. "Thank you for the refreshments."

"Leaving already?" Enzo says, startled, and the loneliness that floods his face makes my heart twist in sympathy.

"It was nice meeting you," I offer, reaching to grasp his wrinkled hand in mine. "I'm sorry we couldn't stay longer, but—"

"Promise to come back and visit, won't you?" Enzo pleads, desperation leaking into his voice. "These days I dread being alone. I always feel like I'm forgetting something when I do."

Part of me wants to say yes, wants to repay his kindness, but the idea of returning to this place fills me with a gripping terror I can't explain. Miyuni and Kye-Shin must sense it too, for they have already backed into the larger connecting room, their bodies leaning towards the nearest exit as if fearing that staying too long within these walls will trap them as they have already trapped Enzo.

I fear they'll trap me too.

With an apologetic cry, I tear my hands from the old man's and vault after the others into the connecting chamber. I'm feet away from the exit when the ship pitches to the side, sending my elbow colliding with the corner of the nearest painting. A loud crack ricochets through the space as the frame breaks against the hardwood floor, sending the canvas careening toward my feet, where it lands facedown.

On the back upper right corner are written two words that have been struck through with an angry line but are still legible all the same. A name.

*Enzo Harper.*

## CHAPTER 20

## THE MAN IN THE PAINTED ROOM

I stare at the name scribbled in ink across the stark, pale space, certain I must be mistaken. The words can't mean what I think.

*I couldn't draw anything if I tried.*

Had Enzo been lying?

A shadow falls over the words as I pick up the canvas, and I flinch—then breathe in relief at finding Kye-Shin beside me, his expression unreadable as he examines the name.

"What are you two gawking at?" Miyuni hisses impatiently, lingering several steps ahead of us. "We should escape now while we have the chance!"

"Turn it over," Kye-Shin whispers, ignoring his sister altogether as he draws close enough to me for his shoulder to brush mine.

With trembling fingers, I obey, readjusting the canvas in my hands until my vision is flooded with the ambers, browns, and reds of a city at sunset. But not just any city. Though I have never been there, I instantly recognize the half-complete spires in the distance, the couples walking hand-in-hand beneath the outline of palms, the child squatting along the partially existing cobblestone street, bright yellow and purple paint splayed all over his hands.

*The city of spires*, it had once been called.

*The city of lovers.*

*The city of artists.*

A place that was once beautiful, once breathtaking—and now nothing more than rubble.

*Tanzet.*

Next to me Kye-Shin lifts another painting from the wall—this one depicting a jungle of turquoise and greens—before turning it over. His jaw clenches as he looks it over before holding the canvas out for me to see the crossed-out words, *Enzo Harper*, again written along the back.

With rising panic, I reach for a sketch, tilting it until I can make out the signature in the corner, then another, followed by a fifth, then sixth...

Every one of them is identical, each containing the same two sets of crossed-out letters written by the same hand in the same ink.

"What happened?" Enzo demands, rushing into the room. "Did something fall?"

"I thought you said you weren't a painter," I utter, looking up to see the old man's face crumple in confusion.

"I am not," he replies, and I search his features for any hint of deceit. I find none.

"But this is your signature, isn't it?" Kye-Shin asks, tilting the canvas toward Enzo. The other man blinks uncomprehendingly, as if he can't decipher the letters written on the back of the canvas—or see them at all.

Still, Kye-Shin's words seem to fracture something inside of him.

"My signature? But...that isn't possible," Enzo begins shakily. At the panic rising in his eyes, I'm overwhelmed with the sensation that we have made a grave mistake, one that will surely bring disaster, or worse.

But it's already too late.

"That can't be," Enzo insists, his pallor paling. "I don't understand. I couldn't—I never painted anything in my life. This isn't possible!"

"It's alright, Mr. Harper," I say, unable to watch any longer. "It's alright. We believe you." I motion for Kye-Shin to set the canvas against the wall with the name on the back, hidden from view. "Please, forget we said anything at all."

"Forget?" the old man shrieks as if the word is poison. "What have I forgotten? Why can't I remem—"

With a loud creak, the room sways, sending Enzo teetering back like a toy doll. But when I reach for him, he swipes his arm with surprising vengeance.

"Stay back!" he roars, his eyes bloodshot. No ounce of his gentle self from seconds ago remains. "Leave me alone. Go!"

"Come on," Kye-Shin urges, grabbing my arm and tugging me away from him as we race towards the exit. Just as we pass through the doorway, I glance back one last time to see Enzo bent over with his head in his hands, his silhouette crumbling in on itself while the paintings covering the walls seem to grow, looming over him until he is gone from my sight.

We continue rushing around countless corners and up the stairs until I halt, realizing we've hurried past the same cabin numbers multiple times.

"We're going in circles," I gasp, resting my hands on my legs as I struggle to catch my breath when another revelation hits me. "But...that can't be." I straighten, peering down the corridor. Navy carpet, maroon doors, and white walls stretch out identically in four directions. "We made different turns each time. We even climbed two flights of stairs. We shouldn't be back here again!"

Enzo's earlier words replay in my mind.

*Every once in a while, this ship has a way of turning you around and spitting you back out in the oddest places.*

"We must have gone back down the stairs without noticing," Miyuni insists, desperation flooding her tone. "Perhaps you're just imagining things. All these corridors look the same anyway. It's only logical you would get them confused."

A lie—and an unconvincing one at that considering from her trembling lips and frantic expression it is obvious Miyuni doesn't really believe it.

I can see her trying to though. I can see her already rejecting the bizarreness, the impossibility, the disturbing truth of what we have seen in favor of a narrative of her own making. One that is palpable and unamazing. One that can be easily dismissed and disregarded altogether.

"Nothing about any of this is logical," Kye-Shin snaps. "How can you delude yourself into believing it is after what we just witnessed? You yourself have always been convinced there's something mystical about *The Fated*."

"Mystical?" Miyuni spits back disbelievingly. "What I saw was a man who has lost his mind! If he can't remember learning how to paint, then who can tell what else he has forgotten? We shouldn't believe anything he says, especially the fact that he thinks he recently left a city that hasn't existed in sixty years!"

"But why couldn't he recognize his own signature on the back of the painting?" I wonder aloud. "His memories about the tea and oranges were so vivid. The fondness in his expression when he spoke of Tanzet —it sounded like he truly lived there."

"Okay, then he's delusional. Problem solved!" Miyuni says.

"This solves nothing, and you know it," Kye-Shin scoffs, glaring at his sister as if she is the one who has lost her mind. "Listen to yourself, Miyuni! The only reason you're even saying any of this is because you know nothing adds up. Missing passengers, visions so vivid they almost look real, and now Enzo—none of it makes sense, and yet you want to act as if everything is alright. Why?"

"Because you promised it would be!" Miyuni shouts, instantly silencing her brother. Even from several feet away, I swear I can sense the breath being knocked out of him, swear I can feel him rock back onto his heels as if another word from Miyuni will send him crashing to the floor altogether.

"Look," I say, feeling guilty. If they hadn't been helping me, they would never have been dragged into this mess, would never have had a reason to fight. "We've all had a long morning. Let's just calm down and—"

"You promised me, Kye," Miyuni pushes on, her voice cracking.

Tears pool in her eyes, and still, her gaze bores into him accusingly. "You promised everything would be alright the moment we stepped on board. This isn't one of your stories. There is no grand mystery waiting to be solved or scheming villain we need to defeat. This is our lives."

"Exactly," Kye-Shin says, as if he can still make her see. "And because it is, don't you want to discover what is really going on? Aren't you curious about who is really running this ship? Why we were chosen in the first place?"

Miyuni's answering smile is heartbreakingly soft. "No." She shakes her head. "What I want is to dance every night until I'm too tired to stand. I want to drink champagne and laugh with handsome boys. I want to be beautiful and adored. I want to be careless. I don't want to obsess anymore about not being good enough to become a ballerina. I'll never be good enough, Kye."

"Miyuni, that isn't tru—" he starts, but she pushes on.

"It's okay. I've accepted it for a while now. So I don't want to think about it anymore. I don't want to think about anything. I just want to be like all the other happy girls I knew while I was growing up. Will you let me at least do that, big brother?"

For one heart-stopping second, as I take in Kye-Shin's clenched jaw and tense gaze, I think he will lash out with the maelstrom of words I can already see whirling in his mind, waiting to be weaponized. Miyuni must sense it too, for her hands curl into fists while her face sets in determination, preparing for the barrage surely to follow. Just when I'm certain the corridor will erupt into all-out war, Kye-Shin sighs. The action seems to steal away every last drop of his anger, leaving him tired and defeated.

"Since when did you ever need my permission for anything?" he finally says with a regretful grin. Miyuni's expression becomes pained, as if she wishes she could take back her words.

"You don't need any more of my help now, do you?" she says, turning to me and gripping my hands in her own shaky ones. "I'll only slow you down and make a fuss when I get easily spooked. I'll be utterly useless, I'm afraid, if I keep tagging along. You understand, don't you? You can forgive me?"

Can I? I want to be angry. I want to rage and demand how I could possibly understand. How could anyone?

*You're the one who offered to help me find my cousin,* I yearn to remind her, yearn to watch the accusation hit its mark as her beautiful face crumples with guilt. *You're the one who said we were friends. Is abandoning each other what friends do?*

But the words stick on my tongue when I recognize the same fear in her eyes as I saw in Leander's when he ran out of the cabin during the storm. One more disturbing revelation will be too much for her, I realize. Even now, after experiencing the visions and meeting Enzo, I can see her clinging onto some semblance of normalcy, some slim, desperate hope of returning to how wonderful everything was when we first boarded *The Fated.* When we still believed everything about this ship was perfect.

As hurt as I am, I can't bring myself to rip that away from her.

"Of course, I can forgive you," I lie, forcing a grin. "Don't worry about me."

Miyuni beams in relief, her smile so bright that for a moment I like to think that if things were different, she might have stayed by my side, and we might have actually been best friends.

"You'll find your cousin. I know you will," she urges, giving my hands one last encouraging squeeze before spinning around and hurrying down the hall.

As soon as she vanishes from view, I half-expect her to appear once again from another direction, caught in the same pattern we've been trying to break out of for the last fifteen minutes. But whatever trick the ship was playing on us must have lifted because Kye-Shin and I remain alone in the hallway, the ever-present creaking of the ship serving as our only company.

The noise reminds me of the dark corridor with the trinkets and objects strung along the walls, and I turn, opening my mouth to ask Kye-Shin if he saw the same scene in his visions. The question, however, dissolves from my mind when I take in his slumped shoulders and vacant gaze, as if his fight with Miyuni has robbed him not only of anger but everything else as well.

"Are you alright?" I ask, concern twisting inside my chest at seeing him so defeated.

Seeing my expression, Kye-Shin chuckles, the sound humorless.

"Not really," he huffs, retreating several steps to lean against the nearest wall and slide down to the floor. Metal flashes in the light where he reaches into his pocket and retrieves the medallion. He repeatedly turns it over so that the side with the Alexandris rises into view, then the compass, then the Alexandris again. After a second or two, he peers past dark locks of hair up at me. "You?"

I nearly laugh too when I hear the question directed back at me and realize its absurdity.

"Not really," I echo, reaching him in two strides and seating myself by his side. Beneath my legs, the carpet feels soft in contrast to the hardness of the wall against my spine. I feel heavy. Like I'm weighed down by thousands of stones and will never rise again.

"Jaslene isn't alive, is she?" I whisper. "After all this...it's impossible, isn't it?"

"Nothing's impossible. Especially on this ship," Kye-Shin sighs, and despite the truth of the words, they fail to bring me any comfort.

"You know, when I was twelve, I went missing." I turn in surprise. At meeting my eyes, his lips widen ever so slightly into a grin that softens his face and makes me want to stare. Instead, I swallow and look away. "Well, to phrase it more accurately, I ran away. But to my parents I was missing for a couple of days."

Past my shock, I struggle to form a response. "What made you run?"

"It was stupid, really," he says, and something in his voice makes me glance at him once again though I try not to, as if I've been caught in the same invisible current that tugs the most unsuspecting objects out to sea. "My parents fought all the time, but luckily for me one of the few things they agreed on was the importance of education. They locked me in my room as punishment for making terrible grades, and I wanted to punish them back by running away. At least for long enough to make them worry."

I huff in amusement. "Did it work?"

"Oh, yes," he nods. "I'm sure they aged several years in those two days they scoured every corner, store, and park in the city searching for me. But I had hidden in the one place they would never think of to look for me. Have you ever been to Nanshyn City?"

I shake my head, recalling the handful of books I'd read and photographs I'd seen depicting the capital of Nanshyn's lantern-covered boulevards, fried-food vendors, and bustling trolleys.

"Well, it has one of the largest libraries in the world," Kye-Shin says, fondness seeping into his voice and eyes. "The entire west wing of the old palace was remodeled and covered with shelves after shelves of books and maps and famous people's journals."

"That sounds amazing," I breathe, already picturing it in my mind and wishing I was there.

How strange, I can't help but think, that now I am on board *The Fated* I'm yearning to be somewhere else—somewhere belonging to the world we left behind.

"It's a sight you can never forget," Kye-Shin agrees. "But when I stumbled inside that day, my only thought was that my parents would never find me. Back then nothing interested me: not the things I was taught in school, not any of the sports my father tried to pressure me into playing, and definitely not books, let alone writing. It wasn't until I was forced to pass the time by reading the stories I saw on the library shelves that I discovered how addicting it could be to lose myself in another's words, in another's life and struggles and adventures."

I understood the feeling well. Not only with books but music. Hadn't I played the piano hundreds of times for the same reason? I wanted to forget my own troubles, to drown out the hunger in my stomach and my mother's swearing when something else yet again in our dilapidated apartment broke. I'd lost myself in the notes, in each new symphony I could arrange them to create...but I had found myself too.

In the end, though, none of it had mattered.

"So what you're saying is," I start, struggling to remember the purpose behind this whole conversation, "Jaslene could be hiding from me?"

"I'm saying that she could be in a place you least expect," Kye-Shin says. "Somewhere that slipped your mind. Somewhere you yourself might never even have been or know of. What I'm saying is," he reaches his hand out and settles it over mine, "that even after everything that's happened, she might still be alive."

As he says the last words, Kye-Shin's gaze once again lifts to my face, and I feel the breath stutter out of me at the intensity of his dark eyes, at the warmth of his skin against mine. Only a week ago, he would have been the last person I would have wanted by my side. Yet in this moment, I'm overwhelmed with the certainty that if he were to abandon me as Leander and Miyuni had, I'd be lost altogether.

"Thank you," I say, and yet the phrase doesn't do justice to the emotions I feel building inside me, doesn't even begin to communicate the extent of my gratitude.

I'm so focused on trying to find the words that do, I barely register Kye-Shin drawing away, the closeness between us shattering as his gaze fixes on something past me in alarm, something quickly approaching.

Then I hear it. A voice calling both our names.

"Amarra? Kye-Shin?"

Emory races towards us, his usually composed expression startled—no, panicked.

His gaze fixes on us, but the disappointment underneath the relief in his eyes tells me we aren't what he was looking for—or rather, *who*.

"What is it?" I ask, though the instant I do I already know. I can already tell from the familiar desperation in his eyes. "What's wrong?"

"It's Leander," Emory breathes, the terror in his voice erasing any doubt. "He's missing."

# CHAPTER 21

## CHASING SHADOWS

Leander Scott's stateroom is every bit as flamboyant as his personality.

Mahogany walls encompass a space filled with expensive objects of luxury and leisure. A pool table sits towards the chamber's center. A cue stick and several brightly colored balls still roll back and forth across its surface along with the ship from where Leander no doubt abandoned them after growing bored. A shelf lined with phonograph records stretches along the wall behind a flying marble staircase that spirals up to a king-size bed. Velvet curtains cover floor length windows that almost certainly open to a grand balcony I wouldn't doubt is over five times the size of ours. Even the massive light fixture looming above is shaped into a crown, and I can't help but huff at how that particular detail is the most fitting of all.

Not a single thing appears out of place, though. There are no signs of distress. No shattered glass or knocked over furniture, nothing hinting at a struggle. Leander seems to have simply strolled out the door and never returned. Not that such an action was unusual for someone like him. From the little I'd learned about Leander, it seemed more probable he was hidden away in some dimly lit lounge on the lower levels or charming women along the pool deck instead of having disappeared altogether. Then again, I hadn't believed Jaslene could go missing at first, either.

"What time did you say you left him last night again?" Kye-Shin asks. He steps away from the table to survey the room again as if taking in the decanters clustered in the corner, the nearly blindingly gold gramophone by the curtain, or the expensive furs peeking out of the closet for the dozenth time will uncover something ground-breaking.

"Around half-past twelve," Emory says, "Maybe a little earlier. When I didn't see him for breakfast this morning or even lunch, I still wasn't too concerned. But when I failed to spot him all day in any of our usual haunts around the ship, I began feeling uneasy."

"The last time I saw Leander, he was on edge too," Emory continues. "It was just after I got back from your cabin, Amarra. Even hours after leaving, he was still anxious, angry even. I couldn't get him to confess why."

Across the room, Kye-Shin meets my eyes, and I can tell both of our minds latch onto the same thought.

"Amarra saw something that day," Kye-Shin offers. "When the lights went out in her cabin, she said her cousin's purse looked like it was melting before eventually returning to normal. Maybe Leander caught a glimpse of it and panicked."

"Melting?" Emory says, turning to me in disbelief. "And you think that might have something to do with why he disappeared?"

"I don't know," I admit.

If Leander had gone missing because he had been one of the few people to see things around the ship melting, then why was I still here? The memory of Leander's expression lingers in my mind: the bitter twist of his lips, the hysterical pitch of his voice, the fury burning in his eyes—and underneath all of it, fear.

Had he been just as terrified when he vanished?

As soon as the thought crosses my mind, I glance at Emory in guilt. But his features remain unchanged, showing no sign that he has sensed my thoughts.

"We'll find him," I say automatically, reaching out a comforting hand. The second I feel the muscles of his arm go rigid beneath my grip though, I feel sick at my own words. After everything that's happened, we're still no closer to finding Jaslene, so why would Leander be any different?

Emory's answering smile is strained. Almost sympathetic. "I know," he responds unconvincingly. Thankfully, Kye-Shin draws Emory's attention before I can mumble anything more foolish.

"I never took Scott to be the innovative type," he says, inspecting several stacks of papers arranged neatly across a nearby table with begrudging admiration.

"Those are mine actually," Emory says, the shadows haunting his face momentarily clearing as he smiles in pride. "My mother always said I started building things before I could walk, or speak for that matter."

Curious, I stalk forward until I can make out the maze of thin pencil lines, curves, and angles zigzagging across the pages.

"What's this?" Kye-Shin asks while I draw close enough to see that in addition to annotations and measurements, the markings altogether form a rectangular device decorated in various buttons and switches with a large round lens staring out from the center.

"It's a compact personal cinema camera," Emory says, pointing at multiple elements of the diagram as he launches into explanation. "You simply hold it here and after flipping this switch, turn the lever clockwise to begin filming your very own miniature movie in the comfort of your home or anywhere else you like."

"Miniature movie?" I repeat in disbelief. "In your home?"

Even now, despite standing on a ship as miraculous as *The Fated*, I can't help but be amazed by such an invention.

"And this," Emory continues, lifting the top paper from the nearest pile to reveal another drawing beneath, "is a multifunctional walking stick that contains a removable umbrella, a small flashlight, and even a compass inside while still remaining easy to maneuver."

"That's amazing," I breathe. "They both are."

"It's nothing compared to the level of technology running this ship," Emory says, seeming almost disappointed as he returns the drawing to the table. "Still, Leander believed in my inventions from the beginning so much that he managed to convince his father into funding my research. But after a round of unsuccessful experiments, the project was cancelled. Leander's father didn't make his fortune by wasting his money on hopeless ventures, you see. He tried to soften the blow by telling me it wasn't personal."

Kye-Shin gives a disgruntled snort. "It never is."

"If you haven't already, you should call and report what's happened," I suggest, nodding to the phone several feet away, its color redder than blood. "They still haven't found any sign of Jaslene, but maybe they'll have more luck with Leander. It can't hurt anyway."

"Yes, of course, you're right," Emory says, hope filling his eyes once again as he rushes to the phone.

I don't have the heart to tell him not to expect too much. Even if we do manage to discover some clue, I doubt we will be any closer to finding Leander, not really. Jaslene's clutch, the stranger's token, even Enzo—everything we have uncovered within the last twenty-four hours has only led to more confusion, more uneasiness. A part of me dreads what our next discovery will bring.

For the first time, I wonder if everything about our voyage—the hope of sailing to the famed lost continent of Melanthros, the intoxicating luxury constantly surrounding us, even being fortunate enough to be chosen to board *The Fated* at all—is a curse.

"Yes, I'm calling to report a missing person," Emory speaks into the mouthpiece. "His name is Leander Scott, and I last saw him in..."

The rest of his words fade into the background as I step into the corridor. The faint echo of jazz music leaks from the atrium, gradually growing in volume as I wander closer towards the elevators. On the opposite end of the hall, a trio of women in feathered headbands and beaded dresses stumble with the ship's movements, their bubbling laughter sounding foreign to my ears.

Had it only been days since I too laughed on a deck beneath the sunshine and blue sky, every bit as careless and happy as the passengers who pass by me lately are? The afternoon I'd spent with Jaslene eating sundaes and ambling through the aquarium; the night I swam beneath the stars, listening to Kye-Shin's and Miyuni's laughter—all of it feels like a mirage, receding and intangible. Another dream I'd mistaken for reality.

A ding rings through the air, announcing an elevator cab's arrival as a group of passengers floods through the sliding doors and bustles into the hall.

"Such a marvelous selection at the buffet again today!" someone says as they brush past me.

"What an exciting round of bingo!" another praises when the ship tilts without warning, and I along with the dozen or so other people sway towards the wall.

Instead of colliding with a solid surface, I stumble into a connecting corridor I failed to notice earlier, one so dimly lit that my eyes instantly land on the one bright area in the space.

A spotlight shines down on an alcove in the corner, a porcelain vase holding a single flower at its center.

I recognize the plant as an almost identical version of the flower I'd seen during my search through Jaslene's room, the one that had cut my finger deep enough to draw blood. Large-petaled and colored the deep red-purple hue of wine, the plant is without blemish and unnaturally tall. It's so tall in fact that it seems to have outgrown the slender curving vase wrapped around the stems which are adorned with thorns.

*What a strange flower*, I can't help but think as I drink in the wide curving petals and the faint streaks of gold stretching from the center. *And what an even stranger location to display it.*

I'm almost close enough to brush my fingers against the petals when the tip of my shoe hits something solid. Half in dread, half in anticipation, I glance down—

—and nearly laugh in embarrassment at finding it's only a bracelet.

It's not until I reach to pick it up that I see the golden watch face staring back at me, its numbers and hands melting into dark globs that stretch toward my fingers just as the ship around us gives a mournful wail.

The watch drops from my hand as I stumble back, watching it bounce along the carpet towards the entrance as Kye-Shin and Emory appear in the doorway. I cough at the rancid taste that fills my mouth.

"Be careful," I hiss in warning as Emory bends towards it, but the instant he grasps the watch in his fingers and turns it over, the clock face has returned to normal.

"Did you see it melting just now?" I ask Kye-Shin, who steps up beside me, but he only shakes his head before saying to Emory, "That's Leander's isn't it?" At the words, I recall seeing the watch on Leander's wrist, gleaming beneath the dim lights in The Nautilus what felt like ages ago.

In response to the question, Emory reluctantly nods, though his eyes never waver from the object, as if trying to summon the watch into revealing its secrets through sheer force of will. Instead of seeming relieved at the discovery, he looks ill.

"It was a gift from his father on his sixteenth birthday," Emory says softly. "The other day he mentioned it had started slowing. He planned to take it by the jewelry shop and get it fixed but obviously..." his voice trails off as he holds the watch limply at his side, and I can see the now un-melted hour hand is fixed between one and two while the minute hand sits several inches past six. The second hand is motionless. Had the watch stopped ticking when Leander disappeared?

A creak groans through the air, sending hairs rising along the back of my neck and arms as my gaze snaps to the end of the corridor. An outline of a familiar figure slips through a door, then disappears just as quickly.

"Where is he going?" I say. "Where does that lead?"

"Where is *who* going?" Kye-Shin says. "I didn't see anyone."

"Neither did I," Emory echoes.

"Amarra, wait—" Kye-Shin shouts behind me, but I'm already moving, some unnamable instinct pulling me through the gaping entrance and into the light.

# CHAPTER 22

# CRIMSON

It takes seconds for my eyes to adjust, and when they do, I discover I'm inside a lounge.

No—not just any lounge: The Sea Dragon. It is where we attended the watch party and celebrated making it to the other side of The Veil.

And the last place I had seen Jaslene.

In my peripheral vision, I barely register the vague shadows of booths, tables, and chairs cluttering the space around me. I barely take notice of the unlit lamps or eerily carved bronze landscape along the back wall depicting a raging ocean crowded with monsters of every kind, including sea dragons and krakens rippling along the sides.

But none of these details matter. Nor does the fact that the figure I saw slipping through the door earlier is nowhere in sight, the memory of him fading like mist in the wake of the scene before me. Windows wrap around the circular space, stretching from carpet to ceiling in almost every direction. Yet unlike the others, the glass here is not concealed behind any curtains or metal barriers.

I wish it was—for the landscape on the other side looks like a sight from an alien world.

A crimson sea stretches out as far as the human eye can detect. Waves break along the surface, giving it the appearance of water at first glance, and yet there is a certain slowness to the ripples' movements that looks anything but natural. The sky, too, glows a pale red hue, and yet no matter where I look, I can't locate the sun or any clouds it could be lurking behind. In the end, however, it is not the sky or even the crimson ocean that fills me with horror.

It is the ships.

Vessels in various stages of decay lay scattered around us. To my right, a brigantine that looks centuries old drifts with one of its masts collapsed and the sails almost completely disintegrated. To the left, what remains of a small fishing boat bobs along the surface, though its stern is missing. Several yards past that, an ocean liner nearly the size and extravagance of *The Fated* stands half-submerged with its bow hoisted into the air, the sleek black and white paint eaten away by rust.

We're wading through an oceanic graveyard—and one not made up of only ships.

Amidst the deteriorating vessels, the right wing of an aeroplane protrudes towards the sky like a bleached bone. On the opposite side, the envelope of a deflated airship sprawls across the red surface like a warped fan.

*There must be a mistake*, I think. There has to be.

Happiness, prosperity, hope—*those* are the things to which *The Fated* is supposed to be leading us according to all the legends and theories. To Melanthros.

Not oceans the color of blood and a fleet of wrecked and decaying ships.

Yet no matter how many broken and half-submerged vessels we pass, *The Fated* does not falter or slow. Instead, it weaves in between the obstacles with ease and grace, as if it has travelled these waters hundreds of times before.

"What the hell?" Emory gasps as he and Kye-Shin shuffle through the doorway, their expressions contorting in dismay then horror. "What is this place? Are we lost? Surely, this has to be some kind of detour..."

Emory's voice trails off while he glances at the ceiling beseechingly, as if praying the Captain's or even Gerald's voice will blast through the air with the answer. For once, however, the invisible speakers are infuriatingly silent, abandoning us to the mercy of our imaginations.

"Look," Kye-Shin says, pointing to where the bow of a submarine sits above the crimson waters. Past the rust eating away at its hull, I struggle to make out faded letters in white.

"Does that say..." I start in disbelief.

"Danmar," Kye-Shin answers, and when his gaze meets mine, I can tell the second we both arrive at the same conclusion.

Sixteen years ago, when the country of Danmar attempted to solve the mystery of *The Fated* by sending a fleet of submarines, planes, and airships full of soldiers and scientists after it into The Veil, not one had returned—because clearly they had all sunken here.

But that was far from a complete explanation.

"Where are the bodies?" I whisper.

The sailboats, the ocean liners, the fallen airships—none of them retain any sign of the people who once operated them. No hollow faces stare out the cracked, cloudy windows. No bones lay scattered throughout the rotted decks or floating along the crimson surface.

It is if all the humans who were ever stranded in this place never existed.

"I thought everyone was supposed to stay inside," Emory says, and I follow his gaze to where a figure has appeared beside the rail on the deck below.

Something about his slumped shoulders and fumbling stride strikes me with familiarity. When he swivels around, I recognize the glasses and pale wrinkled skin now painted scarlet in the light.

Enzo.

"He shouldn't have been able to get out there," Kye-Shin says, his brow furrowing in confusion. "All the doors are sealed."

"We have to help him," I say, remembering the Captain's warning about passing through a high-risk area.

But high risk of what?

My gaze spins around the room until latching onto the phone hanging from the right wall. Within a matter of steps, I reach it, removing the handset and forcing my shaking fingers to enter the numbers for an emergency into the spinning dial. The ringing seems to stretch on for hours before a cheerful feminine voice clicks onto the line.

"Hello, are you in distress?"

"Yes, you need to send someone onto the upper deck immediately," I say. "There's a passenger outside. I don't know how he got out, but he's—"

My voice cuts off when Enzo stumbles violently, his hands grasping at his throat while the rest of his body flails as if his muscles are warring against each other.

"Please remain calm and state your emergency," the female voice says.

"Calm?" I demand, furious. "I just told—" I force in a deep breath, scrambling to drag together the last fraying strands of my patience and sanity. "There's a passenger. Enzo Harper. He's outside on the deck, and something terrible is happening to him. You need to send someone up here now!"

Silence greets my response, and then...the click of the phone on the opposite end of the line being hung up.

"Hello?" I shout. "Hello?"

"What's happening to him?" Emory demands. The phone slips from my hand as I spin to see Enzo still writhing and clutching his neck. His face pales. His lips darken to gray.

"There must be something in the air," Kye-Shin murmurs. "Something that's poisoning him."

Instinctively, I freeze, holding my breath even while I expect any second for a pungent smell to invade my nose while my throat burns as if being seared by a dozen iron brands. But the air inside the lounge remains cool and odorless.

Past the window, Enzo continues convulsing.

Watching him reminds me of the first silent film I ever saw. A comedy, where something as ordinary as a precariously placed bucket of paint or marble rolling along the floor could launch a series of absurd but hilarious events. In one scene, after being bonked on the head with a bowling ball, a man in a suit flailed wildly as he tried to maintain his balance. Even now, I can vividly remember the shrieks of laughter from the audience in the theater, the dramatic strands of violin music playing over the speakers adding to the nonsensicalness of it all. I recall my mother smiling too, her usually melancholy gaze amused.

But to me, the exaggerated bend of the actor's elbows and knees at odd angles had appeared unnerving, inhuman even, as if instead of a man he was a marionette being forced to dance at the whims of a cruel invisible master.

Staring at Enzo—at his bulging eyes and gasping lips while his arms and legs twist in on themselves as he struggles to maintain his footing—I can't help but be overcome by the same sensation of revulsion, of *wrongness.*

This time there is no music or laughter. Only suffocating silence.

I reach towards the glass, wishing I could help him. But there's nothing I can do. The doors are locked and yet...he must have escaped somewhere. I should search for it. I should at least try. My conscience demands that much of me.

My brain though already knows it's too late. Knows if I venture outside I will doom myself to the same fate. Perhaps I will even doom the rest of the passengers if I allow whatever toxins are floating through the atmosphere inside the ship.

So I remain unmoving, watching unblinkingly as the man at last tumbles to the deck where he crawls with shaking hands until eventually collapsing onto his stomach in a defeated heap.

A second passes, then a minute.

Still, he does not move.

"No," Emory whispers, backing away from the glass as if doing so will shield him from the truth. "He can't be..."

"He's dead," Kye-Shin finishes tonelessly, and a wave of guilt and remorse crashes over me.

I spin when something moves at the edge of my vision, and I spot a figure retreating from the nearest doorway, reminding me of the silhouette who lured me to this room in the first place. I barely manage to catch a glimpse of his face before he vanishes from view.

"What is it?" Kye-Shin asks.

"There was someone in the hall," I say, my gaze never wavering from the entrance. "I'm guessing the same person who opened the door to this room in the first place."

Not just *someone*, I realize, belatedly registering the familiarity of the stranger's features. Tall, lithe build. Dark golden hair. Knowing hazel eyes—the eyes I found myself staring into twice before.

"It's the stranger," I breathe, "the one who dropped the token and helped me find The Nautilus on the first night."

But now instead of offering help, he's fleeing, as if he's done something wrong.

Had he been the one to lock Enzo outside?

I bolt towards the exit, catapulting through the door until I'm in the hall, my head spinning like a record as I search for him.

But the corridor is empty, the stranger nowhere in sight, as if he melted into the walls.

## Chapter 23

# Visitor

The walk back to my cabin stretches as long as an eternity.

Despite the corridors' narrow walls and close ceilings, *The Fated* has never seemed so massive. Every step demands more concentration, more effort that drains my already depleted strength. The crimson waves I saw outside minutes ago must have heightened because around me the ship lurches back and forth. With every deep, slow tilt, I can't stop myself from stumbling and sliding. My fingers hurt from constantly grasping the rails lining the walls in order to keep from rolling across the carpet altogether.

"Poor girl," I hear one woman mutter amidst the trio of passengers passing by. Her response is quickly followed by the others' murmurs.

"...complexion is absolutely dreadful."

"...must be seasick."

"...looks as if she has seen a ghost."

I don't bother correcting them. They wouldn't believe me if I tried to tell them the truth anyway. So when the festively dressed strangers brush by me, I don't speak at all. As I listen to their excited voices and laughter gradually fade, I wonder if I'll ever be carefree again.

I had been wrong, I realize only now. In the moment when I first stood in the atrium and held out my hand to catch the glittering confetti, I'd foolishly believed I was free of my sadness, my confusion, my loneliness. No longer would I be forced to remain an outcast as I had been in the department store—as I had been my entire life—unable to do anything but watch as others waltzed and wandered wherever they liked, always heading to or returning from some glamorous event. I would finally belong.

But I don't belong. Jaslene's disappearance, the world I saw outside *The Fated* today, Enzo—those things have made it so that I can no longer simply flit from party to party, go see one film in the cinema after another, or waste hours staring at the brightly colored fish filling the aquarium like all the other blissfully ignorant passengers ever again.

I can almost laugh at the cruelty of it.

I open the cabin door. Silence flows from the connecting door to the neighboring stateroom, and I relax at the possibility that Salenna might have gone out, sparing me from facing her at least for now after the way we parted this morning.

That's when I hear my aunt's cry.

It is a high piercing sound, and listening to it tells me everything I need to know. My cousin, like Enzo, is dead. Her body has been found. Had she simply tripped and fallen on some shadowed stair or had she been kidnapped? Murdered?

In a handful of strides, I'm through the connecting door and inside the next cabin already expecting a man in dark uniform sitting in the chair beside my aunt, his head bent and face tight with sympathy just like the one who appeared on my doorstep over three years ago the day my mother died.

What I'm not expecting is a young woman.

One whose flawless beauty I'd been jealous of throughout my childhood. A young woman who, instead of wearing the same lilac gown and crystal headband I saw on her days ago, dons a short burgundy dress and matching heels along with a triumphant smile.

Jaslene.

# Chapter 24

# Normalcy

Seconds as long as lifetimes pass as I struggle to make sense of the scene before me.

I struggle to register the half-drunken champagne glasses, partially eaten chocolate strawberries, and truffle wrappers scattered along the coffee table. I struggle to register that my aunt isn't actually crying but laughing instead, that her face is beaming—and so is Jaslene's.

"Oh, Amarra, I have the most wonderful news!" my cousin says, launching onto her feet and skipping towards me.

"Are you alright? Are you hurt?" I say, snapping out of my daze to stop Jaslene from throwing her arms around me as I grab her shoulders and study her over, searching for cuts or bruises or tears in her clothes. "What happened? Where have you been for the last two days? Do you know how worried I was?"

"Please don't be angry," Jaslene insists, but I charge on, my fury rising too fast to be shoved aside now.

"Angry?" I shout. "My friends and I searched everywhere on this ship for you. I even called the emergency number and reported you as missing!"

"Foolish girl," Salenna snaps, glaring at me from where she reclines on a settee, a newly filled glass in her hand. "I told you I didn't want you alerting anyone else about our business. Think of the scandal you could have caused!"

"Scandal?" I cry, feeling like I've fallen into another dimension where fish walk along the waves and the sun rises at night. "Jaslene was *missing* for three days! I wasn't about to simply sit back and do nothing."

My aunt's responding smile is scathing. "And what a lot of good all your efforts accomplished, didn't they?"

"Stop it, both of you! None of that matters now," Jaslene says, thrusting her hand in front of my face. I stare uncomprehendingly at the fat diamonds encircling a ring on her finger. "I'm engaged!"

"Wha—" I can't even form the word, can't even stop my mind from reeling faster than a derailing train.

"You mean who," Jaslene corrects, giggling at her own wit, and for one horrible second, I wish my cousin had never returned at all. The thought dissolves instantly of course.

"It's Arthur!" she says, oblivious or uncaring of the worry and despair she's made me suffer over the last three days, and all the confusion and shock she is making me suffer now. "Can you believe it? Everything's happened so fast! We've been busy exploring all the quaint little cafes, winning prizes playing the games at the amusement park, and dancing whenever we get the chance. Then the next thing I know, he's proposing! Bending down on one knee with a ring and confessing that he loves me. Apparently, he's loved me from the very first moment our eyes met, and he never wants to part from m—"

"Wait, wait," I say, some small fragment of my mind restarting again. "I asked Arthur yesterday where you were, and he had no idea. He was even mad at you for not showing up at the theater like you planned to."

"It was a misunderstanding, that's all," Jaslene says, waving her hands as if to ward away my doubts. "We had our times mixed up. It was silly, really. Besides, Arthur could never stay angry with me."

"Of course, he couldn't," Salenna says, taking another sip before sighing in contentment. "My daughter getting married to a duke of all people. I knew all those expensive etiquette and singing lessons couldn't have gone to waste."

"I looked at every café I could think of," I insist, desperate to find some part of my cousin's story that doesn't make my head ache or want to shake Jaslene until she says something that makes sense. "I searched the amusement park multiple times too, and I never saw you or Arthur once. You're really telling me those are the places you've been this entire time?"

"It's a huge ship. You could have easily missed us," Jaslene shrugs before she gives a shy smile, suddenly blushing. "Besides, we didn't spend all our time in the public areas, or else how could we have gotten to know each other better?"

"But it's only been three days," I say, feeling increasingly ill with every second that passes. "You still barely know each other at all. Why the rush? It's not like you—" the words dry up in my throat as a new possibility surfaces in my mind. "Is Arthur forcing you to say this? Did he threaten you?"

"What?" Jaslene cries, offended. "Of course not!"

"Then how do you explain what caused your purse to..." I stop myself before I can say the word *melt*. Because I already know it's pointless. As soon as I mention what happened with the clutch, neither my aunt or cousin will believe me.

"Really, Amarra," my aunt says when I re-enter the sitting room. "You could at least try to hide your jealousy instead of acting out this little charade. It's pitiful."

"I'm not—" I start.

"Gracious me, look at the time," she says, rushing to her feet and looking herself over in the nearest mirror. "We'll be late for dinner!"

Before I can protest, I'm ushered out into the hall by my aunt and Jaslene as we head toward the dining room, the pair of them waltzing arm-in-arm and giggling like schoolgirls while I follow in a haze of confusion and disbelief. Beneath those emotions, I feel another unfurling, one as cold as ice, as smooth and heavy as a pebble plucked from a riverbed. Unease.

I'm dreaming. I have to be, I realize, as we enter the dining room to a smattering of applause and congratulations from our table where Arthur already sits, his face beaming once again when his eyes fall on Jaslene.

"Wonderful news, the engagement!" one man booms.

"You two make a marvelous pair!" a woman praises.

"We couldn't be happier for you!" a couple shouts in tandem.

I feel as if I've stumbled into a play without being given any lines.

The dining room stretches out around and above me like an elaborate set—its high dome ceiling intricately gilded with swirling designs in nearly every shade of gold, silver, and red. Clusters of tiered chandeliers form spirals that descend through the air. In between the marble columns rising from the carpet floor, people lounge in the tables crowded along the circular second level.

By far the most notable props are the tables covered in food: massive platters and bowls overflowing with lobster, filet mignon, rack of lamb, beef wellington, and scallop risotto that's smell wafts through the air, inducing a perpetual mouthwatering state for any occupant. The clatter of silverware scraping against plates and clinking of glasses forms the closest equivalent to a musical score accompanied by the sharp laughter and vibrant buzz of murmuring voices.

The dozen or so passengers reclining around the table I sit at might as well be supporting actors, with their fingers practically dripping with diamonds so bright, and gold so yellow, they are surely costume accessories. Their flamboyant gestures seem more practiced than genuine, their expressions overly exaggerated. Even my aunt appears to be in on the act—playing another character besides her usually cold elegant self as she cackles at a particularly terrible joke one of the middle-aged bachelors seated towards the far end of the table makes.

Finally, in the center of everything just as any star should be, is Jaslene.

To all these strangers, the young woman sitting across from me with my cousin's body and my cousin's mannerisms must appear unchanged from three days ago. She is, after all, still dramatic, still bursting with life —still utterly mesmerizing.

Yet…I can't shake the feeling that something is off. Something is missing, like an intangible piece of my cousin failed to return along with the rest of her, though I try and fail to pinpoint what.

I can sense it in the way her laugh seems just a little too high, her smile a little too wide, as if she stretches her lips any farther her face will split in half. Perhaps that would be better. Perhaps only then I would be able to see what could possibly be going on inside my cousin's head.

"The reason we are here isn't simply a coincidence, you know," a clinical-looking man in a white suit says, drinking from his glass before grinning as if he has deduced the secrets of the world. "The only logical explanation is that we must be special, blessed. We are the best of the human race, and because of that we're being rewarded."

From one end of the table to the other, passengers nod and murmur in agreement, their expressions smug with self-importance at the notion. In the bright lighting, the women's lipstick is too red, the men's teeth too white. I can hardly stand the sight of them.

*Special. Blessed.*

Enzo had looked far from either of those things as he writhed in agony on the deck, his face contorted nearly beyond recognition, his eyes wide with fear.

I can't help but dig my fingers into my chair at the bitter irony of such words. I resist launching to my feet and informing them a man has died while they were busy dreaming about their perfect futures and selecting their fanciest dinner clothes.

I can already feel the accusations forming on my lips, can feel the words taking shape, their edges sharpening, ready to be flung like knives. Beneath me, the legs of the chair screech in protest before sliding across the carpet with a hard push. I lean forward, the tendons in my legs tensing as I prepare to stand. When I glance up though, I freeze as Jaslene's gaze fixes on mine before she quickly refocuses her attention on scooping a spoonful of mango sorbet into her mouth.

"Jaslene—" I start just as a familiar high-pitched wail warbles through the air. Out of instinct, I along with everyone else look towards the ceiling, though as always speakers are nowhere in sight. The piercing noise soon degenerates into static while the sound of someone clearing their throat bleeds onto the line.

This is it, I realize, hardly daring to breathe. This is the moment when the Captain will tell everyone the terrible news—that the body of a passenger has been found on the deck. I wonder if he will explain how Enzo escaped outside in the first place. I wonder whether or not the explanation will be true.

In the end, however, it isn't the Captain's steady tone that soars through the space.

"Hello, my fantastic fellow travelers, this is Gerald speaking again!" the Entertainment Director's voice blasts throughout the dining room with enough force to elicit startled gasps and pained winces from even the most stoic passengers. "Fabulous news! The Captain has successfully steered us through that slightly hazardous area we've been stuck in throughout the day, and as a result you are now free to meander along the decks and balconies to your hearts' delight! Also, later tonight we'll be hosting a special dance extravaganza beneath the stars on the main deck, so grab your jazz shoes and—"

The curtains on either side part, revealing an ocean colored navy blue rather than crimson. Not a single abandoned boat, aeroplane, or other vessel remains in sight. The sky, too, is no longer red but streaked with pinks, purples, and blues, while a burning sun still hovers a distance above the horizon.

In my distracted state, I almost fail to notice Jaslene stand and stride towards the wide revolving doors, not bothering to glance at the windows. By the time I rush through the entranceway as well, I see my cousin disappearing into the corridor leading to the restrooms on the right.

"Jaslene, wait—" I shout, rushing into the narrow hallway only to halt in bewilderment at the fluorescent green jellyfish floating up along the wall beside me. No, not a wall, but a pane of glass, I realize, drinking in the rippling glow of the surface above and the light's reflection along the sandy floor on both sides of the path before me.

I am in a tunnel. It's similar to the one in the aquarium, and yet the water here is barely illuminated at all, for instead light radiates from the creatures themselves. In addition to jellyfish, blue glowing stingrays glide above me while neon orange, yellow, and magenta fish dart away from the path of a tiger shark with stripes as pale as the moon. As I stalk farther into the space, a purple octopus on my right pushes away from the glass, its tentacles pulsing different colors with every movement. On my left, a bright green eel slithers by, its bulbous eye following me curiously.

The coral, too, glows like a miniature underwater metropolis. Thick, vivid red pillars burst from the sand floor while others stretch towards the surface like skeletal fingers. Luminescent—even transparent —anemones, seahorses, shrimp, and other creatures spread out across the aquatic landscape, their small bodies undulating with the current.

Just like everything on this ship, the scenery before me is so alien, so mesmerizing that staring at it nearly makes me forget having any misgivings in the first place.

Could that be the purpose behind such otherworldly lavishness? To distract us from asking too many questions or searching for answers when they failed to emerge.

"Stop!" I shout, rounding a bend in the tunnel to find my cousin at the opposite end. She shows no sign of slowing. "Jaslene, please!"

For a second, I think she will ignore me altogether, but then she swivels around.

"Whatever are you shouting for?" my cousin hisses as I approach. "Let me guess, you're just dying to know how I nabbed a wealthy dashing fiancé practically overnight. I could give you some tips—"

"Will you stop pretending already?" I say, no longer bothering to hide my exasperation. "Why did you really disappear for so long? I promise, whatever it was, however crazy it may sound, I'll believe you. I swear."

In the dim glow of the lights blinking up from the tunnel floor, my cousin's face is a smear of shadows and distorted dimensions. I can make out the familiar slant of eyebrows, the rounded tip of her nose. Even while her lips twist into a smile, her eyes remain cloaked in darkness save for the tiny specks of light reflecting off their surface as if they are nothing more than marbles. Any emotions swirling beneath are obscured entirely.

I might as well be staring at a mannequin rather than a girl of living flesh.

"You're the one sounding crazy," Jaslene scoffs after a beat too long.

"I saw the clutch," I insist, wishing more than anything I could see her gaze clearly. Jaslene had never been a good liar—until now, it seemed. "I saw it melt before my eyes, Jaslene! There's no use hiding the whole story."

"Exactly what *story* could you be referring to?" my cousin says. "Is me becoming happily engaged to a duke not exciting enough for your imagination?"

"Don't even," I warn, losing patience. "You were *missing*, Jaslene. While you were gone, strange things started happening. Leander Scott, you remember him? He's disappeared too. We also ran into another passenger named Enzo who's been on board for over sixty year—"

"Enough!" Jaslene screams. "You've always had a habit of overthinking things, but this is too much even for you! Why can you not just be happy for me?" Jaslene snaps, moving close enough to at last reveal her pained features. "Mother was right when she said you were jealous of me. You've always been jealous that I got to wear beautiful dresses and attend the most wonderful parties and be admired by countless suitors—all while you had to work at the department store."

"That isn't true," I say, even though deep down part of me realizes it is.

Jaslene must know it too because she cackles, the unnerving sound something I would have once thought my cousin incapable of making.

"I remember when you used to hate the gowns and parties your mother forced you into," I say quietly. "Or have you forgotten when you ran to my room crying and telling me you once wanted to be like your father and travel the world? At least I fought for my dream."

"I don't know what you're talking about," Jaslene replies, shaking her head as if the action will vanquish the memory once and for all. "And oh, yes, your dream of being a *concert pianist*, ha! As if I need reminding!"

"What's that supposed to mean?" I snap, suddenly angry.

"It means after failing to achieve something they wanted, most people would move on!" Jaslene accuses with such venom that I stumble back. "What happened to your mother was terrible. What happened at your audition was horrible too, and for the six months you lived with us, I did everything I could think of to cheer you up because I pitied you!"

"Jaslene—" I say, the words cutting deeper than any knife. My cousin, though, is beyond listening.

"Even after that, even when we did manage to have some fun together, you always would go back to your gloomy appearance and sad moods, as if the world had taken everything from you when it hadn't, not when you still had me and Mother. You always hid in your room when I didn't have the energy to drag you back out. You always looked like a storm-cloud whenever someone mentioned music or, Heaven forbid, the piano. If you had just *once* ever made any real effort to try to fit into our family, I could have convinced Mother to want you to stay."

"Why are you saying these things?" I say, feeling as if I no longer know my cousin at all. As if I've never known her.

"Because I'm sick of having to put up with your attitude!" Jaslene cries. "In the beginning, I thought this voyage would be a new start for us, but I can see you're just as pessimistic as you always were, determined to find something wrong even with the amazing opportunity we've been given."

Jaslene steps back, her face becoming shrouded in shadow once more, closed off from me. Perhaps forever. "I feel sorry for you, Amarra. It must be lonely seeing only the bad in everything."

# CHAPTER 25

# ECHOES

I don't know how long I stand in the tunnel once Jaslene leaves.

It could be hours after the rhythm of her heels against the tile floor fades. It could be minutes after she stalked past me as if I were a stranger, or worse, someone she wished she'd never met.

*I did everything I could think of to cheer you up because I pitied you.*

Pity. Was that what Jaslene had looked at me with whenever she pulled me out of the house to go play in the snow like children on one afternoon years ago or that time we strolled through the galleria, sipping lemonade and window shopping at the stores even my aunt couldn't afford to buy anything in? I had always looked back on those memories with fondness, with the knowledge that while my aunt may never have accepted me, Jaslene had and always would.

Now I feel only betrayal and loss. Most of all, I feel a cruel sense of realization.

I can't deny that Jaslene was right when she accused me of having stopped living my life years ago. When my mother died and my dream disintegrated before my eyes, I had raged, flinging every curse I could towards the heavens as if my anger alone could make the world finally stop and listen to me. But the world hadn't stopped, and it hadn't listened. It simply dragged on, uncaring. As I felt myself being pulled along with it, that rage had eventually given way to exhaustion, hollowness—and then...habit.

I had woken up in the morning because I had to. I ate breakfast, lunch, and dinner because I was hungry. I trudged into bed, exhausted and aching until I had to repeat it all again the next day with nothing to look forward to or achieve. I no longer played the piano, no longer wished for anything at all. I had been existing, not living. Not until I held the ticket to *The Fated* in my hand. But even now this memory is marred, my joy and hope in that moment diminished by the frustration and anguish currently drowning me.

I don't know what draws me to The Nautilus.

I move without thinking. Place one foot in front of another as I pass unseeingly by shops and cafés and theaters until the music and laughter from the atrium fades, leaving only the low hum of the ship as I descend down, down, down until I stand before the bronze and blue double doors. I'm already wrapping my fingers around the handles when my eye falls on something I failed to notice before. At a mere glance, the illustration embossed along the entrance appears unchanged. In the upper corner of the right door, *The Fated* sails beneath a sky heavy with storm clouds while angry waves burst from the surface, as if on the verge of flooding the corridor any moment.

Only now, amidst the water's swirls, can I make out the outline of an additional boat. The vessel is small, tiny enough for me to nearly lose sight of it within the vast raging ocean. It is plain too—so plain in fact it begs the question of why the designer bothered to include it at all in an otherwise striking piece.

I brush my fingers over the object, taking note of its smoothness in contrast with the water's sharp curving edges. The poor vessel looks as if it might soon topple over, and the thought evokes memories of the vision from the arcade: the wind slashing across my face, the boat rocking beneath my body, its pitches and rolls sending my own stomach churning. But above everything else had been a yearning, a consuming want for something without name or shape beyond the horizon.

I pull the doors open, sending them shifting with a low groan loud enough to echo through the entire ship. Like everything else on board, I assumed The Nautilus was open throughout the day. But the chamber is empty and dark, save for streaks of aqua light rippling across the shadowed lamps and chairs from the massive window on the right. My footsteps echo along the dance floor as I amble towards the glass, peering into the vast blue for any sign of sea turtles or dolphins like the ones in the aquarium. But unlike before we passed through The Veil, the water is lifeless, the sand floor farther below flat and featureless. Sighing, I turn away, backtracking towards the entrance.

I almost don't see it.

Tucked into the corner between the window curtains and nearby booths, its dark color would render it unnoticeable to anyone else. But never me.

It's a piano.

Within several strides, I have reached the instrument and pushed back the curtains, revealing a stream of white and ebony keys that make my heart rush in familiar joy. Even in the dim lighting, I can tell the piano is magnificent, more magnificent than the one I played at the Institute three years ago.

At the memory of the cold beautiful place where my hopes had been dashed with a mere handful of words and fake smiles, my earlier elation turns sour before dissolving altogether.

Still...I can't resist trailing my fingers along the keys, remembering the sensation of gliding across the smooth wooden blocks to create music that echoed from my soul, that made me feel as if I were more than a girl with worn clothes and a need so desperate it had taken on a dangerous edge.

When I played, I was at peace. Free. Weightless.

But I hadn't played in years.

The last time the notes had come out wrong, sharp and dissonant. My fingers had felt tired and clumsy, as if the tendons and muscles had lost whatever magic once flowed inside.

Would right now be any different?

Holding my breath, I spread my hands over the keys. The first notes are jumbled and imperfect. The pain from listening makes me wince, nearly wanting to stop altogether. But I don't. I force my fingers to keep struggling, to keep trying, until their awkward movements turn graceful and the sound they produce at last makes something deep inside me mend back into place.

"First and Last Wish." The original Lamiran folk tune might have been intended to tell the story of a person's whole life, but for me it was the melody of my childhood. It was the first song I recall ever hearing from my mother's gentle humming at my bedside, then later from a music box I received on my tenth birthday. Despite its seemingly simple and languid tune, it had been the most difficult piece I ever arranged and played, the one I spent hours each night practicing and perfecting until I had been certain it would win the bright future that seemed easily within my grasp.

For the first time in years, I allow myself to imagine what my life could have been if everything had gone right. If only the judges at the audition had understood the origins and meaning—the truth—behind the version of the song I played. If only they had evaluated my ability rather than my lack of appropriate credentials or connections.

If only my mother hadn't left early to sell her paintings on the street that morning six months before. If only the cab driver had eased his foot off the pedal when the rain started falling.

My days would have been filled with symphonies and the steady tick of a metronome rather than customers' rude remarks and an elevator's groan. On the weekends, my mother and I would've gone to the market like always, soaking up the smells and sights before grabbing a cup of hot chocolate or bowl of noodles to ward off the city's constant chill. Classes and practices would have given way to performances and eventually a career doing what I loved. Of course there would have been long days and tiring nights. Moments when my fingers ached from overuse, times when the tiny black notes on the page before me would swim together. But everything would be alright in the end because I had fulfilled my dream, my destiny.

I can envision it now—this very moment in my other life.

Instead of a ship, I would be on a stage. If I try, I can imagine the heat from the spotlights. I can hear the hushed silence from people sitting in the rows upon rows of seats wrapping around the auditorium's floor and balcony. If I were to glance to my right, I would spot my mother in the crowd of blurred faces, her eyes and smile finally free of worry or sadness. Perhaps sitting beside her would be my aunt and cousin, their expressions for once proud as the last notes drift wistfully through the vast space before being swallowed by applause.

I don't even realize I'm crying until the tear falls against my wrist. The coolness brings me back to *The Fated,* back to where I sit alone in the dark while the final strings of the piano fade into oblivion.

A soft clap echoes in the silence, and I hastily wipe my face before I peer into the shadows.

"I've never heard that song played like that before." Something lurches in my chest as Kye-Shin materializes on the opposite side of the room like an apparition I conjured from my loneliness.

"Now that you have, what do you think?" I ask, sucking in a breath as he closes the distance between us. The click of his shoes against the smooth floor lets me know he's real and not a phantom, not some figment of my imagination who will dissolve at the slightest blink or mistake.

"I think it's exceptional," he says, halting close enough to brush his knuckles across the piano's surface as his dark eyes meet mine. "Just like the person playing it."

Heat floods my cheeks at the statement, but when I look up once more, Kye-Shin is drifting towards the window.

"Did you always know music was your calling?" he says, changing the subject so smoothly. I'm grateful.

"Yes," I reply after a moment, maneuvering from behind the piano to stand by his side as the ship gives a low groan.

I know I should tell him about Jaslene, about the doubts and worries and confusion around her reappearance that still plague me, and I will. But, though I know it's foolish, for just a moment longer, I don't want to think about *The Fated* or our future. I don't want to think about the questions that have haunted me from the beginning of the voyage either.

"I wish I'd never learned to play," I admit softly, my eyes never leaving the glass. "Because learning to play gave me something to hope for. Something I learned too late was impossible for someone like me. I think it would have been less cruel, less painful to hope for nothing at all."

The instant the words slip from my lips, I fear I've revealed too much. But when Kye-Shin speaks, I forget to be self-conscious.

"I'm jealous of you, actually," he admits.

"What?" I gasp, certain I must've imagined what he just said. "Why?"

"Because you are still able to do what you love," Kye-Shin says. "Because regardless of whatever unfulfilled dreams you have, your fingers clearly still remember which keys to play. Unlike mine, which can't seem to recall how to fit even a handful of sentences together."

He sighs before turning and placing his hand in his pocket as he studies the water.

"I once thought I could change the world with my words and the stories they told, real or imagined," he says, his lips twisting into a smile that is both bitter and wistful. "I just never expected them to abandon me one day."

He glances at me with a grin still pasted on his face, as if inviting me to laugh at his expense. But I can see only the poorly concealed pain beneath it—the same pain that had crept into my eyes during the minutes, hours, then weeks following the audition and never left.

Out of everyone in my life, only my mother had known what it was like to have a dream you couldn't give up, a dream powerful enough to consume you. More than a calling, it was a hunger to do one single thing even when the world tried to force you into anything else. It was an obsession that demanded your nearly every thought, nearly every breath of each waking and un-waking moment. It was a wish you had held onto for so long that failing to fulfill it would leave you empty and forever incomplete.

Jaslene had turned her back on her dream, so she couldn't understand, but my mother could. In this moment, I know Kye-Shin does too.

I reach out my hand—to comfort him or myself I don't know—when he clears his throat and refocuses his gaze back on the window. My fingers freeze in mid-air before I slowly lower my arm to my side, swallowing my embarrassment.

"My cousin is back," I say eventually, and at the edge of my vision I can see his face swivel towards me again, though this time I don't dare meet his gaze. "She showed up just a couple of hours ago, unharmed and healthy. She's even engaged. It turns out she was never missing at all. I overreacted about nothing."

"I wouldn't say that—" Kye-Shin begins slowly, but I can't stop myself from speaking further, from spilling out the next words before I lose my resolve altogether.

"I'm sorry for causing you and your sister so much trouble," I apologize, remembering their fight in the hall and the haunted, guilty look in Kye-Shin's eyes. "I should never have dragged either of you into this mess. Now that Jaslene's back, I'm sure Leander will turn up any moment as well, no doubt with an explanation of his own. Everything will soon be normal again."

Next to me, a long pause. Then, "normal," Kye-Shin repeats softly as if weighing the word on his tongue. "You don't really believe that."

I don't. And yet...

I understand it now—the reason why Miyuni and Leander chose to pretend nothing was wrong even in the face of the bizarre and incomprehensible. Why they decided to shut down that voice deep within every human mind that couldn't help but thirst for truth.

Because what if knowing only brought misery?

I can't stop myself from foolishly hoping that everything I experienced today will be the end. That tomorrow and the days following will be blissfully free of blood-red oceans, dying painters, or any other horrors.

Only yesterday, I'd been convinced there was something cursed about this ship just like the woman in the department store had said what feels like lifetimes ago.

But that had been before Jaslene's return. Jaslene—whose disappearance, however uncharacteristic and outlandish, has no explanation I can think of other than the reason she already gave.

*You're the one sounding crazy.*

Could there be rational justifications for most of the odd occurrences plaguing me since our departure? Or as rational as anything pertaining to *The Fated* could be.

It wasn't exactly a stretch to assume that whatever mystical nature surrounded Melanthros likely applied to *The Fated* as well—just like Miyuni initially said. What else could explain my repaired music box, the visions we'd seen when we'd left the arcade, or things melting without cause on the ship?

With what happened to Enzo though, perhaps there was no mystical explanation at all. Perhaps Miyuni was right. Perhaps his aging mind could no longer distinguish between fiction and reality, between his memories and the life he was living, or rather *had* lived until this afternoon.

But if the Captain had sealed the doors, how did Enzo wander onto the deck in the first place?

"Amarra." I tense at the difference in Kye-Shin's tone, at the dread I hear in it.

I turn to see his gaze is fixed on something past me and on the other side of the window. An object rises from the ocean floor, followed by a second, then a third.

At first, I think they must be rock formations—that is until my eyes take in the pointed spires, sleek windows, and bizarre architecture.

Buildings.

## Chapter 26

## Abandoned

The city materializes like an apparition.

At first I think it must have sunken beneath the ocean some time ago. But as the simple structures I initially observe quickly give way to bolder, grander buildings tall enough to nearly scrape the ocean's surface, I realize this metropolis was designed to thrive underwater. Bridges spiral past domed stadiums, transparent malls, and other strange structures I can't begin to name. The urban landscape appears both absurd and futuristic, as if it belongs to an era where humankind has developed technology capable of allowing us to breathe beneath water and fly to the moon.

Despite everything that's happened—despite everything that's gone wrong, for a second, hope resurges inside me.

All those stories about *The Fated* carrying passengers to a new and better world race through my mind. All those tales of another, far more perfect, far more mystical and advanced civilization across an endless ocean only one ship knew how to navigate. Could they really have been true this whole time?

"You don't think this could possibly be..." I whisper, stopping

myself from saying *Melanthros* for fear the thought will become reality
—or fear it might not.

"No," Kye-Shin replies, immediately understanding. "It looks
abandoned."

As I study the metropolis gliding by far below more carefully, I
realize he's right. Moss and other algae crawl along the buildings, wrapping around shattered windows and crumbling staircases. A train stands
still in the middle of the track, its originally silver surface tinted with
rust. Its interior dark and hollow.

Most disconcerting of all is the lack of life—and bodies, just like in
the crimson sea.

There are no people strolling along the glass-roofed boulevards
winding through the city. No corpses remain splayed in the transparent
and slightly vehicle-shaped orbs lying half-sunken in the sand floor. No
shadows stir behind balconies or half-open doors.

Cold familiar dread swallows the last of my hope, and I wonder how
many more times during this voyage I will be forced to experience the
awful sensation, how many times I will regret ever stepping foot on this
ship.

The noise initially sounds like thunder—a low rumble that trembles
the water before morphing into a high groan like something being
stretched and twisted until wrenching apart altogether. When my eyes
focus on the movement at the window's edge, I understand why.

A section of seabed partially beneath one building collapses into a
sinkhole without warning, sending the structure swaying like a pendulum. At first it tilts left, then right, before one by one the levels begin
collapsing on each other, creating an avalanche of metal and glass that
careens forward—straight towards *The Fated*.

"Get back!"

A hand latches onto my wrist, and then Kye-Shin is pulling me
away, dragging me off the dance floor just before the window explodes.
In reaction, the ship pitches to the side, sending me stumbling past the
bar and Kye-Shin ducking from a flying lamp. Still, we don't slow. We
can't afford to as the entire ocean rushes into the chamber, sweeping

aside the tables and booths along with anything else unfortunate enough to meet its rage. Seconds before the wall of water overtakes us, we launch through the entrance, catapulting past the heavy doors and into the hall.

Instinct propels my legs up the nearest stairs until my senses are assaulted by salt air and blinding sunshine. Heavy footsteps clamber behind me as Kye-Shin emerges by my side as we both gasp for breath, drawing curious glances from passengers strolling by.

"The ship's going to sink soon!" I shout, rushing up to the nearest group of people wearing sun hats and sipping daiquiris. "You need to get to a lifeboat now!"

Instead of rushing to action, they only stare at me like I'm insane before hurrying away, glancing back every few seconds or so as if I might sprout wings.

"We're in danger!" I insist, turning towards an older couple who only shake their heads and swivel around to hasten in the opposite direction, their muttered words carrying back to me on the wind.

"Young people have such a warped sense of humor these days..."

"I'm being serious! I—"

"Don't bother," Kye-Shin says. "They won't believe just you alone."

I scour the walls behind me along with the rest of the deck for a phone to call the emergency line, but I find none. I could scream from feeling so helpless.

"I have to get Jaslene and my aunt," I say, already backing up towards the stairs. "I have to get to them before—"

"Do you know where they are?" Kye-Shin says.

"Well, no—" I start.

"Then there's no time to go searching," Kye-Shin insists, grabbing my shoulder. "You saw how quickly the water flooded The Nautilus. By the time you got down there, the alarms would have already sounded and everyone would be rushing up to the decks. We need to get to a lifeboat. Come on."

Ignoring the passengers' strange looks, we both launch into a sprint, peering over the rails and along the upper decks for lifeboats, but we find none. In fact, there aren't any lifejackets or buoys to be found either, as if whoever built this ship never considered it could sink at all.

Is that why the alarms still weren't blaring?

*Any moment now they will sound*, I think, as I take in the people milling along the rails and lounging by the pool with glittering drinks in hand. *Any moment now the Captain will make the announcement to evacuate*, I try to convince myself as the couples continue to walk hand in hand, admiring the brightening horizon or wading into the jacuzzi, their expressions calm and untroubled.

I've almost given up waiting altogether when a familiar wail warbles through the air, followed by the static of an incoming announcement.

"Good afternoon, this is the Captain speaking." I breathe in relief. "As you can tell, the current weather is perfect for sailing. Over the next couple of days, we can expect blue skies and a steady wind from the north. There may also be a chance of rain this coming Wednes—"

"What's he doing?" I say, whirling to Kye-Shin in disbelief. Surely, the water would have flooded past The Nautilus' doors and into the hallways by now. Why had no one reported it yet? "We have to tell him."

"Tell who?" Kye-Shin asks, and I give him an incredulous look.

"The Captain, who else?" I say. Calling the emergency number wasn't an option. Not after what happened with Enzo. The Captain was our last hope.

"Amarra, wait—" But I'm already racing across the deck, searching the top levels for where the bridge could possibly be. Somewhere in the front, most likely. In a place high enough to see for miles.

With these guesses in mind, I rush up more stairs and hurtle through the first entrance I find and into a hallway. I try door after door but find them locked or useless in where they lead. More static erupts from the invisible speakers somewhere above me, followed by the shuffle of a microphone.

"Thank you, Captain, for sharing that terrific forecast!" The Entertainment Director's voice bellows through the line, loud enough to send my eardrums ringing. "In order to make the most of it, we've got an *ocean* of exciting activities planned for you the next few days, starting with an island-themed party on the pool dec—"

I reach for the closest doorknob, expecting another storage closet or empty chamber. Instead, I stumble into a wide room crowded with tall brass telegraphs, compasses, and wheels.

The loudness of the intercom, however—the way the noise bounces harshly off the smooth walls and emanates from the opposite end—is what pulls me inside. Somewhere in the back of my mind, past the blaring speakers and my thundering feet against the floor, I realize a crew member should be appearing to stop me, that voices other than the Director's should be filling the air, shouting at me to halt.

But I'm already reaching the door in the farthest corner with the warning *Announcement Room-Do Not Enter* stamped across the front. I twist the handle and swing it open, expecting to find a man wearing a flamboyant suit and fake smile.

The space, however, is empty.

And in place of a man there is only a gramophone sitting on a table with a record spinning along its top.

C H A P T E R  27

———

T H E  W A Y  O U T

I launch towards the device and rip the needle away, cutting the Director's voice off.

For no more than a second.

"...also suggest hopping on the next elevator down to The Nautilus for those looking to party beneath the waves—"

Gasping, I stagger back from the gramophone. The voice isn't radiating from the horn or anything on the device at all. Instead, the sound seeps through the blank walls, pulsing around me. I whirl, rushing out of the room—only to stumble headfirst into a body that wasn't there seconds ago. Hands descend onto my arms, and I shout, trying to twist out of the unrelenting grip.

Past the blaring announcement, I gradually comprehend another voice shouting my name. But it's not until I raise my gaze to find Kye-Shin's face above mine that I at last feel the adrenaline racing through my veins give way to relief. Oxygen eases back into my lungs.

"Are you hurt?" Kye-Shin asks, and when I shake my head, he studies me for several seconds more before stepping away and venturing into the gramophone chamber.

With a mind still numb with shock, I trail beside the window, following it until the glass curves around to stare back over the vessel and carefree people still meandering along the decks. Around us, the sapphire waters reveal no sign of the city beneath. There is no hint that the ship has been hit at all.

A cheerful ring draws my attention back inside, but I can't make out any movement among the blinking lights of the panel or half a dozen telegraphs standing like sentries. Reaching out, I brush my fingers over the nearest one, over the brass surface of the handles and glowing letters along the side.

Apart from where my own skin has lingered, there are no smudges or fingerprints, no sign the device has ever been operated by human hands.

"I don't understand," I whisper.

"I do," Kye-Shin says, stepping out of the room with the gramophone, the lack of surprise on his face startling. "But I should have realized earlier. It all makes sense now."

"Sense?" I repeat disbelievingly.

"Yes," Kye-Shin insists, raking a hand through his hair before unleashing a harsh laugh. "There's no staff on board. There never has been."

"Of course, there has," I snap. "I've seen waiters in the restaurants and clubs—"

"Have you?" Kye-Shin argues. "Really seen them, I mean? Not out of the corner of your eye or some receding figure in a crowd? Have you ever once looked any of them in the eye—or stared at them directly for so much as a second?"

"I..."

Now that I think about it, I can't recall ever clearly seeing a waiter. At every meal, the dishes on the table were always fresh with no staff in sight, no matter how early or late the guests arrived. Whenever I or anyone else wanted a drink or type of food that wasn't available, other people would say they saw a waiter bring the item, or I would catch a glimpse of someone myself.

But that's all it ever was—a glimpse. A hand setting down a glass at the edge of the table. The shadow of a figure reaching over my shoulder to deliver a steaming dish of whatever I asked for. There was never a face or any distinguishable or even memorable features. These appearances were just faint memories that all too quickly slipped from my mind given the overwhelming glamor and excitement of being on board *The Fated*—at least until now.

"What are you saying?" I demand. "That the people we thought we saw are just hallucinations?"

"I don't know," Kye-Shin replies, his gaze haunted. "Maybe whatever made us believe we saw the crew is the same thing that caused our visions after the arcade? But think about it, Amarra. If this ship had a crew, then why wouldn't we be seeing them everywhere?"

He's right. I want more than anything to say that he's not, that he's terribly confused. But like Kye-Shin said, looking back now it all makes a twisted kind of sense.

The lack of a real crew explains why the passenger services desk is always closed the handful of times I pass by. It explains too why music constantly drifts through the lounges and atrium though a band is never in sight. It explains how the cabins can be cleaned so quickly and room service always leaves food outside the door even though I never see any staff passing through the halls. Hadn't I unknowingly sensed the lack of their presence on the first night when unease overwhelmed me after hearing the music box play for the first time in years? This unease had grown when I retraced my footsteps back to a hallway deserted of any other living soul.

Then there were the people I'd heard or spoken to: the Captain, the man who called from room service, the woman I'd talked to several times on the ship's emergency phone line. But just like the Entertainment Director, they had only ever been voices. They were never humans made of flesh and bone standing in front of me, never real.

I shouldn't be so surprised. After all, hadn't I already come to terms with the fact that nothing on this ship belonged to the rational world? Still, a desperate part of me had been holding out hope that the Captain or Gerald or *someone* would be the mastermind behind everything—or at least hold the answers. Because if there is no one else on board other than the passengers, then who or *what* is running this ship?

And where the hell is it taking us?

Beneath us, *The Fated* lurches as it hits another wave, and my eyes stray to the window and the churning water below—water that is flooding into the ship with every second we stand here.

My gaze snaps to Kye-Shin's in panic as I remember Gerald's announcement. "Didn't the Director say a party was going on in The Nautilus right now?"

Alarmed, we both race out of the room and down the corridor to the stairs. Levels and people pass in an incomprehensible blur, yet still no sirens sound. No passengers scream or run in the opposite direction as we draw closer. But it's only when we at last see that the hallway stretching towards the club is completely dry that I feel relief.

"The water must still be sealed inside," I breathe, stumbling to a halt before the entrance.

"No," Kye-Shin says, placing his hand on the embossed surface and leaning towards it. "Listen."

I tilt my ear forward. For a second, nothing, and then...notes gradually drift past the metal, flowing into my ears and flooding my mind with confusion. When I glance back at Kye-Shin, his bewildered expression morphs into one of dread. Together we grip the handles and pull, opening the massive doors with a powerful groan.

Inside, the club—which had been dark and silent minutes ago—pulses with light and jazz music. People crowd into the booths, leaning over the tables with glasses in hand and inane smiles pasted on their faces. Behind them, the window stretches along the right wall, its surface smooth and unfractured. Beyond the glass, the ocean is once again vacant and blue. Not a droplet of water remains in the space.

It's as if the city and crash never happened.

"No," I hear myself whisper as I take a step back, followed by another. "No, it's not possible."

As soon as the stupidity of the words sinks in, I can't help but laugh.

The sound bubbles up and out of my throat like a convulsion, the pitch sharp and hysterical.

Only half an hour ago, I'd been agonizing over whether Jaslene had been right. Over whether every strange thing we had experienced contained some reasonable explanation after all. But I had forgotten *The Fated* itself had never been rational. Not in any of the legends or stories circulating around it since time practically began. No one really knew where it came from. No one really knew where it was headed. Everyone just believed what they wanted to believe—and so had I.

"Let's go," Kye-Shin says, ignoring my nervous breakdown as he grabs my arm and pulls us down the hall away from the music and laughter of The Nautilus. Soon the smooth polished corridors tumble away to reveal the atrium.

People are everywhere, on every level. They crowd into booths filling diners and pasta parlors, forming a line outside beneath the bright flashing lights of the Rhapsody Theater's awning, hunched over the poker tables in the casino. All of them are oblivious to the fact that they would be sinking in water right now if this ship had been any other than *The Fated*.

Steps ahead, Kye-Shin slows to a halt, his head spinning from side to side.

"Where are we going?" I ask, my former hysteria having finally mellowed into exhaustion and exasperation.

"Let's talk in there," he says, nodding to a nearby bistro adorned with lights and flowing with calm music.

"But..." I start. *What's the point?* I want to say. *There's no mystery left we're capable of solving. Nothing else we can rationalize.*

"Please." Kye-Shin's voice has an undercurrent of desperation, and I nod after a second before letting him tug me towards the club.

I've never been here before, and only days ago I would've taken delight in passing beneath a wide sweeping entrance designed like a parting curtain showered with pale lights. I would have felt at home with the soft trickle of piano notes in the air and the relaxing strum of a double bass. Right now, however, I feel only numbness as we brush past guests swaying on the dance floor or giggling in each other's ears at the bar.

The club is smaller than The Nautilus, more intimate. Silk curtains cascade from the ceiling, concealing sections of the room and giving the space a secretive aura. Red roses and golden vines woven with tiny lights span the walls and tables, their fragrant scent mingling with the aroma of food and wine.

Kye-Shin barely offers a cursory glance at the surroundings before sliding into the nearest booth. Seconds after he sits, he reaches into his pocket and retrieves the medallion, spinning it over in his trembling fingers just as I can see his own thoughts doing the same, whirling through his mind and spiraling out of control. Like mine.

Chocolate-covered strawberries along with cookies and cakes litter the table, and yet staring at their powdered sugar-covered tops fails to make me feel so much as an ounce of hunger. Across from me, Kye-Shin too regards the food with disgust until eventually grabbing the nearest glass and downing half of its contents in a single sip.

There is something so tortured about the action that I'm already reaching out to comfort him when I hesitate. What words could I even offer? What consoling thing could I say when I myself have no idea how to react, how to cope?

In the end, though, Kye-Shin speaks first.

"We need to get off this ship."

"What?" I gasp.

"We have to leave as soon as possible," he insists. "We can't stay here."

"But..." I feel as if I'm tilting off the edge of a cliff and scrambling for something to hold on to. "There aren't any lifeboats."

"We'll keep looking," Kye-Shin continues, unfazed. "There must be something on board we can use. We could be gone within a handful of days, maybe less if we're lucky."

"Wait," I state, my eyes dropping to where his palm rests over mine. It feels heavier than before. "What you're saying is—" Preposterous. Unthinkable. Madness. "We can't just step off *The Fated*."

"Why not?" Kye-Shin demands, his gaze growing fervent. "There's no one running this ship. There's no one to stop us."

"That's not the point," I snap, shocked that he doesn't realize the gravity of what he's proposing. "You saw what happened to all those other boats and planes in the crimson sea. You saw what happened to Enzo! We would've died just like him if we hadn't been inside."

"We might still die if we stay here," Kye-Shin says, ripping his hand from mine as if it's poisoned. I shove down the twinge of hurt before it can show on my face. "Open your eyes, Amarra. If what Enzo said was true, he was stuck on this ship for over sixty years. There is no paradise. Not if we remain on board."

"You don't know that!" I shout loud enough to send the occupants in the surrounding booths glancing toward our table. When I speak again, my voice feels strained and unrecognizable to my own ears. "Whatever magic or advanced technology is running this ship could still take us to Melanthros. Enzo could have chosen to stay on board for all those years rather than disembarking. And besides, even if this ship isn't really taking us anywhere, it'll pass through The Veil again in sixteen years. If nothing else, we could just wait and—"

"And what?" Kye-Shin scoffs. "Waltz down the gangplank back into our old lives? If that was an option, why do you think Enzo never took it, or any other passenger for that matter? If they had, everyone back in the world behind The Veil would know the truth of *The Fated* by now. We can't go back. Our only option is to escape while we still can."

"And how long do you think we'll last out there?" I demand. "On the open ocean. Alone. With no map and limited supplies. What if we run into another crimson sea? What if we run into something worse?"

"Well, it's better than sitting here and doing nothing like a—"

Kye-Shin halts before he says the word, but I hear it loud and clear anyway.

*A coward.*

Is that what I am?

I can't deny I'm crippled with fear at the very idea of leaving *The Fated*, of leaving behind the sturdiness of its gilded walls, the comfort of its lounges and theaters along with all the food, drink, and luxury we could ever ask for. I shudder too when I imagine floating adrift among the waves with no land in sight, when I envision death by starvation, drowning, or a fate more gruesome than Enzo's. Even now such things appear far worse to me than mysterious disappearances or crew-less ships.

Across from me, Kye-Shin's frustrated expression becomes conflicted, the distance between us stretching for miles.

The music's tempo has changed.

On the dance floor, people spin and swing to an almost hysterically fast foxtrot that blurs their faces and distorts their bodies, making them appear more like cartoon characters than humans. Stained glass windows streaked with gold and silver styled landscapes illuminate the interior in a rosy glow. For the first time I notice that only couples fill the surrounding booths, their arms intertwined and heads bent affectionately together.

Before I can help it, I glance back at Kye-Shin, my cheeks heating. I shouldn't have bothered. He isn't even looking at me. Instead, he stares unseeingly into the table, his only movement the occasional tap of his finger against the now nearly empty glass. As desperately as I search, I can find no trace of the vulnerability I saw on his face when he told me about running away as a child, no remnant either of the affection that softened his features when he told me I was exceptional.

Now the lines of his face are as sharp and cold as the moment I handed over his ruined papers at the docks, the feelings of friendship and attraction and whatever else might have flourished between us withering before my eyes.

"I'll find a way off this ship on my own then," Kye-Shin says, finally looking back at me. In his gaze, I expect to find anger, or at least resentment.

The lack of any emotion at all is more hurtful than anything I could have braced myself for. We might as well be strangers.

"You can't be serious," I say despite the dread twisting my stomach. Across from me, regret flashes across Kye-Shin's face for the briefest instant before it is gone, and he is moving, fracturing something deep inside me as he does.

"Wait, please, Kye—"

But he's already leaping up from the table and striding away, vanishing behind the curtains and abandoning me to the false comfort of the twinkling lights and cheerful music.

# CHAPTER 28

## AFTERNOON TEA

The cake, like everything else on board, is without flaw.

I scrutinize the slice on the porcelain plate before me, scouring the icing-covered surface for the tiniest unsmooth patch or a single piece of fruit sitting crookedly on the edge. Unsurprisingly, I find none. Every dollop of whipped cream down to the last glittering sprinkle is perfectly placed, reminding me that it wasn't made by human hands.

I purposely knock the fork to my left off the table, compelled by a mixture of boredom and morbid curiosity at seeing what happens next. It clatters onto the floor loudly enough to send the people seated in the garden courtyard around us peering in my direction. I can't bring myself to care.

"I need another fork," I say tonelessly, and the words barely slip my lips before a figure in white appears at the edge of my vision to place the spotless utensil to the left of my plate. Yet when I spin around to look at the waiter, there's no one in sight, like always.

"Really, Amarra," my aunt snaps from where she sits, sipping her tea with the regality of an empress. "I understand how idle you must have been in your job at the department store, but it never fails to amaze me how clueless you are about how to act in polite society."

"Now, Mother," Jaslene says, reaching for the tiered stand in the table's center to daintily pluck a cupcake from the dozens of brightly colored pastries crowding the silver trays. "Amarra's started helping me design the loveliest wedding dress, and she's suggested some marvelous ideas." My cousin offers the last comment with a fond smile at me before biting into the pastry and sighing in pleasure.

"You also have your outfit for the ball to plan as well," my aunt remarks, lifting the teacup to her lips once more.

The invitation had been waiting for us on the coffee table last night after dinner.

Enclosed inside a wax-sealed envelope and trimmed with gold, it read in elegant script:

*Dear Treasured Passengers,*

*Please join us for an enchanting evening in the ballroom at seven o'clock this Sunday!*

With hardly more than a sentence, the entire ship had descended into a frenzy of meaningless gossip about what people planned to wear or who they prayed to dance with.

"Since everyone will be attending, you must look no less than stunning," Salenna says. "After all, this will be you and Arthur's first official appearance together as soon-to-be newlyweds. You wouldn't want to embarrass him."

I glance at my cousin, searching for the familiar spark of irritation that often shadows her expression whenever her mother makes such statements.

*Am I not allowed to be anything more than beautiful?* I remember her shouting during dinner once years ago. The question had launched an hours-long battle between mother and daughter that ended with Jaslene practically barging into my room and collapsing on the bed, her face streaked with tears. In the years since, Jaslene no longer dared to argue with her mother outright. But the resentment had remained, rising to the surface in the form of a subtly worded barb or tightness at the corners of her smile.

Today, however, my cousin offers no clever retort, and her smile holds no trace of anything other than excitement.

"I have the perfect gown in mind," she gushes. "The rose-pink dress should do the job nicely. You remember, the one with the frills and the..."

I jab my fork into the cake and scoop a piece into my mouth with a vengeance, allowing the delicious sweetness to wash over my tongue and distract me from my cousin and aunt's mindless chatter. For the last two days I've heard nothing else. Dinners flooded with sophisticated conversation, luncheons consisting of cucumber sandwiches and scandalous gossip, cocktail parties crowded with potential connections and meaningless acquaintances—these were the events around which my aunt and cousin constructed their days. The same kind of events had made up their lives back in Abeon City—only on a much more luxurious and grander scale.

On board, my aunt no longer had to struggle with deciding whether to spend her deceased husband's gradually depleting fortune on the latest fashionable dresses or to repair the water-stained walls of the top bathroom in the townhouse (since no guests ever saw the top floor anyway). She no longer had to cut back on the amount of food both she and Jaslene ate at home too under the guise of maintaining their slim figures just so she could afford to keep up with the current trends in costume jewelry.

For my aunt and cousin, *The Fated* really was the perfect paradise.

It is mine too...or at least that is what I keep telling myself.

After the argument with Jaslene, my anger had gradually faded until I no longer had the strength to carry it anymore. I expected the opposite from my cousin. Knowing Jaslene's capacity to hold even the pettiest grudges, I had braced myself for more of her reprimands or refusal to speak to me entirely. But she behaved as if the entire argument had never occurred. I had carefully searched my cousin's gaze for any hint of hurt or resentment while she grinned and giggled, but I failed to find either. It was unnerving.

Then there was Kye-Shin.

Kye-Shin, who I haven't seen since two days ago, who despite my best efforts to push out from my mind, lingers at the fringes, echoing like a melody I can't unhear.

*I'll find a way off this ship on my own then.*

Over the last two days, I've been tempted countless times to find him, to make sure he hadn't gone missing, to learn if he might have decided to stay after all. Yet every time I made up my mind to go to him, I hesitated before deciding against it altogether. Because what could I say or do if I found him? As guilty as I felt about the way we parted, I still couldn't bring myself to leave *The Fated.*

Deep down I knew he hadn't changed his mind or gone missing, not when the memory of the determined look in his eyes the last time I saw him remained branded in my mind. Could he have already left without me? If so, was he safe wherever he was, drifting along the open ocean? Or had his lifeless body already sunk to the bottom of the sea?

Laughter bubbles from the opposite end of the courtyard, drawing my attention from our table to where a trio of young people have seated themselves beneath the tent in the far corner bordering the bougainvillea bushes. Past the thin orange and magenta curtains, I make out two girls around my own age practically wrapped around the shoulders of a young man with shining blond hair and a smile as arrogant as a king's.

Leander.

My breath catches. When I decided to stay on board rather than escape with Kye-Shin, I told myself I would stop asking questions. I would stop trying to uncover *The Fated's* secrets, stop trying to pry into the truth behind Jaslene's disappearance now that she had returned safe and unharmed.

And yet...

"It's a pity you didn't have the chance to introduce yourself before becoming engaged," my aunt sighs to my cousin, regarding Leander wistfully as she stirs her tea. "A duke is well enough, but the Scott heir would have been a true conquest. You can be certain his family provided him with a generous fortune before coming on board. Once we reach our destination, he will undoubtedly become every bit as wealthy and successful as his father, if not more."

Salenna's gaze all at once turns calculating. "Jaslene, dear, why don't you wander over there and act as if you are looking for an earring that must have fallen off on the way in. Remember what I taught you."

"Oh, stop it, Mother," my cousin says, blushing. "I actually did meet him briefly, but I'm perfectly happy with my darling Arth—"

I lurch to my feet, my chair scraping across the cobblestones with a loud screech that sends people from the nearby tables wincing and glowering towards me in reproach. I glower right back.

"Where exactly do you think you're going?" my aunt inquires, raising an eyebrow and looking over me as if feathers have sprouted along my entire body.

"To have a word with him," I declare, jerking my chin towards Leander and plopping my napkin on the table.

"*A word*?" my aunt splutters. "You of all people can't simply waltz up to someone like Leander Scott and—"

Her remaining insult is drowned out by other people's conversation and the water trickling from fountains as I stride through the space without looking back. The surrounding foliage resembles a forest more than a garden, with oak, willow, and palm trees alike reaching towards the glass ceiling. Their various colored branches shade the dozens of tables crowded with guests trying to act as if they are occupied sipping their tea or chatting with their friends instead of watching their neighbors.

Then there are the flowers—they're everywhere. Blue moon wisteria hangs from vines twisting along arbors over winding paths. Pink magnolias bloom in vases next to cinnamon churros and pastel macaroons. Yellow hibiscuses rise along the courtyard's fringes, their faces turned to greet those strolling by.

Leander is only a handful of yards ahead of me, his demeanor and handsome face every bit as carefree as on the first night I met him. Gazing at the heir now, you would think he had never fled from me and the others in terror. For the briefest second, anger resurges in me at the memory before fading just as quickly. Unlike when Miyuni abandoned me, Leander's absence had left me startled but not hurt. Perhaps deep down I'd never expected him to stick around anyway.

"Can we talk?" I state the second I draw close enough. My voice is low, too low to overpower the two girls' flirtatious giggling or Leander's boisterous tone. The three instantly fall silent, though, their expressions both confused and startled as they turn to regard me.

Leander's smile wavers, but he eventually nods, and I stalk through the nearest opening between the trees with the thump of his reluctant footsteps trailing behind me.

"Listen, if this is about what happened in your cabin," Leander starts, and I can tell from the forced nonchalance of his tone that he's already planning to spin some lie, some ordinary excuse for why he left instead of mentioning Jaslene's melting purse.

That's not what I'm here for.

"It isn't," I reply, halting before a pond dotted with water lilies and koi fish. I swear I hear Leander sigh behind me in relief.

"Well then make it quick, will you," he grumbles, his voice rising in something sounding suspiciously like a yawn. "I'm afraid I'm still recovering from a night of poor but irresistible decisions. Besides, if people got the wrong idea about us, it would only make you the target of jealous admiration—"

"Where were you two days ago?" I inquire, finally facing him. "Emory was worried enough to ask me and Kye-Shin for help. The day after you ran from my stateroom, remember?"

Across from me, Leander blinks. Then he scoffs.

"My, my, you really have fallen in love with me, haven't you?" he whispers in wonder. "I'm touched by your concern. Really, I am."

"It isn't concern," I snap. "I just need to confirm something."

Leander tilts his head, studying me with renewed interest, but I push on before he can ask anything else.

"Just answer the question."

Leander smirks but otherwise runs a hand through his hair, his expression turning pensive.

"Two days ago...let me think," he sighs. Then he chuckles. "Ah, yes. After stumbling out of a stateroom that definitely wasn't mine, I spent the morning holed away in the quietest lounge I could find before making my way outside to the golf course around noon. Satisfied?"

"What about your watch?" I ask, my gaze fixing on his bare wrists. "While we were searching for you, we found it on the floor in one of the halls—"

"I must have lost it by accident," Leander shrugs before smirking. "As I hinted earlier, my morning was rather...blurry."

"So you didn't encounter anything unusual that sticks out in your memory?" I say. "Something like your watch melting?"

Leander's eyes flash to mine, the amusement on his face draining away. But I keep going.

"I know you saw the same thing happen to my cousin's purse in the cabin," I say, my gaze never wavering from his. "Two days ago, when I picked up your watch from the floor in the corridor, it started melting. Then it returned to normal seconds later. Where did you really disappear off to, Leander?"

"I already told you," he says, his expression slamming closed just like Jaslene's—and that's when I know this conversation is finished. "I should be getting back before my dates think I've abandoned them."

"Wait—" I try again, but he spins on his heel and stalks past red maples and hydrangea bushes. "Leander, please—"

"You would be happier if you stopped, you know," he says, lurching to a halt. "Asking so many questions, I mean."

I roll my eyes, a retort ready on my lips. But my annoyance quickly evaporates when Leander turns and regards me with...concern. Such an emotion on his face appears wrong, unnatural.

"What makes you say that?" I ask.

My voice is barely above a whisper, but the question seems to reverberate through the air. Noise from the courtyard leaks past the foliage surrounding us, but the sounds are muted, indecipherable. Somewhere nearby a bird I can't see launches into song, its tone harsh and dissonant in the quiet.

Leander shakes his head, his expression clearing. His lips spread into the arrogant smile I once thought he was born wearing.

"No reason," he replies, stepping forward and clapping a hand on my shoulder as if we're close friends.

Before I can think of an answer, he stalks away and is swallowed up by the trees.

In the courtyard, my aunt and cousin are too immersed in conversation to notice me. It isn't until I draw close enough to hear the heated words being exchanged that I realize they're arguing.

"...have to know where it is."

"...no idea what you're talking about."

"You ungrateful child!" Salenna spits, fury etched all over her features. "That necklace was a precious gift from your father. I don't care if you have to crawl over the entire ship, you will find it."

"Father never gave me a necklace," Jaslene insists. "Bracelets, dresses, and shoes, sure. But not a pearl necklace! When have you ever seen me wear such a thing?"

"Just several days ago," I interject, recalling the rose-colored pearl gleaming in the light around Jaslene's neck when we left the docks and then again just after we passed through The Veil. "The day you went missing, or at least the day I thought you did. You wore it to the watch party."

"There," my aunt declares triumphantly. "What do you have to say for yourself now?"

"I..." Jaslene starts, reaching for her throat as if trying to remember the feel of a sterling chain against her fingers and failing.

Confusion blooms across her face, wrinkling her brow and twisting her lips. The look is one I've seen before—on Enzo. He had worn the same expression when he hadn't remembered any of his half-complete paintings.

Now it seems Jaslene, too, couldn't remember the necklace she had worn every day since I moved in. That necklace had been her father's last gift to her—the very same necklace that Jaslene had once turned the entire house upside down to find when she misplaced it.

*You would be happier if you stopped, you know,* Leander's words echo in my mind.

I agree. I would be happier if I stopped asking so many questions. If stopped putting the pieces together, pieces that are rapidly evolving into something more terrible than I could have imagined.

But it's too late to stop now.

Across the courtyard, Leander bellows in laughter, and I look up as the girl on his left plucks a cherry from the tray and feeds it to him with a delighted giggle. He doesn't so much as glance in my direction, as if he's forgotten about me entirely.

It's then I realize something: it would have been impossible for him to go golfing at noon two days ago.

Because that was before every door had been unsealed and every window uncovered.

Because if he had gone outside, he would never have made it to the golf course in the first place. Before reaching it, he would have stumbled and fallen onto the deck like Enzo, his face a mask of horror. Then he would have died.

Because at that time, *The Fated* had still been sailing through the crimson sea.

# CHAPTER 29

---

# DECK PARTY

K ye-Shin is nowhere to be found.

Too late, I realize I don't know his cabin number. I don't even know what level his cabin is located on. I search every place I can think of, hoping to see his familiar profile sipping coffee in the Breakfast Room or bent over a desk in the library with a pen in hand. My hope, however, quickly deteriorates into panic with every second I fail to spot his ebony hair or determined gait amidst the crowd.

"Have you seen a tall young Nanshyn man with black hair here recently?" I ask an older woman nearly buried beneath a tower of books, and then later a teenage boy wearing spectacles. "He could've been holding a medallion or writing in a journal. Maybe using a typewriter."

Their answers are almost the same, their gazes friendly but apologetic.

"No, I don't think so."

"I haven't, I'm afraid."

I don't spot Miyuni or Emory either in my search, not in The Nautilus or the spinning rides at the amusement park or anywhere else. Had Kye-Shin taken them both and really left without me? Had they all, like Jaslene and Leander, gone missing instead? Had I made a terrible mistake in waiting so foolishly long to search for them?

My stomach twists at the endless possibilities. I'm so overwhelmed with regret and helplessness I feel like I can't breathe, like my lungs are taking on gravel rather than air until they might rupture from the weight of it all.

I *was* a fool. For believing everything could be fine, that *Jaslene* could be fine after her disappearance and what happened to Enzo. Now that I've discovered the opposite to be true, it is too late. There's no one left I can turn to, at least no one who will believe me.

I stumble away from the bright lights and liveliness before collapsing onto the nearest stairs and throwing my head in my hands. Beneath me, the ship rocks back and forth like the pendulum of a clock. Footsteps approach and recede around me. I hear people's curious whispers and then their giggles at my expense before quiet descends once more. Still, I can't force my legs to stand or put myself back together enough to form some sort of plan. I can't make myself care enough to.

"You don't look like you're having fun."

At the familiar voice, I raise my eyes, blinking as I gradually recognize the short black hair, blue vintage dress and matching bow, and dark eyes as belonging to Lethia.

"Um..." I reply, searching for an excuse. "I'm just tired, that's all."

"That's what my brother says when he's upset about something," she says, tilting her head as she regards me inquisitively. "Are you upset?"

"No," I lie. "I..." I pause, noticing the beach ball she's carrying for the first time.

"Wait, are you going somewhere?"

"The party," Lethia says as if the answer's obvious. Her eyes narrow when she takes in my casual cotton blouse and skirt. "Are you not going?"

"What party?" I ask.

"Grab your bathing suits and dancing shoes, folks!" Gerald's voice blasts through the air as if on cue. "In case you've forgotten, right this very moment, we're hosting a special poolside party featuring the bubbliest champagne and a magnificent display of fireworks along with..."

"Come on!" Lethia says, grabbing my hand and pulling me to my feet with surprising strength as we race up the stairs and through the double doors leading to the deck where the celebration's already in full swing.

Strings of lightbulbs stretch across the level's open top, illuminating the swaying crowd and champagne glasses scattered throughout. Women with feathers in their hair and glittering dresses draped over their figures gasp and laugh while men with slicked-back bangs wearing tuxes twirl them in time with the music.

"Now this looks fun," Lethia says next to me, drinking in the scene with hungry eyes. When several bubbles float by, she pops them with a giggle before pointing to where a dunk tank's been set up in the corner. "Oooh, I love that game. Wanna give it a try?"

I glance again at where over a dozen people in satin dresses and silk suits are lining up to get soaked, cheering when one man plunges through the water.

"Maybe another time," I say, hardly feeling in the mood to play. "But don't let me stop you. You should go if you want."

"I will," Lethia says, grabbing a chocolate chip cookie from a nearby tray and taking a bite as she ventures farther onto the deck before pausing and glancing back at me. "Are you coming to the ball tomorrow?"

"What?" I ask in confusion before remembering my aunt and cousin gossiping about it earlier. "Oh...I guess so."

It's not as if I have anything better to do now that Kye-Shin is gone —and with him, any answers I may have once been able to uncover.

"Good," Lethia says, clearly pleased. "I'll see you there then. Bye for now. And don't think about things that upset you anymore!" she skips off with a wave and tosses her beach ball into the pool where several people begin batting it back and forth.

I can't help but shake my head, all at once both jealous and amused by her unconventional and carefree nature.

Weaving past swaying balloons and drunk passengers, I make my way along the stairs to the upper deck, breathing easier when I have more than enough space to avoid colliding with anyone. My feet seem to move of their own accord, and minutes later, I find myself wandering into the area where Enzo collapsed merely days ago.

Unsurprisingly, there's no sign his body was ever here.

I retrace where he stumbled; walk on the smooth wooden planks where he eventually collapsed and grew still. But there's not an inkling of blood or tendril of gray hair to tell that he was ever there. I wonder if the same fate will befall his half-finished paintings and sketches. Perhaps, like their owner, they too will disappear one by one until the rest of Enzo's belongings and stateroom are swallowed up by the ship for all eternity.

Perhaps they already have been.

A chill breeze slices through my coat, sending strands of hair whipping back from my face as I stalk towards the deck's edge. For once, the surface beneath me does not sway or pitch to the ocean's movements, and after gazing out past the rail, it looks as if *The Fated* has somehow launched into the night sky altogether. Bright, flickering stars along with distant planets float both far above and below, the horizon between them undetectable. Twin pale moons serve as the only indication that the ship still glides across a waveless sea.

The memory of the Alexandris resurfaces in my mind, but I fail to make out its golden glow among the constellations no matter how desperately I search. Yet another thing this voyage has made disappear. Another treasure lost.

A saxophone's trill and other accompanying instruments echo across the motionless water. The couples strolling across the upper deck wear contented expressions as they walk hand in hand, pausing every few minutes to admire the moon or point out the constellations.

Here, in this tranquil setting with the distant notes from an unseen piano wafting through the air, I have never felt so alone.

"You don't look like you're celebrating," a voice drifts beside me, and I turn, not daring to breathe or blink when Kye-Shin steps up beside me.

Even with a mind in chaos and my thoughts as scattered as the stars surrounding us, I can't help but swallow nervously at the sight of him, standing by the rail with his hands in his coat pockets and his tall silhouette outlined by moonlight. "I was afraid you had already left."

"That was the plan, wasn't it?" he says, the edge in his tone slicing right through me. When he swivels his gaze to me, his eyes do the same. "Or are you disappointed I'm not gone?"

Before I can respond, I flinch as a whistle pierces the air. Seconds later, purple and gold fireworks burst across the night sky, then cascade down in brilliant shards that flicker out just before reaching the water. Passengers gasp and cry in excitement as they clamber across the deck and crowd along the rail to gain a better view of the spectacle. As my eyes sweep over their languid smiles and joy-filled gazes, my heart pangs with envy.

I force myself to face Kye-Shin again. "Of course, I'm not disappointed."

Next to me, he huffs in either derision or amusement, I can't tell. I hate the distance that has grown between us in just a handful of days, hate that whatever trust and connection we shared before has fractured, maybe even been broken. I only hope it hasn't shattered beyond repair.

"I'm glad you haven't left yet..." I try again, gathering my courage before meeting his gaze once again. "Because I'm coming with you."

Shock flashes across Kye-Shin's face, and my courage wavers as I look away toward the horizon, as if I stare hard enough I'll be able to decipher the exact point where the sky melts into the sea.

"What happened?" Kye-Shin asks with surprising gentleness in his voice.

"You were right," I admit, unable to shake the memory of Jaslene's face from my mind. "There's something wrong with my cousin. She's become like Enzo. She can't remember certain things."

"What things?"

"Like the necklace her father gave her," I say, my hands tightening on the rail. "She's worn it every day for years. She was wearing it at the watch party on the evening she disappeared, but now it's gone."

"You think someone stole it?"

"No. Well, I don't know," I say, my head aching at the endless possibilities. "It's just—her expression was exactly like Enzo's when I mentioned it. She swears she's never even owned a pearl necklace and had no idea what I was talking about. It was like..."

Like someone had stolen her memories or erased them entirely.

I don't even realize I'm shaking until Kye-Shin pulls me into an embrace, the warmth and solidness of his arms around me sending me shuddering for a whole new reason. When I breathe in, he smells faintly of dried paper, ink, and cologne. I try to force myself to relax and my heart to stop pounding. I fail miserably at both. If Kye-Shin were anyone else, this would be the moment he tells me everything will be alright, that we'll make it out of here for certain.

But Kye-Shin isn't the type of person to make promises he might not be able to keep.

So instead he says, "I'm glad you changed your mind." Against the top of my head, I swear I feel him grin. "If Miyuni and I had to escape alone, I'm not sure we'd get very far before one of us tossed the other into the ocean."

I can't help but laugh at that, the noise muffling against his shirt and making me feel lighter if only for a moment.

Beneath my cheek, Kye-Shin's chest rises and falls as he releases a long sigh.

"I wasn't entirely honest with you before," Kye-Shin speaks in such a quiet tone that it takes several instants for me to register the meaning of his words past the crackling of fireworks. "The real reason why I followed you in the first place, the reason why I stayed by your side as you searched for your cousin despite nearly every self-preserving instinct warning me to turn back was because I couldn't stop myself from being drawn to *you*."

My already pounding heart speeds to a reckless, dangerous pace.

"What are you saying?" I demand quietly, forcing my voice to remain steadier than I feel.

It's not like I haven't felt this kind of attraction before. I have learned all too well how confessions of adoration from men can easily be lies or, at best, temporary truths spoken in the heat of the moment and excitement of the chase.

Yet...despite my better judgment, I can't help but believe every word from Kye-Shin's lips.

"I'm saying," he repeats again, the hope and anxiousness in his eyes shattering the image of the detached façade he projects to the rest of the world. "You were like the heroine in a story I had never known I was searching for. A woman whose quiet strength pulled me into her life, who made me want to take control of my own again rather than simply letting it pass by like the faded pages of an uneventful book. For better or worse, you have changed me, Amarra Obrel, and no matter how much I have tried to ignore it, I am still reeling from the traces of you."

The deck sways, sending my perception of the world shifting along with it. I can't recall the last time I saw myself as the heroine of my own life. Had it been the morning before the audition and my mother's death, when my future still seemed as brilliant as the marquees lining Pearl Street? Or the final moment of my audition, as my fingers waltzed across the piano keys like they had thousands of times before in the deteriorating apartment my mother and I called home?

Boarding onto *The Fated* had not been an act of courage so much as one of desperation from someone who had nothing left and nothing to look forward to.

But I am not that same person any longer.

*A heroine in a story.*

"Kye—" I breathe, rising to the tips of my toes until my lips are inches from his when my voice is swallowed by a deafening roar.

## CHAPTER 30

# MIDNIGHT PROMENADE

*The Fated* is sinking.

I'm certain of it as I clap my palms over my ears against the wail that rumbles from the bowels of the ship. The hull violently pitches to the side, knocking me off balance with a startled shout. I'm already falling when Kye-Shin reaches for me, wrapping his fingers around mine and pulling me back towards him with surprising strength.

"What is that?" I cry, struggling to imagine anything on the ship producing such an unholy noise. The instant Kye-Shin's grip loosens, I pull away, struggling to stand on my own. I have to grab the rail to keep from falling again when the ship tilts.

"A fog horn," Kye-Shin replies, gazing up towards the sky, and for the first time, I notice the stars and moon have vanished behind a blanket of rolling mist. Any sight of the ocean has disappeared as well.

Dampness brushes against my knuckles, and I snatch my hand from the rail. I stagger back as a wall of fog curls towards me, the wisps and billows thick enough to swallow me whole or conceal something that might.

"We should get inside," Kye-Shin says, backing along the deck towards the nearest entrance. When he grabs the handle, however, the door refuses to budge, refuses even to shift against its frame as if rather than being locked it has been sealed shut. An angry buzz cracks from the closest lamp hanging from the wall before the bulb begins flickering.

"There's another set of doors over here," I offer despite the dread already settling in my stomach. Our hurried footsteps sound muffled as we round the corner to find both the upper and lower levels deserted. Below us, flecks of glittering confetti lay scattered across the deck along with broken glasses and scraps of fallen food. Lethia's beach ball floats in the pool's turquoise waters while the pale cloths covering the tables clustered at the corners resemble phantoms rippling in the breeze.

When had everyone left so quickly?

I strain my ears for the faint echo of receding voices, but I hear only the wind's haunting howl and the occasional slosh of the waves against the ship's hull. Even the fog horn has gone silent. The second I draw close enough to the doors, I wrap my fingers around the brass knobs and pull with all my strength. They don't even tremble.

Panic seizes me as Kye-Shin bangs on the doors.

"Hello, is anyone there?" he shouts, pounding his fist against the surface. "If you can hear us, let us in!"

No voice radiates from the other side. No click of a lock being slid out of place signals our salvation.

Everyone else on the ship has abandoned us.

A gust of wind tears through the deck below with enough fury to send tables tumbling, the plates and glasses on them exploding into fragments against the floor. Color flashes at the edge of my vision, and I turn just as a piece of paper hits the rail, the crumpled material wrapping around the metal almost despondently.

It's a flyer for the party earlier. Beneath the words, *Fireworks!* and *Celebration!*, a fancily dressed man and woman dance with wide vacant smiles stretched across their faces. Or rather part of their faces—

—considering the material's edges begin melting just like Jaslene's clutch and Leander's watch.

I stagger back from the rail, my lips opening to breathe Kye-Shin's name. I never get the chance. The deck starts trembling beneath us in the same instant the ship emits a deafening screech like metal sliding against metal.

Then, as quickly as a thread being cut, it stops.

"That," Kye-Shin's quiet voice drifts beside me, "didn't sound reassuring."

The words linger in the space surrounding us, churning and thickening with the fog, which has swallowed nearly half of the deck already and is swallowing still more. Lights from the ship cast odd shadows that constantly morph into different shapes within the haze, making it impossible for me to distinguish between what is real and what is illusion.

I should run. Take cover. I should do anything but continue standing out here in the open, vulnerable and defenseless. Adrenaline thrums through my body. My muscles tense in preparation. My breathing slows, deepens. Yet I cannot, for the life of me, manage to take a single step. Kye-Shin remains immobile as well, as if he too senses the slightest action will set into motion a chain of events for which we are ill prepared.

In the end, the choice is never ours to make.

The rancid smell hits my nose first. A familiar hum erupts from behind us, and I whirl just as the nearest lamp begins flickering like the first. But it's not the light that captures my attention—that instantly makes my mind scream for me to flee and my body go cold with terror. Instead, it is the way the lamp begins melting, the glass splattering onto the deck in giant globs while to the left, the double doors begin doing the same. The bulb inside the lamp gives a loud pop before it goes dark in the same instant my knee collides with a bench—and sticks to it.

"Come on!" Kye-Shin shouts, grabbing my hand before I can protest and dragging me away.

To my relief and disgust, the action detaches my knee from the bench with a wet sopping noise as strands of the melting wood stretch between my skin and the furniture piece like spider legs before breaking with a snap. Bile rises in my throat at the sight, but I shove it down as together, Kye-Shin and I sprint down the melting staircase until reaching the lower level and rushing across the deck as another curtain of fog rolls over us. The sound of sloshing water brings my gaze back to the pool again—and Lethia's beach ball less than a yard away, which is now melting into the blue waters. Something thumps behind us, and I glance over my shoulder, nearly stumbling when I catch sight of a figure.

The silhouette is familiar and vaguely human—until it changes shape by the second, widening and growing over six feet tall in one instant before shortening and thinning to skeletal proportions.

I give a strangled gasp as Kye-Shin catapults us forward into the gray opaqueness. The warm feel of his palm against mine is steady and reassuring, and I've never felt more grateful to have him by my side.

The thought barely forms in my mind, however, before my shoe catches against a fallen vase, and my hand wrenches from his. By the time I regain my balance, Kye-Shin has vanished, the sound of his receding footsteps in the unnerving quiet the only proof of his existence.

"Amarra," I hear him call as if from miles away. "Amarra!"

"Kye!" I shout back, stepping in the direction of his voice.

Silence greets me.

I can no longer hear anything but my hammering heart and strained breathing. Beads of sweat roll down the back of my neck. Against my skin, the mist is so cool it stings. The ship moans, the noise so low it reverberates through my gums and skull before falling silent once again.

Then...footsteps.

I swallow the scream rising on my tongue as I force myself to remain still and soundless.

Is it Kye-Shin or the figure who was following us?

Above me, the whiteness curls apart, revealing the rows of lights spreading across the upper level's edges like sentries, their beams blinding.

This time there is no flicker, no angry buzz.

One clap after the other echoes harshly throughout the space as pair by pair, the pool deck lights on either side shut off in terrifying synchronization like an invisible hand sweeping across the switches.

Then the deck beneath my feet begins melting.

I launch into a sprint—or I try. The bottoms of my heels sink into the floor, followed by my shoes, and then my ankles. Against my skin, the melting deck feels ice cold. I scream, half in fear and half in determination, as I wrench my feet into moving again.

Yards ahead, the figure appears like a ghost.

At first, I'm convinced it must be another vision. The door appears out of nowhere, its circular window a portal into a world bathed in warm light and bursting with glistening halls. The profile of a man stands in the center, his posture poised and commanding like the subject in a portrait, and at the sight my heart leaps in hope.

I recognize the shade of dark golden hair, defined jaw, and long black coat draped over his shoulders. Through the window, the stranger's hazel eyes meet mine. Right now, I find nothing angelic about them.

"Please!" I shout, no longer caring about who or what else may hear me so long as he does. "Help me!"

*Like you did before.*

Instead, he swivels on his heel and stalks down the corridor without a backward glance.

"No!" I scream, closing the remaining distance to the entrance, though, I'm certain he has already locked it. "Stop!"

The tips of my fingers barely brush against the doorknob when something slams into me, and the rest of the lights on the deck go dark.

# CHAPTER 31

———

## IN THE WAKE OF

The scream tearing from my lips is cut short as a hand covers my mouth, and a familiar voice whispers in my ear, close enough for me to shudder at the warmth of his breath along my neck.

"Amarra, it's me."

Kye-Shin.

The light from the window is enough for me to make out the contours of his face, the shadows of his gaze. Beneath my fingers, his arm feels strong and solid. *Alive.*

Behind us, footsteps echo along the deck once more.

Kye-Shin lunges for the door, and to my shock, it swings open, allowing us to fly into the corridor lined with carpet and mahogany walls. I whirl, slamming the door shut and locking it. I can make out the barest silhouette of a figure in the dark just as the ship gives another wail. The noise tears through the air with enough force to send the door and frame quaking.

We don't wait to see if it holds.

Instead, we run again, flying down the stairs then weaving left and right through corridor after corridor. I risk a glance behind once, then twice, fully expecting to see a dark figure on our heels. But the halls are startlingly empty, free from both the usual wandering partygoers and ambling guests alike.

The silence propels my legs further, sends my arms pumping faster. Turn after turn, I find no sign of the golden-haired stranger either. No dropped arcade tokens roll along the floor this time. No coattail disappears around the corner. Our only company is the reflections in the series of mirrors spanning along the walls, depicting two desperate people racing through corridor after endless corridor on a ship that increasingly feels empty.

Without warning, the hallways end, revealing the atrium and passengers bustling back and forth on every level. A sea of noises once again washes over me in a wave, filling my ears with the chatter of voices, ringing arcade games, and music. Still, I keep running, too terrified to halt. Too terrified that whatever chased me on the deck will materialize and drag me away the second I do.

"Amarra!" I hear Kye-Shin holler breathlessly behind me, but I don't slow. I can't. "Amarra, stop!"

His hand latches onto my arm again, and the contact shocks me into hesitating long enough for Kye-Shin to drag me back around to face him.

"Are you all right?" he says, looking me over with concern. "Were you hurt anywhere?"

I'm already opening my lips to tell him I'm fine when I realize my hands are trembling. Of course I'm not all right. I can also tell from the barely restrained panic in Kye-Shin's eyes that he isn't either. No one in their right mind would be, not after what we've seen. Who could the figure on the deck following us have been? Or *what*?

Some of the most obscure legends surrounding Melanthros had occasionally mentioned old gods, but what if there were other supernatural beings on the lost continent too? Beings who were malevolent, monstrous.

What if one of them had snuck on board *The Fated*?

I fail to realize I've spoken all of these questions out loud until Kye-Shin responds.

"I don't know," he says, running his hands through his hair before pulling me out of the way just in time to avoid colliding with a group of passengers cackling and stumbling drunkenly by. "I don't know."

Laughter drifts from a café nearby, and I glance at a couple through the nearest window, at the people inside sipping coffee and eating pastries, oblivious to the terror prowling the decks above them.

I had been wrong. I thought that since there was no Captain or Entertainment Director or crew at all, we were alone—that there were only passengers on the ship, only humans.

"I need to show you something," Kye-Shin says, rescuing from my thoughts as he pulls us across the Boulevard and past the marble columns framing the entrance to the Excursion Rooms.

The second we pass through the revolving doors, my eyes fall on the living, moving dioramas depicting landscapes from every part of the world. On my right, half a dozen people walk across sand dunes snaking along a chamber while in the background, clouds ripple across an azure sky, more lifelike in their movements than any projection back in Abeon City. On my left, a couple stands on a rocky edge overlooking a water-fall, while in the exhibit next to it, people picnic on the lawn of a twenty-foot stone castle, its windows flickering warmly as if lit by candlelight.

"This way," Kye-Shin says as we stroll into a wide hallway lined on either side with trees. Oaks and maples swiftly give way to kapok and banyans. Mist coalesces among the branches. Somewhere, a parakeet's chirp ricochets off the leaves.

Minutes later, we're standing in front of another chamber I've been in before. The *Island Room*, it reads over the doorway, and the description is more than fitting given the space's tropical interior. Like in the Desert Room we passed seconds ago, projection clouds glide along the walls. Instead of being white, they flicker shades of orange, pink, and marigold as if painted by a sunset. Sand covers half of the floor too, speckled with scallop and tulip shells among others, while a river of turquoise water weaves around a cluster of palm trees in the center. Two hammocks hang from their trunks, moving to the tilt and sway of the ship—the same hammocks Jaslene and I swung in the day after we boarded. I swear I can hear the memory of our laughter echoing through the room like a ghost. Perhaps it's just in my mind though, which is now heavy with guilt and regret. Would Jaslene and I ever be happy again?

Kye-Shin doesn't so much as glance at the hammocks or palms swaying in an artificial breeze before stalking to the boat pushed into the corner I failed to notice until now.

It doesn't take me long to recognize its hull and design.

I whirl to him in shock. "This is the boat from one of my visions after we left the arcade," I say, expecting Kye-Shin to nod in agreement.

When I glance back up at him, though, his expression is troubled. "There wasn't a boat in any of my visions," he replies.

The vessel is small, fit to carry a little over half a dozen people at most. Unlike everything else on the ship, its appearance is ordinary and plain—so plain in fact that I can't help but wonder what it is doing here at all. Such a trivial thought, however, is quickly replaced by the much more troubling realization that this tiny, simple, and insubstantial-looking boat will soon be the only thing keeping us alive on the open ocean.

My earlier conviction quakes.

"Believe it or not, in some ways it's more than we could have asked for," Kye-Shin says as he surveys the boat and stalks around the base. "The wood is sturdy. It's in perfect condition without a single scrape or sign of rotting. And it's light," he grips the top of the bow and pulls, causing the front half to lift from the sand with a slight groan. "Light enough for a single person to carry."

Despite my lingering uncertainty, I can't help but smile at the hope and excitement in his eyes. All too quickly, though, his grin fades.

"There's just one problem," he says, motioning me to follow him as he moves behind the stern.

The chain is thick and made of wrought iron, extending from a metal hoop in the center of the bow to the floor. A large lock hangs from two links towards the top.

"I tried everything I could think of," Kye-Shin sighs. "Picking it, breaking it, but nothing worked. I searched for a key too, in here and throughout the other rooms. I scoured the entire ship and still found nothing. If this were any other vessel, I would have guessed one of the crew had it, but now..."

Now we know there is no crew.

But that didn't mean no one else on board had the answers. More specifically, *one* person just might.

"The stranger," I whisper, furious I had failed to think of the possibility before. Kye-Shin seems to read my thoughts.

"You mean the man who dropped the arcade token?" he says, a frown creasing his brow before realization dawns across his face. "The same man you saw the day Enzo died."

I nod, stunned as details about the stranger begin piecing together in my mind. "I saw him tonight too behind the door as we were running across the deck. I yelled at him for help, but he just left." Without hesitation. Without glancing back once.

He clearly hadn't cared at all if we melted too or fell prey to the figure hunting us...

Unless it had been *his* footsteps behind us on the deck in the first place. The fog had been as thick as a blanket by that time, dense enough for him to sneak by both of us unnoticed before reaching the door first.

When I meet Kye-Shin's grim gaze, I can tell he's reached the same conclusion. The thought makes me pulse with anger as well as betrayal. How could I have ever mistaken the stranger for a friend?

"We need to find him." In doing so, we would find answers. I was sure of it. "Even if he caused what happened tonight, he's also the only one who could have the key."

"And how exactly are you planning on taking it from him?" Kye-Shin says. "If he's the one who caused everything that happened on that deck tonight, what's to stop him from doing the same to you?"

"Nothing," I say, shuddering at the thought of my skin melting—at the thought of my eyes sliding out of their sockets and down my face, leaving streaks as they fall just like the beads on Jaslene's purse did days ago. I swallow. "But there's no other choice. We have to try."

From the way Kye-Shin's jaw clenches, I can tell he wants to argue but can't.

Sighing, he rakes his fingers through his hair before asking, "Any ideas where to look? If he knows the ship as well as you're suggesting, he could make it impossible for us to locate him."

It's true. Given *The Fated's* labyrinthine nature, we could easily scour every stairwell and level and still never see him again. Still, now that I think about it, the stranger appeared during some of the most important times during the voyage; the first evening, the watch party as we sailed through The Veil, the day following Jaslene's disappearance, minutes after Enzo's death, and the night we were hunted by something across the deck.

But how could we possibly predict when another one of these instances would happen? Lately, all the announcements had been about insignificant activities, such as an upcoming round of bingo, karaoke tournament, or—

"The ball," I breathe. "It's tomorrow. Practically everyone on board will be there. That might make it the best chance we've got at seeing him again."

The best chance. But was it a good one? After all, what could be important about a dance?

I have no clue, and I can tell from the skepticism on Kye-Shin's face that he doesn't either. As always, whatever we choose, we are left with more questions, more uncertainty.

Finally, Kye-Shin nods. "Okay. We'll plan to leave tomorrow once we get the key."

"What about the others?" I ask, remembering we won't be alone in this.

"Miyuni will be coming with us whether she likes it or not," he replies, his tone brokering no room for any disagreement. "I'll talk to Emory too and Leander if I can. See if they'll be willing to join us."

"But what about my family?" I say, growing anxious. "My aunt and cousin—I know they won't believe me even if I tell them everything."

"Then don't," Kye-Shin says, grabbing my shoulders as I look up at him in surprise. His features are set in determination. His eyes as steady as two anchors. "Tell them it's an excursion. Some kind of activity the ship's hosting. Just do whatever it takes to convince them to come with you down to the promenade deck. Through the door we entered when we boarded the ship, remember?"

"Yes," I say, recalling that moment nearly two weeks ago when I had stepped inside *The Fated* for the first time. Recalling my nervousness and excitement. And *hope*.

I had imagined walking off this ship to a myriad of scenarios: greeted by the applause and the welcoming arms of those who'd previously sailed on *The Fated*; beckoned into a land full of swaying palm trees and the aroma of plumerias. I had wondered if wherever we docked there would be a city or forests, if it would be snowing or flooded with sunshine. If I would feel at peace or be bursting with exhilaration.

But none of that matters now. Tomorrow, when we stepped off *The Fated*, there would be no people or land or sense of peace.

Tomorrow, when we stepped off *The Fated*, we would be nowhere at all.

# CHAPTER 32

## HOPES & PROMISES

I wake before dawn on my last day on *The Fated*.

I drink in the details of my room as I pack. I try to imprint the diamonds dripping from the crescent moon chandelier and softness of the silk jacquard comforter beneath my fingers into my mind. I step onto the balcony, wrap my robe closer around me as I watch the silver horizon lighten to yellow then gold as the sun rises from the water. Most of all, I savor the comfort: the security of four walls around me; the flavor of coffee and taste of a strawberry cream puff on my tongue; the warmth in my bones and fullness of my stomach.

Will I regret leaving all of it behind by this time tomorrow?

"You're up early this morning," Jaslene says, nearly startling me from where she shuffles out of her room. She stretches her arms in the air and yawns.

"It's ten thirty," I say, unable to hide my grin at her uncharacteristically disheveled hair and fluffy slippers.

"Really? Oh, well then *I'm* up early," Jaslene sighs, ambling over to the small kitchen and minibar where I've opened a basket of pastries and plucking up a muffin. "I had every intention of sleeping 'til noon."

"You're not excited about the ball then?" I ask, surprised.

"Of course I am," Jaslene gasps, looking scandalized. "The reason I wanted to get all my rest this morning was so I could stay up the whole night dancing!"

At the last part, she spins away from the counter, knocking over several empty mugs on the coffee table by accident and giggling in the process. I glance at my aunt's door as I bend over and pick them up, expecting her to throw it open any minute and snap for us to be quiet. But the tall door remains shut, her room on the other side silent.

"Is your mother okay?" I say, straightening and placing the mugs back on the counter where they are safe from any more of Jaslene's enthusiasm. "Usually, she's up by now."

"Oh, I'm sure she'll be back soon," my cousin responds.

My head snaps to her. "What do you mean? Where else would she be at this time of morning?"

Jaslene shrugs, unconcerned. "I haven't seen her since yesterday afternoon."

I gape, waiting for my cousin to provide some explanation, or at least act like a normal daughter would in this situation. Instead, she hums a waltz as she makes her way towards the bathroom, throwing in another twirl while she's at it.

Dread drips along my spine along with a memory as I stride toward Salenna's room and throw open the door.

"Did you not hear what I just said?" Jaslene cries from behind me, but I still rush into the chamber and open the top drawer of the dresser, my head spins when I fail to locate my aunt's photograph of Florian.

I tear through the drawers' contents, rifling past scarves, gloves, and fans. I find no trace of the photograph. It's as if it never existed.

Just like Jaslene's necklace. Just like part of my cousin's memories—and my aunt's, I suddenly realize, whenever she returned.

Because she would return. Just like Jaslene and Leander. And like them, she might never be the same.

When the ship beneath me sways, I stumble, my knees all at once feeling weak at the realization—and the guilt.

Jaslene's disappearance may not have been my fault, but my aunt's was. If I had only agreed when Kye-Shin first suggested leaving, we might have found the key and escaped before my aunt disappeared. If I hadn't been able to save Jaslene, I might have at least stopped her from suffering the same fate. But I was too late. Because of my fear and hesitation, I failed them both.

But I have no intention of abandoning them.

"Jaslene," I say, forcing enthusiasm into my voice as I re-enter the sitting room. "I have something exciting to tell you."

"Oh?" My cousin reappears in the bathroom doorway.

For the briefest second, I hesitate, hating what I'm about to say, hating that I'm about to lie. Yet I know from her reaction the last time I tried to tell Jaslene everything, the truth won't work. Not with her or my aunt whenever she comes back.

Kye-Shin's words echo in my mind, urging me forward.

*...do whatever it takes...*

"We got a call this morning saying that our family won a special opportunity to go on an excursion!" I say.

"An excursion?" Jaslene repeats the words as if they feel foreign on her tongue. "What kind?"

"To go stargazing," I say, recalling the story I'd spent most of last night thinking up. "After the ball, we get to take a boat and venture just a little distance away from *The Fated* for a while to admire the constellations."

"But," Jaslene starts in confusion. "We can see the stars perfectly fine from the deck."

Frustration bubbles up within me before I shove it back down. "That's what I thought, but they said the lights from the ship actually prevent us from seeing a more spectacular view. Plus tonight we'll be passing through an area where there will be a lot of shooting stars. We'll be in the perfect spot to watch them!"

Instead of looking thrilled, my cousin's expression grows more puzzled.

"That's strange," she ponders, "I haven't heard anyone talking about any excursions. Did Gerald announce it recently?"

"He mentioned it briefly the other day," I insist, trying my best to sound casual despite the heat I already feel rising to my cheeks and panic twisting my nerves. "But they didn't want to make too big of a deal about it, you know. For the people who didn't win." Remembering Kye-Shin and the others, I add. "I think they said only a handful of other people won the chance to go."

"Oh, I suppose that makes sense," Jaslene replies, nodding and allowing me to relax. Then she glances up and asks, "What about Arthur? He can come too, can't he? After all, since he's my fiancé that counts as family, right?"

I bite my lip to keep from swearing. I had forgotten about Arthur. My aunt and cousin would be more than enough to deal with once they discovered we weren't really going on an excursion. How would Arthur react? Even if we managed to fit him onto the boat, would he become angry enough to turn violent? Would he ruin everything?

I'm already opening my mouth to make up some excuse for why he can't join us, when I pause, taking in Jaslene's expectant expression. If I say no, she might not agree to go at all. Worse, once she realized we were leaving *The Fated* behind forever, she would never forgive me. No, we would just have to take him with us and figure out the rest later.

"Why not?" I say, forcing out a laugh. "I'm sure no one will say anything if we sneak him on board."

Jaslene's eyes narrow, and that's when I know.

She doesn't believe me. She's either caught onto our plan or thinks I'm pulling some kind of prank. Either way, she won't step foot onto the boat now. I've done all of this for nothing.

A minute passes, then my cousin smiles and grabs my hands before spinning us both around like little girls.

"That sounds fantastic!" she cries, twirling us around several more times until she releases me. I collapse on the couch, feeling already exhausted for the day as she skips towards the opposite wall and plucks up the phone. "I have to call Arthur and tell him right away."

"You should pack warm clothes too," I add. "Just in case it gets chilly while we're out there."

"Sure, sure," Jaslene nods absentmindedly as she begins dialing, and I sigh in relief, sinking farther into the couch and closing my eyes to the excited trill of my cousin's voice as she chatters into the transmitter.

The rest of the day crawls by slowly and fleetingly all at once. I don't look for my aunt. I know I won't be able to find her no matter how hard I try, just like I hadn't been able to with Jaslene or Leander. I can only hope she will reappear soon after we find the key. That she will believe a lie as easily as her daughter.

By the time we make it back to the stateroom after wandering aimlessly through the ship all day, we're rushing around the space in a frenzy of hairbrushes, makeup, and skirts to get ready for the ball. The gown I choose is the same one that caught my eye on the first day towards the back of my closet, and as soon as I put it on, I realize it is the most breathtaking dress I have ever seen.

Colored a blue almost as dark as midnight, the gown flows down to my feet in a cascade of shimmering silver beads and soft chiffon. Streams of fabric pour from the back of my shoulders, forming a train that shifts with every movement, making me appear graceful and even regal—two characteristics I'd long ago given up hope of possessing. My hair too has miraculously been tamed into elegant curls while earrings that glitter and sway like miniature chandeliers dangle on either side of my cheeks.

When I glance in the mirror, I'm unrecognizable.

My basic features remain the same. My lips are still rounded, and my nose is still small. My eyes are still the same sapphire shade. Yet the stranger in the mirror is the furthest thing from the girl I've come to know over the last nineteen years. The shadows under my eyes are gone as if I've never suffered a sleepless night. My skin has darkened to a rich olive hue as if I've spent days basking in the sun rather than imprisoned inside an elevator a world away. Even the blue hue of my eyes looks brighter, clearer, as if no longer haunted by unfulfilled desires and past regrets.

Will I still appear this healthy—this *alive*—after I leave *The Fated*? Will I reflect on this moment and regret ever leaving at all?

"You look gorgeous!" Jaslene squeals as soon as she sees me, and I can't help but think the same when I gaze over her rose-pink skirt that falls into tiers like waves and rhinestone-laced bodice.

"So do you," I say, and Jaslene's grin turns devious.

"Well, I couldn't embarrass my fiancé, now could I—"

A knock sends us both looking at the door.

"Oooh, that must be the champagne I ordered," Jaslene says, hurrying towards the hall before I can stop her.

The click of the door opening and shutting echoes through the space before she reappears holding an envelope in her hand.

"I found this in front of the door," she says, bewildered as she holds it out to me. "It's for you."

For a moment, panic grips me. Had the stranger discovered our plan? Had he placed a warning inside this envelope—or a threat?

Yet when my eyes fall on my name written in elegant flourishing script along the front, a whole new thrill runs through me. Though I've only glimpsed it before in crumbled notes or at the edges of a journal page, I would recognize Kye-Shin's handwriting anywhere. With trembling hands, I open the envelope and devour the note tucked inside:

*Amarra,*

*With or without the piano, you are magnificent.*

*P.S. I've included a gift so that you will never be lost without a compass or the stars.*

Less than three sentences should not steal away my breath and make my heart falter. Should not send heat rushing to my cheeks and water flooding behind my eyes.

But it's the necklace that slips from the envelope and into my palm that makes my jaw drop and the world around me shift forever. At the end of the chain is Kye-Shin's medallion, the compass on one side with the Alexandris on the other. It was a good luck charm he'd carried for I can't guess how long, and I'd seen him turn it over in his hand whenever he was deep in thought, when he was troubled, when he wasn't even aware of the action—as if the medallion were an extension of himself.

And he'd given it to me.

"You never said you had an admirer!" Jaslene gasps, snatching the necklace from me and holding it up to the light.

"He is not!" I snap though I'm grinning as I chase her around the coffee table, couch, and kitchen. Our laughter fills the air and fools me into believing that we really might live happily ever after.

# CHAPTER 33

# LAST DANCE

I thought I'd already beheld the full extent of *The Fated's* splendor: in the brilliance and color of the Breakfast Room; in the dazzling lights and beautiful storefronts along the Boulevard; in the embossed entrance and daring design of The Nautilus.

But all of that pales in comparison to the ballroom.

The second I step through the towering silver doors, I'm certain I must have wandered into an underwater palace.

Sapphire walls rise in every direction, covered in stylized waves that curl and crash around colossal windows flooding with the oranges, reds, and purples of a setting sun. The chandeliers are shaped like cresting water with even the tiniest droplets consisting of diamonds reflecting over a thousand colors, each nearly blinding in their brilliance. The floor is pale and radiant, as if it was formed from a giant pearl that has been flattened and stretched along the vast hall.

I'd been right when I told Kye-Shin practically everyone on the ship would be attending, for there are more people in the ballroom than I recall ever seeing in one place on the voyage. Dressed in tuxedos and flowing dresses from nearly every era, they spin in graceful circles to the music. They cluster around tables decked with ice sculptures and champagne fountains. They mingle along the edges, overfilled glasses in hand as they laugh and chatter about everything and nothing at all.

I stutter to a halt when, through the crowd, I spot my aunt chatting with several men in the opposite corner, her head thrown back in laughter. As always, she is like a vision from a magazine or cinema screen with her dark, voluptuous hair cascading down her shoulders and a satin red gown that stands out even amidst the sea of beautiful dresses. As one man leads her onto the dance floor, I realize my aunt appears happier than I remember ever seeing her.

*Changed.* Like a weight has been lifted off her, or rather, certain memories. I can only hope it's not too late. I can only hope that when we leave, whatever happened to her and Jaslene will be reversible.

"I told her about our little stargazing trip," Jaslene says, appearing by my side and adjusting her headband, which is adorned with pearls and gold flowers. "She said it sounds interesting enough to come along."

Relief courses through me at the words. Everything might really go as we planned after all.

"There he is!" Jaslene gasps as Arthur weaves through the crowd toward us, his chestnut hair slicked back and his eyes glued to my cousin.

"Hello, ladies," he greets, barely glancing at me before he leans close to Jaslene and whispers something in her ear that sends her erupting into a fit of giggles.

"Amarra!"

I swivel to find Miyuni hurrying towards me with Leander and Emory ambling behind. She wears a fitted violet gown adorned with white plumerias. In her ecstatic expression and glowing smile, I detect no trace of the anxiety and sadness that clung to her after we left Enzo's stateroom over a week ago—after she refused to question anything more about the ship for fear of uncovering the truth.

Will she refuse to leave *The Fated* with us as well?

"I'm so happy to see you!" Miyuni gushes, grasping my hands and taking in my appearance with wide eyes. "You look positively beautiful! Don't you think so, Kye?"

"Breathtakingly," Kye-Shin says, materializing at his sister's side. I sense his focus sweep over me; over the delicate fabric of my gown; the medallion sloping around my neck; my lips.

I feel my own breath be stolen away as I take in the way his white tuxedo accentuates his tall, elegant frame and makes his already black hair appear impossibly darker, his already piercing gaze impossibly sharper. When I finally gather enough courage to meet his eyes, they bore into mine, the fondness and desire swirling within them intense enough to send heat rushing through me.

"So far this party's a bit tame for my taste," Leander says, holding a cocktail in hand as he surveys the bouquets bursting with cherry blossoms and couples slow-dancing on the floor with boredom.

"That's because for once you're here on time," Emory says, smirking. "You usually show up hours late and only when the people finally get interesting."

"What can I say?" Leander shrugs, not bothering to deny it. "Tonight I was overly optimistic."

As they both chuckle in response to his comment, I study their features, searching for some flicker of nervousness in their smiles, some sliver of dread in their gazes. Their expressions are relaxed though, content—and not of the kind belonging to anyone who might be planning on leaving *The Fated* later tonight.

When I glance at Kye-Shin, he confirms my suspicions by giving a slight shake of his head. Regret tinges his face. He must have tried to convince them into coming with us, and they refused. Disappointment slices through me, followed by a wave of sadness.

"We should celebrate being together again with a toast!" Miyuni says, urging us all to grab glasses filled with blue liqueur from a nearby tray.

"To paradise!" She announces as we tap our glasses together with a clink.

*To paradise.*

The word makes me want to cry. Instead, I drink.

The first taste is sweet. The second is fire.

I wince as the liquid scalds my throat, sending red stars angrily rushing across my vision. By the time my sight finally clears, the others are drifting away, with Jaslene and Arthur being the last.

"Wait!" I nearly shout, reaching toward my cousin as she swivels and gives me a puzzled look. "Don't forget to go down to the promenade deck later for our excursion. You can't forget it."

"I won't, I won't," Jaslene snaps in exasperation, waving away my fussing as she and Arthur melt into the crowd, leaving me alone with my irrational sense of worry at the memory of them doing the same thing the night Jaslene disappeared.

This is part of the plan, I remind myself. Later, once we have the key, we will all be together again.

"What did you tell them?" Kye-Shin wonders aloud.

"I said we'd won the chance to go on a special stargazing excursion," I sigh, still cringing from the guilt of such an innocent-sounding lie.

"Ah." He nods in understanding, crossing the distance between us in a handful of steps. And just like that, all thoughts of Jaslene evaporate at his nearness. "Care to join me for a stroll?"

I manage a nod and swear his lips twitch in amusement before he entwines his right arm seamlessly around mine and pulls us away.

"Thank you for this," I say, instinctively reaching for the medallion hanging around my neck. Against my skin, it feels cool and solid. Steadying. "I know how much it means to you."

"That's why I couldn't give it to anyone else," Kye-Shin says, fixing his eyes on me.

The sound of breaking glass and a high-pitched shriek shatters the moment, sending us whirling to see a woman in a wine-stained skirt shouting at another passenger who laughs it off, his wide and worry-free smile epitomizing the exact opposite of how I feel.

"I hate this waiting," I confess, trying and failing to shake the tendrils of dread already crawling along my spine and the restlessness threatening to suffocate me.

"I know. I feel the same," Kye-Shin says, squeezing my hand in understanding. "But everything's going to be alright. Our plan will work."

The warmth of his fingers brushing over mine has me spinning back around, but his other hand is already dropping to his side as he guides us along, our arms still locked as if we are just another couple mingling on the edges of the dance floor.

The final rays of sun that flooded the ballroom earlier have since faded. But in the windows, I can see a yellow glow still lingering on the fringes of the horizon while dark violet storm clouds descend towards the water. Lightning flickers past the chandeliers and candles reflecting off the glass. *A bad omen*, my mother would say.

"Do you see him?" Kye-Shin's voice is low, and I know who he's talking about without having to ask.

Miyuni glides across the floor hand-in-hand with a handsome young man who drinks in her graceful movements with adoration. Lethia watches from the side, sipping a strawberry milkshake and wearing a matching pink bow and dress. Several feet away, Emory and Leander appear deep in conversation while Jaslene and Arthur spin in dizzying circles before running through the crowd, drunk with giggles.

There is no sign of the stranger.

Had we been wrong from the start? How could I have ever thought he would attend something as insignificant as a ball?

"Well, while we have nothing better to do..." Kye-Shin says, appearing unconcerned as he tugs us onto the floor.

"What are you doing?" I gasp, frantically taking in the twirling couples around us.

"Asking you for a dance," he scoffs as if the answer is obvious. It takes me several seconds too long to realize he has extracted his arm from mine and instead is extending his hand.

The laugh that escapes my lips sounds more like a squawk.

"No, I don't think so," I insist, backing away. "I'm fine! I'm not so great at dancing anyway. I'll just embarrass you. Really!"

"I highly doubt that," Kye-Shin says, snaking an arm around my waist before I comprehend what is happening and pulling me towards him. "But if you're telling the truth, then it's fortunate we're starting with something slower."

The lively quickstep from earlier has since melted into a melody undulating with the low pitch of saxophones and lazy strumming of a double bass. The dazzling chandeliers have dimmed, allowing the candles flickering along the tables to bathe the room in a warm but vibrant glow.

I hardly notice any of it.

How can I when my body is mere inches from Kye-Shin's, close enough for my forehead to brush his lips? Close enough for me to see the curve of his eyelashes, the slight crookedness of his nose. Enough for me to want to lean in and be closer still...

"I came up with an idea for a new novel," he says suddenly, and I instinctively reel back with a force that almost sends us stumbling until Kye-Shin redirects us into a slow spin. "It's the best one I've had in years."

"That's wonderful," I manage after a moment, thankful when my voice comes out steadier than I feel. Kye-Shin's eyes gleam knowingly.

"I finally found a story worth telling," he breathes, raising his arm to send me into a twirl that makes the edges of my dress ripple outward before pulling me back to him once again. His voice softens to a murmur against my ear. "Yours."

When I falter this time, Kye-Shin pauses with me, his dark eyes peering into mine, burning with the same desire and admiration I had only seen a glimpse of during the night on the deck.

"It's *you* I want to write about," he says. "Your hopes, your disappointments, your triumphs. I can't stop myself from wanting to capture you on every page, from thinking of every word to describe the exact shade of your eyes or the right pitch of your laughter when you no longer care who is listening."

"I..." I start, only to hesitate.

*I think about you too,* I want to say, because it's true.

At some unidentifiable moment during this voyage, I'd begun thinking about where Kye-Shin was and what he was doing nearly every hour of every day. I often wondered whether he was scribbling notes down on the nearest piece of paper he could find or strolling along the deck, breathing in the salt air.

I feel the words rise in my throat, crowding along the back of my tongue, begging to be released into the world. I can feel Kye-Shin draw in a deep breath, as if waiting to hear them. But the sentences stick on the roof of my mouth, and no matter how desperately I try to shake them loose, they won't budge.

I had let my emotions get the better of me once. I had hoped and dreamed and *wanted*—only to watch as everything I wished for drew close enough to shatter in my hands.

I don't want to risk breaking whatever this new, exhilarating—and terrifying—feeling growing between us is by doing the same. By reaching too far, too recklessly. So I don't reach at all, at least not now. Not when so much else is at stake.

At my silence, the disappointment in Kye-Shin's gaze is fleeting, hardly even noticeable. I've never felt more ashamed.

"Last night, I dreamed of what our life would be like once we were no longer on board *The Fated*," he says, moving us in time with the music once again. "In this new world, wherever it was, I was sitting at a desk, writing my book while you were playing the piano. There were birds singing outside a window and sunlight dancing through the curtains. We were both happy."

"Aren't you afraid that might be too much to ask for?" I say, at last giving voice to the dread that has haunted me the entire day. "For us both to be happy?"

At the uncertainty in my voice, Kye-Shin's expression clouds, and as I watch him struggle to find the right words to erase my doubts, I yearn to smooth away the crease between his brows with my fingers and melt away the downward curve of his lips with my own.

I've barely started rising on my toes and leaning forward when the clashing of cymbals signals the song's end. Voices and clapping erupt along the dance floor as around us, couples break away from each other.

I clear my throat, reluctantly loosening my grip on Kye-Shin's shoulder before moving to step away.

I never get the chance.

Kye-Shin's hand is no longer on my waist but against my cheek, his touch as gentle as it is unyielding.

"No," he speaks softly, resolve brimming in his eyes as if arriving at some silent decision. "It isn't too much to ask for."

Kye-Shin dissolves the inches between us and descends his lips onto mine. I wrap my arms around his neck without a second thought. I run my fingers through his hair like I've always wanted to. I marvel at the ease with which my body molds into his, the way our pounding hearts accelerate before falling into perfect sync with each other.

But it's the intensity of his kiss that demands the majority of my attention. Every brush, every push of his lips against mine promises a future where we are at last safe and content. A future filled with laughter and sunshine and *love.*

A life beyond *The Fated.*

Kye-Shin pulls back abruptly, and for one terrifying second, I think he is regretting everything.

My panic disintegrates though when I see his face break into the most radiant smile I have ever seen. In response, I feel my lips spread into a grin of my own, and for several seconds more we linger together, basking in the glow of the candles and each other's company. Yet all too quickly, we pull apart, Kye-Shin's eyes focusing on something behind me.

"What is it?" I ask in alarm, following his gaze but failing to place anything unusual among the mass of swaying couples.

"It's nothing," he insists, shaking his head as his expression clears. "I just haven't seen Miyuni for several minutes. I'm sure I'm being paranoid, but I'd feel better if I checked on her."

"I'll come with you," I offer. Kye-Shin nods before taking my hand and pulling us to the edge of the dance floor. The chandeliers brighten once again while the first beginnings of violin strings bleed into the air, sending the passengers around us buzzing with anticipation.

"Can Amarra spare one last dance?"

The voice that drifts behind me is calm, quiet even.

Yet Kye-Shin and I both lurch to a halt immediately.

Together we slowly turn, me already knowing who the speaker is even before I drink in the dark golden hair, black tuxedo, and green-amber eyes regarding us with amusement.

The stranger.

# CHAPTER 34

## THE STRANGER

I should speak. I should spread my lips into a convincing smile and say something clever or charming in reply. But my fear makes me hesitate too long.

The stranger looks disappointed.

"Come now," he pleads, tilting his head at me. "After all the help I gave you, I thought you would at least consider me a friend."

I'd thought so too once. But now—as I take in the sharp intelligence behind his gaze, the way his very presence seems to swallow up the massive room and send any passengers unfortunate enough to drift too close reeling back as if compelled by an invisible force—the only emotion I feel is fear.

Before I can step back, my eye snags on an object glimmering from inside his vest pocket before it quickly disappears beneath his jacket: a key.

So I had guessed right after all. Still, suspicion makes me hesitate. What if the stranger had let me see the key on purpose? Somehow he could have known our intentions and was using the key as bait simply to lure me into his clutches. After all, if he was the mastermind behind *The Fated*, then he had known enough about us to design our rooms, our clothes, and even steal our most precious belongings. Could he sense our current thoughts too?

I shudder at the possibility.

But what other choice did I have? Waiting, allowing myself and everyone else to have our memories stolen instead wasn't an option. Shoving down my fear, I brush past Kye-Shin and place my hand into the stranger's outstretched palm.

For the briefest moment, I half-expect my hand to start melting the instant my fingers touch his. I can't help but sigh in relief when they don't.

"Of course we're friends," I say, forcing a smile before spinning back to Kye-Shin and saying, "Go on without me. I'll be here waiting when you get back."

Kye-Shin looks as if he's about to protest, but when I glance toward the key, his eyes follow my gaze. Understanding blooms across his expression. From the way his jaw clenches and the glare he directs towards the stranger, I can tell he doesn't like the idea of leaving me here alone. Neither do I. But none of that matters.

"I won't be gone long," Kye-Shin finally relents, and I nod, swallowing the heaviness in my throat as I watch him turn and weave through the crowd, his white tuxedo eventually disappearing altogether.

Despite every instinct urging me to do otherwise, I allow the stranger to pull me back into the center of the room.

"Your friend seems a little on edge," he comments, spinning me without warning and so fast I struggle not to stumble.

"He's charming, really," I say, almost defensively before adding, "though not the best at first impressions." The stranger looks amused.

"This waltz has always been one of my favorites," he says as the violin strings are soon joined by the sounds of an orchestra, and before I can so much as protest, we fly across the floor.

The style of the music is beautiful but old—so old in fact that the people around us look to each other in confusion before attempting to muddle through the steps. In contrast, the stranger moves without mistake or hesitation as he advances and pivots, leading me in a perfectly choreographed routine only he knows.

Dancing with him is nothing like dancing with Kye-Shin. Whereas Kye's hand over mine had been gentle and warm, the stranger's hold is firm and commanding, capable of catapulting me into a dizzying spin with the slightest push. His skin too is neither hot nor cold, as if he's made of something other than flesh altogether.

"You look happy," he observes. I have to keep myself from laughing at the absurdity of the comment, given the tenseness in my shoulders and painful staccato of my heart.

Instead, I offer a careless smile like the ones I've seen Jaslene wear countless times before. "Do I?"

The stranger nods, spinning me outwards before pulling me back in once again. "Still, you shouldn't wander along the decks after midnight. Unpleasant things tend to reveal their ugliest nature in the dark."

My fingers are inches away from his pocket when the words register in my mind, startling me for a second too long as he shifts out of reach. He's toying with me. He has to be.

*You're behind everything that's happened, aren't you?* I want to demand from him. *The melting, the disappearances. You're the one who abandoned Enzo on the deck and who keeps kidnapping people and bringing them back changed, as if some vital piece of them has been stripped away. You're the one who invited us onto this ship in the first place —but why?*

Still, I don't dare voice these questions for fear of losing him before I can steal the key, or worse, inadvertently alerting him of our escape plans in the slim chance he doesn't suspect them already. I feign ignorance.

"I'm not sure I understand what you mean," I say carefully, struggling to suppress my frustration when he recaptures my hand in his own.

His fingers have barely clasped around me before he dips me backward and brings our faces inches apart.

"I think you do," the stranger responds, his amber-green eyes boring into mine with an intensity that makes me feel as if I'm both freezing and being burned alive. "I think you have suspected for some time this ship is anything but what it seems."

*He knows.* The thought tears through my mind, paralyzing me with panic and confirming my earlier fears. *He's known everything all along.*

The stranger lifts me back up with ease, and it takes several seconds before I manage to regain my balance and some semblance of a half-decent response.

"It's definitely mysterious," I say vaguely, managing an embarrassed laugh. "I admit on the deck, I let my imagination get carried away. I thought I saw a shape in the fog and fled before I could make out any details. Looking back, I'm sure it was just a shadow or something even more silly."

"I see," the stranger replies after a minute. "So you are content? With the ship I mean?"

"How could I not be?" The lie slips from my lips easily enough. "I can spend the whole day reclining in the sun or watch as many movies as I want. I can eat whatever kind of food or drink I desire. I have every luxury imaginable at my fingertips. What more could someone like me ask for? It's a dream come true."

This time when he delivers me into another twirl, I'm ready. As I spin close enough for my shoulder to brush his jacket, I reach towards his vest, plucking the key from his pocket and tucking it behind my back.

Not an instant later, the song ends, and I struggle to keep from showing my nervousness as I bend my knees in a curtsy, mimicking the actions of the couples on either side of us.

"I'm sorry you feel that way," the stranger says, straightening from his bow. I look at him in confusion.

His expression seems almost...disappointed. I have no idea why. Wasn't the purpose of such overexaggerated extravagance to make the people on board want to stay, to trap us?

I can't puzzle out the stranger's reaction. I don't want to.

"Thanks for the dance, but I should be going," I say, sliding my hand from his while tightening my fingers around the key. "My friends are probably looking for me."

For a long moment as the stranger continues to stare at me, I'm certain I have failed. That he can see through my charade as easily as the thinnest gauze.

"Don't let me keep you any longer then," he says at last, giving another dip of his head before swiveling and stalking away without a backward glance. I watch him retreat for several seconds more until finally releasing a breath and turning, clutching the key to my stomach as I walk in the opposite direction.

I take three steps before his voice drifts from behind, close enough for me to whirl and stumble back at finding him standing less than a foot away.

"By the way, Amarra, you play the piano wonderfully," he says, sending a bolt of shock through my body. "It would be a shame to throw away such a talent."

"How did you kn—"

"Unfortunately, that key won't be of any help to you, I'm afraid," the stranger pushes on mercilessly, his gaze lowering to where my hand is still poised behind my waist. I swear I almost detect a hint of regret in his tone. "It is too late to escape anyway. You cannot stop what will happen next."

"What do you want from us?" I snap just as the ballroom pitches to the side, sending trays and glasses alike flying through the air while passengers stumble across the marble floor, shrieking or laughing as if we are on a carnival ride.

The stranger, however, does not move, does not so much as sway even when the tables slide and the glass spanning the windows rattles.

Just as quickly as it tilts, the ship rights itself once more, causing me to trip on my skirt and careen backwards, watching helplessly as far above the swinging chandeliers and gilded ceiling speed past. Fingers snake around my wrist, halting my fall, and I lower my startled gaze to find the stranger grasping my arm, his previously impassive expression conflicted.

He might help me after all, I think—that is until his lips part to speak seven awful words: "Do not try to save your friend."

I jerk out of his grip in desperation, practically twisting my ankles in haste to put as much distance as I can between myself and him. The man doesn't follow, but his eyes do, and when I lose sight of him behind the writhing bodies of people dancing and crowding around to watch, I can still feel his attention on me, watching. I break into a run.

I scour the crowd for Kye-Shin in his white tuxedo, searching every face for familiar brown eyes and a half-smile. He's not among the people gathered around tables flooded with food and desserts. Nor is he lingering on the fringes, reclining on the velvet settees packed with guests fanning themselves or peering out the windows as lightning skitters across the ocean and illuminates the dark waters in a skeletal glow. Kye-Shin is nowhere to be found inside the ballroom, and neither is Miyuni.

I quicken my pace.

Beneath me, the floor continues to pitch and roll, threatening to send me off balance again, but I force myself to keep moving even when my lungs scream at me to halt and my muscles shudder. Above me, the lights are not only no longer dim, but blinding and hot—hot enough to sear my skin as well as my eyes. The violin strings and flute chords from earlier have been replaced by screeching trumpets and accelerated drums. Someone's elbow rams into my shoulder. A shoe steps on the edge of my train followed by the sound of ripping fabric. Around me, passengers laugh and chatter as they stumble along with the ship, their expressions unconcerned, their smiles overly wide.

I've never felt so helpless or afraid.

In contrast to the brightness and chaos flooding the ballroom, the hallway is dark and quiet. The only other occupants are a couple strolling towards the far end, their voices fading as they round the corner. Thunder booms from outside, causing the crystals hanging from the wall sconces to tremble. I break into a sprint, my heels clicking violently against the granite floor.

I almost believe I imagine the figure in white who materializes at the end of the passageway, his head bent as he studies something in his hand. Even from a distance, I would know him anywhere.

Kye-Shin.

Nearly crying in relief, I step forward to call his name when a low buzz slithers into my ear, the sound of it far too familiar. Slowly, I turn my head to where the nearest lamp begins flickering—then melting altogether, along with the mirrored walls.

When I spin back around, I feel my heart drop at the sight of Kye-Shin's shoes sinking through the floor just as the familiar rancid smell washes over me. The ship gives a mournful wail that sends my ears ringing and teeth rattling against each other.

*Do not try to save your friend.*

"No!" I roar as Kye-Shin shouts, trying to escape—only for his calves to fall through the floor followed by his knees. "Amarra, stay back!"

I don't. Yet with every step I draw closer, the floor drags him down faster, submerging his waist, then his stomach. In desperation, I stretch out my arm. I can still reach him. I'm close enough. Only a handful of steps more...

"Leave without me," he whispers, and something inside me shatters as Kye-Shin's face contorts in agony before the ship swallows him whole.

# Chapter 35

## The Lowest Level

I'm falling too.

I don't realize it until I slam against the now solid floor, which pitches up with the ship to rush toward me. A ring splits through my skull. Teeth sink into my lips. The taste of blood and tears floods my tongue.

Past my throbbing bones and reeling vision, I gradually register the coolness of granite beneath my left hip and elbow, along with the distant warbled echo of music from the ballroom. A shadow shifts at the corner of my vision, and I look up, tensing in alarm.

But it's only my reflection in the mirrored walls that have since resolidified. The radiant woman I was merely hours ago has since diminished into a broken one with a haunted gaze and aching body. I trace my eyes over the tear stretching up the side of my skirt and the medallion swinging from my neck like the pendulum of a clock, stealing away time. My chest clenches at the thought of Kye-Shin threading the chain through the top with care, at the thought of him writing the note and tucking it into the envelope with a slight smile.

*With or without the piano, you are magnificent.*

Now he's gone—no, not gone. He's been stolen.

Like Jaslene and Leander. Like countless others who returned... changed.

But Kye-Shin wouldn't be like the others. *I* would be the one to bring him back, unchanged and unharmed. I had to. I pick up the key from where it has fallen on the ground next to me. In spite of the stranger's words, I can't bear to leave it behind, can't bear to give into the possibility that we might never escape this ship. So I grip the iron in my fingers instead, letting its coolness distract me as I struggle onto my hands, knees, and my aching feet.

A soft crunch beneath my shoe makes me halt. For a second, when I glance down to find crumbled petals, I fail to understand. Why would Kye-Shin be holding a flower of all things before he was captured?

But it is only when I lift the plant up towards the light to reveal wine-colored petals and a long, slender stem adorned with thorns that the revelation hits me.

I've seen this plant twice before.

The first one scratched me with its thorns when I accidentally pushed over the vase of flowers in Jaslene's room soon after her disappearance. The second had been in the hallway leading to the Sea Dragon lounge seconds before I found Leander's watch.

Leander. Jaslene. Kye-Shin.

How did I not realize sooner? In addition to the melting and eerie moans from the ship, the flowers had been at the sight of each disappearance. Kye-Shin had been holding it just before something stole him away.

I rush to the nearest elevator and stumble inside just as the ship pitches with another wave from the storm again, impatiently hitting the button until the doors close. I watch as we glide up and up high above the skating rink and arcade, past the theater and giant chandeliers until finally stopping at the level immediately below the sun deck. The doors open with a cheerful ding, revealing a stone path lined on each side by emerald branches and flowering bushes.

Inside the paneled glass walls, the gardens are deserted, which is unusual for this time in the evening but not surprising given the ongoing ball. I pass by no one as I stride along the walkway, wincing at every other step from my increasingly painful heels. When I reach the courtyard, the white tables and benches clustered around the fountain contain no occupants. Past the glass ceiling, lightning from the still-raging storm flashes, briefly throwing the warmly lit area into an uncanny glow. I flinch at the clap of thunder that soon follows, its violence contrasting with the soothing trickle of water and tranquil harp music drifting through the space.

The gardens, like so many of the corridors on *The Fated*, form a complicated labyrinth, and even though I've been here several times, no path ever seems to remain the same. Walkways that should logically loop back to the courtyard vanish beneath thickening foliage. Paths weaving in opposite directions somehow lead back to the entrance.

Beneath me, the trail shakes as the ship hits another wave, and I barely manage to avoid collapsing again by grasping onto the nearest lamppost. As I wait for the ground to stop moving, my eyes fall on the marigolds and half-crushed pansies next to my feet.

The flowers closest to me are flatter than those merely feet away, as if they've been repeatedly crushed by someone walking over them to reach the trees. No, not the trees, I realize, but rather something hidden behind them.

Lifting up my skirt, I wade into the foliage, following the pressed flowers until the grass and petals beneath me give way to soil while the branches of oaks, willows, and red maples close in from above. I wince as my hair catches on a twig and my ankle twists on a root. Hardly any light seeps in between the trees, forcing me to lean on the trunks and vines in order to navigate through the shadows until I stumble into an open area I have never seen before.

It's another garden—one solely containing wine-colored flowers.

Hundreds upon hundreds of the tall, almost grotesque plants grow in rows spanning the floor and walls, their petals stretching outwards like tongues. Despite their overwhelming number, I can't help but notice the distinct lack of smell, as if whatever twisted force of nature was responsible for the flowers' creation forgot to add one final touch.

A low moan sends me whirling, panic shooting through my body as I expect to find either the stranger or something even more terrifying bearing down on me. But the noise only comes from a door standing ajar against the wall in the far corner. As I drift towards the entrance, wind whistles through the opening, causing the door to swing inward until I can make out a descending stairwell lit by dim, crackling lightbulbs.

At any other time, taking the stairs would seem like the last thing I should do, but I can think of no better option.

Taking a deep breath, I step forward, then gasp in pain when the back of my shoe digs into my already raw skin. Finding Kye-Shin will do no good if I can no longer walk. So I gingerly remove my heels—careful to avoid further aggravating the blisters already forming— before beginning my descent.

Unlike the rest of the ship, this space is far from extravagant. Beneath my feet, the metal stairs are cold and damp. Grime and dust mingle along the rails and walls. Cracks fissure across the surface of several lightbulbs while others are burnt out entirely, casting the winding passageway in fluctuating darkness. The echo of dripping water haunts me throughout every turn, though I never spot the source.

*Drip. Drip. Drip.*

Around me, the already narrow walls seem to fold in closer, the dripping sound becomes louder as the stairs stretch on and on...

I'm suddenly hit with the image of descending the stairs for days then months without arriving at the bottom. Could this be another of *The Fated's* tricks? Maybe this is a trap. Maybe there truly is no end at all. In panic, I'm about to spin around and retrace my footsteps when the chute unexpectedly expands into a wide hall cloaked in shadow.

Several yards ahead, a lamp buzzes along the wall. Around me, the ship groans and creaks, sounding more alive than ever. As if from a world away, I can make out the noises of the raging storm above, can feel the distant power of the thunder and waves in the reverberations that tremble the floor. Beneath all those sounds, there are others too—soft clinks and rattles that I initially fail to notice but soon become impossible to ignore. A familiar, musty smell floods my nose.

When I draw close enough to the light, I discover why.

It's the scene from my vision come to life.

Objects of every shape and size cover the walls. No, not simply objects, I realize, but belongings. Earrings, pointe shoes, a stuffed rabbit —I spot them all along with hundreds of others swinging from thin cords like decaying ornaments. I see the same cracked moonstone ring, rusted compass, and broken violin from my vision hanging among them as well. Like in the vision, the sight fills me with a sense of terror.

But now I think I might be able to explain it, that I might finally understand the reason why everything about this place, this *ship,* has always seemed too good to be true.

With every step I take towards the corridor's end, my heart pounds quicker, my breath shallower. Sweat trickles down the nape of my neck. Every instinct screams for me to flee.

*You can still turn back,* a voice urges from the depths of my mind. I have the key. All I have to do is take my family, the boat, and go.

Yet...deep down a part of me knows it's too late.

For Jaslene. For my aunt. For Kye-Shin.

And for me—because despite my overwhelming fear, there is something else, something stronger: a desire to know. Why we were chosen to board this cursed ship in the first place. Where the ship came from, where it is taking us now. What will happen to us by the end.

Which is why I force foot after agonizing foot forward until at last rounding the corner at the end of the hall. Why I barely hesitate to step through the entrance into a room pulsing with machinery.

Steam billows from massive boilers scattered throughout the space while the rhythmic chug of engines vibrates the air. Like in the hallway, trinkets and once-prized possessions clutter walls towering over twenty feet high, and I'm in the midst of struggling to wrap my mind around the sheer vastness of their number when my eye falls on the rose pearl dangling from a gold chain to my right. The sight smothers the breath on my lips.

Jaslene's necklace.

But that isn't the only thing that catches my eye. With horror, I recognize other items strewn along the wall. My aunt's photo of her lover, Florian. Leander's square gold ring with his initials carved into the surface. And a painting, one of Tanzet at sunset as well as a complete and better version of the one I picked up in Enzo's stateroom. The spires are fully formed and masterful in design. Some of the couples have been re-drawn as dancing instead of strolling along the amber and gold-hued city. Even the child, who was before squatting on the cobblestone street, is instead now standing, his face raised towards the sunset with a dreamy expression.

Slow, measured footsteps approach from behind, and I whirl, furious at the stranger for doing all of this. But the figure that appears through the steam distorts in physique just like on the deck that night. Growing tall one second, then wide the next before ultimately shrinking down to a far too small, far too delicate form to be the stranger's.

I barely register the familiar green dress and matching bow before the vapor parts to reveal the young girl's pleased expression.

"Hello, friend," Lethia says.

# CHAPTER 36

## ONLY A SMALL SACRIFICE

"Oh dear," Lethia remarks, tilting her head as she regards me with a stunned expression. "Were you expecting someone else?"

"No," I gasp disbelievingly. "It can't be. You're a passenger like me. You said you came on board with your family. You're only a..."

*Only a child.*

But the only child on board, I register too late—all the passengers are either teenagers or older. A child who is always alone, whose brother or family I have never actually seen. A child who repeatedly wears the same style of vintage clothes, whose skin was freezing despite being outside on a hot day.

"What are you?" I whisper.

"Your friend, silly," Lethia says, stepping closer and causing me to instinctively back away. The younger girl *tsks* in disapproval. "Don't tell me you make a habit of forgetting your friends so quickly."

The words are similar to the stranger's during the ball, and I recall Lethia standing on the edge of the dance floor, watching Miyuni minutes before she went missing and Kye-Shin soon after.

"Where are they?" I say. "My *real* friends, what have you done with them?"

"Did you enjoy the celebration I threw for you?" Lethia poses instead, crossing her arms behind her and stalking along the wall to inspect the antiques hanging from the walls. They are her trophies, I realize. "You humans are always so easy to delight with galas and champagne and diamonds. I could have made this ship half as grand as it is, and still you would trample each other to get a peek inside."

"My friends," I say, my voice deadly. "Where. Are. They?"

"The sister and brother have already made their choice," Lethia responds, her tone almost bored. "Although the boy's was rather...unexpected." Her thin lips spread into something barely resembling a grin as she twirls back around. "Now it's your turn."

"What choice?"

"The most life-changing one you will ever make," Lethia says before sighing at my wary expression. "Despite what you may think, I'm not evil. I will not force you to remain on board, Amarra, if you do not wish to."

"Is that what you told Enzo?" I sneer, the memory of the terror on his face still vivid in my mind.

"He made his decision," Lethia says. "He practically handpicked that fate himself. He chose to stay on my ship for the rest of his days, one hundred nine years to be exact. I even let him remain the same age he was when he stepped on board. By remaining on *The Fated*, by choosing a carefree blissful existence, he lived more happily than could have been possible anywhere else."

"And you took his mind in return," I say.

"Not his mind," Lethia counters calmly. "I took something much smaller. Something insignificant, really and yet a thousand times more crippling than any blade or weapon. It was a delusion, an obsession—a foolish idea he had ever since he was a boy of becoming a famous painter admired by everyone who saw his work."

"You took away his dream," I murmur, finally voicing the truth I'd been too afraid to put words to until now.

Jaslene's most precious wish had been to travel the world with her father. But Lethia had stolen that dream away along with her necklace. Not only that, she had erased all of my cousin's memories having to do with it from her mind. My aunt too had once dreamed of being together with her former lover—and now her photograph was just another decoration on Lethia's wall.

"A dream, yes. That is what you humans so fondly call the things that bring you misery," the girl remarks in disdain. "You should feel honored. Most people never get an invitation for my ship. I only invite the most desperate and unhappiest of guests, guests who wouldn't dare refuse one of my tickets."

"Why?" I demand, confused. "If it's dreams you want, then why not take as many passengers as you can? Why not stop sending tickets at all and just open the doors to everyone?"

"Because I only take the most delicious and dangerous dreams," Lethia says, holding her arms out as if the answer is obvious. "The ones that cling to their owners, refusing to be forgotten or let go. The ones that remain forever unfulfilled and yet are either shoved into hiding like a shameful secret or worn everyday like a gaping wound. Dreams like yours."

"Dreams aren't dangerous," I argue, but Lethia wags her index finger at me as if I'm the child.

"When Enzo boarded my ship, he was a broken man," she says. "In his younger years, he had been bursting with potential. At the prestigious art school he attended, all the instructors fawned over his talent, proclaiming him to be the next great prodigy.

But he wasn't. Not one of his works ever became well known. Not one ever graced the walls of a museum. He became obsessed with the idea of creating a painting without any flaws, so obsessed in fact that for decades he never finished anything he started and struck through every signature in despair when he became convinced it was a failure. You saw all the unfinished works he dragged on board, unfinished works he both loathed yet couldn't bear to leave behind. When he finally completed his supposedly perfect painting twenty years later, it still didn't bring him the success he desired. He spent all that time in deteriorating apartment after deteriorating apartment, desperately slaving away at the canvas and destroying himself in the process for no reason at all."

"Let me guess," I say, already sensing her justification. "You convinced yourself you were doing him a favor by making him forget."

"As I recall, the first time we met it seemed you would have agreed," is Lethia's response.

"I—that was—" I sputter, recalling the words I spoke recklessly days ago.

*"What were you thinking about?"*

*"Memories from my past...Most days, I wish I could forget them entirely."*

"I didn't mean what I said," I insist.

"Didn't you?" Lethia asks, taking another step forward as she gazes at me, curiosity swirling in her black eyes. "To let go of something painful is a kindness. Take your dream for example. What did striving to become a concert pianist ever do for you except bring you disappointment and heartbreak?"

As much as I try, I can find no words to deny it.

Lethia nods, unsurprised. "Your cousin and aunt couldn't answer that same question about their own dreams when I asked them either," she says, "which is why I've always loved bringing families and friends on board. It never ceases to intrigue me how humans can live in pain so close together and yet never really understand the depths of each other's secret desires and unfulfilled dreams."

She extends her hand to me.

"I gave both your cousin and aunt a choice, and now I lay that same choice before you. I can make it as if you never learned how to play at all, as if you never dreamed of being anything more," Lethia says softly. "I won't take more memories than necessary—only the ones tainted by the curse you call a dream. All those wasted nights tied to the piano when you could have been just a girl who was carefree and content, not someone cursed with wanting the impossible. All those wasted years following the audition, forced to be reminded of your failure every time you saw your reflection in the elevator of that wretched department store, every time you passed by the Institute on your way home to see the bright, bustling students living the life you could never have.

I can make all that needless pain, bitterness, and sorrow melt away. If you choose to stay on my ship, you can never leave or go back home, not even when *The Fated* returns to the known world every sixteen years. But you will never want to, not when your family and life are here. Humans only hold on to their dreams because they believe achieving them will bring them happiness, but I can give you happiness. I can give you paradise."

"How?" I breathe.

"Only a small sacrifice is required," Lethia says, nodding to my arm. "A trivial possession you no longer need. The one in your palm will work nicely."

Confused, I lift up the key I stole from the stranger, but the younger girl wrinkles her nose in disgust.

"Not that one." She shakes her head, motioning towards my other arm.

"I don't have anything else with—" I begin only to pause when I notice the weight in my right hand.

I stare, stunned, at the tiny music box in my palm—*my* music box with the dandelions and hummingbird carved into the smooth wood. The lever begins revolving of its own accord, releasing the familiar melody into the air while my fingers trace over the scratches spanning the bottom corner. I can't help but wince from the memory of throwing the box against the floor in my rage after the audition. I had been so angry, so full of heartbreak and loneliness that night.

But I would never have to know heartbreak or anger or loneliness again if I stayed on *The Fated*.

I could trade memories of nights spent gasping for air through my tears in exchange for endless days basking in the sun and an ocean breeze. I could swap a damaged music box and worn clothes for silk gowns and sapphires.

I can envision it now: the life that would be mine if I stayed.

I would never want for any comfort, would never be belittled again or forced to work a miserable job in order to keep a roof over my head. If I remained on *The Fated* I would be safe and happy. I could make a fresh start with my family, spend every day laughing and having fun with Jaslene like she always wanted, while trying to be a more sympathetic niece to my aunt. I could laze away my afternoons sipping wine in the gardens or gliding on amusement park rides with my friends. If Kye-Shin stayed too, I could dance with him in the ballroom every night, stroll along the deck with him hand in hand to watch the sunrise each morning.

A tranquil, painless life.

"Yes," Lethia says, her dark gaze studying mine in understanding. "Just give the music box to me and that future will be yours. I give you my word."

My hand slowly drifts towards her outstretched fingers. It would be so easy, I realize, to let it all go. In a way, it was one of the easiest things I had ever been asked to do.

The music box is inches from Lethia's reach when I gasp, startled when the key in my opposite hand grows hot. The ensuing pain makes me loosen my grip enough to send the key clattering against the floor before it dissolves altogether.

In its place sits a flower.

It's the same kind of flower Kye-Shin had been holding when he disappeared—the same kind of flower I just saw hundreds upon hundreds of in the garden.

"Don't!" Lethia warns, but my fingers are already wrapping around the stem, careful to avoid the thorns.

As I lift it, the thin bright lines streaking out from the center seem to flow like liquid gold while I swear the wine-colored petals pulse. For the first time, a sweet fragrance floods the air, slamming into me with enough force to send me stumbling back as a long-forgotten memory consumes my mind:

I'm playing the piano while my mother dances in the living room of our cramped apartment, a wider smile on her face than a twelve-year-old me recalls ever seeing before. We're celebrating a special occasion—the unexpected arrival of an art collector who wandered across my mother's stand that afternoon and declared her paintings perfect for the new gallery he was opening soon.

*Do you know what this means?* My mother had said with wide, glittering eyes as she swept into the room to grab my small hands and twirled me around. *This marks the start of our lives changing for the better.*

It hadn't.

Still in this instant, I glow with happiness, and though I'm too young to fully comprehend why, I am old enough to recognize the emotion as rare. Precious.

That's why, when my mother switches on the old gramophone in the corner and begins dancing to a jazz tune, I join her without hesitation. Why, even when the antique device abruptly stops working, I rush over to the piano and begin playing what little segments I know of my mother's favorite songs. The notes my unskilled fingers produce sound clunky and uneven. But they keep my mother smiling, keep her laughing—and in that moment I cannot wish for anything more.

Lethia claimed she would only take the memories tainted by my dream. She could make it as if I'd never learned to play the piano.

But my life had always been the piano—and my dream of becoming a pianist had long ceased simply being a dream. It was a thousand memories wrapped into one wish. Memories of my childhood...and most importantly, my mother.

Countless days spent playing by the living room window, I'd grown up seeing the world through music. I watched, spellbound, as snow fell over the city, dusting the roofs and streets like powdered sugar while my fingers glided along the keys in a waltz. I beheld slivers of sun pierce through the clouds onto the purple and yellow petunias lining the windowsill to the notes of a sonata. I had practiced to the soft pitter-patter of rain, witnessing the world become blurred and distorted by streaks of water painting the glass. I saw the moon rise on a clear night to the slow cadence of a nocturne, as if the very music had summoned it into existence.

I'd played while my mother painted or lounged on the couch listening to the radio. I had played when I was happy, when I was sad, when I was restless. From the moment my mother taught me that first handful of notes, the music had become a part of me, like the color of my eyes or rhythm of my heart. The music was a piece of me that, even after all the pain and heartbreak it had brought, even if I never played again—I still couldn't force myself to part with, not even for paradise.

Giving away my dream to Lethia would rob me of all the memories I'd carried along with it. Memories that—however much agony, happiness, or sorrow they had brought me over the years and would bring me in the future—were all worth keeping.

"No." The word is faint, barely a whisper. Yet the sound gives me enough strength to pull my hand holding the music box back and out of Lethia's reach. "I won't do it."

Across from me, any kindness in the younger girl's expression drains away.

"Then what will you do?" she asks coldly. "Sail into the sunset on that rickety boat you found? What makes you think what waits for you out there will be any better? What makes you certain Melanthros even exists? The people in your known world may have remembered a handful of stories about the lost continent before The Veil. But *I* am the one who spun them all into sickening optimism about *The Fated* sailing to a perfect continent across the sea. A more advanced civilization, a mystical utopia—those were all lies I've whispered into humanity's ears for as long as *The Fated* has existed just to get them foaming at the mouth like animals to step on board.

But you saw the crimson sea and what it did to Enzo. You saw the crumbling city without a living soul beneath the waves. Why risk certain death when you could stay with me and be safe?"

It's true. I will be safer if I remain. This ship, with its limitless supply of food, drink, and luxury, is practically a giant, beautifully gilded box designed to shield me from everything that could ever bring me harm.

But I refuse to be trapped inside any more gilded boxes.

"Since you said you wouldn't force me to stay," I say, cautiously taking one step back followed by another, "I'm leaving."

I force my feet to remain steady as I turn around and walk away. One step, two steps, three...

I'm yards from the corridor entrance when Lethia's voice glides through the air.

"Under normal circumstances, the contract would force me to keep my word." I stutter to a halt at the regret in her tone, my stomach twisting in dread as I glance behind me to see Lethia releasing a long sigh. "But it only covers the passengers I bring down here. The fact that you sought me out of your own free will changes things. Leaves a sort of...loophole, I should say. Or at least, room for interpretation."

My breath falters. How could I have been so naïve to think I might escape?

"I am flattered you came all this way down to visit me, really," Lethia continues, kicking the flower aside with disgust before inching towards me. "No one has been considerate enough to do that in decades. It makes everything so much more exciting!"

I stumble back, then gasp at finding the steam has expanded into a churning cloud around us as the ship gives a low groan. An all too familiar rancid smell drowns my nose and mouth.

"Your dreams would have tasted far sweeter," Lethia laments. "But I suppose I'll have to take what I can get."

I spin around, barely comprehending the hunger burning in Lethia's gaze before the entire bottom level begins melting.

# CHAPTER 37

# GODS & DEMONS

I'm reliving the nightmare on the deck all over again.

My heart pounds. My breathing turns ragged. Adrenaline propels my legs and body into a run. Steam rather than mist obscures my vision this time, searing my skin and making my eyes water.

Like before, I'm being hunted—only this time, I'm truly alone.

I move toward the corridor, but the entranceway is already nearly collapsed with the edges of the frame sliding toward the floor like a warped waterfall. Around me, the ship wails as if in either rage or anguish I can't tell, making my ears ring and my head pulse from the vibration. Melted drops of the ceiling fall onto my shoulders, freezing cold against my skin even as I try and fail to brush them off with a cry. I spin and race into the opposite direction until the steam finally parts to reveal rows upon rows of boilers and engines on either side.

Boilers and engines begin melting as well. The stench of smoke and sulfur makes me cough, and tears blur my vision. The heat from the distorting machinery grows unbearable. Sweat trickles along my neck. The slowing chug of the engines reverberates through my body like a second heartbeat as I weave through the rows in a desperate attempt to find another way out.

But one doesn't exist. Every turn either leads me to more machinery or windowless walls adorned with trinkets. Despair pierces me when I spot a typewriter sliding along the melting wall beside me, its keys covered in Nanshyn characters.

*No.*

Surely, Kye-Shin wouldn't have given in. Surely, he had refused—

*Apart from the sweet deliciousness of your dreams, do you know what I love most?*

The voice that slithers in my mind is Lethia's, but different. This one is older, stronger.

I swerve into the next row, scanning left then right for a small figure in a green dress and failing to find any sight of her. Her footsteps though echo through the space, reverberating louder and hollower with my every step, my every turn, as my fear spikes to a crescendo.

Then, as if by a miracle, I spot an open doorway a short distance ahead.

*It is the look of adoration on your faces whenever my ship arrives at the docks. Even with all your technology and grand achievements, you humans are as simple as you always were. Still unhappy with your tiresome little lives, still greedy for more than you can swallow.*

I break into a sprint, my gaze boring into the entrance as it draws closer and closer...

*Do you really believe you can outrun me?*

The cold metal floor beneath my feet softens and wrinkles like cloth, rippling backwards with every step I take. Around me, the boilers rumble while the engines speed to a violent rhythm even as their exteriors melt away.

*I made this ship into my masterpiece,* Lethia hisses. *Every feather inside the pillow that cradled your head. Every crumb of the pastries you so eagerly consumed. Every bead and sequin on the dress you are currently wearing.*

*In order to convince you, I just might bring the entire vessel down right now.*

A groan tears through the space as the ceiling bends inward, more of its paint and melted parts splattering onto the floor around me. Fire erupts from a nearby deteriorating engine, the flames reaching towards me like tentacles. When I try to stumble back, I can't. Not because my shoes have sunk through the melting floor.

No, because it is *I* who is melting.

Terror grips me when I look down to find my shoes and feet inside them softening to something like plasma, the sensation feeling like nothing at all considering the numbness spreading through my body. I watch the music box liquify into my palm like a puddle of paint. In horror, I lift up my hands in front of my face, helpless to do anything but watch my nails peel off like dead shells while the sides of my fingers liquify into rivulets that stream down my palms.

I scream. Yet the noise too quickly takes on an unnatural pitch as I feel my lips melting and elongating farther, farther—

Until everything stops.

I open my eyes to a world on pause. The walls are half-melted, warped in shape but frozen and unmoving. The engine fire's tendrils hang in the air motionlessly a handful of feet away. Even the rancid smell and taste flooding my mouth and nose have since evaporated.

But most importantly, I am no longer melting. My feet, hands, and lips are solid and whole once again. Any trace of numbness in my body has vanished as well, leaving only a dull ache that I have a feeling will linger for days to come.

When I look up, my eyes latch onto the familiar features of the figure standing between me and Lethia. Dark golden hair, sharp jawline, tall lithe build.

The stranger.

"You've had enough fun for one night," he says impassively. "But the game is over now, and you have lost not only one but two rounds. How humiliating."

*The girl foolishly wandered down here of her own free will,* Lethia's voice hisses through my thoughts. *She's as good as mine.*

The stranger almost smiles. "If that were true, she would have been dead already."

*Give me this insignificant girl, and I will let you have the next three without a fight,* Lethia offers. *It has been decades since I tasted flesh and bone.*

"Their lives are not yours to trade," he says, looking over me with something close to admiration. "You only have the power to offer them the choice, not make it for them." He redirects his glare toward Lethia. "Or are you willing to suffer the consequences of breaking our deal?"

The roar that erupts from the ship around us shakes the ceiling and floor, flooding my ears so violently I'm certain my skull will burst.

The stranger sighs.

"Take the girl if you wish," he says, and I jerk away from him in shock and betrayal. He doesn't seem to notice. "Break the contract for all I care. In fact, nothing would delight me more than to finally see this wretched abomination at the bottom of the ocean where it belongs."

As if summoned by his words, a crack fissures along the right and left walls seconds before they split open with a boom. Water rushes in, flooding over the half-melted boilers and drowning the flames. The ship dives, sending the floor swinging away and me stumbling with a cry.

I don't have time to run or take one last deep breath as a tidal wave of water and debris slams over me—

—Then parts inches before touching my skin. When I look ahead, I see the water doesn't brush against the stranger or Lethia either, no matter how much it tosses and turns around us like a cyclone. Droplets spatter onto the uneven floor beside my toes. The roar of the ocean blares through my ears. Past the surface, I can make out the trinkets from Lethia's victims speeding by: a tiny carousel horse, a heart-shaped pendant, a diary, a pocket watch.

The ship releases a dying groan as it sinks farther.

*Fine. FINE!* Lethia hisses. *The deal still holds. Drag the girl from my sight before I change my mind.*

The stranger smiles. The sight is anything but heartwarming.

"Until next time then," he says, tugging me along with him as he strides towards the exit while the floor smooths and steadies beneath his every step. With a flick of his hand, the water revolving around us flies backwards, each liquid particle slipping back between the cracks spidering along the ship until the openings reseal and the walls are whole once more. The stranger makes a point of stepping over the mementos now scattered along the floor with distaste. "And clean up the rest of your mess, will you?"

Lethia's responding hiss rumbles from behind, but to my amazement, the objects rise and reattach themselves to the walls. The boiler that exploded minutes ago reassembles, and the ceiling resolidifies with a resounding snap.

*Farewell, friend.*

The voice drifts across my mind in the same instant I pass through the doorway, and I whip my head around, expecting to see a monster or a girl watching us leave.

But the vast engine room is once again fully restored and empty.

"We need to hurry," the stranger urges, breaking through my daze long enough for me to remember how to move one step then another until the world narrows to a winding corridor.

Something wet drips onto my right foot, and when I glance down to find the bottom of my skirt melting, I cry out in panic. Had Lethia gone back on her word? Was she going to melt the rest of me after all—

"Amarra, it's okay," the stranger says, returning the fringes of my dress back to normal with a wave of his hand. "You're safe now. I promise."

His words still fail to bring me relief until I open my hand to see that the music box has returned to being solid and intact. I look up at him in confusion. "But then why..."

"There are limitations to even Lethia's power," the stranger replies, understanding my question. "She may have created everything on this ship, but she struggles with controlling it all sometimes as well as keeping her true form in check, which looks nothing like the little girl you just saw. Her mere proximity to things can at times cause the melting. Although the night she nearly liquified the entire deck was an embarrassingly huge loss of control even for her."

Still, that would explain why Jaslene's clutch had melted in my hand. Lethia must have been near it when she stole my cousin away so soon after the voyage started.

"But what about Leander's watch?" I ask. "She didn't create it. He'd had it long before he boarded the ship, so how could she have melted it?"

"She nearly melted you, didn't she?" is the stranger's response. "True, melting a human would have taken more effort on her part than a mere object, but nothing on board is immune from her moods."

"Except for you it seems," I say before I can think better of it. "You said she created everything on *The Fated*. But does that mean she... created you?"

The corner of the stranger's lips lift in amusement. "No," he replies. "Fortunately, for the rest of us, that is another one of her limitations. She can create all the chandeliers, marble floors, and boulevards she wishes. But if she were to conjure up an illusion of a human before you right now, you would instantly know from the glassy look in their eyes and unnatural mannerisms that something was off. This is the reason why the glimpses of crew you remember seeing were only glimpses. Her power caused vague figures to appear at the edge of your vision or in the distance only when seeing no one at all would be more suspicious."

"I was suspicious of you for a while," I admit, beginning to fit together the pieces I previously misinterpreted. "But I was wrong. You were trying to help the entire time."

The directions he gave me on the first night had led me not only to The Nautilus but Kye-Shin and the others. The arcade token he dropped had led me to the visions, to Enzo, and through him, closer to the truth. He had been the one to open the door to the Sea Dragon lounge so that we could see the Crimson Sea beyond as well as witness Enzo's death.

On the deck as we raced through the fog, he had *unlocked* the door to let Kye-Shin and I inside, I realize now. Most importantly, just when I had been about to give in to Lethia, the flower he must have conjured into my hand had produced a smell that reminded me of my fondest memory with my mother and the piano, of the vital part of myself I nearly sacrificed.

"You weren't the one who trapped Enzo outside, were you?" I say.

"No," the stranger speaks. In the dim lighting, I can see his features tense in regret. "Besides, I couldn't have done anything if I tried since he'd already chosen to stay long ago."

"Is that what happens to everyone who stays?" I can't help but ask. "Does she kill them as violently as what she did to Enzo?"

The stranger's eyes flash towards me, his expression grim. "Not always. Lethia keeps her end of the bargain. She showers the passengers who choose to stay with every luxury and comfort for the rest of their long lives. Still, their lives all end on this ship, and the manner of their deaths varies...usually depending on Lethia's mood."

"But that is not to be your fate," he continues quickly. "The instant you said no to Lethia, you fell under my protection."

"Protection?" I repeat in confusion before another realization resurfaces in my mind. "At the ball, you said it would be a shame to throw away my talent." At the time, I'd mistaken the words for a threat rather than a warning.

"It would have been," he agrees, climbing stairs that seem to rise from the floor in the blink of an eye. "Had you taken up Lethia's offer and chosen to forget ever learning to play the piano at all. That is why I gifted you the flower to remind you of the best memory, the best piece of you that you would be giving up."

"What about my cousin?" I ask, thinking of Jaslene, of the flower in her vase when she went missing and everything she had forgotten once she came back. "Did you give her the same chance? Did you remind her of what she would be sacrificing as well?"

The stranger's gaze is unflinching as he meets mine. "Yes," he says, and despair mingled with disappointment slices through me at the word. "Smell carries the strongest link to memories out of all humanity's senses, which is why I give every passenger a flower to remind them of the best memories tied to their dreams."

The stranger shakes his head. "But all too often even that doesn't stop them from taking Lethia's offer," he says. "With every century, she makes this wretched ship larger, its interior grander."

"Why are you helping, anyway?" I say, following him. "Why do you care what happens to any of us?"

"Because it is my job," is the stranger's answer.

"But if your job is to protect us from Lethia, why have you never warned people from getting on the ship in the first place?" I demand, my mind spinning. "Why not tell the rest of the known world the truth?"

"The terms of my service on this ship wouldn't allow it," the stranger replies. "Besides, I am as much of a prisoner here as Lethia," he glances at me. "But you aren't. Not now that you've made your choice."

Before I can ask him more about what exactly the terms of his service are, he pulls a door open out of seemingly nowhere, revealing the atrium bustling with people beyond. After the darkness of the lowest level, the bright lights hurt my eyes. The surrounding music and laughter sound overly amplified as well, like a radio dialed up too high.

"We don't have much time," he says, ushering me through the entrance. "You can't stay for too long after you've made the choice to leave. Another stipulation in the contract, I'm afraid."

"What contract?" I demand, my head still spinning with everything I just learned. "What's going on? What about Kye-Shin and Miyuni? Where are they? And what about my cousin and aunt? Are they coming too?"

"You know where the Rhapsody Theater is, yes?" the stranger pushes on, ignoring my questions. "In an hour, go through the main entrance and down the fourth hall to the right until you reach the door at the end. From there, you will leave *The Fated* behind forever. Only pack your most precious possessions. The food and supplies for you has already been prepared. Go. Hurry. Whatever happens, don't be late."

"Wait," I say, whirling around.

But when I turn back, the door has disappeared along with the stranger, leaving me blinking at a wall covered with flower moldings and tapestries, alone once more.

# CHAPTER 38

# FAREWELL

I stare at my suitcase, at the meager handful of belongings making up my life.

Along with my favorite handful of books, the same six outfits and two pairs of shoes are arranged like before. For the first time since stepping foot on this ship, I'm wearing my own plain dress. My own plain coat and worn boots along with a scarf and gloves. Taking any more clothes from the closet had felt wrong somehow—as if whenever I wore them, I would still feel haunted by Lethia's presence in every touch of the fabric against my skin, still hear her laughter in every swish of a skirt. My eyes fall on the sheet music tucked securely in the side pocket, then on my music box sitting in the center. The sight of them does not fill my heart with nearly as much pain as they had weeks ago.

There are souvenirs from the voyage as well. Small things I can't bear to part with even though technically they are Lethia's creations, like everything else. Pictures of me and the others taken at the photo booth in the amusement park. The moonstone bracelet I took from the jewelry store during Jaslene's and my first visit. The flower the stranger had given me. Its fragrance is gone now—its power too. Even still, for as long as I live, whenever I see it, I will remember what I nearly forgot, what I almost chose to lose.

I slowly click my suitcase shut, wanting to linger in this moment for just a little longer. In the next room, my aunt and Jaslene bustle around, getting ready to leave for the Breakfast Room and then yet another tango party in the Sea Dragon lounge. Listening to their familiar chatter and footsteps fills me with wistfulness.

"Amarra, have you seen my silver flats—" Jaslene asks, rushing to my doorway before pausing when she spots my suitcase. "Where are you going?"

"I'm leaving," I say, searching her expression for some sign she understands. Would she even remember sacrificing her dream—or that she ever had a dream to sacrifice at all?

"Is this about the excursion last night?" Jaslene asks, frowning. "Are you still mad we didn't meet you at the deck? I told you Mother and I were terribly sorry we forgot all about it…"

"No, this isn't about the excursion," I say. "We can't stay on *The Fated* any longer. We have to escape as soon as possible."

"Escape *The Fated*?" Jaslene gasps, looking horrified. "You can't be serious! We have everything we could ever want here. All the dresses I could dream of wearing, all the dances and fun activities imaginable!"

"Just forget about the dresses and dances for a minute," I urge, growing more exasperated with every second. "Jaslene, *please*. We need to go now before Lethia finds out."

"Lethia?" Jaslene repeats in confusion, confirming my fears, but I press on.

Lethia had promised she would only take memories connected to our dreams, but had she also made it so that Jaslene could no longer remember meeting her or making the choice to stay in the first place? I can't be sure.

"There is no paradise," I snap. "This entire voyage has been a lie. *The Fated* is dangerous. It traps people into staying on board for the rest of their lives by stealing people's dreams and memories. It's already stolen some of yours!"

"Stolen—" Jaslene repeats, something like realization flashing across her face for the briefest instant before her face crumbles in confusion again. "Amarra, I don't understand."

"I know, but you have to trust me," I say, my hope rekindling at the slightest possibility that Jaslene's memories might not have been entirely erased altogether. "It isn't too late." I cross the distance between us and grab her hands. "You and Aunt Salenna could both still slip out with me, but we have to leave now!"

I would defy Lethia and her rules. I would defy even the stranger in order to sneak my family off this ship if he tried to stop me.

I've already grabbed my suitcase and am pulling Jaslene out the door when she rips her hand from mine, making me nearly stumble from the force of her action.

"I don't want to go!" my cousin snaps, anger flashing across her face. My hope fractures when she stares at me with pleading eyes. As if *I'm* the one who harmed her. Who is harming her still. "Don't you see, Amarra? I'm happy here. *This* is the paradise we were hoping for!"

"But what about your memories? What about traveling the world?" I try one last time, praying for her to recall at least something. Anything. "Aren't you curious about what else could be waiting for us out there? Even just a little bit?"

But Jaslene shakes her head as if the thought never crossed her mind. "Of course not."

That's when I realize I've lost.

No matter what I say, my cousin will never leave *The Fated* willingly. As much as I wish I could blame Lethia, Jaslene had decided her own destiny, even if it wasn't the one I wanted for her. Even if she had sacrificed her dream, her memories, and part of her identity in order to achieve it.

Throwing my arms around her, I pull my cousin into a hug. I commit to memory the familiar jasmine scent of her hair, the solidness of her body against mine, the jingling of the charms along her bracelet as she slowly pats my back, awkwardly offering comfort for something she still doesn't understand.

"Take care of yourself, okay?" I whisper, swallowing back tears. "Live a long and wonderful life. I'll be wishing only the best for you every day."

In my grip, Jaslene shifts and pulls away. I tense, expecting any moment for her to yell at me in anger or betrayal or beg me to stay. She doesn't even look in my direction.

"Oh, there are my flats!" she says, peering over my shoulder before brushing past and scooping up the shoes beyond the corridor.

My cousin doesn't so much as glance back at me while she hums a waltz and twirls back into her bedroom. I tell myself it isn't her fault. Lethia's magic must be the reason why Jaslene seems to have already forgotten about all mention of escaping—and me.

Was that what happened to the passengers who chose to stay on board? Would they eventually forget about those who had chosen to leave as well as their dreams?

A piece of my heart shatters at the thought.

With a final click, I close my bedroom door behind me. I brush my fingertips along the plaque spelling my name and flinch away when the painted letters fade beneath my skin. Fragment by fragment, my presence on the ship is already fading.

"Going somewhere, are you?" my aunt says, eyeing my coat and suitcase when I stalk through the sitting room.

"Yes," I reply. "I'm leaving *The Fated*. I'm afraid this is...goodbye."

For the second time in the last five minutes, I tense, waiting for screams and shouts to be flung at me, for insults to fall down on me like rain.

But unlike Jaslene, my aunt doesn't question or snap at me. In fact, she shows no reaction at all. From where she sits drinking her coffee, she makes no move to stand or bid me farewell. Even now, after so many years, the woman's coldness slices through me like a blade. Still, she had taken in a girl with no mother or other family and given her food and shelter.

"Thank you for everything, Aunt," I say before making my way towards the door. I barely take two strides when cool fingers wrap around my wrist, stopping me mid-motion.

"Don't make the same mistake your mother did," Salenna warns, and I spin, shocked to see her beautiful face twisted in grief and worry. "Ever since we were children, she followed her dreams no matter how exotic and impossible they were. I used to admire that about her. But that very courage and stubbornness led to her downfall. Don't let those same things lead to yours. Don't wish for more than this life can give. Think about everything you're throwing away here. Stay. Nothing good waits for you outside these walls."

As she speaks, Salenna's gaze bores into mine, imploring me to understand—and I do.

I once thought my aunt was perfectly happy with the world and her place in it. But now, with startling clarity, I can see she was once like me. She too had once dreamed only to give those hopes up. How different would her life have been if she had run away with her childhood love instead?

It's a question that will never haunt my aunt again.

It's a question that will haunt me for some time longer.

"I'm sorry," I say, once again shocked and touched by my aunt's affection and yet heartbroken that, like always, I must disappoint her. "But I have to do this."

Salenna releases my arm as if she's been stung.

"I shouldn't have wasted my breath then," my aunt says, her face melting into the callous expression I know well. "Well, what are you waiting for? Go."

I obey, stalking towards the door and opening it without a word. Just before closing it, I glance back half in hope, but no one bothers watching me leave.

I pass through the ship like a ghost.

Amidst the throngs of laughing and smiling people drifting from one exciting event after another, I alone study the exquisite interior for the last time. I try to commit as much of it as I can to memory: the aroma of fresh coffee wafting from a corner café, filled with couples sipping in leisure that only comes from having all the time in the world; the gentle rocking of the gold-streaked marble floor beneath my feet; the echo of jazz music bouncing off the vast walls.

To me, everything already feels like a dream, one gradually fading with every step I take.

As on the first day, confetti flutters through the atrium and down onto the people dancing along the bottom floor. My breath catches at the sight of a familiar figure with black hair in the center. It's Miyuni, twirling around in circles with a beaming smile on her face, looking happier than ever before. I hope she is.

For a moment, fear and regret seize me at the realization that I am likely making a terrible mistake. That leaving behind so much luxury and safety is not only naïve but idiotic, suicidal.

And yet...

If Lethia were to appear before me now with the same offer, I still couldn't bring myself to sacrifice my failed dream or my memories. Even now, standing beneath such boundless opulence and guaranteed happiness, I can't help but feel...restless. Curious. Hungry to discover what else lies beyond The Veil whether it be Melanthros or some other uncharted land or nothing else at all.

After everything that's happened, I need to know.

"Goodbye," I whisper softly, turning away.

Kye-Shin.

I nearly imagine him in every face I pass, in every tall dark figure walking away from me that makes my heart soar in hope, if only for seconds. He never appears, though, to rescue me from the torture of my spiraling thoughts.

*I finally found a story worth telling: yours.*

My heart lurches at the memory of how warm his hands felt against mine and the emotions brimming in his eyes as he spoke those words at the ball. But perhaps he's chosen to forget about telling stories altogether. Perhaps he has chosen to forget about me.

Ahead, the theater's bright awning materializes into view, and I rush forward, allowing the voices and lights to drown out my thoughts as I move past the lines of passengers waiting to see a movie, past the popcorn bags and soda cups adorning the concession stand until I reach the fourth corridor on my right.

Unlike the countless winding others on board, this hall is utterly straight, allowing me to watch the reflection mirrored on the door at the opposite end grow inch by inch until I stand before a version of myself that for once looks like *me*.

*My* hair falls in wild waves around my face rather than being forced back into the dull respectable style I'd grown to hate these last few years. *My* rich olive skin is not nearly as flawless as my cousin's, yet beautiful all the same. *My* sapphire eyes burn with uncertainty and excitement and *life*.

Taking a deep breath, I pull the door open to reveal a dark chamber. Salt air washes over me, flooding my nose and lungs like elixir. The sound of splashing water reverberates against the walls along with the low murmur of voices, and when I round the corner I see why.

A little over a dozen people mill around the room while beyond them, the opposite wall opens to a tranquil sea slowly being enveloped in fog. *The Fated* appears to have halted altogether.

"Amarra."

My breath stutters to a halt. I'm certain I must be imagining things.

But when I slowly turn, Kye-Shin stands merely feet away from me. His brown eyes drink me in with wonder and disbelief, as if he had not dared to hope he would ever see me again. In an instant both of us are moving, catapulting into each other's arms with the force of a tidal wave.

"I thought—I wasn't sure..." I say, unable to say the rest as tears stream down my cheeks before I bury my face against his chest, striving to match the pounding of my own heart with the steady rhythm of his.

"I know," Kye-Shin says hoarsely above me, his lips trembling ever so slightly against my head. "Neither was I."

Footsteps close by send him breaking away, and I look up in confusion to find Emory at our side, a small grin stretching his face.

I can't help but laugh in relief as I pull him into a hug as well.

"I'm sorry I didn't say anything at the ball," he breathes, returning my embrace. "When Kye-Shin asked me to escape with you both, I had already faced Lethia and made my choice. I knew it was only a matter of time before you were forced to do the same."

"I understand," I say before another thought crosses my mind. "What about Leander? Is he joining us or..."

When I pull back though, the sadness in Emory's gaze tells me what I already know: the Scott heir won't be joining us—and neither will Miyuni. From now on, we have only each other.

"So what's next?" Emory says, looking between us as well as our surroundings. For the first time, I notice that the others, like me, are dressed in warm clothes and carrying suitcases at their sides.

Out of the thousands of people on board, are these the only passengers who made the same choice as we did? The only people who refused to forget? The loud creak of a door sends everyone looking to where a figure clad in black with golden hair steps through an entrance I swear didn't exist seconds ago.

"I'm glad you arrived on time," the stranger says, his amber-green eyes brushing over me before surveying the rest of the group. "Please." He directs our puzzled gazes outside, "Do get on board."

I catch a glimpse of a key glimmering beneath his jacket—the same key I stole from him during the ball, which he later replaced with the flower after I confronted Lethia. The sight soon makes sense because where a moment before there was only water outside, a boat now bobs along the surface, tethered to the ship. I recognize it as the one from Island Room, though it has grown large enough to hold over a dozen people, along with the food and water I already see packed inside, just like the stranger said.

"I'm afraid it is hardly as luxurious as you have grown accustomed to, but don't worry," the stranger offers. "It's strong enough to last the journey."

"The journey to where?" someone asks, but the stranger gives no reply as he begins ushering people onto the small vessel.

"Is there no way to save anyone else on *The Fated*?" Kye-Shin says in desperation. "Will one choice really trap them on this ship for the rest of their lives?"

"You cannot undo your sister's decision," the stranger replies, and I feel Kye-Shin's pain radiate from beside me. "Those who sacrifice their dreams become destined to remain here until they die."

The finality of the words cuts through me like a scythe. I can't help but imagine my aunt and Jaslene strolling along the deck years from now, looking every bit as young as they did this morning, every bit as beautiful—until the day Lethia decides their time is up, just like Enzo's. Around me, everyone else has fallen into solemn silence as well, their expressions haunted.

"If, however, a person were to make a new dream," the stranger adds, the barest glint in his eye. "If, say, a person began to yearn for something not contained within the ship's gilded walls, for something more than endless galas, gardens, and days at the pool..."

"What?" Emory says. "What would happen?"

"Who knows?" the stranger replies just as curiously. "The contract doesn't take into account such a possibility."

Without warning, the air and metal around us trembles from the fog horn's roar, drawing startled gasps from me along with the others while the stranger glances at his watch.

"You should be going," he says, holding out his hand for me to grab as I step onto the wobbling boat after everyone else.

"Who are you really?" I ask, searching his face for the answer I have been wondering ever since he saved me. If he was powerful enough to oppose Lethia, then what exactly did that make him? An angel? A god? Something else? "How can we ever repay you?"

"I told you, I'm your friend," the stranger says, a trace of a smile on his lips. "And as for repaying me, just follow the current and keep a steady gaze on the horizon."

"What are we looking for?" I ask, but he is already untying the rope and pushing the boat out to sea.

Beneath my legs, the vessel's swaying grows more pronounced. Against my face, the wind turns colder. On each side, tendrils of fog close in like a rippling curtain. Yet my eyes remain fixed on where the stranger's retreating figure raises a hand in farewell before melting back into the ship forever.

# CHAPTER 39

# AT SEA

When I recall my last image of *The Fated*, I see its dark, towering profile receding into the pale mist. I remember the lack of any light leaking through its windows, the lack of any passengers wandering its usually lively decks, as if it were a phantom ship from legend with no living soul on board.

I remember seeing the silhouette of a young girl strolling along the deck's edge, humming a familiar tune as both she and the ship vanish into the fog one final time.

The following days blurred in my memory, swirling together until they became indistinguishable. I remember the boat's constant rocking becoming as natural to me as a second heartbeat. I recall watching the heavens shift like a reversible raincoat, as clear and blue as another ocean one hour and rolling with storm clouds the next. I remember the fog, the taste of it, the sensation of its coldness seeping into my clothes—then the sun, its burning heat beating down on my back, its brightness blinding my eyes.

There were bizarre and fascinating sights to behold as well. Waterspouts twisted in the distance across a silver ocean as smooth as glass. Mirages of palaces or entire cities lingered among the waves only to disappear within minutes, never to be seen again. Fluorescent icebergs broke apart against the backdrop of an ink black sky.

Yet…within such infinite spaces, no sign of life.

No fish. No birds. Nothing at all.

Among those countless nights, I once woke to the moon floating above in a sea of foreign constellations. Unable to return to sleep, I sat at the bow and stared straight ahead past the water, as if I focused intensely enough I could see beyond the horizon to the future we had chosen and whether or not it had been worth fighting for.

More days followed, harsher days. Days full of doubt, regret, and thinning supplies.

Why had we done this to ourselves? Had we really traded all the luxuries in the world for this? For a small, cramped boat wandering aimlessly through a never-ending sea? Our bodies grew tired, our gazes dull. Still the current dragged us on, through rain, sleet, and snow.

Even now, a lifetime later, I can remember the moment everything changes.

It's the moment I finally spot the Alexandris again since that night on the deck with Kye-Shin what feels like ages ago. It glows in one final burst of gold far above the horizon just before dawn like a beacon. *A lucky sign*, my mother would say. For the first time since the day of my audition, I believe her.

The boat creaks, swaying ever so slightly to the gentle ripples scattering across the water's surface, so different from the waves raging last night. Next to me, Kye-Shin stirs, his eyes finding mine in the dark. Around us, the slumped figures of other passengers slowly rise to life, blinking in confusion as if awakened by an instinct they can't comprehend.

I lean against Kye-Shin's side, my face directed towards the glowing horizon, my body savoring the uncharacteristic warmth in the air. I sense the transformation in him—his tensing muscles, a sharp intake of breath—before I pinpoint the cause. It starts out as a sliver, barely perceptible in between where the orange sky rises from an obsidian ocean. It can't be real, I think. It is just a mirage like the others. Yet instead of vanishing, it grows, taking shape and solidifying.

Still, it isn't until I make out the twinkling lights that I at last realize it is no illusion, but rather something impossible, something we had once hoped for but long forgotten the sight of. Something miraculous.

Land.

Keep reading for a sneak peek of my novella

# THE PHOENIX
# &
# THE NEVERENDING WINTER

# THANK YOU!

Thank you so much for purchasing this book! Since I was a child, I've dreamed of sharing my stories and books with the world, and thanks to you, my dream is now a reality. One of the most important things that can help an author is reviews. Would you please consider leaving a review on whichever retailer site you purchased this from or Goodreads? Even a short review would boost this work's search results and credibility more than you realize. Regardless of whether or not you leave a review, thank you again for purchasing this story and helping my dream come true.

Warmly,

Katelynsam

# Acknowledgments

Writing can often feel like such a lonely and grueling profession. Yet in publishing this book, I've grown more aware than ever before that I wouldn't have had the courage to keep writing despite so many setbacks without the support of many people I've been blessed to have in my life.

First and foremost, thank you, Mom and Dad—Mom, for always being my first proofreader, editor, and champion for whatever I write, and Dad, for your endless love and encouragement over the years. Your unwavering belief in me has always fueled my belief in myself, and you both are the greatest parents I could have ever asked for. Thank you, Grandma, for loving my stories and to the rest of my amazing family for being who you are.

Thank you to all the numerous people who have supported my writing career in one way or another over the years. There are too many of you to name, but please know that I am grateful for each and every one of you.

Thank you, Katerina and Leor, for your uplifting words and unwavering friendship. Thank you, Brian, for always cheering me on, listening to my rants, and reading my stories and asking questions that will inevitably make them better. Thank you, Janet and Kerry, for all the movie nights and conversations about books, TV shows, and urban legends. Thank you, Marie, for taking the time to leave your wonderful redlines and comments in "Last Masquerade at the Carousel House" and for being an ARC Reader for *The Fated*. Thank you, Pearl, for all the late night movie talks and laughs in between classes and for always being so invested in my stories. Thank you, Meghann, for deciding during college orientation that we should be the best of friends and supporting my dreams of a writing career ever since. Thank you, the two Emilys in my life, for your encouraging words and friendship over the years. Thank you, Professor Randell, for saying you hoped I would continue writing even after I graduated and for being so supportive of my unconventional journey to publication.

Thank you, my fantastic ARC readers, for being among the first brave and generous souls to read this story and help share it with the world. Thank you so much to my fellow writers and readers I've connected with on social media and through my Dear Writing Diary series on Substack for your supportive and kind comments that always make my day. I love being a part of your wonderful and inspiring communities. Finally, to my readers, thank you for being an integral part of my journey as well and for embarking on *The Fated* with me.

# MEET THE AUTHOR

Photo Credit: Elena Uvarova

As a child, Katelynsam fell in love with stories, and to this day, her passion for creating imaginary worlds and vivid characters has never faded. She wrote her first book at 12 years old, and at the age of 15, she started her long journey towards publishing. After overcoming many obstacles, she is now thrilled to be publishing her stories and sharing them with the world. Her debut novel, *The Fated*, was nominated as a semi-finalist for the 2025 Book Bloggers' Novel of the Year Award.

When not writing, she loves reading, seeking out sunsets, and most recently, learning graphic design to create the covers of her stories. If you would like to hear more about Katelynsam's day-to-day writing adventures, check out her Dear Writing Diary blog and newsletter on Substack at https://katelynsam.substack.com/.

katelynsam.com
Instagram: @_katelynsam_
TikTok: @katelynsamauthor
Pinterest: katelynsamauthor

Also follow me on Goodreads and BookBub!

If you enjoyed

THE FATED

Check out the following excerpt from my novella

## THE PHOENIX
## &
## THE NEVERENDING WINTER

Available now

# EXCERPT FROM THE PHOENIX & THE NEVERENDING WINTER

*Up again so late, my darling? Had another nightmare and cannot go back to sleep? I can't say I blame you. This place, with its cobwebs, creaking floorboards, and dark shadows, is nothing at all like the grand and warmly lit rooms of our home. My goodness, your hands are so cold, and I can feel you shivering underneath the blankets.*

*How about I stoke the fire and then tell you a story to take your mind somewhere else for a bit? You like that idea? Good. I must admit I planned to wait and tell you the full version of this tale when you were a little older. But I suppose tonight will do. After all, I will tell it to you more than once, just as my father did to me, and his mother did to him.*

*The story goes like this:*

On the plains of the Shaolyu Empire, there are two birds made of fire. One is deep crimson, while the other is the vivid blue of a summer sky. They were not always as they are now though.

Once, the red phoenix was just a girl.

She was born during The Neverending Winter, and by all accounts, she was a normal human child like you, although rather fragile. At this time, you must remember, the entire empire had been covered in snow and ice for as long as anyone could recall—everyone, that is, except the Emperor, who had lived for thousands of years.

Many people say that her story actually begins with him, which makes sense given the Emperor caused The Neverending Winter in the first place. No one else knew this, of course. At that time, everyone believed the winter and his reign had no beginning or end.

This was a lie—and one which the Emperor had carefully and cruelly maintained for centuries.

But let's return to the girl.

Her name was Meiawen, and she was born on the third night of a terrible blizzard. She came into the world shivering and almost so blue that her parents feared she wouldn't live to see the morning. The girl, however, did live. She eventually even grew to be unusually tall and thin for her age, with pale skin that contrasted with her midnight black hair. But when she became too cold, her skin would take on a blue tint that resembled her complexion at birth.

The circumstances of the night she was born also caused a condition that made her even more susceptible to the winter climate. A strong gust of chill wind would send her coughing for a week. A short walk in the snow would leave her feet numb for hours afterward. Even certain rooms in her parents' country house were perpetually too cold for her. As a result, Meiawen spent most of her days inside, either in her bed— which was heated by a stove underneath like most ancient houses at this time—or beside the fireplace, wishing she could remain as warm as she was by the flames wherever she went.

Her brothers and sisters often spotted her staring out the windows at the plains beyond, watching the silver eagles with envy as they soared over the world. *How many places and people had they seen?* She wondered. *How many villages, cities, and palaces had they glided over?* Perhaps they had laid their eyes on every province within the Shaolyu Empire and even the Emperor himself. Perhaps they had soared far enough to explore the lands and kingdoms beyond the empire as well—lands and kingdoms that were not covered in ice and snow but instead with golden sand and forests as green as emeralds.

These were places Meiawen, as well as nearly everyone else in Shaolyu, had only ever read about in a handful of antique books or heard whispered about around fireplaces late at night when no guests or servants were listening. After all, the Emperor was infamous for flying into rages whenever he received reports of anyone mentioning the warmer climates of these other places—or worse, the fact they actually had *multiple* seasons.

Decades ago, when an unfortunate bard recited an ancient and forgotten poem miles away from the capital about the summer days in the neighboring kingdom of Telira, the Emperor sent his guards to remove his tongue. Decades before that, an entire noble family was imprisoned for life when the father requested his daughter be allowed to travel to the Castor Territories west of the border. She had simply wanted to watch the gold and red leaves fall from the trees during the season known as autumn.

The Emperor refused to let anyone travel outside the ice walls he had built around the empire unless it was for diplomatic reasons. But Meiawen still dreamed of one day seeing the changing seasons of different places just as she dreamed of one day becoming strong enough to walk along the snow-covered plains beneath the eagles.

Yet as the years passed, her condition failed to improve. Her siblings grew up around her, marrying off into other families within the same province or setting out on their own adventures across the empire. She would have given anything to be able to experience such adventures for herself rather than staying inside by the fire, growing more impatient and restless with each passing moment.

Still, Meiawen never complained. In fact, she developed an unhealthy fear of becoming even more of a burden than she already believed she was. Her condition had caused her family to worry so much over the years, she hated making a fuss over anything else she feared would upset or hurt them. When her sister sewed a dress for her, Meiawen wore it with a smile even though it dug into her ribs and caused her skin to itch. When her father accidentally spilled too much salt in the bone broth soup he made for her one day, she barely winced before eating the whole bowlful.

Perhaps another reason why she never complained was because deep down she was afraid to. Afraid that if she did, they would grow to resent her for being the burden she knew she was. They never told her that, of course. But she could sense it in her mother's worried sighs and her father's concerned glances.

So no, Meiawen didn't dare give voice to the occasional impatient or unkind words that formed on her tongue before they dissolved just as quickly.

The day she looked forward to most every year was her birthday—not because she would be lavished with gifts and praise—but rather because the Emperor Moon Festival was always on the same day. The festival was held in Tianko, the largest town bordering the plains, and it was celebrated beneath the Emperor Moon, the fullest moon of the year.

Normally, Meiawen couldn't stay outside for more than twenty minutes without suffering dearly, but to her joy, the festival had always been the exception. Enough campfires and food carts were set up around the festivities that she could warm herself by the flames anytime she needed. Whenever the wind chilled her bones, she could take shelter in the open shops along the streets. Whenever her throat grew sore, she could soothe it with a warm bowl of stir-fried noodles and freshly steamed buns.

At the festival, Meiawen could pretend, if only for a little while, that she was like everyone else. This was why she loved it.

On the night of her nineteenth birthday, though, not even the cheerfully colored lanterns or beautiful carved ice dragon sculptures could dissipate Meiawen's growing listlessness with her own life. She kept thinking about tomorrow, dreading the very thought of sitting again by the fireplace with nothing else to do except read books about other people's adventures and stare through the windows at the world outside. The following day would be the same too, and the day after that, and on and on until the days melted into years that stretched through the entirety of her life like the ocean to the horizon.

Was this truly all she was destined for?

Meiawen was so consumed by this thought that she failed to notice when the game over a dozen people were playing yards away drew too close to where she stood by a bonfire. She failed to notice as well when one of the players kicked the woven leather ball the game was centered around too hard and too fast for any of the other players to stop. Seconds after it sped through the air, it slammed into her back.

Meiawen gasped, stumbling forward. She tried to regain her balance. But it was too late. Heat engulfed her as she fell towards the flames.